BEWARE THE NIGHT

BEWARE

THE

NIGHT

JESSIKA
FLECK

SQUARE
FISH

SWOON READS
NEW YORK

SQUARE
FISH

An imprint of Macmillan Publishing Group, LLC
120 Broadway, New York, NY 10271
fiercereads.com

Square Fish and the Square Fish logo are trademarks of Macmillan and
are used by Swoon Reads under license from Macmillan.

Our books may be purchased in bulk for promotional, educational, or business use. Please
contact your local bookseller or the Macmillan Corporate and Premium Sales Department at
(800) 221-7945 ext. 5442 or by email at MacmillanSpecialMarkets@macmillan.com.

Library of Congress Control Number: 2018944955
ISBN 978-1-250-23333-2 (paperback)   ISBN 978-1-250-15474-3 (ebook)

Originally published in the United States by Swoon Reads
First Square Fish edition, 2020
Book designed by Liz Dresner
Square Fish logo designed by Filomena Tuosto

1 3 5 7 9 10 8 6 4 2

FOR AINSLEY & SIERRA.

AD ASTRA, MY LOVES.

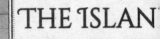

THE ISLAND
OF SOL

The Coliseum

THE GR
SEA

TH
HO

★ VEDA'S HOME
⊙ NICO'S HOME
◆ MAIN HOURGLASS
■ FISHING TIMERS
☀ PIAZZA FOUNTAIN

OF BELLONA

The Crag

Imperi Palace

Dogio Village

The Market

Main Tunnel

East Woods

Ferry Dock

Basso South Village

CHAPTER 1

C*rack.*

    My jaw.

The snap echoes between the walls of my skull as white-hot pain shoots down my throat and into my ears, pushing water from my eyes.

One shaky whimper flees my lips. Just one.

His boot—now a vise with the ground—clamps my cheeks between the hard grate of its sole and the sharp, icy gravel beneath me.

Snow drifts down, sweeping me with cruel, frosted kisses.

The Coliseum is taller, more menacing, than ever. This time, I'm the cause of all the commotion.

Down here, the large stone arena orbits me, the traitor, mocking the Sun instead of honoring it. Each towering arch surrounding me is an ashen rainbow, cracks and all. And below each arch, the stands are crammed, stippled with faces like small dewdrops piled on grass. The Coliseum is strong as always, but today, it's suffocating, the unbreachable walls yards away yet closing in on us.

We're positioned front and center, the main attraction: a girl and her executioner. Our stage: snow and dirt. Our audience: the blood-hungry citizens of Bellona.

I'm numb and frozen and burning all at once. Long strands of red-tinted hair stick to my forehead and hang over my eyes. Blood trickles thick from my nose down the back of my throat. It tastes of tin. I spit it out and blood sprays the snowy ground.

The crowd cheers.

"More!" several shout as one.

"Traitor!" a woman calls out.

A child lets out a high-pitched "Off with her head!"

Mass laughter ensues.

They lust for this, are entertained by it, feed on and frenzy over it.

But all of that is background noise. At this moment it's only me and one other—the Imperi officer who holds me with the intensity of his eyes. Each fleck, each shadow. I know so much and so little of those eyes.

Tears collect in my own, blurring his image. Bloodying every memory. It's better. I can't stand seeing him.

As if on cue, the gray clouds break. The Sun shines down, casting a fiery ring around us; a spotlight illuminating the place where I lie and my executioner crouches over me, his boot at my jaw like a hunter with fresh-killed game.

The Coliseum quiets.

All of Bellona hushes.

A newly hung banner flaps in the wind, the red words IN SUN'S NAME, THE IMPERI WILL PROTECT YOU FROM THE NIGHT distorting with each whipping gust.

"Veda . . ." My name cuts through the silence as a whisper in my ear.

I strain my eyes to see past his exterior. To find the boy I thought I knew so well within the enemy. But I can't begin to pluck a single piece of him from the fray. Instead, my sight settles on the altar, the slate pedestal to our right, the large sacred hourglass suspended above. Red sand fills the bottom bulb.

A single bell rings.

It's time for the finale.

CHAPTER 2

BEFORE

The icy hand of early morning slaps my face the instant I step outside. I gasp and then force an exhale that leaves gray clouds hovering on the other side of my lips. It's dark. It's freezing. I'm breaking the law.

Quickly, quietly, I make my way from shadow to shadow toward the woods. My face stings with numbness, my nose already tingling, but I ignore it. I've gotten used to that, ignoring discomfort, because there's always something more important. This morning, it's bait.

The one bait that trumps the worms I sell at the market. The worms do fine, but the fish are tired of them, fewer and fewer biting with each passing day. And who are they to be so picky? It's a free meal after all. But Poppy and I need to eat too. And right now, our hunger trumps stinkin' finicky fish. It also trumps the law.

Not only am I out before the Sun, but I'm headed to the Hill, the Dogio side of the island. The side Basso folk like me aren't supposed to wander. If we're found near the Hill it can only mean one of two things in the eyes of the law. We're either stealing or looking to steal. No one gets lost on this island; it's too small. No one walks around after dark; it's too dangerous. If I'm caught by an Imperi guard, I have no excuse. If I'm caught by the Night, I die.

A branch snaps in the distance and I skid to a stop, hiding behind a tree. For a moment I question everything. Can Poppy and I continue living on scraps if I don't catch any fish today? The cellar is emptier than ever. Even the mice have moved on. But is this truly worth it? My stomach grumbles in answer.

Yes.

A plump mud beetle will assure me at least one decent catch.

As I keep to the edge of the woods, steering clear of any lamplight or main walkways, I can't ignore the crudely posted signs. Paint on parchment. Some of it still fresh and sticky.

Names . . . Photos . . . More and more Basso have gone missing. Taken by the Night. Snatched from their beds or from tunnels or while sneaking around after sunset, forced into illegal deeds to stay alive. A gust of wind blasts from nowhere right through the trees above me, casting leaves down like heavy raindrops. I startle when they hit me, but as fast as they've fallen, I brush them away, silently cursing the cold breeze for scaring me. For reminding me of childhood bedtime stories.

When evening's wind laps through the trees, the Night's light footsteps hide 'neath the breeze.

I force away the shiver.

No.

Fear is a luxury I can't afford at the moment.

Besides, how many times have I gone out before morning bells? Countless. How many times have I encountered the Night? Never.

Making my way deeper into the woods, I take in the crispness of impending winter, the clean smell of snow that hasn't yet fallen but brews someplace not far off. The canal whispers to my right. At first, it sounds like a warning, hissing *stop*. Then it quickens, the rush of water urging me to *move*.

I stop when I reach the pond, which is only a small pool off the main canal that runs like a thick vein through our island. I crouch, my knees sinking into cold, damp earth. The mud beetles always nest in the soft dirt near fresh water. Not only is the soil richer on the Dogio side of the island, there's more fresh water. It'd take me days to find a mud beetle in the dry, unforgiving sandy stuff we Basso call soil.

Pulling my blade from my belt, I use it as a shovel. As I dig deeper and deeper, a black, iridescent beetle scurries and burrows farther into the ground. But before I can claw my fingers in to pinch the thing, a sound steals my concentration.

Just below the whistling wind, footsteps crunch over dry leaves behind me.

My heart lunges into my throat and the words ... *the Night's light footsteps hide 'neath the breeze* ... repeat on a loop in my mind.

I search my surroundings. Too quickly, the gray of night is churning into early morning indigo, shadows showing all over the place, distorting everything around me into Imperi soldiers sent to arrest unruly girls who leave before the morning bells. Or worse. Because there's always worse.

The footsteps crunch again. Closer now.

I tell myself to focus. To pay attention. "Look sharp," Poppy would say. But all I can picture is the brutality of the Night. Of bedtime horror stories about heathenish, moon-worshipping monsters cloaked in black like death. How they snatch children from their beds and put them to work underground, milking mud beetles and feeding the toes of naughty children to snakes and fanged groundhogs.

Bait, Veda. Bait.

With a deep breath and clumsy fingers, I claw my way into the ground in search of the pest. Determined, dirt caking my hands, finally, I get ahold of what I know is a mud beetle, its spindly legs fighting for dear life. With a gentle yet quick pinch, I yank the bug out of the earth and shove it into a jar. One'll have to do. But it's alive. Fresh is always better.

Fast as I can, I throw the jar in my bag, wipe my hands over my wool shawl, and shove my gloves on to cover the evidence. Step-by-slow-calculated-step, I inch my way to a tree and duck behind it.

Another loud crunch sounds. If it's an animal, it's large.

My breath catches.

I wait, silent as night itself, not daring so much as a long breath. As the Sun rises, I use the increased light to check the small hourglass slung around my neck. Holding the metal frame between my finger and thumb, I strain to see that the brown sand has nearly reached the one-hour line. Only a few minutes until the all clear.

Dropping the pendant, tucking it back under my shawl, I peek around the tree trunk, allowing one eye to sneak a look.

Whoever or whatever it was that made those footfalls is gone. I want to think it was an animal, a fox or deer. But sense tells me I'd have heard it run away. Even an Imperi soldier at their sneakiest would have made more noise. No, this was something stealthy. Something heavily cloaked. Sly and devilish.

Rumor is the Night melt into shadows like pitch in a crack, taking whomever they can skewer their bony fingers into right along with them. Usually unsuspecting Basso like me.

I shiver.

The Sun's risen.

Morning bells ring. Quick as I can, I flee the forest and make my way to the Hole.

CHAPTER 3

My feet tread lightly along the stone streets, buildings towering on each side like the walls of an enormous labyrinth. Promises of *I'll meet you at morning bells* nag the back of my mind. But there was no time to meet Nico when there was bait to steal and fishing holes to get to.

Faster still, I wind my way through alleyways and over bridges. Despite the cool morning, escaped hair sticks to sweat dewing the back of my neck. Not daring to slow my pace, I gather and twist it all into a thick rope, tucking it back under my knit hat.

I don't stop until the alley opens into a large square. It's nothing but a bit of open space, all cracked stone and an old, dried-out fountain, vines growing up and over it. A tunnel, its mouth wide and dark, closes the other side into a dead end. I stride across the square, standing tall, readying to face what every Basso fears: this damn tunnel.

Like a grim warning, two altars flank the entrance. One is a Sun altar, no different from any of thousands filling corners and crevices all over Bellona. Piled on top of the stone pedestal is a framed image of the Sun; an hourglass; and a small bouquet of sunrise flowers, the red-yellow petals browned, long dead. Mounds of candles, many of them lit, are stacked atop melted wax that flows the length of the altar like a waterfall. Various types of shells have been stuck into the wax as if barnacles on the rocky shore of the Great Sea. At the base, several offerings have fallen—a couple of soap carvings, a large rusty nail, a walnut still in its shell, and a ball of string.

I kneel before the altar, close my eyes, and ask the Sun to guide me through unharmed.

I search my pockets for something to offer. With nothing but lint, the hourglass quickly sifting, I hastily take off a glove, ball up the pilled wool, and make a small bead of beige fleece. I leave the blessing next to one of the shells. Then I scoop the rest of the trinkets—discarded prayers—up off the ground and pile them back on the altar for good measure.

I try to ignore the other altar, but my curiosity gets the better of me. It's an altar to the missing. These have been popping up on more and more corners as the Night grow increasingly aggressive. Photos, scraps of paper, personal mementos, and other items overwhelm the top and are nailed and pinned up and down the sides of the wooden structure. Hanging above it is a fresh missing persons bulletin, several names scrolled beneath the large red block letters that read BEWARE THE NIGHT!

The tangled black yarn of a doll's hair catches my eyes before I force myself to glance away and refocus on the task at hand. The tunnel. Fishing.

The tight passage snakes through the bottom of the old housing building like a dark secret, the entrance a crumbling mosaic archway.

I light my lantern, take a deep breath, and enter.

Several paces in and it's already pitch black save the flickering of my lamp. The lights mounted along the walls are out, meaning one of two things: The unpredictable generator is down or they've been destroyed again, the bulbs busted by the Night.

Lantern in hand, I try my best to be as quiet as possible, but my boots squeak with each step as lures and hooks jingle from my belt.

One third of the way through, I round the corner, and the opening at the end of the tunnel pops into view like a heavenly beacon sent down from the Sun himself. I'm desperate to make my way there, but it's still so far.

Before I can bolt toward the light, quick footsteps dart between the tunnel walls and my chest. "Who's—" I bite my tongue and a bit of metallic warmth blooms inside my mouth. I skid over gravel and run toward the exit.

The footfalls get closer.

I run faster until the steps are on my heels and heavy breath hits the back of my neck.

I skid to a stop, pivot, and punch whoever it is straight in the stomach, their momentum helping me out, but stinging my knuckles something fierce.

There's a groan of pain and the shadow doubles over before my lamplight.

"Gah . . . Blessed . . . Sun . . . ," he coughs.

"Nico?"

He glances up at me, dark eyes watering.

"What the hell?" I say.

"I . . ." He pauses to catch his breath and slowly stands. "I was just . . . trying to catch up with you."

"Well done." I fail at holding in a small laugh.

He glares.

"What? You don't get to be mad. *You* scared me!"

His expression softens. "All right . . . It was stupid."

"Not to mention mean."

"Fine . . . Mean *and* stupid."

"Indeed." I won't admit I'm comforted by his sudden presence. And not only because my chances of meeting my end decrease exponentially with a Dogio by my side.

"Speaking of mean . . . ?" Nico holds up his hourglass so it dangles in my face from his forefinger.

"I was detained." I wiggle my mud-caked fingers in his face.

9

"Come on, Veda..." He breathes my name as a disappointed sigh, eyebrows slanted into an exaggerated V. "Again?"

I shrug.

"You promised you wouldn't anymore."

I lift an eyebrow. "No, I didn't."

His jaw goes slack. "Yes, you did."

"No... I promised I wouldn't leave during the night anymore. And I didn't. I left in the morning."

"Before the Sun was up."

"I'm not an idiot."

"I told you I can get the beetles for you. Jars full."

"And I told you no." He glowers, but the way he works at the corner of his lower lip, I know he wants to smile too. "Hey." I take a step closer and adjust my gear over my shoulder. "I'm sorry I didn't meet you. It's just..." I pause to choose my words carefully.

Before I can get out the thoughts I'm struggling to form, Nico takes my hand, brushes off a bit of the mud, and finishes the sentence for me. "... You had more important things to do." He looks straight at me through the dim lamplight, his eyes near-black, lashes thickly folding above them. Despite the darkness, I can distinctly make out the indent of the dimple on his left cheek. It shows deepest when he's happy and when he's disappointed. Pretty sure he's not happy.

We're both silent a beat too long, the wind howling in the background.

Nico places his hand on my shoulder. Layers below, my skin tingles with welcomed warmth. "You could have asked me to come along." He always says this. "Let me help you." He says this even more often.

"No." And I repeatedly refuse his offer. "We'd both be in trouble if caught." Nico's brow furrows. "Actually, I'd still be the one in trouble." I tap his Dogio badge.

"Veda..." His voice trails off because he can't begin to argue.

But I'm sure to change the subject before he tries. "Why are you wasting your time at the Hole anyway?" I continue toward the exit.

"I told you . . ." He leans in, reluctant grin dancing at the corners of his mouth. "My Sun, Veda, don't you ever listen?"

"What's that?" I bite the inside of my cheek to fight a smile.

He shakes his head but laughs under his breath. "I'm going because James is assisting with the hourglass. I promised him I'd watch, say hi after." Ah, right. Nico's young protégé. Dogio are assigned a mentee as part of their training or something. As if going to school nonstop through their sixteenth year isn't enough, then they mentor (basically more school), and eventually either join the Imperi or apprentice and take on a profession. So, basically, school from birth to death.

"We definitely don't want to miss that, eh?" I say.

"Exactly. A promise is a promise." He eyes me, but instead of the disappointment I expect to see, Nico takes the burden of my fishing basket off my arm and clasps my hand in his.

I hesitate at his touch. The fact that I want to hold his hand and the fact that I know I shouldn't wage a small war.

But here in the dark, not a soul around, I close my fingers over his.

And for the first time all morning, I breathe.

OPENING INTO THE Great Sea, the Hole is a water-filled cavern, the shape of a crescent, tall ridges rising up around its perimeter allowing for a natural platform for fishing.

Just to our left, the Crag, a peaked, dormant volcano, rises out of the ground like a hooked claw, shading one half of the Hole so it appears to be a quarter moon. The dormant volcano is off-limits, forbidden after the first war and the mines the Imperi buried in the sand surrounding it to protect their weapons cache inside. Supposedly many mines were never found and might still go off if stepped on just right.

"The boundaries are this," Poppy would say. "If the Crag hits the sand with its forbidden shadow, you're too close." The rule was further hammered in at school when we went on that side of the island to collect clams: Never step in the shadow of the Crag. As if the moment your toes hit darkness the entire world would erupt in flames. Still, no one ever dared.

Bodies cram from one end of the horseshoe-shaped fishing hole to the other. Like small strokes in a smudged, heavily layered painting, faces blur and blend until they're only stipples of color. A sea of variegated, earthen hues. My fellow Basso.

The tide is high, but the water is calm, glassy, with one blinding line of light streaking through the middle as the Sun strikes down from the cloudless blue sky. If I squint just right, I can make out the dark silhouette of the Island of Sol; the tall arches of the Coliseum are dark, empty cavities, a series of large jaws yawning toward the Sun.

We arrive and an Imperi soldier slams the gate closed directly behind us, the bolt locking with a loud click of finality, announcing no others will enter. He then rings a loud bell to announce fishing will soon commence.

Nico and I immediately part ways. With a slight nod and a smile, he moves toward the viewing pier above, where Dogio and Imperi officers sit, as I find a good place to fish.

Once settled, I look for Nico, but he's blended into a sea of black, red, and gold.

Above the fishing ridge where the Basso stand, suspended from an iron frame is an hourglass. It towers no less than twenty feet in height. Positioned before the hourglass, fists at her hips, is the Imperi Regent of Fisheries. She's tall, slender, with a long, slick braid that stands out over the shoulder of her crisp black suit. The Imperi government crest, similar to Nico's Dogio badge, a gold embroidered sun, is loudly emblazoned over her heart, setting off the delicate, golden thread that webs her crimson sash.

As the Head of Fisheries counts down, four Imperi soldiers—all wearing black uniforms and boots—tip the hourglass. From high atop

12

ladders, they heave a rope and pulley, sending black sand spilling down the glass bulb.

This is when I spot James. He's in a similar uniform, but with a flash of red round his waist—an officer in training—and all of twelve, he proudly coils the rope into perfect circles. Nico sits in the front row, eyes intent on his mentee, red scarf piled high around his neck. When James steps away from the rope, hands tucked behind his back, Nico stands and says something into the boy's ear. Nico seems so proper, so important, standing shoulder to shoulder with the other Dogio. At the same time my stomach spins at the sight of him, my hands squeeze into fists around my pole. This version, while strangely alluring, is at constant odds with the Nico from the tunnel moments ago. The Nico I know so well.

And who is this version? Truly?

I'm both dying to know and terrified to find out.

For now, I'll keep him at a distance. Closely observe the Dogio version as if he's some other person and continue digging deeper to know the boy who holds my hands in tunnels and adores my grandfather almost as much as I do.

Surely, at some point, they meld into one.

Nico catches my eye, and my breath hitches like I've been caught thinking about him.

Which I have.

Then, subtly, so inconspicuous only I'd ever notice, he arcs his thumb over his heart, *Ad astra, to the stars, no troubles, be well.* Both my Nico and this version use the gesture to convey at least ten different expressions.

Ad astra . . . That sign . . . I'd never seen anything like it until the day I met Nico. We were tiny underneath the canopy of trees next to the pond behind his house. It was then, when he didn't turn me in for illegally fishing on Dogio-owned soil, when he ran his thumb over his heart and spoke those two words, that I understood I could trust him. It was then I knew we'd always be friends. Always be together.

But that was a lifetime ago.

I give him a slight grin and quickly glance away, realizing I'm the only one down here paying any mind to the Regent and the Dogio. With everyone's focus on their own poles and nets, finding a good spot, now is the perfect time to dig the beetle out of my bag and bait my hook.

Kneeling on the ground, surrounded by gear, I reach into my bag. When I find the small jar, I open it and pull the beetle out, skewering it with my hook.

Saying a small prayer to the Sun for one good catch, giving thanks for the plump beetle, I set my sights on a particular spot. I can tell it's deep, the perfect home for a large fish.

As I pull back to cast, something cracks to my right, breaking my concentration. I know that gut-wrenching sound.

I turn to find the glassblower's apprentice kneeling over what is now two pieces of a fishing pole.

When he glances up, our eyes meet. I see him around the island from time to time; we schooled together the few years Basso attend school before learning a trade or beginning work. Mostly, I remember him as the boy who threw rocks to scare the birds out of the trees in front of the glass shop. I yelled at him once to stop, and he sent a handful of rocks my way. I haven't spoken to him since.

I glance back at the bird bully, and he's actually trying to mend his pole with his line. *He can't be serious.*

He looks back up at me. His knit hat slumps lazily down the back of his neck, and blond hair peeks out over his ears, but it's his eyes that catch me. They're brilliant. Like silvery-blue agate. "I'm not so great at this," he says, holding the two sad pieces of wood up, clearly at a loss.

"Seems that way," I say, smiling, wondering if he knows who I am. Remembers the child version of me yelling at him to leave the damn birds alone. That I specifically remember. Poppy wasn't always the best influence. "Here." I dig into my pocket and pull out a small ball of twine. "You can try to mend it and hope you don't hook anything too heavy, or it'll snap again for sure."

Reaching for the twine, his hands are worn as if from hard work, the sleeves of his tattered muslin shirt rolled up to his elbows. "Thanks."

"No problem."

When I glance toward the hourglass, Nico's there. His eyes are already on mine and he motions toward the sand, how it's quickly dwindling.

I've wasted several precious minutes helping the bird bully mend his probably hopeless fishing pole. Focusing back on that spot in the water, I cast my line and hit my mark.

"Should do the trick." The bird bully breaks my concentration, but I don't take my eyes off my line. "At least for today." I watch from my periphery as he holds his fishing pole out in front of him and bends it back and forth so it bows without giving but still moans angrily.

"Dorian." He shoves his hand out to shake mine.

"I'm Veda. Glad it helped." Our hands only touch for a second when, without warning, I lurch forward, my line taut like wire. Dorian lunges and wraps his arms around my waist, keeping me from falling into the water. I barely get a second to catch my breath and say thanks when my line is jerked toward the edge again. Dorian makes to grab for my pole, but I dig my heels into the ground before he can try to help. "I've got it!"

He steps aside.

I skid closer to the cliff, but use my body weight to counter the monster of a fish. I will not lose this fight—Sun knows we need this beast roasting over our fire tonight.

My pole creaks and whines a painful cry, threatening to crack in two. Dorian steps closer. "You still got it?"

I don't have time to answer, but I know I've got it when I spot the creature flop at the water's surface. It's a true beauty.

The palms of my hands go raw, my legs are about to give, but I hold strong. Taking a long breath in, closing my eyes despite it going against every instinct I have at the moment, I heed the first lesson Poppy taught me about fishing . . .

I wait. I listen.

The sea stills and the beast finally tires itself out.

I open my eyes to find Dorian staring right at me, but I don't have a second to spare on him because the fish is so heavy it takes all my strength and attention. The beast is a long-whiskered pantera, and as I pull it in, the line cuts into my palm. Ignoring the blood trickling from my hand, I drop the fish to the ground. It jumps twice before I snare it under my boot; I can't stand to watch them suffer.

Long whiskers limp, near-black scales like inky ice, the beast is still. Jagged teeth poke up from its mouth, pushing its snout into a permanent snarl. It's one of the loveliest ugly things I've ever seen.

I recite a silent prayer, thanking the beast for its offering, the Sun for his blessings. Gratitude is the root of all living, Poppy taught me. Take nothing for granted. Without appreciation, he says, all humanity is lost.

CHAPTER 4

Nico and I meet on the other side of the gate to the Hole, under the same tree as always. He tags along most days, but his excuses for being here are growing thin as his Dogio engagements only increase. Sure, today he had a valid story to be at the Hole, but what will he come up with tomorrow?

"How was James?" I ask as Nico approaches.

He smiles proudly, showing the deep dimple in his cheek. It's adorable when he's happy. Nico's smile: one of my favorite sights in the world. "Nervous, but he did well."

"You went over it enough with him—he could probably do the motions in his sleep."

He laughs. "Sort of—he said he dreamed about it last night. Maybe I was a little too hard on the kid. He'll make a fine Imperi officer in a few years though."

At the word *officer* my stomach falls. My smile must falter because Nico's dimple disappears. Expression replaced with concern, he steps closer. "What's the—"

"I'm fine." It's like an automatic response these days.

"The Imperi stuff?"

I shake my head and shrug, but . . . "There's no point getting into it." I glance over his shoulder. "Especially not here." His friend Arlen is quickly striding toward us. Always in a hurry. Always dragging Nico off to one thing or another after fishing, like clockwork.

"Denali!" Arlen shouts Nico's last name. "Blessed be the light!"

"Blessed be the light." Nico throws the greeting out even though he's still facing me. He then takes a step away and frowns, disappointment showing in his dimple. Raising his eyebrows, he turns toward Arlen. "Let me guess—my father sent you."

"What can I say; he knows who to turn to to get things done." So humble. "Hey, Veda." Arlen makes sure to stare several seconds extra at the place where my shawl is unraveling. "Blessed be the light."

"Blessed be the light, Arlen." I sort of smile by setting my mouth into a hard line, because he's perpetually two steps behind Nico. Always spying over Nico's shoulder. All thanks to Lord Denali. Since Nico's father can't be sure his son stays on task himself, he's employed an annoying substitute. "Where to today?"

Arlen laughs. "Where to today . . ." He seems to size me up to see whether I'm being serious or not. I'm not. Of course, I know what event Nico's being summoned to instead of attending his usual mentoring classes, but I keep the guy hanging for fun by shrugging. "Ever. Sol. Feast."

"Oh . . . Right." I catch Nico's eye. He folds his arms over his chest, avoiding eye contact with me, probably to hold back a laugh.

"Are you serious, Veda? It only happens every year," Arlen goes on. And on . . . He talks about how he'll forgive me for not remembering . . . That he forgets Basso don't celebrate the great feast when everyone brings blessings of lavish food and prays to the Sun to please shine throughout this dark night . . . That when it does happen—and it will happen, *Arlen believes, he truly does*—the Sun will finally snuff out the Night and their evil ways for good.

We should be so lucky.

Meanwhile, Nico and I are communicating without words. He raises an eyebrow, what I assume to mean *Are you and Poppy ready for tonight?*

I give a slight nod. *Kind of. Are we ever?*

He smiles softly, more concerned than pleased. *But if you'd only let me help . . .*

Yeah, right. Like you could. Like your father would allow you to be five feet from your front door tonight.

You're right. I hate that you're right . . .

Or something like that. We've had this conversation before, so it's easy to fill in the blanks.

"Enough about all of that—I've got bigger news," Arlen says, breaking into my and Nico's silent conversation. "I've done it. I've joined!" He flashes a piece of paper and a badge in Nico's face.

The surprise in Nico's eyes quickly fades into an enthusiastic smile. I can't tell if it's genuine or not. "Arlen, you chose the army! You'll make an excellent soldier."

"The best. First step, soldier. Next step, get chosen as heir. Then . . ."

"The world ends," I mumble. They both hear. Arlen ignores me; Nico stifles a laugh. It's been all the talk among Basso and Dogio alike. Who will the Imperi High Regent appoint as his heir? When will it happen? How? It's unprecedented that a Bellonian Ruler doesn't have family to pass his ruling duties along to. And knowing High Regent Raevald, it'll be a grand spectacle when it does occur.

Dogio like Arlen are foaming at the mouth for the chance.

Basso are terrified someone like Arlen might be appointed.

Nico doesn't talk about it.

"*Regent-in-Training Rivera.* You've got to admit"—Arlen pins the new soldier's badge to his chest and then smacks it for good measure—"it's got a nice ring to it." He turns and faces Nico. "Now, to talk you into—"

"Veda—" Nico turns to me, so blatantly cutting Arlen off, it'd be comical if it wasn't one of the only things we ever argue over. "That fish you caught today . . . Arlen, you've got to see it!"

I show Arlen the beast of a pantera, and he proceeds to tell me about the time his uncle caught one five times as big. It's then I notice, aside from his new, shiny badge, he's also had his hair cut. It's much shorter than usual, no longer sticking out over his ears, and mimics the same fashion as the other Imperi soldiers, which makes sense. When he's finished with his own fishing story, he checks his hourglass and hurries Nico away.

"Later, Veda!" Arlen calls over his shoulder. "Happy Ever-Sol!"

"We don't . . ." But he's already gone.

They disappear behind a copse of trees when, not a minute later, Nico comes bounding back, calling something to Arlen about how he's right behind him.

I'm crouched over my basket, shoving the monster of a fish back in when Nico bends down next to me to help me close the flaps. He leans in, breath so close the warmth brushes my cheek, sending my stomach into yet another spin. "Tomorrow morning?"

"Tomorrow."

"Be careful tonight, Veda."

"Always."

"Promise me you won't go out before the Sun again? Just not tonight, please?"

"I promise." And I mean it this time.

He gazes into my eyes for a lingering second as if searching for the truth in my words, and when satisfied, he turns and leaves, disappearing a second time around the corner.

In his sudden absence, everything tumbles down around me. I can't believe it's been an entire year already. Last Night of Reckoning, the Night used fire as their weapon of choice, ravaging several villages. The time before, they swooped in like shadows, taking a record number of Basso from their homes, never to be seen again. No telling what this year will bring.

Imperi Regent Raevald explains that the Night want one thing more than anything: to create as much fear as possible. With fear comes power. But we aren't to fight back.

Fighting back would incite all-out war.

And the Sun doesn't want war.

Not yet anyway.

Maybe he will after tonight's Dogio feast. Because if soul after soul vanishing doesn't make an impression, a five-tiered chocolate cake and the words *Blessed be the light* surely will.

I gather my things, stand, and take all of three steps when I'm tapped on the shoulder. I turn to find Dorian holding his hand out.

"Your string."

"Oh yeah. Thanks." I reach out to take the ball of twine, and when I do, my bag slips off my shoulder, pulling the neck of my shirt to the side with it. When I lean forward to take the string, stuff it into my bag, Dorian's eyes linger. Just below where my shirt tie has loosened, the material folds over, exposing my skin. More specifically, the jagged scar that stains that spot. I adjust my shirt to cover it back up, meet his stare. There's no avoiding how blatant the moment is.

His eyes quickly dart away, then veer back to mine. "I'm sorry . . . I didn't mean to . . ."

"It's fine. Old injury." It's not *that* low on my chest but is still a little uncomfortable to talk about.

He nods, now staring at the ground. His neck and ears have gone red. "Hey, thanks to you"—Dorian clears his throat—"my uncle and I will eat tonight."

Our eyes meet again. "Well, that's something." I smile softly.

"You headed home?" Dorian motions toward the tunnel, pulling off his hat and running his hands through his hair, which is disheveled on one side and shaved on the other. Still, as much as he's changed, I can see the little boy I remember from childhood and I can't help wondering if he still pelts birds with rocks.

"I am . . ." I glance toward the darkness. "Well . . ." I begin walking. "See you around." *Bird bully.* But maybe the name no longer suits him. I mean, I don't jump in ponds wearing nothing but underclothes anymore.

"Do you mind if I walk with you?" Dorian shudders. "I hate that

21

damn tunnel." But he gazes my way, narrowing his eyes. "Unless you'd rather walk alone? I can't imagine this tunnel worries you too much after the way you hooked that fish." He raises an eyebrow. "Most grown men I know would have let the thing go, pole and all."

I cross my arms over my chest. "I can be a bit stubborn when it comes to fishing." But the fish is impressive, I can't deny it. "Normally, I'd brave the tunnel, but I walked most of it alone this morning. I think I've had my fill of adventure for the day."

He laughs. "Right." Lighting his lantern first, Dorian then glares toward the tunnel. "Shall we?" He glances over.

I nod and we enter.

The tunnel seems to go by faster on the way back, Nico and I always notice. We've decided it has something to do with heading closer to home instead of away from it. As if our feet move more quickly.

But it's not the case this time.

The tunnel is a decent five-minute walk, and today I feel every second of it. I can't remember the last time I walked it side by side with someone I didn't know. Not to mention the kid who used to terrorize birds. And it's too late to turn back.

It takes me the first fourth of the tunnel to come up with a topic of conversation (glassblowing) and the second fourth listening to Dorian's response (he's been learning the trade for years ... He loves it when he can make his own creations ... Hates it when he has to make fancy wares for the Dogio ... Seems a waste ...), so the next time there's an awkward silence between us, we're maybe halfway through.

Thankfully, some of the lights have been replaced so it's not black as night like it was this morning. Still ... I hadn't thought this through fully. Being alone with Nico in the dark is as natural as fishing. But being with someone else ... Some other boy ...

I panic.

"Give and Take?" I ask.

"I'm sorry, what?"

"Oh, Give and Take . . . It's a game. You know, for conversation?"

He slows. "Wow. Is it that awkward?"

"No, I just . . ."

He flashes a wide grin under the flickering light above us. "It's one of my favorites. Fair warning: I'm good."

We'll see about that. "Challenge accepted." A question flies out of my mouth. "Do you still throw rocks at poor defenseless birds?"

He stops dead, clutches at his heart, and stares right at me. "Brutal."

"Oh . . . Too personal? Should I go easier on you?" I smirk. Just a little bit.

Quickly recovering, Dorian adjusts his knit cap so it's tipped precariously to one side. "Pfft! You didn't say you were good too."

"I didn't feel the need to."

"Touché." He fights a smile by glancing away.

We resume walking.

"Obviously, I'd hoped you'd forgotten my sordid past." He side-eyes me. "Yes, yes . . . I used to throw rocks at birds. In my defense, I lacked parental guidance. My uncle meant well, but I was a handful." Dorian pauses, staring ahead as if lost in some distant memory. "As for your question? No. I do not still torment the poor things. Not for years."

"I'm so relieved to hear it . . . For the birds, of course." I nod, satisfied, and begin to toss another question his way before he steals the turn, but he beats me to it.

"I remember you too, you know . . . Hair a ginger rat's nest, a bit of dirt always smeared cross your cheek, sea salt stuck to your clothes."

I shake my head and laugh, part embarrassed, part surprised he'd remember such detail. "I used to skip school lessons to fish at the beach. I'd wade in up to my waist, get soaked to the bone. Poppy was forever torn between scolding me and encouraging me." I glance over, furrowing my brow. "That wasn't a question. You're stalling."

Dorian throws his hands up in mock surrender. "It was my lead-in to the real question . . . Poppy . . . Your grandfather?"

"My grandfather, yes." I raise an eyebrow at his sad attempt. "Didn't you say you were good?"

Dorian laughs. "You've had a long day." He glances at my fishing basket. "Figured I'd go easy on you."

I nod, eyes narrowed. "Of course." He either can't think of a question or is afraid to ask what's truly on his mind.

We finally exit the tunnel into the square. I adjust my hat to shade the Sun as he extinguishes the lantern, hooks it to his bag. While he's distracted, I seize the opportunity. "What's your favorite glassware to make?"

He swears under his breath, gazing over at me, feigning shock, his expression humored. "I thought the game was finished!" He crosses his arms over his chest. "Who'd have thought . . . the Protector of Birds is downright vicious at Give and Take."

I shrug. He knows full well it's not finished until the person who started it declares it, the cheat. But again, he's stalling. I stare without a word.

"All right . . ." We start walking toward the south Basso village, bypassing the market. "I like making most things, but what do I love crafting? Tiny figurines. Usually animals." He fishes something from his back pocket and presents a tiny black piece of glass from his open palm.

I pluck it from his hand and hold it up toward the light. The thing is so small yet so incredibly realistic—the tiniest of shimmering scales, gills, even small whiskers glisten under the Sun. "Pantera . . . ," I whisper.

"Thought you'd appreciate that. I always bring one fishing for good luck."

I'm still staring, turning it over in my hand, studying the miniature version of the fish I caught this morning. "The detail is . . . unreal."

"Thanks. That's my favorite part. The challenge of the details. When I get it right, it's really rewarding."

I smile, handing it back.

"No. Keep it."

"I couldn't."

"Please. As a thank-you for helping me out today." He smiles so it reaches his eyes, and I can't possibly refuse.

"It'll go on my altar. A prayer for future pantera." I tuck it safely into my pocket.

"Good. I actually went through a fish phase. Made so many that sometimes I pass them out to kids at the market." I realize I'm staring over at him when, I swear, the slightest flush overtakes his cheeks. He clears his throat. "I mean, I pelt them at stray kittens."

I laugh. "I knew it! The truth comes out."

He laughs back, the flush traveling down his neck; something about the image of him giving small blessings in the form of glass trinkets to children is irrefutably endearing and instantly warms my own face.

"Ah! I've got one!" Dorian nearly shouts, pulling me back into the present and Give and Take. "What's the story with you and Nico Denali?"

"Oh . . ." I don't know why the question catches me like it does, but my pace slows.

"I'm sorry . . ." Dorian backpedals. "It's none of my business. Got caught up in the game."

"No. Not at all." I quicken my steps, force myself to stand taller. "First rule of Give and Take: Nothing's too personal."

"Right." He nods.

Our boots crunch over gravel as the stone path turns more rugged and I try to collect my thoughts. "Nico and me . . . It's hard to explain. We've known each other since we were kids, when none of this"—I motion down at my clothing—"really mattered. Or, at least, we didn't realize it did. He's always there for me. Always the first to stand up for me. He's my closest friend."

"It's nice you have someone you can trust. It's important." But I recognize the skepticism in his eyes as if he doesn't buy it. As if he's wondering what's possibly in it for me . . . for Nico . . . that could be worth the scrutiny we must face. Questions of *What do you expect to gain?* And *How the Sun does it even work? Don't you know your days are numbered?*

Or maybe those are my own questions.

"I'm very aware our friendship is risky," I blurt out.

If he's surprised by my change in tone, my sudden defensiveness, he doesn't show it. "I've found sometimes risk is worth it." The Sun sends rays through the trees, casting an iridescent sheen over his already ghostly eyes as he cocks one eyebrow up in a knowing way. Like he's read my mind. Which he has. And like he knows it. Which he does. I glance over my shoulder and cut off our connection.

Now I'm the one clearing my throat. "I'm just a few houses down, there with the lamp still lit."

"Ah, good." He makes to turn and leave.

"Hey," I say, and Dorian looks back. "Thanks for the walk."

"Sure. Thanks for the game. Rematch sometime?"

"Definitely."

He removes his knit hat, unleashing his hair. The longer side is light, the color of the Sun at midday. It's a mess of waves, in complete contrast to the stubble of the shaved side. Raking his fingers through, mussing it even more, he smiles and shoves his cap into his back pocket.

I realize I'm staring and I catch myself. "See you around." I give a half grin, then turn away and head toward home.

A fresh BEWARE THE NIGHT OF RECKONING poster nailed to a nearby tree steals my attention and it hits me: Somehow, beyond all reason, I'd managed to forget what day it is for a brief moment in time.

Without thinking, I glance back.

He's still standing there, all tall and messy haired, and hands shoved into his pockets. "Be safe tonight, V," he calls, his tone gentle, concerned.

V? No one's ever really given me a nickname before. "You too . . ." I try to match his tone. I give a half wave and surprise even myself at how quickly I bolt through the front door, shutting and locking it behind me.

It's not the abruptness of my actions but the butterflies fluttering in my gut that shock me. It's a feeling only associated with Nico. Until just now.

I pause, my back to the door, and think on his nickname for me. V. I turn it over in my head a few times and decide I like the familiarity of it, the simplicity of it, when I look up to find Poppy marching straight toward me, arms piled high with wooden slats, his words a running tally of tasks to be completed.

As comforting as it was to lose myself in Give and Take and pantera fish and the flutter of butterflies, there's no escaping reality.

At sundown, the Night will attack.

POPPY AND I SKIN, clean, and cook the pantera fish in record time. The beast provides enough to barely satiate us now and salt and store for later. But we don't get to enjoy the small feast, not really, because we're eating while boarding up the windows, covering what little furniture we have with old canvas. We jar the fish, store the firewood (last year the Night used it as kindling to stoke the fires), and wrap up breakables.

Everything is moving smoothly until, when I run to the shed for more lamp oil, I find the can's bone dry.

"Already? It goes so quickly," Poppy says when I tell him. "We have candles."

"Not near enough," I say, tipping the basket so he can see the three lonely candles at the bottom. "This won't last us a quarter of the night. We have to get oil."

"I'll quickly run to the market," he says. "I need to pick up more canvas anyway, for the kitchen table." I decide not to tell him it probably won't make a difference. If the Night get in our home, a bit of fabric isn't going to protect anything.

"No, no, I'll go. Plus, I need to pick something up."

"Veda . . ." He knows what it is, but doesn't chide me because, though he'd never admit it, he looks forward to it all year.

"Poppy . . . We both know I'll be much faster. You should stay here and keep preparing." I look toward the windows, the walls: Everything from curtains to the few framed photos we have hanging needs to come down. "I'll be back before you know it."

He grumbles under his breath, but finally says something that sounds like, "All right . . . Be quick . . ."

I fill my bag with jarred worms and fishhooks for trade. As I bound out the door, Poppy shouts, "Be careful and get back here fast, eh!"

"I will, I promise!" I call back.

FAST AS MY LEGS will carry me, I travel from our village into town. I make it to the market just in time to trade worms for one of the last cans of lamp oil and pick up the handful of candied lemon I've been saving months for. Sunrise bread. I bake it once a year, the morning after the Night of Reckoning. Traditionally, it's supposed to have a lemon custard inside. Poppy could never figure out the custard—his was more a glue— and we'd end up throwing that part away. When I started baking it, I bypassed custard altogether and added the candied lemon slices. I place them into a perfect ring right along the middle of the round loaf, so when cut into, each slice should have a sunshine-lemony surprise. It's cheaper and easier and it's been tradition ever since.

Unfortunately, the sweetshop is packed with Dogio and by the time I buy the candies and head to the fabric store it's already locked and boarded up for the night. I swear under my breath for Poppy's sake, but we'll have to make do without the canvas.

When I turn to head home, a strange sight breaks my stride.

Imperi soldiers are pasting more warning signs, but also something new. Fresh, white postings cover the sides of buildings, are strung along the fence around the market like garland. JOIN THE IMPERI ARMY! they say. I walk closer to one of the papers. DOGIO AND BASSO

WELCOME. INQUIRE AT IMPERI HILL. I read it again just to be sure I'm truly seeing it correctly.

Dogio *and* Basso.

Unheard of. Basso have never been allowed to serve. Never.

Then it hits me: The Night must be stronger than ever, a huge threat, if the Imperi wants Basso to join their precious army, to break the rules of society as we know them. Faith in the Sun seeing us through this must be at an all-time low.

A hammer sounds in the distance, startling me, just as a woman's laughter slices through the air. Who the hell could find anything enjoyable at a time like this?

I'd like to spit in her general direction, but, heeding Poppy's warning, I start back toward our village.

Not five steps forward, I encounter the woman whose laughter set me on edge. Actually, several women, men, and children. All draped in their finest black, red, and gold. Carrying packages and food and gifts up to the Dogio side of the island.

Ever-Sol Feast.

I actually did forget about it. Oh, how Arlen would love to tease me over that.

The woman laughs again.

I glance around the side of a building at her, at the procession. I suppose there is joy to be had this evening. You just need live on the right side of the island to find it.

As if from the very pit of my soul, something clicks inside me. I'm not sure if it's the woman's jubilant cackling, the golden sheen of her dress, the fact that the Imperi is finally allowing Basso to join the army now that they really need us—like they're doing us a favor—or the stress of an impending Night of Reckoning, but I follow the crowd.

I need to see for myself what's so great. What is so funny that the woman in gold would laugh all the way up that hill?

I stick to the woods a good distance behind, not daring a step onto the path that leads to the Dogio village. Tree to tree, shadow to shadow, avoiding where the Sun shines through the branches, I sneak like the sneak I'm being, following people I shouldn't follow to a place I know I'm not welcome.

But I'm not ashamed of my sneaking. I am worried I'll get caught. I'm a bit concerned I might run into Nico, and there's no excuse that would ever suffice for my being here now. Yet I keep following. For once, I'm not questioning my desire to know more about these other people I share this small island with. I always keep to my own Basso business.

Not this time.

But the woman has stopped laughing. In fact, I've lost her completely and I realize why. Two by two, the Dogio procession snakes right through Nico's front door—into Denali Manor—with an endless round of *Blessed be the lights*.

I stop behind a nearby copse of trees, stealing glances when it's safe. The inside of Nico's home—which I've only ever seen through the windows from the pond out back—is ablaze with the golden brilliance of a hundred candles. Guest after guest leaves their gifts of offering, blessings for the Ever-Sol Feast, on a long table near the front door. Some gifts are immaculately wrapped, tied up in gilded ribbon; others are on display: sugared fruit and fresh breads and cheeses piled high in baskets. It's then I realize my mouth is watering from the aromas alone.

And I hear it, the woman's laughter. It's so distinct, airy and light and jingly like cheery bells. Before I can spot her, the door slams shut.

Glancing to the Sun, then the hourglass round my neck, I realize that if I'm quick about it I've got just enough time to go around the back to steal one more peek.

And I get more than a glimpse.

The back of Nico's home is all windows. The place spreads up and out like a table-topped hill. The roof is rich red clay tiles, and the grounds are protected by a black iron fence. Glass extends floor to ceiling, the Sun invited to shine directly in to greet the Denalis each morning. Many Dogio houses are built this way, with the Sun in mind.

Our cottage is surrounded by forest, the Sun only finding its way to our roof midday, nothing to warm but a thick slab of cracked stucco.

As I make my way closer to the fence, boots crunching over fallen leaves, hidden by the shadows of trees overhead, the chatter grows louder despite the windows being closed.

Then a chiming—metal fork against a glass—and all goes silent.

Tiptoeing closer, I'm only one short step away from the fence, barely concealed by the trunk of a tree, when the low murmur of a man's voice cuts through the quiet of late afternoon. Inch by inch, I move out from behind the tree until, if I squint, I've got a perfect view of Nico's family at the head table and the beginning of the feast.

Lord Denali welcomes the crowd who sits before him at round tables adorned with gold linens and even more candles, centerpieces a cascading of fresh sunrise flowers, crystal flutes filled to the brim with the same sunny, candied lemon slices I just spent a small savings on (for six pieces).

After a short speech, Nico's father bows his head in thanks, but he continues speaking. Nico sits to Lord Denali's right, and when his father motions to him, he stands. Taller than his father by a good three inches, Nico squares his shoulders and nods, agreeing with whatever Lord Denali's saying. And I find myself dying to know what that is. So much so that I've moved out from behind the tree, completely exposed, my head nearly shoved right through two bars of the gate.

Still, I can only make out every few words, and without any context, they're nonsense. And I know it's getting late . . . And I know Poppy'll wring my neck . . . And I know I'm being reckless and stupid by sneaking and eavesdropping and staying out long past when my grandfather expected me home.

Yet, I don't move.

I'm frozen.

Because Nico's caught my eyes.

Across the countless Dogio focused on him, his father's announcements, blessings, and sunrise flowers, his backyard with the garden and trellises, and out to the tall iron fence that closes it all off, I swear, Nico sees me.

A bit of shame mixed with a deep blush creeps up into my face, and I scramble to leave, but not before I spot the woman in the gold dress. She's seated, her back to me, right before the closest window, and when she turns her head, showing a wide, genuinely gleeful smile, it hits me as if it's been there all along. It's not a punch line I've missed. There's no riddle to crack. She's simply happy. Content on this very same night Poppy and I will board up our home and hide for our lives from the Night.

And it's all wrong.

I run the whole way home, not once looking back.

Vesper bells ring mere minutes after I slam our back door shut. They sound three rounds on the Night of Reckoning.

Three.

Two.

One.

CHAPTER 5

Once I close and lock the door behind me, Poppy's right there with the boards to reinforce it. As he hastily hammers nails into the wall, almost catching his thumb more than once, my conscience pangs with the guilt of how stupid it was for me to waste time spying on Nico, on the Dogio feast. How Poppy must have been watching each grain of sand drop through the hourglass waiting for me to return.

Worse, right beneath the guilt of worrying him so is a sickening humiliation over being caught by Nico, which only makes me more ashamed.

And all of this on the most dangerous night of the year.

The Night have lived in opposition of the Imperi, hidden underground in what's believed to be a complex series of tunnels, for as long as the Imperi have been in power. Since before the Great Flood that overtook our island on this day centuries ago.

Dogio celebrate with candles and sweets and sunrise flowers.

Basso huddle in their boarded-up homes.

The Night have their Night of Reckoning.

And the Imperi guard their weapons cache, the High Regent, and powerful Dogio citizens and villages like Nico's.

Honestly, who knows what came first—the Imperi, the flood, the Night, the Sun himself? I just want Poppy and me to live through to first light. To have food on the table. To not have to work all hours in order to afford six measly pieces of candied fruit to stick in the middle of a yearly loaf of sunrise bread.

A final series of bells echoes over the island the moment the Sun fully sets each night—vesper bells. Tonight is no different.

"Downstairs. Now—" are Poppy's first and only words after he shoves the hammer through his belt loop. He then crams a chair under the door handle and checks to be sure I'm carrying the lamp oil I was sent for what feels like forever ago.

His expression alone—tired, concern lining his forehead—is punishment enough for my sneaking. When this is over, I'm going to catch him a fish twice as big as the pantera this morning and then cook his favorite stew to go with the sunrise bread.

I pull the rug that covers the basement door aside, as a series of windows breaks from somewhere down the street.

It's begun.

And it was a night similar to this that my parents were taken. It was the attack that spurred the first war. The Night surfaced, revolted.

Somewhere during those hours of terror, they snatched my mother and father up in the dead of dark. Dragged them away and tortured and killed them in Sun knows how many horrible ways.

Poppy blows out the lamp on the kitchen table, the sudden blackness sending a visceral shiver down my back. I force my fear, my nightmarish memories conjured from Poppy's stories of the last time he saw my mother—his daughter—aside. He's only once spoken of my father. And in an expletive-laced rant under his breath, no less. Poppy didn't know I was listening outside his door when he lost his temper. There was mention of my father, that my parents died before they could marry, and that if it wasn't for *him* maybe things would have been different. Not too long after, I worked up the nerve to ask him about it. He apologized that I'd overheard, that he'd used such language. There was truth to his words, he admitted, but also explained he'd been angry and missing my mother. My grandfather completely buried the subject from that moment on.

Aside from that memory, I know nothing of the man.

Vincent. His name was Vincent. That's all I've ever gotten out of Poppy.

I've not been able to glean a whole lot more out of my grandfather about my mother either. She was kind. Brave. We share the same dark red hair. There's only one photo of her in the house, stuck in an old book Poppy likes to read about sea navigation. In it, she's standing tall, strong, holding a weapon she used for hunting. An atlatl, Poppy explained when he caught me staring at it one afternoon. It's a long wooden thrower with a hook that flings thick, sharp spears.

She also used it to protect her and Poppy against the Night.

I slide open the wood-planked basement door. We hurry down the ladder, Poppy pulling the carpet back over, locking the door behind us.

Within the cellar is one lantern, a jug of water, jarred food, and a couple of blankets.

The space is cramped, no larger than a broom closet, but it's the safest place right now. Last year when several homes burned to the ground, the only saving grace was that the families hid in their cellars. They lived. If you don't have a cellar, on this night, you know someone who does.

I stare across the short distance to Poppy. His eyes are heavy; he's probably exhausted from the work of getting the house boarded up, worrying over me cutting things much too close, on top of laboring the day away selling worms at the bait stand.

I wish I could give him a barrel of candied lemon.

"You sit," I say, pushing the one stool toward him. He doesn't protest. I hand him a blanket and I sit on top of the other on the floor. "Will they ever stop?"

"Afraid not," Poppy says through work-weathered hands as he rubs his eyes. "Not until they get what they want."

"What more could they possibly want? I know they hate us, but to what end?"

"Power, my Veda. It's all about power."

"I don't get it. Who the hell cares about all that?"

Poppy snorts in that way he does when he agrees with me and also eyes me for saying *hell*. "The Night. The Imperi. Those who already have it and fear losing it."

I roll my eyes. "At least the Imperi protect us . . . Sort of." But do they? Sure, they'd insist they do, but with each day that passes, each morning I have to sneak out for bait, it feels less true. More and more I can't help but feel we're just pawns to their king. We do all the work while they roam wherever they please, laughing and celebrating, bellies full of candied lemon. Yeah, they'll recruit us to fight, to tend their gardens, to bake their bread, but never—never—to share their gold-linen-adorned table.

"Mmm . . ." Poppy nods. He takes my hands in his and is about to say something, go into one of his stories from my childhood, probably, when there's a blast above. What I assume is the back door, those boards Poppy so hastily used to barricade it, left a mess of splinters on the floor.

The noise travels down into the cellar, rapping against my ribs. Poppy's eyes are wide, his forefinger hovering at his mouth. I blow out the lamp.

The world is painted pitch black.

Booted footsteps knock against the planked floor over our heads.

The darkness is so dense, so all-encompassing, I can't see even inches in front of me.

More footsteps. There must be at least six Night soldiers marching around our home as we wait like sitting ducks below.

Something falls over. A shelf? Our kitchen table?

I pull my knife from my boot.

Poppy squeezes my shoulder as if reminding me not to do anything reckless or hasty.

A window breaks.

Another.

More boot clatter.

Another item crashes to the floor.

Then . . . silence.

My heartbeat is all I can feel. All I can hear, the *thump-thump-thump* between my ears.

I'm about to dare a whisper to check on Poppy when something slick and cool drips through the slats of the ceiling onto the top of my head. Then again.

Poppy must feel it too because he strikes a single match for light. I glance to his face, gasp, and then look down at my hands where I've wiped the warm liquid off my head. It's red.

Bloodred.

CHAPTER 6

Lucky souls who live through the Reckoning must tread timidly at first Sun's beckon-
ing. For when they wake from a long eve's bed, thanks to the Night, the canal runs red.

I STIFLE THE scream in my throat and focus on cleaning the blood off my hands by smearing my sticky palms against my skirt.

Not a word and nary a sound exchanges between Poppy and me as, silently, we try to figure out how in Sun's name blood was spilled on the floor upstairs and, more, who it belongs to.

I risk lighting another match.

Poppy leans in and, of all things, sniffs my hand, then nods knowingly.

Paint, he mouths.

I lift my hands to my nose and instantly recognize the sour, metallic scent. My panic, the buildup of the evening, definitely ran away with my imagination and had me thinking the worst. Poppy doesn't dare relight the lantern.

Silence saturates the house, the world, until the neighbor's rooster crows, alerting us that at least he made it through the night. Then the bells ring.

Poppy lights the lantern.

"I'll go up first," I say, jumping up off the floor.

But Poppy's already climbing the ladder. "Wait here, Veda. Please." He's sure to make eye contact—he knows I'm less likely to go against him when he does this. Knife at the ready, I don't dare even a breath.

He unlocks the door, slides it open with a bit of trouble like something's blocking it, and then vanishes into our house.

I wait. And wait.

It's too quiet. Too still. And as much as I want to heed Poppy's warning, I can't. I take the ladder, two rungs at a time.

I scramble up from the cellar to find a shocked Poppy, staring helplessly from one disaster to the next.

It's as if our home's been doused in blood, picked up, turned upside down, and dropped back again. My face flushes with anger, but it isn't until I see remnants of the altar from my bedroom . . . a photo of me and Poppy, a scrap of map that belonged to my father, a chunk of rose quartz (my mother's), a stone from the pond in Nico's backyard, and the glass fish Dorian gave me only hours ago, that everything hits me.

Walking over, I bend down and pick up the items one by one, setting them in a neat pile to the side, sticking the glass fish in my pocket, so tiny and delicate compared to the others, I worry it'll be lost for sure. My throat tightens as Poppy's heavy steps grow closer. I don't know what to say, but the warmth of his hand on my shoulder says it for both of us.

"Ah! It's about time!" he says. "That altar needed a good dusting!"

I look back at him, my eyes burning from holding back angry tears.

He runs his finger along the frame of the cross-stitched Sun I made when I was nine, showing a layer of gray dust. "Heh?" Eyebrows raised, his forehead a sea of lines, he waves the frame in the air. "We should thank the Night." He breathes in. "Thank you! You damn hellions *are* good for something after all," Poppy says.

But, too quickly, his expression grows somber. Leaning closer, he stares into my eyes, his dark, always so stoic. "These are just things. Sure, they hold memories, but it could be so much worse. Yes?"

I nod, my forehead nearly touching his. "Yes."

"Good . . . Good . . ." He hands me the cross-stitched Sun and leaves a kiss on the top of my head.

Poppy begins picking things up—a broken chair, a shattered lantern—while I tuck the rest of my altar blessings into a neat pile on the side table that's mostly still standing.

Unsure of where exactly to start, I glance around our home. It's stark, a blank canvas of earthen hues. Except in the room where the Night dumped buckets of paint. That spot, our main living area, is the scene of a massacre.

So much red.

THE SUNRISE BREAD is in the oven baking, filling the house with the most delicious, warm aroma, masking the ugly remnants of last night. I'm dipping the mop into a bucket of soapy, bloodred water when Poppy busts through the front door from taking out the first load of trash.

"Medallions!"

I stop dead.

The mop slips from my hands and lands with a loud whack against the floor; paint-soaked water spills across my bare feet like a fresh splattering of blood.

"Why?" I ask as he's bounding straight for me.

Gripping my shoulders, Poppy stares firmly—lovingly, but firmly. "The Night of Reckoning was the worst yet. The Sun's not pleased."

I nod. "When?"

He only shakes his head, a halo of silvery hair atop his speckled brow. "Soon. The Imperi soldier's been spotted. Just down the way."

I push a knot of emotion to the back of my throat and take Poppy by the arm. Walking toward the front door, we sit before the Sun altar that greets us each time we enter, and light several candles.

And we wait.

One of us could die today.

Any minute now two gold medallions will drop through the mail slot in our door. If the one with Poppy's name on it bears the stamped image of the Sun, it's his time. If not, it's my time.

If neither shows the Sun, we breathe easy the rest of the day. Well, in theory.

Because no one truly breathes easy on Offering days.

Time passes. No idea how much; there's no hourglass in the compact entry to our home and I don't bother glancing at the one round my neck. All I know is time passes slow and fast at once. Dragging but also speeding by more swiftly than I can keep track.

But all time stands still when the purposeful boot steps of an Imperi soldier march up our walkway.

Onto our porch.

There's a pause and then the hinges on the mail slot squeal.

Large gold medallions drop. One, two.

They hit the floor. One lands flat. The other spins like a top, then slows, teeters, and falls.

Neither of us moves.

Poppy takes my hand. I give his a light squeeze. Then I stand, take a few steps, and bend down, picking up the coins, not looking too closely.

Holding one in each fist behind my back, I return to Poppy, sit before him so our knees are nearly touching.

He points to my left hand.

I give him the one in my right and he lets out a small guffaw.

"Ready?" he asks.

"Ready."

"Three, two, one."

We hold the coins out flat on our palms.

The medallion in my hand reads JAC ADELINE.

In his, VEDA ADELINE.

Neither shows the Sun.

"Blessed be the light," Poppy whispers.

"Blessed be the light," I repeat.

CHAPTER 7

As with most of Bellona's history, the Offering dates back to the Great Flood.

The story goes that our island was birthed of the Sun. A star itself, born of the most important star, Bellona was holy, but it didn't ascend to the night sky. Instead, it was pulled downward, toward the land below.

Ashamed, the Sun cast his only child into the sea. But the small star wouldn't descend to the ocean floor either. It was stuck. An unremarkable speck amid vast blue.

Its fire went out, but still Bellona floated, a flat, dark disgrace of a star.

Soon it sprouted roots and came to life, bearing plants and animals and the most beautiful of trees and waterways. People even came, built a society. Lived off the shunned star.

The Sun, in his humility, instantly regretted the shame he'd felt. He vowed to protect his one and only child—a beautiful land star—for all time. For it was one of a kind.

When the island was hit with the Great Flood, it was seen as punishment, a sign from the Sun that he was displeased with his Bellona, with the people he'd chosen and entrusted to take care of it.

Thus the Offerings were born. To please the Sun, to prove how thankful they were, what a blessing it was to live on this holy island, the people of Bellona would offer their god the greatest of sacrifices. Life.

It's said one day a new child of the Sun will be born. A star unlike any before or after.

That it will ascend into the heavens, but not before bringing about a great reawakening over all of Bellona.

I'm not sure if that's meant to be a good thing or a bad thing.

Or maybe it's just a nice nighttime story.

SIDE BY SIDE, my and Poppy's footsteps echo in the stillness that haunts the air. Every soul in Bellona is required by law to attend the Offering. There's a steady stream of Bellonians making their way toward the boats that will transport us to the Island of Sol for the ceremony. But no one speaks. The Offering is a reverent time, a time of prayer and reflection, silent respect for the Sun.

The market is secured and boarded. The iron fence surrounding its perimeter stands tall, the gates locked with a complicated metal device crowded with cranks and levers. The Sun shines down on it at the perfect angle so it blinds us with its silvery glare.

As ominous as the silence is, it's nothing compared to last night's destruction. Signs of the Night of Reckoning hit us around every corner.

Anti-Night postings, normally tacked to the sides of buildings, are torn to shreds and littering the streets like fallen leaves. A few of the altars for the missing have been tipped over, photos and blessings and candles scattered.

The main hourglass that controls the bells, the curfews, has been defaced. Written in black and red paint against the light pine frame are large ornate letters spelling out the words BEWARE OUR RECKONING!— the g in reckoning is a perfect crescent moon and the word beware is written in red and drips like a freshly sliced cut.

We arrive at the dock just in time to catch the second-to-last transport to the Island of Sol—a small mound of earth a mile out, the only thing there, the Coliseum. There's nothing else surrounding Bellona save unforgiving, rough seas. Nowhere to travel. Nowhere to start anew. Nowhere to hide. It's just us, the Night, and the Sun's mercy.

Before too long we spot the festively colored Coliseum flags adorning the uppermost wall: red, orange, and yellow repeating along the massive circumference of the open dome. The large triangles whip with the wind.

As a child, I would jump up and down at the sight. The day was a holiday, an exciting outing when I'd wave my homemade white flag hastily embroidered with the Imperi Sun. But that was then ... I didn't know anything about the world, how things would play out, how pleasing the Sun meant someone had to die. That the Night were so cruel. Or that I'd one day be friends with a Dogio whose dimple I shouldn't think about, whose hand I certainly shouldn't hold.

I was oblivious.

Blissfully oblivious.

Poppy and I make our way from the dock to the Coliseum, where separate lines have formed.

There are two sections of the Coliseum and two types of tickets: The cheap seats are free since attendance is required, and the costly seats are stocked with extra amenities for those who can afford it.

Anyone is free to sit where they like, but the reality is that Dogio are on one side, Basso on the other.

We take our place in the free-seat line, slowly working our way to the open-arched doors. Standing on my toes, I squint to spot Nico and his parents in the crowded line next to us. But I don't see him. I try to peek inside, get a glimpse of the mosaic Sun in the entryway, where we always meet before we're pulled our separate ways. But the Basso line lurches forward before I see anything.

To gain entrance, we hand over the same medallions that fell through our door this morning to an Imperi soldier who drops them into a metal box and waves us through.

Poppy hands his over, tipping his old straw hat.

I turn mine over to the same soldier.

The instant I'm through the archway, I'm greeted from across the open space by a smiling Nico. Poppy eyes Nico and then me, mumbling, "Be quick about it, eh?" under his breath, and then disappears up the stairs to our section.

I bound toward Nico, who's a decent ten feet away, but slow down when I hear the clatter of my boots echoing against the stone tile, at numerous eyes watching us, at how my stomach suddenly tightens with the guilt and embarrassment of spying on him yesterday.

Surrounded by silent murmurs, the wind whispering through the vast hallways of the Coliseum, Basso herding one way, Dogio the other, it's like Nico and I are stuck in the middle. Caught in the eye of the storm.

"Hey," he whispers, thankfully not leading with questions about my sneaking.

"Hey." I give a cordial nod.

"Are you all right? Was anyone hurt last night?" He leans in, searching my face, my clothing as if looking for signs of distress.

"It's not great. They broke into our house."

He leans in even closer. "What?"

I nod, then allow my sight to wander. A Basso girl watches me from the corner of her eyes as she kneels before the multicolored tiled image of the Sun.

Not too far past the girl, Nico's father glares our way, and then, taking Lady Denali's arm, turns and heads up the stairs.

"Do you need to . . . ?" I motion toward his parents.

Nico follows my eyes. "I said I'd meet them at our seats." He glances back to where the Dogio—a sea of darkness flecked with bright red—flow up the stairs through the archway, the words BLESSED BE THE LIGHT carved in the stone over them. "Actually . . ." Nico looks into my eyes. "I'm sitting with you." He takes hold of my hand beneath my shawl. And before I can question his decision, we're following the other Basso up the opposite stairs and to our seats.

"Your parents," I hiss to Nico under my breath. "They'll kill you."

Nico stays quiet, but his jaw tightens like he's working the idea over. Like he knows I'm right. But like he doesn't care.

I lead the way to our usual spot—where the section above provides the tiniest bit of shade—and Poppy's jaw goes slack at the sight of Nico behind me. But he recovers quickly. "Ah! Nico, welcome." His eyes crinkle under the pressure of a genuine smile.

Nico adjusts his black hat so the rim better shields his face. "Morning, sir."

My grandfather cocks an eyebrow, snorting under his breath, his usual response over Nico calling him *sir*. Poppy's long since given up telling Nico not to bother.

We sit down, me next to Poppy, Nico next to me.

People stare. A child two rows down keeps glancing back, staring at Nico's red scarf—a gaping wound awash the muted olives and tans and beiges of traditional Basso garb. The boy tugs on his father's sweater, points, and urges the man to glance back. The father scowls and then picks the boy up and places him on his lap.

And they're not the only ones.

Word's spreading.

Dogio never sit on our side, and I can't tell if they're curious or angry or simply confused over it.

I lean in toward Nico. "This was a bad idea."

"Charging money for better seats when Basso have to bake in the sun is a bad idea. It's not right."

"Since when do you scoff over your cushy, shaded chairs?"

Nico takes in our surroundings again, working over his jaw. "Since now. I want to be here, Veda. You're not able to sit with me, so I'll sit with you. It's not a sacrifice, it's a choice."

"I'm glad you're here, but—" I'm about to comment on how nice it is he has that choice when my grandfather cuts me off.

"Psst!" Poppy brushes my face with the essence of the peppermint leaf he's chewing, setting his sights to the highest perch in the Coliseum. Imperi High Regent Raevald enters.

"Welcome, citizens of Bellona." Raevald's voice blares out over us, golden speaking-trumpet placed to his mouth. "Dogio." He raises his right arm toward the paid-seating side of the dome. "Basso." He does the same for our side. High above us all, wearing a black suit, his dark, slick, graying hair hidden underneath a bright crimson hat, the High Regent towers in a balcony, flanked by Imperi officers. He stands behind a podium, and as he preaches, he scans the crowd laid out before him. "As we bring out the Offered, that praiseworthy soul, we shall pay homage to the Sun."

Each person stands, head bowed in respect, prepared to follow along with the Prayers.

"Almighty Sun, life force to all beings, we implore thee. Bless us with your light. Provide for us plentiful harvests, protection from the Night, and prosperous life. In return, we vow to keep this society strong, for we are ever indebted."

There's a pause, a moment of silence in reverence for the Sun, for the Offered, and then the Regent adds, "As we bear witness to this sacrifice, we remember: 'A thriving Bellona is only as strong as the light that shines upon it. Blessed be the light.'"

"Blessed be the light," we repeat.

We resume our seats. The Coliseum is silent, at rest, barely a breath taken. Even the wind ceases.

A golden-pink sunstone altar stands in the middle of the Coliseum; to its left, a large hourglass. To the altar's right is a dried-out canal. When the hourglass is turned upside down and the gold sand spills into the bottom bulb, the floodgate is opened. Sea water rushes through the door, filling the canal so it runs over onto the gravel floor.

Across the Coliseum, another door opens.

A woman enters the arena. She's draped in all white—traditional of the Offered—and is flanked by two Imperi soldiers. The soldiers don't touch her; in fact, they walk slightly behind. At this moment in time she is a sacred being. Neither Basso nor Dogio. Chosen by the Sun through the Imperi for Offering.

But as the woman comes closer, I catch her face and the sight sends my heart to the floor. I must make a pained noise because both Poppy and Nico glance at me.

The woman lives in the south village. Our village. Maisy Jarrow. She raises chickens and sells eggs in the market. I've known her for as long as I can remember. Despite that hers was one of the homes burned down last year by the Night, I cannot recall a time she's been without that warm smile across her face.

Until now.

I wouldn't say she looks sad or afraid or even angry. Just . . . different. As if in a trance. And maybe that's the state you'd need to be in to do such a thing . . . Sacrifice yourself for the greater good of your people. Walk straight to your death and not turn back screaming, "I change my mind!"

Because, yes, Maisy Jarrow received a medallion with a bright Sun imprinted on one side this morning, but she also agreed to be the sacrifice.

If the Offered doesn't agree to volunteer after being chosen, another medallion is plucked from the chest. It's rare, but it does happen. Though the fallout isn't pretty. Those who refuse their fate face unofficial shunning. Sometimes worse. Because no one turns their back on the Sun. Or the Imperi.

Out of nowhere, a pained scream overtakes the Coliseum. The startling sound sends my heart to beat in my ears. In special seats, front and center, sits Maisy's family: her husband, elderly mother, and teenage son.

It's the older woman who cries out for her daughter. "No! Not my Maisy!" she wails.

Maisy doesn't react. She doesn't face her family. She's so incredibly focused, she strides straight to the altar and holds her hands, palms up, over the top.

Simultaneously, the soldiers slice each of her palms. Without so much as flinching, Maisy places her hands upon the sacred sunstone altar. Maisy's blood, symbolic of her gift to the people and island of Bellona, is forever imprinted.

Her mother's cries peter out, and when I gaze down to their seats, I see she's slumped over herself, praying, refusing to watch.

A raft is brought in by golden cart, set afloat in the newly filled canal before the altar. It's tethered to a stake in the ground, and a black crescent moon is carved and painted into the top, a sign that this Offering is a sacrifice for protection against the Night.

The raft, ornate and made of the finest materials, is designed to give way the hour the Sun rises next morning. This provides the Offered long enough to appreciate the Sun and reflect on their sacrifice, how they've given the ultimate gift for the betterment of their community. It is then the rope, tied to last a full rotation of the Sun at most, will unravel and the raft will collapse, sending the Offered to the Great Sea in recognition of the Great Flood, and as an appeal to ward off another. Everyone's— Dogio's, Basso's, Imperi's, and, I'd dare a guess, the Night's—greatest fear.

At the sight of the raft, her final resting place, Maisy raises her bloodied hands to the sky. Her hair is light and graying, twisted into a bun atop her head, a single sunset flower placed in the center like she was born with it. Red drips down her wrists, streaking her forearms, staining the pristine petals.

The soldiers help Maisy onto the raft, where she kneels, hands lightly folded in her lap.

The last of the gold sand fills the bottom bulb of the hourglass.

A single bell rings, reverberating around the circle of the Coliseum. Birds flee from the trees behind the dome.

My skin prickles.

One slice of the rope and the raft is set free.

Slowly, the raft is carried down the canal, under the floodgate, and eventually makes its way out to sea.

Maisy the kind egg lady is no more. She's now known as the most recent Offering. Sacrifice for protection against the Night.

I close my eyes as the floodgate is cranked closed. Under the veil of darkness—the scraping of metal on metal filling the background—I hope and pray that this one will take. That Maisy's sacrifice will be the last. That—*please, please*—the Sun will be satisfied and the Night will leave us be.

But in my heart, I know it isn't so.

I don't open my eyes until I know she's gone and that the gate is closed. Some will stay until the last boat back to Bellona and watch, sit at the cliff's edge, squint and shade their eyes, until the Sun sets on the horizon and until the Offered is nothing but a speck in the distance. Many have brought blessings to throw into the sea after Maisy.

As the canal drains, the crowd stands, applauding, praising the day's Offering.

I stand out of respect, expectation, but can't begin to bring my hands together.

Nico finds my hand and gives my fingers a slight squeeze, sending a tingling warmth over me, but lets go just when I've accepted how nice it feels. If even for a second, I covet the warmth that lingers.

I glance up toward the High Regent's balcony to gauge his reaction.

He's vanished.

No sooner than the raft is set to sea, the inner ring of the Coliseum is transformed into a celebration, the altar and hourglass left for viewing. We're allowed to touch the altar, and many do, believing it holds special blessings all its own, gifts from the many souls who have given their lives there.

But it's mostly the Dogio who will enjoy the celebration today. Us Basso have much cleaning up to do. Besides, my stomach is in knots, the fresh impression of Maisy's handprints enough to set my eyes stinging.

I can't face the celebration, can't begin to understand how anyone can. Carts of food line the middle of the arena, as market merchants set up around the edge and musicians play for entertainment. Right now, it's a lyre duet. The scents are overwhelming: cinnamon-glazed almonds, grilled sausages, fresh-baked strawberry pies. Giggling children run, winding in and out of stands, waving flags, their faces sticky from sugary treats. I used to be one of them.

Things were simpler a lifetime ago.

The Sun shines down on the scene, Maisy's memory buried beneath the bitter of curried meats, her blood on the altar, her last mark on this world gradually wiped away with each touch.

Poppy didn't want to stay for the celebration either. He'll wait for me at the dock while I wait for Nico to check in with his parents. Supposedly he's going to come back to the village with us, help clean up, but I'm not sure Lord and Lady Denali will allow it. Especially after the disappearing act he pulled on them earlier.

"Sick, isn't it?" I startle at the low murmur near my ear. I glance up to see Dorian, a hardness to his expression, completely opposite from yesterday. Still, at the sight of him, recalling yesterday, our walk through the tunnel, a couple of butterflies stir.

"Is it?" I reply, pushing the stirring away. That stirring's reserved for Nico. I don't want to have butterflies for anyone else right now. They're obviously confused.

My eyes once again find the rust-red-stained altar. Though, questioning him isn't what I intend. I want to agree, but can't find the words, the courage to do it, especially with so many Imperi soldiers sauntering about.

"It's for the best, I suppose, especially after last night," I hear myself say, as if on autopilot.

Besides, if I confide anything to anyone today, it'll be to Nico. My first words? Something like, "I was a complete sneak last night, but it was beyond my control. I'm embarrassed, but I don't regret it." I saw too much.

Dorian raises an eyebrow. "We can only hope."

I nod. *That* I can agree with.

Grabbing two fresh-baked rolls from the cart beside us, Dorian motions toward a bench away from the throng.

As we make our way through the shoulder-to-shoulder crowd, my eyes are on high alert for Nico—he'll be searching for me.

We sit on the bench and Dorian hands me one of the rolls, but I shake my head and fold my arms around my middle. "No thanks."

"Not hungry? I get it, but"—he tosses a chunk of bread into his mouth—"free food is free food."

I accept the roll, but hold it between my palms. "I'll take it to my grandfather."

Dorian nods. We sit in silence a few moments until he asks, "How bad were you hit last night?"

"Bad. They wrecked our home, but we're safe."

Dorian turns his head to face me. "Can I help you clean up? Our damage wasn't horrible. Only the outside of our shop was painted up, posters torn down."

"Oh, thank you, but Nico's ..."

"Veda—" Nico and an Imperi-uniform-clad Arlen approach. Nico's just taken a bite of a turkey leg and has two others wrapped up. His eyes briefly take in Dorian sitting next to me.

I stand, step toward Nico. "I didn't think you'd be able to get away."

"My parents weren't happy but I convinced them I needed to do more, help with the cleanup, especially since you were so badly hit and our village got next to nothing." I don't say it, but we're always badly hit and his village never sees damage.

"Wait—did something happen last night?" Arlen jokes.

I glare, shocked but also not. I've daydreamed about punching Imperi soldiers in the gut, but never have my fingers itched so badly to actually go through with it.

Dorian snorts in disgust under his breath, and both Nico and Arlen glance at him. Sitting on the bench, finishing his roll, surveying the crowd, he looks back at us, then stands. "Dorian." He shoves his hand out for Nico to shake.

Nico accepts and introduces himself and then Arlen. Dorian doesn't offer his hand to Arlen, and Arlen keeps his thumbs firmly hooked over his weapons belt at his middle.

There's an extended silence between the four of us until Dorian says to Nico, "I heard you braved the cheap seats today."

"That news traveled fast." Nico side-eyes Arlen.

"Oh, it was all the talk. But it's about time."

Nico's jaw clenches slightly, but he smiles. "I agree."

"I don't know what he was thinking!" Arlen cuts in, hand now clenched over the blade strapped to his belt. "Why would anyone choose those seats over the comfort of the others?"

"Some don't get a choice."

Arlen cocks his head toward Dorian, part amused, part something sinister, based on how his eyes have narrowed, and his finger twitches over his sword.

"Well," I break in, "we should get going. Poppy's waiting for us," I say to Nico. "Thanks for the bread." I hold it up and tell Dorian goodbye.

Arlen and I exchange only a moment of eye contact.

Imperi soldiers and Basso aren't supposed to socialize. A glance here and there, a sterile comment about Coliseum seating, a crack over the Night of Reckoning, that'll be the extent of our engagement from now on. Basically, not much will change.

As we pass the Offering Wall—the memorial for those who've

volunteered for sacrifice—a newly added bronze plaque, Maisy's name freshly engraved into it, is being added. I'm reminded that I won't ever buy eggs from her again, hear her hearty laugh, or smile back at her infectious grin.

In the distance, Maisy's family kneels at the edge of the island, her elderly mother balled into her knees, hands against the earth. The image, sad as it is, isn't what catches me. It's what the woman is mumbling into the ground.

"Fear the Night . . . Fear the Night . . . Fear the Night . . ."

CHAPTER 8

The short voyage from the Island of Sol back to Bellona is mostly silent save the loud whimpering of an unhappy baby.

Poppy, Nico, and I pick at our turkey, stare at the foamy water as it sloshes over the deck, glance out across the endless sea. But none of us speaks.

When we arrive at the port closest to the Basso village, we're greeted by several small fires. People have already started burning garbage, broken furniture, and ruined belongings. Poppy decides to check on the bait stand, assess the damage at the market, while Nico and I get started cleaning up at home.

I cover my mouth with my shawl to filter the smoke and the stench.

We've walked no more than a quarter mile down the road when Nico skids to a stop.

One of the large Imperi hourglasses from the fishing hole stands before us, so inexplicably out of place it'd be humorous if it wasn't so menacing. It's cracked, the black sand spilled into a large mound on the ground. Painted across the glass in what looks like blood, but I assume—hope—is the same red paint used in our home, is the ominous warning TIME'S RUNNING OUT!, the words hugged between two red crescent moons. Next to the hourglass is a long list of unaccounted-for Basso, one of the altars for the missing already forming, candles lit and dripping wax onto photos.

"I had no idea," Nico breathes, taking in the scene. "How did they . . . ?"

"I don't know. They defy reason . . . and gravity. It's worse than last year." I inhale deeply. Force myself to stand straighter, peel my eyes away from the scene. "But we'll come together. Work to clean it up. We always do." Then I remember. "You've never seen this before." Nico doesn't respond. "This doesn't happen up on the Hill. Not like this anyway, eh?"

Still staring at the red words, his eyes narrow and his hands form into fists at his sides. "No."

I turn and face him. "You still haven't told me . . . Why did you sit with us today?"

He gazes down at me. "I think I sort of snapped. That Basso girl inside the Coliseum kneeling, praying to the Sun for protection against the Night . . . This . . ." He motions to the disaster that is our village. "You . . ." He glances away. "Outside my house last night." I nearly choke on my own saliva at the mention of it. Again, Nico finds my eyes and this time I look away. "I've enjoyed that feast every year . . . The tiny frosted cakes shaped like Suns, how when I was small my parents would let me stay up until I couldn't keep my eyes open, and how now, I'm given a glass of my father's coveted port like it's a rite of passage." He shakes his head as if recalling memories I can't begin to fathom much less put an image to. "But last night was different. Someone who knows another side of me witnessed part of it, and for one of the first times in my life, I wasn't proud to be Dogio. Those cakes I used to fill my pockets with as a kid had a bitter aftertaste."

"Nico . . . I didn't mean to make you feel that way . . ."

"You didn't. I mean, yes, you being there brought it to my attention, but only by allowing me to get a glimpse through your eyes. Because, Veda, when I saw you outside my gate, two things hit me. The first

56

was, 'Why the hell isn't my best friend inside my house, enjoying this feast with me?'"

"And the second?"

"That you wouldn't be allowed. But even if you were, you couldn't because you were about to be attacked." He shoves his hands into his pockets, staring back at the pictures on the altar. "No Dogio have gone missing... We never do. Why is that?"

I shrug. "You have better protection, I guess. More Imperi soldiers roaming your streets... Better locks on your doors. I suppose we're easy prey."

"It's not right."

"I know."

"Want to know the worst of it?" I don't answer, but I hold his gaze. "Here I am, my family brushing shoulders with the highest Imperi officials, helping pass laws and regulations and plans for the island. I should be able to do something. My parents should *want* to do something. But they don't. I can't. Not yet."

"One day maybe. Maybe you'll be the one who sparks change."

"Maybe." But the word sounds hopeless.

"Still, you didn't have to sit with us at the Offering, break from tradition." I turn my head and look into his eyes. "Don't get me wrong, you're always welcome. But I'm not sure it was the smartest, most productive way to change things."

"I know... I wasn't thinking of the consequences, I just wanted to be near you and Poppy."

"I'm glad you were."

"I'll try to do more, Veda, I promise." I want so badly to believe he can do more. "And with the Offering today... Last night's Ever-Sol Feast... I'm hopeful things will get better for Basso. We'll be seeing less of the Night, I believe that."

I want to believe that too. Have the same hope he's got. The same faith in the Sun I once had. But just how Nico's tiny frosted Sun cakes are suddenly bitter, something changed for me as well today with Maisy's Offering.

It's like my eyes opened.

And what I'm seeing? It's not hopeful.

As Nico and I make our way back to Poppy, many are hard at work repairing the damage. Some only stare hopelessly into nothing in a dead daze. Others sob uncontrollably. The latter are the unluckiest of all. I assume they've lost loved ones. No one knows what becomes of them. What is known is they're never seen again. Lost to the Night.

I try my best to search, hoping beyond all reason I'll find one of those faces from the photos on the altar, when my sight is pulled to the Hill and the northern Dogio perch of the island. So sleepy. So still and safe and content. No smoke billowing from stinking garbage. No screams for missing loved ones.

Nothing.

A short walk up the hill yet an entire world away.

THE MORE WORK we do around our cottage, the more damage we seem to uncover. The Night weren't here long, but they made the best of those few minutes.

Poppy's working and swearing diligently as he hammers our kitchen table back together. I'm chipping away at the now-dried, caked paint staining our floors.

Nico is a machine, bounding up and down the stairs, bringing our supplies back from the cellar and refilling it with everything we took out to make space. Jars of pickled vegetables, firewood, Poppy's rusty tools. Nico makes several trips from the kitchen to the cellar to the backyard to the cellar without issue or complaint.

He's removed his jacket and scarf and only wears a light tunic, one that fits him expertly. It's clearly tailored to his exact specifications, show-ing the angles of his arms and chest, but in a subtle way, yet one that still manages to pleasingly cast heat over my face. He's rolled his sleeves above his elbows. The buttons at his chest, having come undone, show his skin, a bit of collarbone, all of it speckled in a light sheen of sweat. I try not to dwell on this, but can't begin to help it, especially as, I swear, he's intentionally walking past me more than he has to.

I'm in our common area mending the fabric of Poppy's favorite chair—slashed down the back with a knife, its insides spilled—when Nico bounds up the stairs.

"Veda?" He stands across the room, several ancient tools in his arms. "Can you get me the keys to the shed? I put them in my jacket pocket."

I nod and make my way to the kitchen, where his coat is slumped over a chair. Reaching into his pocket, I pull out the keys, but something else, a tightly folded piece of paper, falls to the ground. When I pick it up, the words DEPARTMENT OF THE IMPERI ARMY stare up at me.

I know I shouldn't, but I do it. I unfold the paper. In Nico's chicken scratch of handwriting, I see his name written across the top. Then his address. It's an official army officer's agreement.

"Veda—"

"Yesterday when you cut Arlen off after his army announcement, is this what you were trying to avoid me finding out?" I wave the form at him.

"No." He pauses. "Well, sort of. It's not how it looks."

Blood rushes to my head and pounds in my ears. "I mean, really, Nico." I raise my voice. "I'm very interested to see how you're going to do more to help us Basso when you're legally barred from socializing with us . . . With me."

Poppy walks in, probably curious as to why I'm shouting at my best friend.

"Nicoli. Take those tools out to the shed, please?"

"Yes, sir."

I throw the keys for the shed at him, but he catches them before they hit him square in the chest. His jaw tenses as he turns and leaves.

"Veda . . ." Poppy comes over and puts his arm around me, motioning I sit with him.

I show Poppy the agreement.

"I know."

"You know?"

"No . . . I mean, I'm not surprised." His voice is gentle and soft. "He's not only Dogio, but a Denali. And very loyal, protective. It was only a matter of time."

"But why would his parents allow him to join? Their plan is for him to take over their business. To marry a Dogio girl and have Dogio Denali babies. To carry on their legacy, not to fight, to govern. It doesn't make sense."

"Duty. It's in his blood." He pats my hand, and something about him admitting it forces a rock to lodge in my throat. Duty . . . Dogio have duty. Basso have . . . I glance around our broken home, but my eyes settle on Poppy. Basso have one another. But even that's dwindling.

And I have a feeling, with the Night leaving their mark more and more, the Sun clearly not satisfied with the state of things, that war is only around the corner.

Nico walks back into the house, pile of wood stacked to his chin. He sets it on the floor next to the hearth and brushes debris off his shirt.

Poppy stands, picks up a couple of logs, and descends to the basement, giving us a moment to talk, clearing his throat so obviously as he leaves that it's almost comical.

I make eye contact with Nico, who's moved into the kitchen. He's standing at the window and has taken off his tunic only to be left wearing a white cotton undershirt.

I walk into the kitchen and settle next to him, shoulder to shoulder. "Nico . . ."

He turns his head toward me, and it's then I see his eyes are red. Nico knows I see, that I understand why, but he doesn't look away and instead searches my face.

Turning toward me, he takes my hands in his. I inch closer and so does he. Before I know it we're embracing, arms wrapped around each other. With Nico's strong arms around my waist, chest pressed against mine, we've never been so physically close and I never want to move from this spot, this moment. My face at his chin, I can smell the woods on his neck, the saltiness of his skin.

I wrap my arms around Nico's back, pulling him closer, tighter; I'm on the cusp of tears. There's a burning in my throat that extends up into my nose, toward my ears. I clear it, take a deep breath, and pull away only to be greeted by a letdown Nico.

"Nico—"

He places the tips of his fingers over my mouth.

"Please don't mention it. Not now . . . Tomorrow . . . We'll figure it out tomorrow."

"But . . ." I pull the army agreement from my pocket. "Don't you see? It *is* tomorrow. Sooner or later we're going to have to face this." If Nico joins the army? If we'd been caught two minutes earlier within each other's arms—he an Imperi officer, me Basso—one of us would immediately be arrested for stepping over the line. For being so outrageously out of bounds. Bellonians have been executed over it: sabotaging an officer's duty. And we both know which of us it'd be.

"No." He yanks the paper from my hand, wads it up into a tiny ball, and throws it on the floor.

As I watch it land, roll underneath the lip of the cabinet, something I can't believe didn't occur to me before slaps me square in the face. "Wait." I glance at the hourglass around my neck. The sand is quickly draining the top bulb, filling the bottom, and nearing the vesper bells line. When it reaches it, I'll turn the thing over for the night. "How are you here right now?"

"What?" Nico nervously laughs under his breath, a sure sign I've caught him in something.

"How the hell are you able to be here with me? On the Basso side of the island? On Offering day? Shouldn't you be at . . . something? Some Dogio event? Meeting? Feast? You've always got *something*, especially on Offering days."

He's thinking hard. Spinning a lie. I know him too well not to spot it. All he gets out is "Just trust me" before he's saved by the shattering of glass from the other side of my house.

We rush to the scene to find Poppy's accidentally knocked out an entire windowpane, glass and all.

Poppy's not hurt. The window's done for. And Nico's temporarily off the hook.

"You're avoiding cleaning your room," Nico says as we make our way toward the front door. He knows me so well it's almost frightening.

"Maybe," I joke. He raises an eyebrow and I sigh. "All right. I can't face it." I'm exhausted after not sleeping all night, followed up by a particularly hard Offering, and then the hours of cleanup, Nico's army agreement. "Honestly, all I want to do is curl up into a ball on that chair in front of the fire and sleep until I wake up."

"You should."

I laugh. "Right." As if I could. As if napping's a luxury I can afford.

"Why not?" He takes my hand. "You'll feel better. Even if you only sleep an hour." He leads me to the chair and I don't even try to resist. I drop down into the old cushion, let my neck rest against the back.

He smiles and I laugh lightly. "Great. Are you happy now? I'll never get back up."

He flashes a crooked smile, his dimple showing spectacularly. "My evil plan worked, then." He spreads a knit blanket over me. "I'll be back in a few hours." But he doesn't leave, not right away. Instead Nico just stands there, hovering over me, gazing down at me, and I swear he wants to kiss me, or he's going to kiss me, or in the least he's thinking about kissing me, and I'd be lying if I said I wasn't thinking about it too.

He leans closer. So close I can feel the warmth of his breath brush my forehead.

"Thanks for your help today," I say, because the silence between us is drowning me.

He only nods, eyes unwavering, set on mine.

I swallow.

He leans in even closer.

And . . . kisses me on my cheek.

As he lingers there, breath warm against my face, my stomach dances and dips with both excitement and disappointment and *What the hell were you thinking, you can't kiss Nico, soon to be an Imperi officer!*

Things are already complicated enough.

I turn to the side, shut my eyes, and wrap myself up in the blanket. "See you later?" I say, my insides a mess of tangles, my heart telling my mouth to shut up and kiss him already, my head snuffing that idea out before I do something I can't take back.

"See you later," he says. My eyes are closed, but I can tell he's smiling. I keep them shut until I hear him walk away and then open and close the door behind him.

Once Nico's gone, I jump up—as if I could actually take a nap—and rush to the front window.

I watch as he quickly walks toward the Hill. Before long he turns the corner, the flash of his red scarf disappearing behind some trees. In a matter of one mile or so, Nico will be back to his world. A magical place where candied lemons come by the handful, naps are taken at one's leisure, and no one's worrying themselves over mopping up paint-stained floors and boarding up broken windows because they can't fathom affording a new pane of glass.

Honestly, I don't blame him if he chooses not to return tonight.

But the thought leaves an aching in my throat.

CHAPTER 9

TAP-TAP-TAP.

I drop the scrub brush into the bucket of soapy water with a clunk that splashes my knees.

Slowly, I stand and make my way to the window, but once there, I hesitate, my fingers hovering at the frayed edge of the drapes. I figure it's Nico . . . He'd said he'd be back. But it's after dark now.

After. Dark.

What if it's not him?

TAP-TAP-TAP.

A shiver travels the length of my spine as those lines from childhood bedtime stories fill my head . . . *A bony finger upon pane of glass at first night's nap. TAP-TAP-TAP.*

"Veda!" Nico hisses from the other side of the thin glass.

I jump out of my skin.

"Nico!" I hiss right back. Then, throwing the curtains to the side, I lift the window open in one motion. A chilly breeze takes my breath and sucks any heat that filled my room right out with it.

"Hey." Cast in shadows, Nico stands before me, his arms crossed over his chest, impish grin across his face. I assume if I were to peek out the window and downward, he'd also be tapping his toe against the ground. Nico squints at my thick sweater, the fingerless gloves covering my hands.

"What? It's cold."

"Veda . . ." He bends to his knees and leans forward so his head is inside my bedroom, elbows resting on the windowsill. "You promised." Small clouds flow from his mouth with warm breath, and his dark hair, a mane of unruly waves, falls into his equally dark eyes. I resist the urge to brush it off his forehead and to the side for him, but my fingers itch for the contact all the same.

I wrap my sweater more tightly around me, hugging my middle for warmth. "Oh stop—I'm not going anywhere. It's just cold." I playfully glare at him. "You're one to talk! Who's out after dark right now?"

He worries his bottom lip like he's working something out. "It's easier for me, I guess . . . I'm not in danger, and if caught I won't be in much trouble." He says it like he's just now realizing it. And maybe he is. Did he truly not know we Basso are always on guard? Whether it's an Imperi soldier or the Night, someone's always hovering over our shoulder, threatening to fine us or jail us or, worse, snatch us right up like shadows in the night.

Though I guess he wouldn't realize that.

Another cool breeze snakes its way into my room. I shiver then make to close the window right on top of him. "In or out, Denali?"

He flashes a crooked smile. Deep dimple and all. I swear he knows I'm helpless to it.

I step back.

He climbs in.

I close the window behind him.

This is a first . . . A boy—actually, anyone other than Poppy—in my room after vesper bells. But it's Nico and Nico isn't any boy. He's my one constant, unwavering friendship since childhood.

Nico, whom I almost kissed earlier.

Nico, who's sitting on my bed, glancing around the space as if it's different after the Sun's set. And it is different from usual . . . Signs of the Night's handiwork are all over, from the broken chest to the papers thrown about to the muddy, paint-stained boot prints covering the floor. Why we'd left cleaning my room for last, I don't know. It made sense at the time, especially when Nico said he'd be back after dinner to help me, which, in this house, was hours ago.

Nico, who shouldn't be out, much less on this side of the island, much less in my bedroom.

What I wouldn't do to see his bedroom . . . But that's beyond the point at the moment. Beyond reality, even. I nearly giggle imagining a scenario in which Lord and Lady Denali would invite me into their home, much less allow me to be in Nico's bedroom. The end of times. After "High Regent Arlen Rivera's" short reign. Maybe.

I march over to Nico and shove him in the chest. "What in Sun's name are you doing here?"

He falls flat onto his back against my bed, but recovers quickly, leaning up on his elbows. "What? I told you I was coming back."

"After dinner."

"Yeah. It took me a while to get away."

"Get away?" I sit next to him, stare into his eyes. "Are you telling me your parents don't know you're here?"

"Sun, no."

"Nico!"

"They think I'm in bed. It's fine."

"And where did they think you were earlier?"

He only cringes.

I raise my eyebrows, waiting.

"The Imperi recruitment office—*which I was.*" He looks away. "Yesterday."

"Nico . . ." I must wear the same shock on my face that's tightening my chest because he sits up and scoots closer, takes my hand.

"It'll be fine. I promise. My family's long asleep. They have no reason to suspect anything."

"But. How . . . ?"

Nico grins. "You're not the only one who can successfully sneak around the island, Adeline. Arlen does it all the time. He'd die if he knew I was here. He's been trying to get me to sneak out for years. But all he does is skulk around for the sake of defying the law. I think he stole some eggs once and threw them into the tunnel so it'd stink. Stupid things like that, though I guess he won't be doing much of that anymore." He shakes his head. "Anyway, I figure, if you have a good reason to break the laws, it's justified."

Fair enough. And easy for him to say when his worst punishment would be a good talking-to. Maybe community service.

Nico grabs a scrub brush and gets to work where I left off.

I decide to drop it. The army papers, the sneaking around, the lying to his parents. Sun knows I'm no saint. And I'm definitely not a hypocrite. I'm also appreciative at how hard he's working to scrub those boot prints off my floor.

But they don't come off.

Not completely.

THE CROW OF a rooster shocks me awake.

Heart racing, I sit straight up to see out the window.

Relief blankets me.

It's still dark. Stupid, mixed-up rooster.

A sleeping Nico lies curled up on the floor beside me, his chest against my back, and we're surrounded by cleaning supplies and a pile of trash.

The quilt from my bed's tucked snuggly over us.

As motionless as possible, I lift Nico's arm from around my waist. The night was cold, so it's not surprising we huddled together while we slept.

I hold my breath and scoot inch by inch out from under the blanket.

"Going so soon?" He lifts his hourglass from round his neck. "We've got at least an hour until morning bells." Nico's voice has a satisfaction to it like he's humored over how flustered I am, and I can tell he's smiling.

"I . . . I . . ." I have no excuse.

"Yes?"

"We fell asleep." I shake my head.

"Actually, *you* fell asleep. I kept cleaning." He smiles. "Then I fell asleep too."

I stand, cinching my sweater at my neck, suddenly feeling extremely modest, warmth traveling up from my chest to my face.

It's then I see his shirt's unbuttoned and there's no undershirt beneath his tunic this time. My eyes linger a breath too long before I glance away and the image is burned into my memories like a photo. Nico's skin is smooth, muscles defined, but lean, and—

"Are you all right?" He's staring, brow furrowed.

"I'm fine . . . Just can't believe we fell asleep like that. Thank the Sun for that damn rooster." I release the grip on my sweater, suddenly very warm. Keeping my back to him, I reorganize the things on my altar, something I definitely need to do right at this moment.

"Yes. We owe the rooster." From my periphery, I see he's buttoning the front of his shirt.

I look back at him.

Nico scruffs his hair, leaving it a mess of black curls, and kicks off the blanket. I'm relieved to find the rest of him covered.

Truly, I am.

Moving on, I try to ignore the way my heart has quickened.

Nico puts his face in his hands, rubbing his eyes. He then looks up and watches as I unwind my braids, slip a skirt over my pants, and pull on my socks and boots.

I've no idea what to do with myself so I start toward the door, make a hasty decision for both of us. "I've gotta get my bait. If we leave now, we can walk together to the Hill. By the time you're home, the Sun will be rising and I can safely head to the Hole."

Nico stands, begins putting on his boots. "I'll be able to sneak back in before my parents are up."

I nod and start for the door.

"Wait." Nico walks toward me, pulling a small velvet pouch from his back pocket. I spot a tag with my name neatly scrolled across it attached to a ribbon around the top.

Odd.

He hands me the pouch. I take it and move to my bed, sit down. I frown at the tiny blue bag. "What is it?"

"Open it." He sits down, nudges me in the ribs.

I untie the ribbon and open the pouch. When I reach inside, I find something small wrapped in a square of silk. I slide the item into my hand and look up at Nico.

"Go on."

With one deep breath, I unwrap the silk. Within it is an oval crystal, cut into a hundred angles, set within a gold casing and hanging from a golden chain. The crystal is the faintest, most beautiful blue I've ever seen.

"Nico . . ."

He places his hand over mine, our fingers clasping, the necklace tucked within my palm. I swallow hard.

"It's your birthday gift," he says. "I know it's early, but I couldn't wait."

"It's . . ."—I hold the pendant out before my eyes—"magical."

"It was my mother's. She gave it to me a while ago. I used to love it when I was little. If you look through it, it gives the effect of a kaleidoscope." He breathes out. "It reminds me of the sea, which always reminds me of you."

Closing one eye, I peer through it with the other. On the opposite side of the crystal, Nico's distorted, mixed into a hundred Nicos all staring straight at me from different angles.

"I love it." I hold it up toward the light shining through the window, and it casts several shimmering rainbows on my wall.

I swivel to the side and lean my head down. Lacing it around my neck, I hold my hair up so Nico can clasp it.

He does, and the way his fingers, light as feathers, graze the back of my neck gives me a shiver and a fresh layer of goose bumps.

"There," he says.

I turn back toward him and he's smiling. "It suits you." But he's not looking at the necklace, he's gazing into my eyes. "Happy early birthday, Veda."

"Thank you. Truly. It's so special." I cup the stone in my palm over my chest. It's heavy, but so incredibly fragile, the cuts precise and delicate, the chain a hundred tiny gold links perfectly pieced together.

But this gift, one that should, and does, make me happy, is also singed with sadness. Deep down I fear this gift means more than happy birthday. Nico's army agreement, left crumpled on our kitchen floor, still nags at me.

I fear this gift—on some level, maybe even one we're unaware of—means goodbye.

As Nico and I make our way out my window and into the dark night, I clutch the pendant in my fist, determined not to let that happen.

It's COMPLETELY DIFFERENT sneaking around the island with Nico by my side. I don't glance over my shoulder nearly as much. I don't jump at each and every sound that catches me off guard.

And while we don't dare speak a word, we're able to communicate as easily as ever.

I point up at the moon. It's full and so bright, only a scattering of clouds surrounding it. Nico takes my hand as we pass over a pond, stepping across slippery rocks. And he doesn't let go once we're on the other side.

In this moment, surrounded by the darkness I so often fear, Nico and I are together. Without worry or wandering eyes or Dogio obligation, Basso judgment. Right now, us being something, being more, doesn't feel so completely impossible.

It's too good to be true.

Because this is reality, where Dogio and Basso are never *more*.

A whistle blows to our right.

Then another to our left.

Nico and I share a look of pure panic, dart into thicker wooded forest, when "Hey! Stop!" rings out right behind us. A soldier grabs Nico by the arm, jerking him to a stop. My best friend no longer by my side, on instinct or stupidity—I'm not sure which—my feet slow. I look over my shoulder back at Nico.

He's not even struggling. In fact, he's got his arms up in surrender and is talking with the soldier who stopped him, giving some kind of excuse. Almost as if he's stalling . . .

Almost like he's making it so I can get away.

I turn to run when the other soldier comes out of nowhere and I slam right into him, knocking us both off-balance.

Nico shouts, "Go! Run!"

I scramble to my feet and take off in the opposite direction, only catching Nico's eyes long enough to see a flash of the reflection of the silvery, full moon.

I'm forced to leave the forest and travel the main walkway. It's reckless . . . I'll be seen by another soldier or the Night for sure. But I have no choice.

My boots echo with each quick, hard step against the stone. I splash through puddles. I'm completely out of breath and breaking all the rules I'd vowed to keep when out before sunrise.

Before too long, the soldier's whistle sounds again.

I take a hard right into the dark square.

At least two more whistles blow. More footfalls.

The tunnel is nearly within reach and I can't believe I'm going to run through it at night, alone. But—I gaze back—the alternative is jail. Worse.

Three Imperi soldiers enter the square.

"Stop!" one shouts. The others blow their whistles.

The candles that mound on the tops of the altars usually provide light, but they've long burned out. The tunnel is nothing but a black hole in the stone wall.

Without hesitation, I sprint toward the entrance.

A tall figure steps out of the shadows.

I gasp and skid to a stop before slamming into him.

CHAPTER 10

Out of tunnels, from the ground they'll crawl, dark as night, death to all. Run, hide, scream for help, straight down a devil's den is the fate you're dealt.

I'M STOPPED.

Frozen between something dark and menacing and several soldiers. The Night and the Imperi. A death sentence.

But when the figure steps into the pearly moonlight, I'm greeted by a pair of silver-blue eyes. Even though the person is cloaked in black, hooded, I know those eyes. Blue agate.

"What're you waiting for—come on!" Dorian hisses, hand outstretched.

Still in shock, confusion muddling my brain, I take his hand and run into the tunnel.

The last I see of the Imperi soldiers is them sprinting toward us, but before I can panic, Dorian throws something at them, a large flume of blue smoke the result. The soldiers cough and sputter.

It's the last I hear before the ground drops out from under me.

The world as I know it disappears and I'm sent from the tunnel, down, down, down, the slick metal beneath me refusing to allow my fingers an ounce of purchase. Any hope to claw my way back up is dashed when it hits me.

Devil's den.

I can't breathe; my chest burns, constricted from shock, from running across the island. From the terror ripping through me because I'm sliding down one of the Night's devil's dens—undetectable snakeholes that lead right to their underground caves—and there's nothing I can do about it. I've only ever heard tales, rumors of these holes that appear from nowhere only to vanish just the same. Imperi soldiers can't seem to track them down. I'd assumed they were legend, another wild story, but they're real.

Real as Dorian's arms wrapped tightly around me. Real as the roots and vines and Sun knows what else scratching past my body, cutting any exposed skin with the sting of sharp needles. Real as the scream inching up my throat. But I don't dare release it for fear of what underground horrors it might stir all around me.

When the sliding stops, there's a moment of freefall before we land on top of something soft. I bounce twice, then still.

The minute Dorian lets go, I scramble, my hands and knees falling through what must be a large net. I'm unable to move toward escape before Dorian, suddenly standing before me, lit lamp in hand, says, "There's literally nowhere to go but down." I back away, tripping over my own feet.

This is it. The end. Dorian is a member of the Night, and no one comes back from the Night.

All I can do is stare, search my surroundings for some way out, which of course there isn't. We're underground.

He shrugs, hands up as if he's showing me he's not carrying any weapons. "I know you must be shocked." I keep staring. "You're probably afraid." He then moves to the center of the cavern where a long rope hangs like a noose. My hands instantly go to my neck, but he simply pulls it, releasing what I assume is a door far above that closes and latches.

Slowly, cautiously, he approaches me. "I'm not quite sure what to say here . . . This isn't exactly how I planned for you to find out."

I'm shaking my head, straining my eyes to see through the darkness, waiting for an explanation. "But . . . ?" I urge, my voice quaking.

"It's a shock, I know."

I nod, jaw slack.

He holds the lantern up between us. "I know I've got a lot to answer for—and I will—but it's most important you understand that I *will not* hurt you."

Isn't that exactly what someone who doesn't want me to know they're going to hurt me says? Question after question fills my head, but there's a horrible crash right above us.

"We need to go."

"But . . . Wait . . . I don't understand. What the Sun is going on?"

"How about you interrogate me as we move? That smoke isn't going to hold them off very long. Deal?"

Before I can comment, he's rushing forward, down a slight decline, but enough of one that I keep one hand flat against the wall next to me for balance.

I follow Dorian through the black tunnel as he continues on about the explosive. "The blue smoke is a mix of black pepper, sulfur, and crushed graphite, pressure packed so when it's lit and hits a hard surface, it explodes. It's impressive, but clears quickly."

We make our way around numerous crooks and turns, up then down rough slopes.

Finally, I spit out the loudest question ringing in my mind. "*Who* are you?"

"Did you hit your head on the way down? I thought it was obvious." He glances back at me, and even through the darkness, I can see humor mixed with concern in his expression. Did I hit my head? Is this a nightmare?

Sun, I hope so.

"Do you find this funny?" I ask.

"No." He wipes the almost-smile off his face. "I'm sorry. It's not funny. Not at all. It's just . . . I was only doing a tunnel check and there you were. I'm not sure which one of us was more surprised."

"*Me. I* was more surprised. I'm still . . ." My heart raps like a drum in my ears. ". . . How can this be? You're the glassmaker's apprentice . . . Basso . . . How can you also be a member of the Night?" He's a traitor. And a liar.

The terrain changes from dirt-caked walls to rusty, crumbly rock and then to yellowed stone. The lower we decline, the thicker and damper the air gets, the richer the scents of sour minerals and salt. Everything is sulfur down here.

"Who says I can't be both?"

"Everyone. The laws of nature. Every story about the Night I've ever heard."

He laughs.

I clutch his hand, forcing him to skid to a halt, bumping right into him in the process. Dorian turns and faces me. "Look, you're right. This is serious." Holding the lantern over his shoulder, he searches my face, almost as if he's testing if he can trust me.

Him. Worried about trusting *me*.

"So . . . ?" I ask, waiting for an answer.

"What if I told you I can be both Basso and Night soldier?"

I shake my head.

"Veda." He leans down to meet my eyes. "It's true. It's not the Night who's kidnapping Basso or burning down their homes."

"You're mad."

He narrows his gaze. "I'm definitely not mad."

I raise an eyebrow. "Then prove it."

"Follow me." Dorian turns and continues walking.

"Why should I? How do I know you're not lying just to capture me? Enslave me. Gnaw my toes off. You know the stories."

Again, he turns to face me. Lantern held out in front of him, expression shadowed, morphing from calm to creepy to distorted. "You probably shouldn't trust me. Hell, I wouldn't trust me. But it doesn't seem you've got much of a choice." He glances back from where we came. The tunnel with the soldiers in it.

At this point, I'm not sure which is worse: following Dorian into the belly of the beast or clawing my way back up to Bellona and into the hands of the Imperi for definite punishment.

I stare across the darkness at Dorian.

And I nudge my head forward. "Let's go."

WE HIT A door that's been pieced together with scraps of metal, a padlock keeping it closed. Dorian unlocks it with a key from a ring hooked to his belt. We go through and he replaces the same lock on the other side of the door.

"One way?" I ask, taking in his clothing for the first time. He's wearing all black, a military-style patch sewn over his chest. It's small, nothing but a row of colored stripes as if marking rank, maybe missions. In addition, a crudely hammered silver pin—a crescent moon—is stuck to his collar.

"Only one way," Dorian confirms, catching my eyes on his uniform.

"That's comforting and . . . not." We continue walking. I take note of his keys, which are hooked to his pants on one of the left belt loops closest to me. If he didn't expect it, I could easily clutch hold of them and tear them off.

"It's to keep others out, not to keep you in. If another member of the Night goes down the same den, they'll know an alternative way to get to the Lower. Anyone else makes it that far? Well, they'll be stuck there until eventually found."

I stifle a shiver.

But it isn't until we go through another, similarly patchworked door, that fear truly seizes me.

On the other side, we're greeted by a group of Night soldiers. Twenty or so. All in black. Hoods over their heads. Lanterns scattered about the crowd, giving each of them the deep eye sockets and sunken faces of skeletons.

I grip the arm of Dorian's jacket and then quickly let go. I reach to clutch his keys, but he's already turned away. There's no way I can get to them without causing a scene, and I'm outnumbered exponentially.

Backing up, I take short, calculated steps until I'm flat against the cold, metal door.

He's one of them.

Keys or no keys, before I can make a break for it, try to kick the rickety lock off the rusted door and happily bolt into the open arms of a couple of Imperi soldiers, the Night rushes toward us.

I cover my head with my fists, huddling into the door, but soon realize I'm not being torn limb by limb. My toes are definitely still attached to my feet. Instead, whoops and shouts of "Welcome home!" and "Dorian!" fill the small cavern and echo off the walls.

Daring to open my eyes, I find all manner of hugging and tackling and scuffing of Dorian at the hands of the Night. He's laughing so hard, tears stream down his face. "All right . . . All right . . . I missed you too . . ."

My jaw practically on the floor, I force myself to straighten, then take a couple of steps toward the commotion where Dorian's and my eyes connect.

Cheeks flush, hair a complete mess, he clears his throat and puts his hands up to halt the love fest. "Everyone," he says, surveying the crowd, "this is Veda Adeline. We just evaded a couple of Imperi soldiers. She's probably a little spooked right now . . ." He looks at me, smile dancing at the corners of his lips. "But my hope is she'll soon find we're not the monsters the Imperi make us out to be."

And then I receive a similar, much less personal but equally warm welcoming to the Lower.

To the Night.

✦ ✦ ✦

As one large group, walking in two by two, we descend deeper into the underside of the island, the Lower, they call it. The whispers of quiet chatter snake their way in and out of the line as our damp footsteps scrape against the stone floor.

I strain my ears to hear, hone in on at least one conversation, pick out a few key words that might alert me to what's to come, good or bad. Something to hint at whether I can trust any of these people or not. Right now all I can think of is torture chambers and dank cells and being forced to milk mud beetles until my fingers rot and fall off.

I find myself squinting through the dark to spot the spindly black things. Because if I do see any, that might mean we're getting close to where the Night keep the Basso. Where they're put to work or worse.

And to think, a mere couple of days ago I was digging for beetles like my life depended on it. If I see another the rest of my life, it'll be too soon.

I know immediately when we pass from the tunnels leading to the Lower and enter into actual Night territory.

Curving around a sharp corner, we're immediately greeted by a large mural. A depiction of the phases of the moon is painted in an arc on the rough stone wall. Stars cascade overhead—all around—and actually seem to twinkle from the reflection of the lit candles adorning the floor below, the natural moisture clinging to the walls. Along with the candles are roots and plants, scraps of clothing, handmade knickknacks, all similar to the blessings left on the Sun altars up on Bellona.

Several tunnels identical to the one we're leaving surround the space, all ending at the mural.

We descend a few steps, and when I look down, careful not to trip, I catch two mud beetles skittering along the bottom of the wall.

I swallow back a gasp, grip my hands into fists. *It's only mud beetles*, I remind myself. *Keep it together, Veda.*

But I don't have it together. Not even close. I lean in toward Dorian. "Take me home. Now."

Dorian glances at me from the corner of his eyes and barely nods.

Then we all start moving again.

He's not taking me home now.

Images of Poppy's nighttime horror stories tick behind my eyes like illustrations from a sick book. Basso strung by their toes until they're severed clean off . . . Mud beetles using their pincers to chew the eyelids off Basso corpses . . . Those who couldn't bear the demands of the Night are punished in the cruelest of ways . . . Disposed of inside these tunnels. Left to starve and die . . .

My mouth is dry as cotton, palms slick with sweat, breathing near hyperventilation. My heart races as if trying to escape my body.

Where the Sun are they taking me?

CHAPTER 11

It takes a few minutes, but I manage to calm my heart, steady my breathing.

Nothing's happening, I remind myself. No one's scheming quietly up ahead or measuring lengths of rope to my neck or sharpening a blade. I've no reason to think I'm in immediate danger. Not yet anyway.

But we are moving toward something. Someplace.

Keeping my eyes on the line of bodies ahead of me, with Dorian and me in the very back, I know this is the time to get him alone. Perhaps my only chance. I need answers. Now.

Just as I'm calculating how to make a move, get him away from all these Night soldiers, when exactly to bolt down another tunnel and either force him to follow me on his own or find my way out of here, he bids the others goodbye, but a couple straggle behind.

"See you tonight, Veda?" a girl about my height says, her tone sweet and calm, catching me completely off guard as if I'd expected her voice to be low and menacing by sheer association. The fact that she's wearing a black hood over her head.

"Oh . . . I'm not sure . . ."

She nods, giving a small smile and swooshing her short bangs away from her eyes.

The boy, maybe eighteen or so, standing next to her chimes in equally pleasant, "Well, we hope you come. It's going to be a great celebration."

But I'm shaking my head. "I doubt I'll be able to . . ."

Dorian cuts in before I can politely decline. "Well . . . it's not so much a celebration as it is a small gathering." He shrugs. "Nothing to get too excited about." He pointedly eyes the two Night soliders, smiles in a reserved sort of way. "You guys need to get back. Veda and I have a lot to discuss."

They nod respectfully and turn on their heels, march after the rest of the Night soldiers down the tunnel to the left as Dorian and I take the one to the right.

Just the two of us.

"Dorian?"

"Yeah, Veda?"

"Why in the Sun are they acting like I'm here to stay?"

"Were they?" He avoids my eyes.

I quick step in front of him, stretch my arms out so my hands are against each wall of the narrow tunnel, and force him to stop. "You need to explain some things."

He pauses for breath, gazing down at my lips, and I realize how ridiculously close we are to each other. I swallow, drop my arms, and take a step back. "You're right." He finds my eyes, gives a single nod. "Come with me and you'll get all the proof you need." He steps forward, marching down the tunnel at a quick pace. I'm fast to catch up, and once again beside him, I catch him looking down at me.

I look right back. "Why do I feel like you're luring me to my death?"

This, he seems to take seriously. Dorian keeps walking but slows slightly. "Listen. I know what you've been raised to believe about the Night, what the Imperi works hard to this day to have you believe about us—I learned it all too." Now he stops completely and turns to face me. "It's not true. None of it. Those people back there . . . Did they seem like monsters to you?"

"Well . . . No, but . . ."

82

"But nothing. I know we just met, that you have no reason to trust me. I promise, once you see the truth you won't want to go back up there."

I'm already shaking my head before he finishes the sentence. "I doubt that."

"Just . . . a little longer. And if you don't want to stay, I'll personally take you home." He holds his hand flat next to his face. "Night's honor."

I don't trust him one bit.

But I want to.

And what am I going to do? Find my way back to that devil's den we came down? I'd no sooner get lost or trapped, eaten by fanged groundhogs or a swarm of mud beetles or whatever other horrors live down here. Besides, if he *is* lying, I'll have information to take back—and I will find my way back—to share with other Basso to keep them from disappearing at the hands of the Night.

And if he's being honest? Well, we'll just see what he has to show me.

"All right," I say. "But the minute I tell you I'm through, you'll take me home?"

"The minute." He gives a small closed-lipped smile.

I nod and we continue on.

When we reach a set of steps, Dorian assures me it's not much farther. At the bottom of the stairs is a small cavern. Faded murals adorn the walls, depicting nighttime scenes, stars dancing down on dark treetops, the moon a yellow crescent, smiling upon a sleepy forest. If I didn't know better and if there weren't four caves like black holes peeking back at me, I'd think the world turned on edge and I was indeed staring at the nighttime sky.

Above each save one of the caves is a wooden plank nailed to the wall, labels burned into the signs. Over the tunnel to the far right is the word SOLDIERS; to the far left, OFFICERS; next to that reads GARDENS; and the one next to that has no sign. A mystery door.

"This way first." Dorian walks straight for the gardens' tunnel, which confuses me because how can one grow a garden without the Sun?

We're in an ink-black tunnel, the only light a flickering bulb several yards away and Dorian's lantern.

We stop at a wooden door under the flickering light, which goes out.

"Damn generator," he mumbles, adjusting the bulb to no avail. In the pitch-dark, holding the lantern in one hand, Dorian sifts through that ring of keys. Squinting under the dim light, he finally finds the right one and opens the door. Nothing but darkness claws out at us.

"After you."

Yeah, right. "No, no, after *you*."

Dorian smiles like he knows what I'm thinking and strides past me into the blackness.

Feet planted in the doorway, I'm expecting this "garden" to be a cache of weapons, maybe a block of cells where they keep the Basso they kidnap. Or worse.

But when Dorian cranks something, a metal lever I think, large lamps mounted around the room slowly flicker to life.

What I find before me is indeed a garden.

The plants are duller versions of the crisp, vibrant ones I'm used to seeing up on Bellona. I spot beet greens that are pale yellow. Underripe tomatoes more resembling peaches. And banana trees, the leaves browned, the fruit a muted green.

"Not what you expected?" Dorian asks.

"Would you have expected this?"

He nods. "Fair enough."

I walk farther into the cavern, taking in more of the space. There are wires trailing like a thick web down one of the cave walls, connecting the lamps to the generator; tubes hooked to barrels that I assume hold water line the perimeter.

"But how does it work? There's no Sun."

"No. No Sun. It's kind of a backward greenhouse. Take a closer look."

I take a few steps toward one of the lamps. It flickers with intermittent power, but it's definitely the source of heat and light, the warmth radiating off it intensely and I'm still several feet away.

They've created an underground Sun. Fake Sun? Blasphemous in the eyes of the Imperi. In my eyes? Unfathomable, pure magic.

Turning in a circle, I'm able to make out three walls in the far-off distance, the fourth covered with climbing greenery and what appears to be blackberries hanging from the vines.

I move toward one of the large garden boxes where carrot greens peek out of the earth, lining several rows on one side, the other filled with tomato plants, their stalks tied to small handmade trellises. I bend down closer and find what I thought was soil is sand. I touch it, and the delicate granules slide through my fingers. But nothing grows in sand. Not that I've ever seen. Yet, I'm staring at a tomato plant; its fruit is small, a muted red, but ripe enough to eat.

Shocked, I look at Dorian. His expression is one of pride.

"We've been adapting down here for a while, finding new ways to survive."

"Survive?"

"Well, we've gotta eat, right? And we can't always risk going above."

It's nearly impossible to think of the Night as anything but demons living on insects and vermin, the blood of their captives.

A shiver runs up my spine and I side-eye Dorian.

He catches me staring. "What *were* you expecting?"

"Oh . . . I don't know . . ." Like I'm going to say.

He walks on, taking long, lanky strides. "Let me guess. You were picturing torture devices? A pit of venomous snakes?"

"No." Yes.

"But close."

"All right. Maybe a little."

When we reach the other side of the cave, Dorian cranks the lamps back off.

"Don't the plants need light to grow?"

He stops midcrank, the lamps flickering. "Yeah, but someone else tends it in shifts. Electricity is so unpredictable down here, we've got to conserve." He unlocks and opens a similar door as the first.

"How do you have electricity when we barely get it up top?"

He cocks an eyebrow. "We have the Imperi to thank for that." And he cranks the lights completely off.

"Wait." I shove my boot in the door before he can close it. Dorian's eyes bear down on me, and I can't tell if it's anger or humor I sense in them. "So, the Night have gardens and not torture chambers. Not here anyway. I don't see how this proves anything other than that you have a decent source of food."

"I'm not finished. This was only part one."

"There's more?"

"You expected me to woo you into trusting the *evil Night* by showing you our gardens? Give me a little credit, V." He lightly tosses a firm, nearly white plum at me, which I barely manage to catch. Something about it, about *him*, makes my insides both seethe with anger and light up with excitement.

"All right." I bite into the plum. It's more tart than I'd prefer, but is indeed a plum, a pleasant sweetness soon taking over the sour. Still, my lips slightly pucker. "What's next, then?"

"Torture chambers . . . A toe feast . . ." He stares a beat, taking in my reaction to the fruit, then grins. "Follow me."

We take a tunnel that's one long curve as if we're circling back around.

"So . . . Back up on the island . . . What were you doing out after dark anyway?" Dorian asks.

"What were *you* doing out after dark?"

"I asked you first." He slows down, gazing over at me. "And you call yourself Give and Take champion of Bellona?"

I snort. "I don't believe I ever claimed that sort of fame."

"Oh." He shoots a crooked smile my way. I begin to smile back but bite the inside of my cheek to stop, force myself to remember where

I am—not in the tunnel up on the island, but belowground. Where nightmares come true.

"I was walking Nico back to his house," I answer. Dorian stays silent but gives a slight nod. "He'd stayed late at my house to help clean up after the Night of Reckoning." Another slight nod. "Anyway, we got caught by the Imperi. Nico handed himself over so I could get away."

"He'll be fine, by the way."

"Hope so," I say. "I think it's safe to assume worse case for him was an escort straight home. But with the Imperi you never know."

Dorian shakes his head knowingly. "You mean, *we* never know." I sigh. He's got that right. "Take comfort in who he is, who his family is. They probably didn't even tell his parents."

"Probably not." And I catch myself rolling my eyes. Because it's not fair, is it? That Nico gets a friendly escort home and I had to run for my life. I've always known that's how it would play out, but I never realized how it'd make me feel if and when it did.

Like *less than*.

I swallow hard, pushing the notion from my head, regaining focus and coming back to my surroundings, reality, the fact that I'm underground in Night territory. I put my guard back up like a wall, because I definitely slipped a few beats there. "All right, your turn to answer. Why were you out before the Sun?"

"I'm a member of the Night, remember?" This time he gives me a full smile.

But I don't return it. Instead I lift an eyebrow. "I won't soon forget." This wipes the smile from his face, and I swear if the light was brighter I might spot a bit of warmth speckling his cheeks. So cocky. So infuriating. So . . .

I steal a glance to spot him worrying his bottom lip. Jaw flexed, he runs a hand through his hair, the longer side falling delicately over his ear.

Despite that tiny spark of intrigue daring to awaken those stupid butterflies in my stomach, I will keep him in his place at least until I'm sure I'm not in danger.

He stares over at me, catching me watching him. I look away.

FROM THE TUNNEL, we enter a narrow stairwell. The steps have been pieced together with scraps of wood, metal, what looks like old, broken doors, pieces of discarded furniture. They're creaky, mostly steady. The cave joins another cave, and before I can find my bearings we're back at the cavern where we started, stars and moon mural before us. Four tunnels, one of them labeled GARDENS.

"It's like a labyrinth," I breathe.

"You have no idea." Dorian motions to the soldiers' cave. "This one next."

"Okay . . ."

"Ninth room down."

Room? More like cave. Like a long hallway, cavern after small cavern opens up from the main tunnel as Dorian and I make our way to the ninth one. There are numbers painted on the walls outside each "room." The air is cool and damp, and water trickles down rocks from somewhere not too far off. Once we reach cave number nine, I hesitate.

It's dark, bone-chillingly eerie down here alone with Dorian, member of the Night. And suddenly I'm not so sure I've made a good choice making that deal with him.

Just as I'm about to back away, take myself quickly down the path we just walked, a group of girls comes up from behind us. They're chattering. Laughing. The sudden noise puts me on edge, and, on instinct, I hug the cold wall behind me.

They approach and one of them, the tallest, nudges Dorian in the back of his knee, making his leg bow forward completely out of his control.

In normal life I'd laugh at how completely awkward and out of character it is to see him flop forward like that.

But this isn't normal life and nothing about it humors me.

The girl and I make eye contact and she smiles, two small dimples hooking the corners of her eyes like perfect crescent moons. Under different circumstances, I'd return her smile. Instead, I only nod.

Dorian shoots the girl a seriously devious look. "I will get you back for that."

"Pfft!" She stops, telling the others she'll catch up later.

"When you least expect it . . . ," Dorian singsongs, but in a grave, sinister voice.

"Yeah . . . yeah . . ." Ignoring him, she turns to me. "I'm Bronwyn." She shoves her hand out to shake mine. I hesitate but accept.

"I'm—"

"Veda, I know. I'm so glad to finally meet you. Dorian's said so—"

"All right . . ." He cuts in before I can ask how the Sun she knows my name and, more, what in the world Dorian's been saying about me. "You've probably got to get ready, eh, Bron?"

"Oh! Right. See you in a bit!" And she's gone, fast as she arrived.

I stare over at Dorian, waiting for an explanation about the whirlwind-girl.

"Bronwyn." I cock my head slightly. "My sister."

"Ah." Makes sense.

"She's a pest." He shakes his head. "Shall we?"

"Hold on. How did she know me?"

"Remember our deal, Veda? Details?"

I narrow my eyes at the slight edge in his tone. "I do."

"Well." He clears his throat, softening his voice. "Inside there . . ." He nudges his head into cave number nine ". . . I promise things will make more sense."

I straighten my shoulders, take a deep breath, and march into the cave, not glancing back.

Inside is a lantern, a couple of candles, a mat on the floor made out of wool or animal skin. Atop the mat is a mound of what appears to be black clothing. But none of that is remarkable in the least.

What does stop me in my tracks is the ceiling-to-floor mural.

Dorian stares at it with me. "Each room has one."

"Really? It's beautiful."

He nods, chest slowly rising and falling but with purpose.

Like the murals I've seen so far down here this one too is so much freer, the paint showing movement as opposed to the harsh angles and coldness of the Sun mosaics up on the island. Above me is the night sky, full moon, swirling stars, perhaps a planet or two.

Beyond the stars, on the main wall, is a battle scene. But instead of people with swords drawn, the moon and the Sun are at war. They aren't personified, but represented by different colors, warm and cool. The Sun is all fire: reds and yellows and oranges. The moon, all ice: blues and purples and grays. Two sides exploding into one mess of color where they meet. And in the middle, at the place they completely touch, is a five-pointed star.

I walk straight up to the star, something about it pulling me closer.

Dorian stands behind me. "The mark of the Moon's daughter. The one who will lead the Night to victory. Who will ensure we defeat the Imperi once and for all." His tone is low, soothing, as he breathes the words out.

"That sounds like horseshit," I say. Dorian literally responds with a laugh, a genuine "Ha!" It catches me so off guard that I allow a small laugh too. "If you'd said that to anyone else, V, they'd have thrown you back up that devil's den fast as a ground snake can slither."

"Can you blame me?"

"No." He steps forward so he's next to me.

I turn and face him, widen my eyes like, *so?*

He raises his brow right back.

I blink. "Then you understand why I'm at a loss. Everyone knows those legends are all made up. Stories from long ago, concocted to explain the unexplainable. Like the creation story of Bellona?" He opens his

90

mouth to argue, but I continue before he can get a word out. "The myths I've been taught about the Night?"

Dorian takes a long, deep breath in. "All right, that's fair." He touches the star. "But this is different. Trust me."

"How so? And why should I?"

He nods confidently, stepping closer so we're barely six inches apart. "You'll see how this is different if you stay a little longer." He shrugs. "You don't have to trust me, I understand why you wouldn't, but I hope you'll learn to."

I want to say something smart like "probably not" or "we'll see," but the seriousness cast over his face is sobering. Instead, I only nod once.

"Now, remember, you promised you'd hear me out."

"I did."

"Please . . . Sit with me?" He strides to the mat and sits, setting the lantern down next to him.

Potential information, I remind myself. *You could help save others.*

I sit on the mat across from Dorian, counting down the minutes before I demand he take me back up to Bellona. Because, sure, he might have saved me from a couple of Imperi soldiers. Yes, we made a deal, but I'm gonna need more than fairy tales to settle the favor.

Yet, I'll hear him out.

"I was born up on the island but spent half my time down here. My parents were Night soldiers, and when my sister was born they decided I'd be raised by my uncle and Bronwyn would live in the Lower with them. I visited, but I was Basso. Still am." He flashes a smile. "They figured I'd be a better member of the Night for it. Once I was old enough to train, I did. As a soldier, I'm free to go back and forth when safe."

I realize I'm shaking my head again. "Why are you telling me this?"

"You mean, what's to stop you from taking all this information back up with you?"

"Well . . ." I shrug.

"I've already blown my cover. You know who I am. My parents taught us that to earn trust, you must give it." He pauses. "Veda . . . This is me, handing you some of my biggest secrets. It's my risk to take."

"I'm not sure you should." I hate that I'm suddenly guilt ridden over my plan, that I feel sort of bad for saying his legend is horseshit. I hate that I wish he'd shut up and stop talking. And I hate that I really don't want him to shut up and stop talking.

"Just hear me out? It's all I ask."

My stomach churns over what he's yet to tell me; still, I long to hear it. "Fine." And he's right. It's his choice to tell me. I'm not forcing him to speak.

He nods, eyes locked on mine. "Part of being raised here in the Lower is being a part of a community. My community. We're a loyal people. A strong, united people. Family. And like all families, we have a history. Stories that've been passed down. But the one that's been told most . . . the bedtime story my mother would recite on sleepless nights was about"—he leans in, gazing even more intently over the lantern between us—"the Lunalette."

"What's that?" I scoot back a few inches. Because it sounds sinister.

He raises an eyebrow. "You promised to hear me out."

Shaking my head, I chew on the inside of my cheek to keep from arguing. Because I do want to hear the rest. I release a breath. "Go on."

"The Night have been around for a long time. Centuries. Since the Great Flood and when the Imperi began showing its earliest signs of hardened rule and oppression under the guise of an almighty and vengeful Sun. For countless years the Night lived peacefully and kept to itself. It was separate from Bellona, its own society, one ruled not by oppression and harsh laws, but as a community working together. Skip ahead a few hundred years and to the current High Regent and things have quickly changed. As Raevald has built up his Imperi force, taken more and more rights away from the Basso, and spread his lies about the Night, we've been training for battle."

"But there *was* a battle," I say. "The first war, when I was a baby. The Night killed my parents. It's how I ended up living with my grandfather."

He nods knowingly. "I'm so sorry, Veda." Dorian pauses as if collecting his thoughts, choosing his words carefully. Then he scoots closer, barely whispering. "I know your loss. Growing up without parents is painful and confusing enough without it being under horrible circumstances. But your parents weren't killed by the Night. I can't say for certain what happened to them, but they weren't taken. We don't take people as prisoners and torture and kill them. I promise."

"But . . . No. Poppy told me they disappeared during the war."

"There was a war, yes. Many battles. We lost half our force." He glances toward the floor. "It's how my parents died too."

"I'm so sorry." The words come out less meaningful than I intend. I wouldn't wish that void on my worst enemy. But I'm still caught up in "your parents weren't killed by the Night."

"Thank you." He looks back up at me, eyes even more sympathetic now as I stare through him trying to comprehend exactly what he just told me. "If they were taken, they were taken by the Imperi, not the Night."

I have no words to give him. He doesn't have any reason to lie about my parents. So far what I've seen down here mirrors the Night he describes. But if Dorian is speaking the truth, what of the truths I've been taught?

They'd all be lies.

Many from my own grandfather.

"Are you all right?" he asks.

"Yeah . . ." I take a deep breath in, then exhale before I speak. "It's just a lot to hear."

He nods, brow furrowed. "Sorry . . . I hadn't planned to lay this all out like that. I don't know how or why your parents died, but you deserve the truth."

"Thanks."

"It's literally the least I can do." He catches my eye, his expression almost sheepish as he glances from me to the mural and back again. "You okay if I continue?" Dorian's shoulders have softened, his jaw's less flexed than usual. It's like he's at ease. Not tense or on guard. Not like someone who's lying or deceiving. Unless he's really good at it. And maybe he is.

But with mention of my parents, he's got my full attention. "Yes, go on."

"As I was saying," he continues. "The Night's been training for battle since the end of the first war. Preparing to take back the island. But we've not been ready until now. We've been waiting for something. Someone . . ." Again, he gazes at the mural behind me. Dorian leans in, resting his elbows on his knees, hands clasped. "The short version of the story is this . . . Long ago the Sun and Moon were lovers, of one mind, body, and soul, but were forced to split. When the people of Bellona separated, so too did the Sun and Moon. They took sides. Light versus dark. Imperi versus Night. And it would continue that way for centuries. That is, until the Lunalette returns." Dorian's eyes drift over to mine.

"*Lunalette* . . ." He nods. Yeah, I don't buy it. Yet I worry the inside of my cheek. "Sounds like just another old story."

"Is it . . . ?" The way he raises an eyebrow gives me pause. As if he knows I'm kidding myself. But am I? They are just silly stories. No more factual than the ones in my fables book or the lesson-laden nursery rhymes Poppy used to repeat when I was small.

Dorian leans back against the wall, arms crossed over his chest. "That's all I've got. The short version of our history. We made a deal. Your move, V." Ah, there's the Dorian I recognize. "I know I joke a lot but I always keep my promises."

I'm stuck. Torn. Split between what I've always known to be true and what might actually be the truth. And, mostly, sticking around to figure out which is which.

Dorian stands. "How about this . . . I'm going to step out, take care of a few things. Why don't you stay here and think on everything. There's fresh clothes for you." He points to the black pile on the floor beside him. "I have someplace to be in about an hour, but I'll be back to check on you in . . ." He glances at his hourglass. "Twenty minutes. If you want to stay longer, great. If not, I'll take you back up."

Seems fair. Either I stay and find out more or leave. At this point, I feel mostly confident I'm not going to be tortured or fed to anything fanged and poisonous. I pull my shawl tightly around my shoulders, cross my arms over my chest. "I'll take that deal, but on one condition." Dorian stares back at me. "Word must be sent to my grandfather letting him know I'm safe."

"Done."

I lean forward. "And to Nico."

"Mmm . . . I wish we could, but you're both safer if he doesn't know." I wish he wasn't right, but I know he is. I simply nod.

"I'll be back in a bit. Meet you outside in the tunnel?"

"All right."

He smiles close-lipped. Yet the way it reaches his eyes, not in happiness but out of respect, with a certain knowingness, one that conveys, *I trust you'll make the right choice*, puts a heavier weight on my shoulders.

Then he turns and leaves.

Alone in the cave now, I take the opportunity to explore things more closely. On the wall next to the mat there are small sections of rocks jutting out like natural shelves. Placed on some of them are stones, crystals, roots . . . Like the blessings we leave on our Sun altars, but all things from the earth.

When I turn around to face the fresh clothes, something on top catches my eye. Crouching down, I grasp the delicate, sharp-edged thing.

Holding it over a nearby candle, I see that it's a tiny glass trinket: a small orange-gold Sun. It's no larger than an inch in width, including the eight sunrays that snake out from the middle. I squeeze it gently in my palm, the sharp points sticking my skin like tiny twigs. I know exactly where it came from and who made it. But I've no idea when he slipped it on top of the clothes without me noticing.

Dorian's sleight of hand aside, something occurs to me. Why in the world would he save me from Imperi soldiers at his own risk, show me the Night's vegetable gardens, and then bring me to this cave—obviously their personal quarters—if he only meant me harm? And now this? A gift handmade for me in the likeness of the Sun—perhaps a reminder of home? I hold it to my chest, which is warm from the thought of Dorian spending time blowing and shaping this glass with me, my happiness, in mind.

I know what I have to do.

I just hope I'm not wrong.

MY DECISION MADE, I step behind a burlap curtain nailed to the ceiling and change out of my usual clothes into the ones Dorian left for me. The ones the Night wear.

And after running through the woods, sliding down dens, and climbing through caves all evening, getting out of my old clothes is actually a relief.

The Night uniform fits well enough, but it's strange to be wearing so much black, traditionally a Dogio color. The clothes—close-fitting pants, long-sleeved shirt, and a button-up jacket—are thicker than my other clothes, perfect for staying warm without needing to layer four things on top of one another. They're worn, a bit faded in areas. I relace my boots and head out of the cave and toward the tunnel. "Dorian?" I call.

"Oh hi!" But it's not Dorian, it's Bronwyn. "Dorian sent me for you." She looks me up and down, likely taking in my new clothes. Bronwyn can't be more than a year younger than me, but she's a good five inches taller. A huge smile overtakes her face, those dimples at the corners of her eyes in fine form. "He had to go to the meeting early. Officer stuff."

He didn't mention he was an officer. Maybe that was what the patch on his chest meant? "Oh, okay." Instantly I glance down at Bronwyn's clothes. She wears the same moon pin on her collar but only has one small stripe affixed to her uniform.

"I've only gone on one mission. Soldiering isn't quite my calling. I'd rather tend the gardens, raise chickens . . . I've switched to learning those instead."

"Sounds nice."

"Of course, should battle call . . ." She bites her lip. "I'm pretty sure I'm not supposed to talk to you about battles and war. Dorian told me not to scare you off."

"We pretty much covered that already." She eyes me from her periphery. "But he's worried about me getting spooked, eh?"

"Hopelessly . . ." She smiles and the way she says it, it's as if she knows more about her brother's actions than she's letting on.

Bronwyn motions to the right. "This way—" I'm about to ask her to expand on what she meant by "hopelessly," then decide against it (we did just meet) when we hit a spiral tunnel that corkscrews in a tight succession of turns. Dorian wasn't kidding when he said I had no idea how much of a labyrinth this place was.

Once through the spiral, Bronwyn and I snake and climb and scurry through the caves, accidentally squishing creepy-crawly bugs I'm so glad I can't see. It stays mostly dark save our lantern, and I cannot imagine living without the Sun or fresh air day after day.

When I ask Bronwyn about this, she explains, "We take special vitamins made of roots and fruit and minerals from the garden and the ground. Keeps us healthy." She certainly looks healthy. I'd have no idea she's been raised underground. "Plus, there is one place on the Upper where we're able to sneak to, but only a few at a time. We rotate it out."

"Where's that?"

"Just a section of beach. On the very edge of the island, beyond the Crag. We usually go right before sunrise."

"*Beyond* the Crag? Wait. Isn't it surrounded by land mines from the first war? The Imperi stored weapons there, planted mines all around it to keep the Night away."

She only shakes her head. "It's abandoned now. We dug the mines out ages ago; they're stored in a special cave though, far away from anything living. As for the Crag, some of our tunnels extend into it. In fact, the Sindaco—head of the Night; you'll meet him later—his main dwelling is there."

"Okay..." With each new tidbit of information, my mind whirls. Everything down here directly contradicts everything up there.

"Ah. Finally. We're here." Bronwyn stops abruptly. "Ready?"

"For the meeting?"

She nods. Really enthusiastically.

"Dorian said it's nothing special."

Nod-nod-nod.

"Just a small gathering."

Nod-nod.

"Okay... Yeah, I'm ready."

But something's strange. Before I can probe her for details, we turn the corner and I'm stopped dead in my tracks. We've stepped into a large cavern—the largest I've seen yet—and there are five, maybe ten times the number of Night members than Dorian and I encountered on our arrival. This time though, I'm not so much afraid as I am confused. Curious even. Slightly spooked. Because the minute we enter, the air changes. Eyes glance toward me and a hushed murmur becomes audible. It's not overtly threatening, but notably strange, and I'd bet my only fishing pole it has something to do with me, the outsider. Maybe something Dorian said back in the cave. He did disappear fast afterward.

It's then I fully take in the space.

There are candles on every ledge and table, some on the floor, enough to illuminate the cave like midday. Following the sight upward, I'm mesmerized by how the light from the flames cascades up the walls and laps at the ceiling. There, I spot another mural. Painted in an arc across the highest reaches of the cave is the moon in all its phases.

Walking in farther I notice there's a large tapestry hanging from the far wall, its image covered by the crowd and shadows.

Then there's the people, Dorian's people. The Night. Monsters of the underworld. But they seem anything but. Sure, they stare, but not rudely. More expectantly. Like they're waiting. Watching.

It's a bit unsettling, but I suppose they're as curious about me as I am about them.

Most smile as Bronwyn and I walk past. Some ask to shake my hand, introducing themselves. Others seem shy within my presence. Everyone is welcoming.

There's food and drink, music being played on instruments I've never seen or heard before. They're pieced together, hand carved, made of clay. But the music is plucky and joyful and reverberates from wall to floor to ceiling. In the oddest way, it reminds me of the Dogio Ever-Sol Feast at Nico's house, but completely flipped upside down.

Glancing from face to face, smile to smile, a sea of black clothing beneath the shimmering glow of countless candles, I spot Dorian. From across the expanse, our eyes meet and a curious dancing takes hold of my stomach. It's a mix of nerves and excitement, the desire to smile in his direction battling with wanting to punch him in the arm for not warning me of all this. *Just a small gathering . . .*

He excuses himself from the man he's speaking with and makes his way over. The commotion from my stomach expands, sending prickly heat up my neck, into my ears.

Briefly, I think of Nico. How he'd feel if he only knew the way my insides suddenly swirled because of someone else.

But, no. It's only nerves. I'm completely on edge.

As if it knows better, the spinning stills.

Just behind my eyes my last memory of Nico comes into focus. It was only hours earlier that we were caught outside before morning bells. Mere moments ago, he glanced around the soldiers through the darkness at me, expression intense, eyes set right on mine, silently pleading I run.

The stillness where the spinning had churned now pangs with guilt and sadness. I already miss him.

Dorian's wearing the same uniform he had on earlier, but has added a black sash adorned with even more pins and military ribbons.

He stops before me, blatantly staring at my clothing, small grin playing at his mouth. "The outfit suits you."

"Don't gloat," I joke, and motion to his sash. "And what's all this?"

"Oh." He glances down, humbly waving it away. "I've done some stuff." Yet there's a definite air of pride beneath his words.

"Oooh—moon biscuits," Bronwyn cuts in. "I'm going to get some. Would you like anything, Veda?"

"I'm fine. Thanks though."

And Bronwyn scurries off toward a table of food.

"No, no . . ." Dorian waves a hand toward his sister's back. "I don't want anything. Thanks for asking, Bron." He stares after her, shaking his head.

I laugh. "She must be hungry."

"Moon biscuits. They only come out on special occasions. Our mother used to make them."

I nod. I'm not sure whether it's worse to have known your mother and then lost her or to have never known her at all. "All Poppy ever makes is fish stew. And he uses ALL the parts of the fish he can. Once he tried to make seaweed cookies. They made me throw up."

"Not much of a baker, eh?"

I laugh. "Not at all." Then something occurs to me about the biscuits. Something he said that went right over my head when he said it. "Wait. What's the special occasion?"

"What's that?" He refuses to meet my gaze, eyes dancing from one corner of the room to the next.

"You just said the moon biscuits are only made on special occasions. So . . . ?" I motion toward the celebration in full swing before us.

"Right." He glances toward the food table. "I did say that, didn't I?"

He's hiding something. I wait for an explanation, but Bronwyn comes striding back, hands full of cookies. "There's stars too." She passes a couple to me. They're small sugar-coated biscuits. The size of a sand dollar. One, the shape of a crescent moon. The other, a five-pointed star. A close replica of the star from the story Dorian told, the mural in the cave, all sharp edges.

Is bringing me here just another attempt to convince me to stay? But why the secrecy? Unless there's more. Worse.

As I search my mind for bedtime stories about Night rituals, my eyes find Dorian's.

He's eating a cookie, as if suddenly starved for sweets, his mouth conveniently full, white powdered sugar stuck to his fingertips. But before he can do or say anything, before I can prod him for more information, for some clue, a hint into what horrors surely await, the crowd quiets, all attention centered toward one man.

"The Sindaco," Bronwyn whispers near my ear.

The man—the Sindaco—stands still as more and more people gather around him. Hands clasped in front, he wears a sash similar to Dorian's, but his is crowded with military pins and patches, barely an inch of black fabric showing. His dark hair is fading to silver around the edges, and he wears something no one else does. A flash of red fabric wrapped thickly around his waist, part belt, part ornament.

The Sindaco waits patiently until the entire cavern goes silent. He seems nonthreatening. There isn't anything about his appearance that screams sinister or dangerous, but something—*something*—prickles the back of my neck and sends my nerves on notice. Perhaps it's that he's wearing Dogio and Imperi colors? I learned from a young age to watch out for black and red. Be on my best behavior in the presence of black and red. Don't dare make the wrong move in the vicinity of black and red.

Nico, of course, was always the exception. The way he wore it was never threatening. Never with the air of authority or force. Just Nico.

The Sindaco clears his throat, unclasping his hands and placing them on his hips. "What a night." He glances around the room. "What a celebration." Several people shout out a "hear! hear!" and "huzzah!" Someone hands the Sindaco a drink and he tips his glass, but doesn't take a sip. "It's been too long, but"—he pauses for breath, almost like he's swallowing his emotion—"well worth the wait. And we have Captain Winters to thank." He holds his hand out toward Dorian, and I realize Captain Winters and Dorian are one and the same.

Dorian nods, then finds me from the corner of his eyes.

I turn my head fully toward him as several things happen in quick succession . . .

Bronwyn crunches the point of one of the star biscuits between her teeth.

"Nearly seventeen years we've been waiting," the Sindaco says. The crowd mumbles in agreement. "Finally, the day has come—our Lunalette has returned home."

As if I'm in a bizarre nightmare, the Sindaco raises his glass directly at me. I glance to my left and then to my right. Surely, he's motioning toward Dorian, but both Dorian and Bronwyn have stepped away so I stand alone. Stranded. An island in a sea of Night. Collective, expectant eyes right on me.

When I look across the space at the Sindaco, he nods, not leaving any room for interpretation. He meant me when he said *Lunalette*.

And I'm getting out of here.

I search the nearest route to flee, but before I can get away, the cave erupts in applause, which quickly dies down when everyone realizes I don't know what's going on, that I'm about to run for it. There's soft murmuring, questioning, whispers.

I begin turning away when the Sindaco says something about a star-shaped scar and I stop dead.

Dorian slowly glances over at me. He taps his chest, mirroring the place where my own star-shaped scar is. How could he . . . ?

But a memory hits me square between the eyes like a sharp headache: that day at the Hole . . . When he returned my twine he saw my scar.

I must be shaking my head no, because he nods an emphatic yes as if reminding me of that horseshit story he told, that he wasn't lying, that not all legends are fable. His expression, all sensitive-eyed and strong-browed, is a firm yet sympathetic *I tried to give you a hint*.

But . . . No.

Hint or no hint. Star or scar.

No.

The Sindaco continues. He's still staring straight at me, speaking directly to me, but, my heart racing, ears ringing, I only get snippets of what he says. ". . . We didn't intend for you to find out this way . . . It must be a shock . . . We apologize . . . Have been waiting so long . . . Fate . . . Opportunity . . . Lunalette . . . Welcome . . ."

The ringing in my ears turns to a high-pitched buzzing as my eyes dart from face to face, cave arch to cave arch. I follow the intricately painted phases of the moon, and like a trail of bread crumbs, it leads down the back wall with the tapestry and to an exit.

I bolt straight for the metal door because there's no way. These people are either terribly mistaken or terribly delusional. Either way, I'm not about to stick around to see which it is.

I'm not their Lunalette.

Whatever that even means.

I'm only two short strides away from the door when a little girl breaks from her parents, rushing right up to me and blocking my grand exit.

I've no choice but to skid to a stop or plow her down.

I wouldn't normally plow a defenseless child down, but this isn't a normal situation, now, is it? Poor little thing . . . But she'll be all right.

I'm about to try my best to skirt around her, accepting she might fall over as collateral.

Until, she stares up at me. Doe-eyed. Defenseless. Pure innocence. I stop.

Forced to take a breath, I decide whether I'm going to walk right past her or address her. My head tells me not to take a second glance, but it's too late. I've looked down.

She's tiny, no older than seven, a bit of dirt smudging her nose. Face framed by dark ringlets, when she gives me a well-practiced yet wobbly curtsy, her curls spring up and down with the motion.

"I'm Ruby," she says, her voice strong and squeaky at once. She hands me a rolled-up scrap of cloth.

"For me?" I say, holding it in my hand.

She nods. But the way she stares, starry-eyed, clearly expecting more, I realize to simply ask if the gift is meant for me isn't near enough.

Right.

I quickly untie the twine. Ruby watches quietly, her eyes wide as saucers, and I decide, despite the chaos unfolding all around us, within me, that whatever I find inside this cloth, she deserves a gushing reaction.

Unrolling the white square of muslin, I see that it's a handkerchief, upon it the blue embroidered image of the phases of the moon, the word *Lunalette* roughly stitched in light purple thread below the careful arc.

I smile down at her and not entirely for show.

"This took you a long time to make, eh?"

Her dark eyes light up. "How'd you know?"

I lean down on one knee to her level. "I embroider too. It's harder than it looks. If you miss one stitch, then—"

"—the whole thing's ruined." She nods emphatically.

"Yes!" I stand back up. "Thank you so much, Ruby. I'll treasure it always."

She grins, all teeth, and runs back to her parents, who nod and smile at me.

Slowly returning to the present, when I take a look around, the worn tapestry, now in full view, catches my attention.

Stretched out before me is a battle scene. Not of the moon and the Sun like the painting Dorian showed me back in the cave, but an actual battle scene with people and weapons and blood, one side clearly winning.

It's in the faded shades of four colors only: mostly black and white, but with flashes of red, one flash of gold. The Night is led by a young woman with the mark of a star over her heart—the solitary bit of golden thread in the entire thing. Unlike the more traditional five-pointed star back on the cave wall, cut out as cookies, this one is less perfect. More haggard. Asymmetric. A near twin to the scar I was given by an adult pantera fish's teeth when I was two. The losing army is the Imperi. They're awash in red and black and even more red spilled on the ground beneath them where the edges of the hanging fray.

The cave is quiet, all eyes on me and me alone. As much as I want to sprint straight through that door, somehow I gather the strength to turn and face the crowd.

I have no plan. No words. Just a scrap of muslin, a tightness in my chest, and an angry and confused knot in my throat.

My hands visibly shake, but I clutch the handkerchief between them, clasp it at my waist to calm my nerves. Women, men, and children stare. Some appear to be anticipating something. Something I'm sure I won't deliver. Others wear confusion, what looks like disappointment; a few avert their eyes when they realize I'm seeing them right back.

The Sindaco clears his throat, thankfully pulling the attention off me. "Veda . . ." When he says my name, the way it echoes off the walls and all around the cavern makes my insides squirm. In this moment, all I want to do is hide, curl up into a ball, pinch myself, and make this strangest of strange nightmares end. But I'm not asleep. And he continues, "We were so worried we wouldn't be welcoming enough that I think we overdid it." He holds his hands up like he's treading lightly, choosing his words carefully. "You must know we've all been awaiting this day, prayed and hoped for this day. We know you'll need time, maybe you won't want to stay here a minute longer—" Several some-ones near the back murmur in dissatisfaction. "No, no . . ." He glances in the general direction of the gasp. "We mustn't question fate." A low mumbling of agreement overpowers the naysayers. The Sindaco turns his sight back on me. "Whatever you choose, it's what's meant to hap-pen. We trust in the legend. The Lunalette."

I nod.

I don't buy anything he's saying one bit.

But I nod.

Because I just want this moment to end.

As the Sindaco continues his speech, I'm thankful when the crowd finally puts all their attention on him as he speaks to the future . . . the revolution . . . the rising up of the Night . . . how the Imperi's oppression was built over centuries and how reclaiming that power won't happen overnight.

With his words, there's less disappointment weighing down the air in the room. More hope lightening the space.

Such a fine line with those two emotions.

I BARELY UTTER a word as Dorian, Bronwyn, and I walk back to the caves of the soldiers' tunnel. I'm in a complete fog, the moments that unfolded in the cavern not an hour earlier replaying in a loop in my mind.

At one point, after asking me how surprised I was by the celebration, to which I reply with something like, "I don't even . . . ," Bronwyn reveals she's smuggled a napkin filled with moon and star biscuits out of the cavern.

"My Moon, Bronwyn. You have a serious problem," Dorian says, roll-ing his eyes, but snatches one right as she's about to pop it in her mouth.

She knuckles him in the arm, reminding me of how much I want to smack him right now. The sheer anger welling up from the pit of my stomach over him not giving me more warning before that total bom-bardment back there is reaching a boil.

But I talk myself down.

Keep it all in.

Just until we're alone.

It's then, as Bronwyn's going on and on about how they remind her of their mother and it's so rare they get such a treat and she couldn't possibly have let them go to waste, that I catch a mutual look and shrug of the shoulders between brother and sister. The gesture's over me, I assume. Because it's definitely the unspoken subject at the moment.

Had they expected me to jump up and down? Start writing up battle plans? Enthusiastically plot how to ruin the only home I've ever known? I release a huff out of my nose at the thought and they both glance over at me.

I ignore them.

Once we reach cave number nine, Dorian heads inside and Bronwyn mentions she's going to make tea. But before I can catch Dorian—I'm fully prepared to lay into him the minute we're inside—Bronwyn says, "Hey, Veda?"

I step back out of the cave and face her. "Yes?"

Her brow is lined with emotion like there's something she'd like to say, but doesn't. Or maybe can't. Instead of speaking, Bronwyn hands me the last of the biscuits. "I'm glad you're here."

I look at the small pile of cookies. There's a crack down the middle of one of the moons, and a few star points have broken off. But I know how much they mean to her. And like with the little girl in the cavern earlier, I'm forced to pause. To venture outside of myself. "Thanks," I say.

She smiles and I can't help but smile back.

When I enter the cave, Dorian's back is to me as he stares quietly at the painting on the wall. I stop right next to him, our arms nearly touching. "What the hell just happened?"

"I really did try to warn you."

I glance up at him. "With a story," I snap. My voice is already breaking

107

with emotion, and I refuse to let that happen. To let him see that under the anger, I'm also upset. I take a deep breath, straighten my shoulders, focus on that rage lodged in my chest.

"A true story." His voice is stupidly soft. As if that's going to make me less angry. "I'd hoped it was enough of a hint."

"It was vague at best. And, besides, you know I didn't believe you." He continues avoiding my eyes. "Would *you* have believed me?"

Dorian opens his mouth like he's going to argue, but only says, "No." He finally looks at me. "I'd have said you were out of your mind and made you take me home." He turns and faces me. "I should have warned you about the celebration—I was afraid you wouldn't go, that you'd demand I take you back up. But, I promise you, celebration aside, I've told you everything."

"Everything?"

He nods. "Everything I know, yes."

"Does someone else know more?"

"Only the Sindaco." He eyes the floor. Right. "Take me to him."

"I can't, Veda."

"Why not?"

"He's very busy . . . And it's just not something we do, show up unannounced. I'm supposed to take you to meet him in the morning."

"I'm busy too, you know. In fact, I might be gone by morning." This gets his attention; Dorian's eyes dart to mine. "I need answers."

"I understand and I know it's a lot." I raise my eyebrows. He holds my gaze. "I can't even imagine, Veda. Look . . ." He rakes his hands through his hair. "I'll see what I can do."

I'm about to tell him he'd better get going on that, when Bronwyn returns with a teakettle and three cups. "Something to relax all our nerves and dilute the sugar from those mounds of biscuits we ate."

Dorian and I both look over at her.

". . . Fine. *I* ate." She sets the tea down on the small tree stump serving as a table. "Still, based on the tension in this room, you two could definitely use a bit of moonroot." No one says a word. "All . . . right. I'm going to leave this here, then." Bronwyn pours herself a cup and leaves.

Alone with me again, Dorian fills the remaining two cups with tea. When he offers me one, I refuse. Still holding my cup, he sips his as if to let me know it's not poisoned or something.

"I know it's been a long day," he says. "Just . . . let me know what you're thinking?"

"I'm thinking . . ." With a deep breath, I move across the cave, sit on the mat. Dorian follows, setting my tea on the floor next to us. "You need to start from the beginning."

He exhales, shoulders softening, then gives a slight nod. "It wasn't an accident I ran into you the other day at the Hole."

"Yeah, I put that much together."

"Right. Well, according to the Lunalette legend, you're to arrive here on your seventeenth birthday."

"Tomorrow."

"Yes. I was given until then to find a way to convince you to join the Night. But . . . I waited too long." He shifts uncomfortably. "In all my training, believe it or not, convincing someone everything they've been taught is a lie wasn't part of it. I did my best, but I can't see how I could have earned your trust like I needed to. That would take years." Instantly I think of Nico. "Then with the Night of Reckoning, the Offering that followed, the fact that you're at Nico's side most of the time . . . I was about to have to resort to less desirable tactics."

I furrow my brow. "Like what?" I say through a tightened jaw.

"I was told to do what I must to get you down here safely. So you could see the truth for yourself."

I gape. Do what he *must*?

Hands held up in front of him, he speaks quickly. "I swear to you, V, I wouldn't have done anything dangerous. Whether you're the Lunalette or not, I would never harm you." The way he says it stings with honesty, but he's right, I don't trust him. I can't. Especially after hearing his do-anything-he-must plan.

I take my time sizing Dorian up, not moving my sight off him as the silence stretches between us. He's fidgety. Surely unsure what I'm thinking, worried I'll take off any minute—and, I won't lie, I'm enjoying it. He avoids my eyes. Picks at the wool sprigs of the mat beneath us as he fails at stealing glances.

When he finally looks right up at me, it catches me by surprise because it's like a switch has been flipped. Anxiety wiped clean. Now, brow strong, eyes set on mine, shoulders squared, he looks like he's ready to accept my answer, whatever it is.

What I give is a curt nod. I still don't trust him, but I also don't think he'd hurt me. Not to get me down here and not now. "So, you being in the tunnel when I was running from those soldiers this morning... Planned?"

Dorian's shoulders soften as if he's relieved to be moving on, and I wonder how long the guilt's been eating at him. "My being in the tunnel earlier was one hundred percent accidental. I was spying on Imperi soldiers for information." He scoots forward. "As if it was *meant to be*, just as I was getting desperate to get you down here, you literally fell into my lap."

"Ah . . . The legend." I raise a sarcastic eyebrow.

"Fate," he throws back at me, voice low, confidence unwavering.

It's then I realize I've still got a fistful of cookies. When I open my hand to set them on the ground, only part of one of the stars remains, the rest a pile of crumbs. And as I stare at the one star, something hits me. "Dorian—"

"Yes?"

"If your finding me was one hundred percent accidental and these cookies are such a rarity, how did they know to make them for today?" He cocks his head like he's not following. "How in the world was the cele-

bration and that mural, all those cookies, ready to go if no one knew for sure I'd be here?"

"I . . . They were alerted this morning. Tomorrow's your birthday, the day you're said to return. They obviously had more faith in me getting you here than I had in myself."

I'm not so sure I'm buying it. Plus, "What do you mean, *return*? That's the second time I've heard that. The Sindaco said I'd come home. But I've never been here."

He sighs.

Is he actually annoyed by me? Are all these questions of mine so terribly aggravating? I cross my arms over my chest.

"Listen, you're the Lunalette. One of us. Even if this is your first time here physically, you've always lived here in these caves, a part of the Night." I shake my head, trying to comprehend it all. Dorian pushes the tea toward me. "Have a sip? It's Bronwyn's special concoction. Please, it'll calm your nerves, help you think more clearly." This sets me off.

"I *am* thinking clearly," I say through clenched teeth, "but how in the Sun can I possibly wrap my mind around this?" I throw my arm toward the mural when, at the same time, Dorian shoves the mug closer. "I don't need tea—" And I slam my palm into the cup, sending it flying and spilling all over Dorian's neck and shirt, the ceramic mug shattering against the stone floor.

He swears under his breath and stands, not bothering to clean up himself or the broken cup. "I don't know what else to tell you, Veda. It's the truth—I swear on the Moon."

I look away.

"No one's going to force you to stay. All we wanted was to give you the truth. Everyone deserves to know the truth." Dorian sort of nods to himself, then turns to leave, but stops short, glancing over his shoulder. "If you want to go, say the word." He pauses as if waiting, expecting me to ask him to take me home.

When I don't (which even surprises me), he walks out.

Still, I don't run after him but stay in the cave, stare at the painting. I pick up the kettle, open the lid, and sip the tea.

I stand, walk up to the mural. The moon is mostly blues and grays with soft gold highlights where it touches the bright star connecting it to the Sun.

I place my hand over my scar, and it jabs me with a quick burn. Phantom pains, Poppy calls them. He claims injuries like that make a memory just like your mind does when something traumatic happens, but instead of an image, it's a feeling.

Or maybe it's more. A sign. A push. I'm not even sure if I believe in that . . . Dorian had said it was fate we were at the entrance to the tunnel at the exact same moment earlier.

Or was it simply coincidence?

Is there much of a difference?

I look toward the top of the mural. One side is blue sky, the other nighttime, hundreds of golden stars dotting the background. It occurs to me I've never really taken the time to gaze up at the night sky while out after the Sun's set.

Because I'm always glancing over my shoulder on guard, on the run, fearful of being caught or worse.

Between the Sun and moon's battle is the star, my star, the one I've always known and never really thought twice about. So familiar that when I was small and saw other children shirtless on hot summer days along the beach, I always thought *their* chests looked strange without the small, jagged scar.

But I was different, not them.

And maybe I still am.

There's a bit of crimson bleeding into the golds and yellows of the star, right down the middle as if the Sun and moon are tearing it in two. A sensation I know well. The pain of being pulled apart, cut down the middle, tugged in opposite directions . . . My feelings for Nico, being left parentless at such a young age, having the desire to fight for what's right

but fearing the consequences too much to try, to even consider it. Knowing I shouldn't be out after vesper bells and doing it anyway because we needed food.

Sure, it's a story. Maybe it's fate, maybe coincidence. Likely complete horseshit. Truth or fable, who knows, but does it matter if I could finally make a difference for others like me? Those who know too well the torture of being pulled in two?

My scar gives another phantom pain.

Or maybe it's real.

AT SOME POINT, teapot nearly dry and amid thoughts of becoming a member of the Night, how things might go (good, bad, ugly . . .), the lies of the Imperi, what Poppy and Nico must be thinking, and that haunting image of the battle mural, I fall into restless sleep.

I awaken to Dorian gently shaking my shoulder, saying my name. "Veda, the Sindaco will see you."

"What?" I sit up, disoriented. I look at Dorian, my surroundings, everything from the past few hours barreling down on me all over again.

"The Sindaco. I spoke with him and he's agreed to see you."

I slowly nod my head. "Okay."

Dorian lifts the teakettle. "How much of this did you drink?"

". . . approximately one kettle minus two cups' worth . . . I think."

"That explains it . . ."

"What?" Now he's mad I drank it?

"You . . . Here." He walks up to me and brushes my chin, the corner of my mouth. "Powdered sugar."

Instantly, I glance toward the place where I'd left the pile of broken cookies. It's mostly gone. "Oh yeah . . . I ate those. So strange, it feels like a dream."

"Bronwyn made the tea extra strong. I'd have warned you, but I didn't think you were going to drink it. Actually." He meets my eyes. "I wasn't sure I'd find you here."

I stare back, my face warming. "I've been thinking..."

"Moonroot'll do that."

I nod. No kidding. "I'm considering staying. Maybe. Just a little longer."

His eyes light up, a genuine smile stretching across his face. "I'm so glad."

"Don't get ahead of yourself. Absolutely no promises. It's a lot... I have a lot to consider... To work through." I narrow my eyes at him. "I'm still very angry and confused."

"Yes, I understand. I'd be too." Dorian hands me a canteen of water. I take a long drink and then pour some into my hands, scrub the sleep from my eyes, the sugar from my mouth.

"Let's meet this Sindaco of yours."

"Ours."

"We'll see."

CHAPTER 12

Once Dorian and I have twisted down several tunnels we hit a steep, winding incline that's part rocks, part cave, and goes nowhere but up.

And up we climb. At one point, the moment when I'm sure my legs are going to burst into flames and melt to ash, Dorian stops out of pity or amusement, or maybe he's tired too, I'm not sure, but I welcome the rest.

"Drink?" He thrusts his canteen out at me.

As I chug, he talks. "It's not much farther."

"For someone who chooses to live underground"—I glance down, then back up—"he sure prefers to be elevated."

"It's mostly for security, but we are at the mercy of the tunnels and can only expand so far. But if we are invaded by Imperi troops, they'd most likely come through one of the dens on the ground level. This part of the Lower is the farthest from the den holes, giving the Sindaco time to get to his security bunker or, if forced to, exit out of the top."

I raise my eyebrows. "The top . . . of the volcano . . ."

"It would be a last resort, but would assure he's not captured, tortured for information, and then publicly executed."

"He has a lot of valuable information, eh?"

"Well, he's our leader, a valuable asset. Like the Regent is to the Imperi"—Dorian nudges his head to the ceiling and toward Bellona—"But the Sindaco is less . . . let's-terrorize-half-the-island."

"Very comforting."

Dorian shrugs. "Mostly, he wants to help Basso and end the corruption of the Imperi. That's enough for me to respect and follow him. We're the good guys, V."

"Yeah." I hand back the canteen and he takes a drink. "I'm still trying to wrap my mind around that concept."

"I get it." Dorian starts moving again. "Just a couple more turns, a short climb up a ladder, and we'll be there."

Finally, reaching the top, we're greeted by a large metal door. Unlike the rusty, pieced-together, padlocked doors I've seen thus far, this one is more finely crafted. There's a brass knob and a keyhole as well as an ornate etching of the phases of the moon scrawled down the middle of the door.

I run my fingers across the moons, the metal smoother, colder than I expect it to be.

Dorian knocks three times.

"Come in," a man's voice calls from the other side.

Dorian opens the door to reveal the Sindaco, sitting behind a worn desk, same clothing as earlier, same hardened yet resolute expression on his face.

He watches me as we step toward him as if he's sizing me up. Not in a bad way, but more a curious way. Regardless, something about his stare makes me feel unconscionably small.

But as I get closer and closer to the Sindaco's desk, the pendant Nico gave me sits heavy against my heart, a reminder I'm not alone. Also, a reminder of how far from this place, from me, Nico is in more way than one.

As if he senses my unease, Dorian glances over at me, his eyes warm

and reassuring. Even though we just met, I'm less alone with him by my side. Not to mention, there's a whole island above me full of Basso. Part of why I'm standing here—they deserve the truth as much as I do.

I take a deep breath and square my shoulders.

This is bigger than me.

CHAPTER 13

The Sindaco's cave, like everything else down here, is dim, cast in shadows. I am able to make out several maps adorning the stone walls, lanterns and candles sitting in the places where a bit of rock protrudes into the room. Because of this, the cave has the radiance of sunset, all golds and yellows and pinks.

"That will be all; thank you, Dorian," the Sindaco says.

"Wait!" I blurt out, catching us all off guard. "I'd prefer he stay."

Dorian stares from the Sindaco to me and back again. Sure, the Sindaco's like the High Regent and I'd never speak in such a way to the ruler of Bellona, but Raevald's never put me in a position to, oh, I don't know, lead an army to victory for him.

The Sindaco nods, eyes heavy, expression unreadable. "Very well. Dorian, you may stay." I can't tell if I've angered him or impressed him with my request.

I glance back at Dorian, who'd taken a few steps toward the exit, and I catch a glimpse of the back of the door. There's a large posting tacked to the metal. Not so dissimilar from the ones now nailed all over the island, but this one reads JOIN THE REVOLUTION!

Below the heading is the image of three shadowed figures holding hands beneath a crescent moon. The person in the center, a girl, I think, based on her long hair and delicate features, has a golden star painted on her chest. Underneath the picture, in smaller print, it reads THE MOON WILL RISE AGAIN!

I turn and face the Sindaco, my stare hard, focused. I'm the one sizing him up now. Let him see how it feels.

"Please . . . sit," he says in a quiet yet stern voice, ignoring Dorian and meeting my stare, challenging me to break away first.

I won't. He wants me to be some strong Lunalette? Fling me into that role without warning? He's gonna get just that.

Stepping forward, I sit and slide back into one of the cold, weathered chairs in front of his desk. I clasp my hands in my lap. Dorian takes the seat next to me.

"Veda Adeline," the Sindaco says, his dark eyes piercing. "You must have so many questions—"

"A few," I break in.

The corner of his mouth twitches, but he continues speaking before I can decide whether it was going to inch into a grin or grimace. "I expect that Dorian explained the basics, but, please, ask me whatever you like."

I sit up and scoot to the edge of my seat. "Dorian's been great. He's told me a lot. And you're right, I have so many questions." I scoot even closer. "But the one I seem to keep dwelling on is something you said at the celebration, that the Lunalette has come home. If that's me, if I'm this . . . *Lunalette* . . . and I've never been here before in my life, what in the Sun could you possibly mean?"

He gives a curt nod. "Let's backtrack a bit, shall we?"

I fold my arms over my chest, and I can't help wonder if we're both fighting for a bit of control here. Actually, I'm quite sure of it. I lean back in my chair. "All right." I'll play along.

"Dorian told you the story of the legend, yes?"

"He did. It was quite a tale." I swear I catch Dorian cringe out of the corner of my eyes. And, all right, maybe I am pushing the Sindaco a bit. But from where I'm sitting, I don't owe him my trust, certainly not my loyalty. If anything, he owes me.

Another short nod. "Good, good . . . I'm not sure Dorian's aware, but since I became head of the Night, and especially after the uprising that cost us so many lives, finding our Lunalette has been one of my top priorities." Now I'm the one stiffly nodding once. "I truly believe, Veda, that you are the key to revolution. To giving Basso the freedom and respect they deserve. To finally freeing an entire group of people out from under the oppressive thumb of the Imperi."

"How are you so sure I'm this person?"

"There are several signs that line up, but most telling is the scar over your heart. The legend speaks directly to it."

I eye Dorian. "But there are similar stories on Bellona. I know how these things go . . . Stories are repeated, made grander with each telling."

"You don't believe in fate? Prophecies?"

I shrug. I catch Dorian gawking at me from my periphery. I ignore it, answering the Sindaco. "I wouldn't say I don't believe, but I've never been around when one came true."

"Ah, I see. Well, let me ask you this: Did you believe the stories the Imperi told about the Night?"

I hesitate, but answer truthfully. "Yes." This seems to please the Sindaco. "But people were disappearing around me. Our villages were being burned, property destroyed. My parents were taken and killed by the—"

"Your parents were never taken by us. They were members of the Night."

"No." I shake my head. "I mean, Dorian told me the Night didn't kill them, but . . . members? There's no way." I'm still shaking my head. "It's not possible."

He stays silent like he's waiting for me to come around to the idea.

I continue talking myself out of it. "I've always been told my parents were taken, brutally killed by the Night." I look into his eyes. "If what you're saying is true, that they were actually *members* of the Night, then who killed them?" I assume he's going to give the same answer Dorian did, that if anyone took my parents it was the Imperi, but I test him anyway.

"The Imperi. During the first war." His words are softer than I expect, like he's delivering bad news. I suppose he is. But I never knew my parents. They've been dead all my life, buried with any infant memories I might have had of them. The hows and whys don't change their absence, the senselessness of their early deaths.

Still, I'm forced to take a deep breath. Fight the heat barely simmering behind my eyes. Stay focused in the present.

What would he gain by telling me my parents were members if they weren't? I'm not sure, but if what he's told me is true, then all I've known to this point is lies, the truth stolen, tossed upside down, and scrambled into nonsense. "Why? Why would the Imperi kill my parents?" It comes out as an accusation and maybe it is.

The Sindaco doesn't answer right away, but takes his time as if choosing his next words carefully. Then he simply shakes his head. "Your mother was a member of the Night. She was captured by the Imperi in battle." He clears his throat, staring toward an empty corner of the cave. "I apologize, Veda, but she was tortured and then executed like so many of our soldiers during that time." The Sindaco looks back at me.

Meanwhile, I'm not even sure how to take this information much less whether to believe him or not. I stay cautious. Skeptical. Skim over the details he just shared because I can't begin to delve into their meanings right now. It's what Poppy would tell me to do. Not to be too spontaneous or careless with my reaction.

He'd say, *Wait. Listen.*

"And my father?" I'm 100 percent confident the Sindaco won't have any information, because the man's a ghost. If his own daughter's only knowledge is his first name, that he wasn't married to my mother, how would this stranger have anything new to offer?

The Sindaco shakes his head. "I don't know," he says simply.

No one does.

I push the ghost of my father back into the shadows of my mind and focus on this new maybe-true information about my mother. A member of the Night? A soldier? Could she have been? It would partially explain Poppy's silence over the years about her, his always avoiding the subject, only ever answering my questions with the same quick, short mumblings.

I do my best to pull away from all those unknowns, but my heart races at the sheer idea of it, the image of my mother running around under the cloak of night, atlatl at the ready, fighting the Imperi. My stomach sinks, my chest tightens; severe doubt and wanting badly to know the truth battle within my mind.

"Your grandfather was sworn to secrecy," the Sindaco says as if reading my expression, sensing how my insides are turning end over end. "He knew what was at stake if anyone ever found out, so he locked the truth—your mother's secret, your secret—deep down."

I nod once, head swimming, and all I can think is how horrible Poppy is at keeping secrets. But when I look across the desk and to the Sindaco I can see he's pleased. Not in a smug way but in a way that feels like he thinks I'm coming around. Like he's won and I've lost, and I won't have that. Not until I'm sure of the truth. Sure I can fully accept all of this.

With a deep breath, I shove my questions, my emotions down for safekeeping. I've got to be strong. Stronger than this leader of the Night before me.

You've got the upper hand, I remind myself. "My secret?" I quirk an eyebrow. "That I'm the Lunalette." It's almost humorous to hear such an outlandish revelation leave my own mouth. Almost.

"Exactly," he says drily.

"Here's the problem with that whole thing . . . The difference between what I thought I knew of the Night and this Lunalette myth is that I had fast and solid proof the Night was evil. As far as I know, this Lunalette prophecy is only a story. One I just heard. Nothing but words with zero facts to support it."

"Your scar is proof. Though, I get it, as you just discovered with the Imperi's propaganda, proof can be false."

I sigh heavily, roll my eyes. "I see what you're trying to do. Flip everything around on me, so I'll believe your version. It's a little Imperiesque, don't you think, Sindaco?" I settle back into the chair.

The way the Sindaco's jaw sets and his eyes focus in on mine, how his right hand flexes into a fist, I can tell I've gotten his attention. It's also clear I've crossed a line with him.

I'm not looking directly at Dorian, but I can tell his jaw's nearly hitting the floor.

But as quickly as he turned annoyed, with a deep breath the Sindaco's composure changes again, voice now with less of an edge to it. "You will believe, Veda. I have faith in you. We all do," he says with utmost confidence, folding his hands under his chin, palm to palm, as if in prayer. "But I appreciate your point. Most stories are made grander over time. However, the truth reveals itself in one way or another. I've found over the years that fate doesn't always come around the way you think it will. It may be late. May be confusing. It even might be fickle. But it always shows up."

"I guess I can buy that."

He picks a pencil up from his desk and jots something on a map. Shakes his head. "I'm not trying to sell you on this idea, Veda."

"Aren't you?" Again, Dorian side-eyes me. I'm not intimidated by the Sindaco. If anything, for once in my life, I've got a bit of power. Control.

The Sindaco catches me off guard by laughing under his breath at my comment. "I suppose if you don't believe what I'm telling you, then I *am* trying my best to convince you of it."

"So let's pretend, for conversation's sake, that I am this Lunalette." I pull my hood over my head, tug the strings so it barely tightens around my face like I'm getting into costume, though there is a cold draft. "What next?"

"You'll become a member of the Night, join our community, train to learn to defend yourself from the Imperi."

"Defend myself from the Imperi . . ." I laugh under my breath. "I've been doing that all my life. Fighting the Imperi is a recurring dream of mine."

"Yes, but you won't be fighting the Imperi . . . You won't even be facing the Imperi much if things go as planned . . . We just want you to be ready, to be able to defend yourself if need be."

"Wait. You want me to lead a revolution and not fight?"

"Exactly." He says it as if he's bartering fish for wool. As if it's the simplest, most normal thing ever. "You're a symbol to the Night, Veda. Something sacred, someone our people have revered and prayed to and painfully waited over a decade for. I'm not about to toss you into battle and lose you."

"You're asking me to flip my world upside down . . . To abandon my grandfather . . . My life . . . My home . . . Only to stand by and do nothing at all? To be a symbol?" I shake my head at the sheer idiocy of it. "I don't think so." Dorian shifts uncomfortably in his chair. "If I'm going to be your Lunalette, I'm doing it on my terms."

"Veda—"

"No. Do you know how many times in my life I've hoped and prayed for some scenario where I'd have the slightest chance to fight back? To be in a position to stand up for myself against the Imperi? Now you're going to hand that opportunity to me on a silver platter but with ridiculous conditions?" I harden my stare, glare across the short distance between us.

I hadn't noticed when, but Dorian's placed his hand over mine atop the armrest. He's patting me gently. It's comforting. Calming. But I don't want to be consoled right now. I remove my fingers from under his when I readjust how I'm sitting, shove my hands into my pockets. Breathe deep.

The Sindaco leans forward, softens his expression, his voice. "Don't you see? You'll be saving all those things most dear to you. You'll be a hero, Veda, the one who finally broke your people free of their invisible chains, the shanks dragging them down to the bottom of society. In this way, you will fight the Imperi. Maybe more effectively. More ruthlessly than in combat. You will be responsible for Basso finally having food, decent living conditions, and, mostly, the Imperi won't keep them in fear under the guise of the Night." He finds my eyes, holds my stare. "But we need you alive to do that. Think of yourself not as a follower but as a leader, as being in charge." That's a completely foreign notion. "It won't be simple. I know from experience that being the one everyone looks to isn't easy. There are days I'd much rather switch places with Dorian." He stands up behind his desk. "I long to fight, to throw up my hands and draw my sword because I'm fed up too"—and I see it in his expression, feel it in the emotion beneath his words—"maybe even more so because when you're the one calling the shots, you bear the consequences, good and bad." He leans forward, hands flat against the top of his desk. "But someone must. And, believe it's true or not, you, Veda, have been chosen." He zeroes in on me as if going for the kill. "Can we count on you?"

I won't deny it, he's good. The Sindaco's stare is expectant, his words still sinking in, and I realize my breathing's picked up, my hands, no longer shoved in my pockets, are clutching the edge of my seat because what he said called to me. Regardless of how much I don't want to believe what the leader of the Night who's like-the-High-Regent-but-not is saying, my emotions, all I know and have experienced up to this point in my life, beg otherwise. But I refuse to get completely caught up in all of that. Not yet.

Slowly, I fold my hands in my lap, take a deep breath to calm my nerves. "Before I answer that question, I need to know . . . What did you mean by 'our Lunalette has returned home'?" Because he never answered.

The Sindaco looks away. "I don't have a simple answer to that question except that you've been a part of the Night longer than you can imagine. You're our daughter, sister, friend, cousin . . . A part of our society.

A member of the family. To us, you *have* returned home. The legend foretold it and now we'll live it." It's exactly what Dorian told me.

I have no words.

"That scar over your heart is no accident, Veda. It was divinely placed there as a symbol, a responsibility." The Sindaco stands. "I sincerely hope you'll consider everything I've told you with an open heart. This is bigger than only you. Bigger than any of us." The back of my neck prickles because hadn't I just thought those exact words?

The Sindaco doesn't push me to give him an answer at this exact moment. Instead, he dismisses Dorian and me, explaining he has much to do and that he hopes to see me again very soon. But not before wishing me a happy birthday.

I smile, then mumble something about it not being until tomorrow under my breath, but he either doesn't hear or chooses not to acknowledge it. Dorian definitely hears my comment and once again gives me a horrified look over possibly disrespecting his leader.

I ignore him.

On my way out, I catch something I didn't see when I entered. He has a small altar in the corner of his cave. But it's not a Night altar, it's a Bellonian altar, a Sun altar. My first thought is of home, how much I miss it after only a day—this place a world away. But upon a closer look, behind a row of candles, a hunk of quartz, one of Dorian's glass trinkets (a five-pointed star), next to an etching of the Sun, is a Dogio crest.

"I FEEL LIKE he's keeping something from me." I've been rolling the conversation over and over in my head the entire way back to my cave, and without missing a beat Dorian's quick to point out I've referred to it as "my" cave twice now. "Do you know what it is? What he's not telling me?"

"I told you, I've given you everything I know. If the Sindaco has some other information, it's not my—"

"*Story to tell.* I know . . ." He whips his head toward mine, eyes wide, slight grin tickling at his lips. I suppose he didn't expect me to guess his next words. But, like my spinning thoughts, Dorian and I have been talking in endless circles.

When we reach cave number nine, there's a small package waiting just inside. I pick it up and read the tag: HAPPY BIRTHDAY.

Dorian clears his throat. "Bronwyn has a penchant for gift giving. You'll get used to it . . . Oh, and, happy birthday, by the way."

"Thanks, but . . ."

"It's-not-until-tomorrow." I knit my brow. "We know." He pushes his lips together, shoves his hands in his pockets, like he's trying not to be smug about it. It doesn't work. "I should also warn you, Bron's horrible at waiting to give gifts."

I smile down at the box. "She's sweet." Then I stare back up at Dorian. "But if it's more tea, I'm not touching it."

"A smart choice." I untie the twine and open the linen to find a small, perfect loaf of bread. I lift it to my nose. It's all spices and pumpkin, maybe a bit of apple, and my mouth's instantly watering despite the tight knots in my gut. "It smells delicious."

"Expect more where that came from. I could be wrong, but I think she wants you to stay," Dorian says lightly.

"Seems she's not the only one."

"I . . . I mean, of course I want you to stay—for the revolution. The legend." Dorian avoids my eyes as he runs his hand through the long side of his hair so it flops in the opposite direction. His face is flushed and he's fidgeting with the corner of stone sticking out from the wall. Vulnerable. Embarrassed. Completely endearing. And I'm loving every second of it so much that I allow him to squirm just a little longer.

"Dorian?"

"Yeah—" He continues avoiding my eyes.

"I was referring to the Sindaco."

"Right. Of course. I mean, all of us—the Night, in general—agree with the Sindaco." He steps farther into the cave, starts checking the oil in the lamp, replacing a low-burning candle with a fresh one from his pack.

It's then—Dorian's charming energy putting those silly butterflies in my empty stomach on notice, pushing some of that worry to the side—that I realize how very hungry I am. I begin tearing into the bread. Somehow it even tastes better than it smells.

I gaze back to Dorian, offering him a piece to which he politely refuses. "Thanks, by the way," I say. He's standing by the door, hands shoved back in his pockets, expression oblivious. "For the glass Sun."

He takes a few steps closer. "If it were me and I'd had to leave everything I know out of the blue, I know I'd want a special reminder of home."

I'm only able to nod. The mere mention of home sends me into a sudden bout of homesickness. Not because I've been away so long, but for the notion of what's to come. Of the days, weeks, months leading up to the revolution and the what-ifs over how all of that might look, over possible failure. The unknown. And, of course, of what all of this means for Nico and me.

That, as much as I know I should ignore and push it aside, I can't deny the butterflies and fluttery swirling that takes over when Dorian looks at me that way he does. How my cheeks heat up without my permission when he smiles that crooked smile because of something I've said or done. But Nico . . . There's a very real emptiness in my heart right now for him. And maybe that's why I bridge the space between Dorian and me, meeting him where he stands just inside the doorway. "It is special," I finally manage, the effort of swallowing back my brimming emotion causing my voice to hiccup. "I know each one of these creations must take a lot of time and thought, concentration and effort. It means so much that you'd do that for me." I look him in the eyes. "Truly, it does." Dorian catches my eyes with his own. The deepness of his silver-blue gaze sends a slew of goose bumps up and down my arms. It's like he's seeing so much more than I'm intending to reveal. My cheeks grow warm, the heat reach-

128

ing up into my ears, down my neck. I take a step away more abruptly than I mean to.

Dorian's eyes, no longer searing into mine, glance toward the mat in front of the mural.

"Do you have more questions?" He speaks softly, moving into the room and toward the mat as I follow. "Ones I can maybe answer? Anything that might ease your decision?" We sit down across from each other.

I think for a moment. In my conversation with the Sindaco I'd mentioned the proof (while false) of the Night's harmful actions helped me believe the stories. And perhaps if I believed this Lunalette story, I'd be able to more fully jump on board. "Is there anything written of this legend? A book or a scroll?" I ask.

"Proof?"

I nod. "Anything?"

"Other than the murals and tapestries, you mean?"

Oh yeah, those. I shrug. "More would be nice."

"It's all been passed down by word of mouth. We've been thorough about not being found . . . Not leaving a trail." Dorian shakes his head. "I don't envy you, Veda. It's a heavy burden to bear. One I know most people couldn't handle, let alone rise up for." My stomach sinks because he's pretty much just spoken the doubts swirling in my head. This must show on my face because he leans forward, tone strong yet calm. "What I can promise you is that I'll be next to you every step of the way. Through training. Through missions. Preparing for battle. I will fight in your name—the symbol of revolution. Retribution. Freedom." The way Dorian looks back at me, his eyes blue like ice yet so warm, so trusting, once again, I'm lost in them.

"That means a lot." I manage to get the words out in a whisper.

"I mean every word with all I have." He nods, unblinking, not taking his eyes off mine, and I realize I've leaned closer too. "Will you be staying the night or going back home?"

I swallow, take in my surroundings, the mural on the wall. I recall all those faces earlier at the celebration, the Sindaco's words, Dorian's stories, Bronwyn's kindness, the name *Lunalette* embroidered by a child's hand.

I think of my parents. That they were killed by the Imperi.

Then I think of Poppy. How he deserves so much better than the life he's been dealt. How if there's even the slightest chance I could change that . . .

I glance back at Dorian. "I'll stay. For now. But on one condition. That I can be assured my grandfather will be fed. Taken care of in my absence."

He nods once. "Done."

CHAPTER 14

I've yet to commit, to even consider agreeing to being the Night's famed Lunalette, but, four days later, I'm still here. I've been assured a message was sent to Poppy stating I was safe. That I'll get another chance to meet with the Sindaco "soon." That I've spent more time with the leader of the Night than Dorian does each week serving under him. There's a bit of envy in how he says it, which I immediately tease him about and he vehemently denies.

My birthday passed like any other day, save that morning when I awoke to Bronwyn and a second gift—a fresh blueberry muffin and her admission (I didn't even have to attempt prying it out of her) that the Night had wanted to hold a large celebration in my honor. Much to her disappointment, the Sindaco had decided against it. Bronwyn explained he worried it might be too much for me.

I assured her he was right.

Dorian wished me happy birthday *several* times throughout the day and insisted I noted he had the date correct. He was a complete ass about it, but it kept me smiling, a gift all its own.

Mostly, I thought of Poppy all day. How each year he'd have me blow out a candle before dinner and we'd thank the Sun for another year. Then I'd go to my room for bed and find he'd snuck something small onto my altar. A new fishing hook he'd traded worms for, a pretty shell, the last of the sunrise flowers before they all wilted away from frost.

Strange thing is I was more upset for Poppy's sadness about missing my birthday than my own.

Somehow all of that—turning seventeen, a rare blueberry muffin for breakfast, my Poppy missing the day for the first time in my life—feels like ages ago.

Yet, it's been four short days. Living with the Night on the other side of Bellona in this place they call the Lower.

It feels like so much longer.

And even though I should be lying obediently on the mat in my cave, once again I'm wandering along a maze of tunnels. This is the second time I've ended up here in as many days. I can't sleep in this place. It's too dark. Too quiet. Too . . . underground. There are times, I'd swear on all the pantera fish in the Great Sea, that the twenty feet or so of dirt and rock and insects piled above my head is going to cave in right on top of me.

Despite my constant questions to Dorian, unremitting seeking out of the Sindaco (I'm convinced the man is a ghost), and general trying to wrap my mind around this flipped-upside-down world I've landed in, I'm hopelessly restless at lights-out.

My first night gone rogue, I took a wrong turn and ended up here: a dark and winding tunnel with more caves leading off it. I wound along the web of halls like an aimless ant until I hit a dead end: a large metal door without a knob or lever. Only a keyhole. It's probably nothing. A closet full of gardening tools or extra dishes or, Sun help me, piles of soiled laundry. Despite the likelihood it's nothing, I can't stay away. I've tried picking the lock with the tip of my blade, peeking through the keyhole for a hint, but have been wildly unsuccessful.

Walking softly, I try to keep my boots from squeaking, my shaky breath from sounding too heavily. I traverse the labyrinth, a little ant winding along, going about her business, searching for the door with all the secrets. The tunnels are dark save for an occasional flicker of light mounted on a wall every so often. It's only myself and the dim glow of my lamp, the oil burning quickly.

I turn the corner to find this next tunnel is completely dark, no flickers to be had. Then the next, same thing, pitch-dark like black ink bleeding all around me.

At the next curve I'm greeted with a single light to illuminate the way to—yes—the secret door. No longer worried about the sound of my feet, I speed toward the door, determined that this time it's going to open.

Hand outstretched, I hold my breath, sending small, silent wishes up toward the Sun that when I push the door it'll give way and swing open.

I push it.

It doesn't budge.

Someone taps my shoulder.

I whip around in one quick motion. I'm not sure if it's the adrenaline or the fright, but I accidentally elbow whoever it is in the gut. Hard.

There's a groan of pain, several swears, and a hunched-over Dorian, about to punch the wall.

"Dorian! Holy hell, you scared me!"

He only responds by holding up a single finger as if asking me to wait.

As my heart calms, Dorian slowly recovers, until he's standing but leaning against the wall. "I really tried *not* to scare you. That's why I tapped you instead of shouting your name. I'm sorry."

"My Sun, next time just shout my name." He glares up at me. I give an apologetic smile. "I didn't mean to hurt you, but it's my instinct to punch anyone who sneaks up on me in the dark . . ." I pause. "Wait. What are you doing down here?"

"Guard duty."

"Oh, really . . . ?" Right. "Down here."

He nods.

"Middle of the night."

Nod-nod.

"Yeah, I don't buy it."

"It's true." But the crooked grin taunting the corners of his lips would suggest otherwise.

I slide down the wall and sit next to him. "What could you possibly be guarding in these empty caves?"

He glances over, slowly regaining his composure. "You." I gape back at him. He sighs deeply. "Trust me, I'd rather be sleeping." He narrows his eyes, small smile finally surfacing. "But the Sindaco wants you to go wherever you want, but doesn't want you to get lost. Alas . . ." He shrugs.

I narrow my eyes. "You're guarding me."

"Sort of." He smirks playfully. "It sounds creepier when you say it like that." He peels himself away from the wall, wincing, stretching from side to side. "We'd hate for you to get stuck in some cave. You'd starve . . . There'd be a huge, highly inconvenient search. Someone, probably me, would have to identify your body . . . It's just better for everyone if we avoid all that."

"Sure . . . What a pain that'd be." I return his playful smile, notice how his hair is disheveled, less perfectly kempt than usual, features softer when he's not so on guard. I'm also very aware of how seeing Dorian like this sets off a pleasingly warm swirling in my chest. Especially when his smile widens, how he glances at me from the corner of his eyes, part playful, part trying to read me as if he's feeling the same.

"So." He clears his throat. "What's your excuse? Going somewhere?"

"Maybe. I do miss my bed, my room, reliable plumbing . . ." Well, *mostly* reliable plumbing. "But, no, I'd probably end up in that same scenario you so poetically described." I sigh, rubbing my tired, heavy eyes. "I can't sleep, so I've been exploring. I found this door and . . ." I hesitate for a minute, unsure if I want to open up to him, when, his eyes bearing into mine, I think of what he said my first day here. That you have to give trust to receive it, to earn it back. I choose to give, take a small risk with the hope it'll pay off in the end. " . . . I kind of hoped there'd be something amazing and magical behind it." He only stares. I glance away, instantly regretting the risk. "It's stupid, I know. I'm tired. Delirious, probably."

"It's not stupid." He brings his hand up like he's going to touch my shoulder or graze my cheek with his fingers, but seems to change his mind, which leaves me disappointed, which morphs into confusion. "Not at all. In fact"—he pulls his keys from his pocket, holding a single one up in front of him—"here."

"What?"

"You do the honors."

I take the key out of his palm. My hand shakes as I insert it into the door, turn it to the left. The lock clicks and lifts. I look at Dorian. He raises his eyebrows and I push the door open.

It's not what I expect.

There's no fairy dust or magic . . . No scrolls or thick tomes for me to thumb through . . .

But my breath catches all the same.

The corners of my eyes sting, emotion and memories, so many prayers, filling the air like wishes in a well. You can't see any of it, but you know it's there. Countless blessings. There's an indescribable tangibility to it. I feel Dorian's eyes on me, and I open my mouth to speak, to try to voice my thoughts, but all the right words escape me.

"I know." His words are simple, light. But the way he says them, somehow so knowing and understanding, it calms me.

A MEMORIAL ROOM.

There are lamps mounted to the walls of the cave, illuminating name after name carved into the stone. There's an altar up front, not unlike the ones for missing Basso that have sprung up all over the island. Woven mats line the edge of the floor along the wall.

"The memorial room," Dorian says so lightly it's almost a whisper.

Without another word he leaves my side and walks to a far wall. Crouching on one knee atop a mat, he touches a couple of names, bows his head, and says a few words under his breath.

He glances back at me and I walk over, stop next to him, kneel on the mat beside his.

"My parents." Voice scratchy with emotion, he doesn't take his eyes off the names.

I look over at him. "Dorian...I..." I have no idea what to say. Hearing him say it's his parents, the hurt beneath his voice, it's suddenly very real. I take his hand in mine, then set my sights on the wall as well, read his parents' names, the dedications written beneath. The inscriptions aren't graphic, but Laurel and Ren Winters were brutally killed by the Imperi, their remains never recovered. "I'm so sorry for you...For Bronwyn..." My voice quakes from sadness, but the words seem so small compared to the weight of the loss.

Dorian turns his head, eyes red around the edges, and his words about giving trust to receive it ring true. "Thank you. It means a lot—I know you understand my loss better than most." He catches my eyes, giving a small nod, then stands. I release his hand, standing up along with him.

I glance around at the names, none of them familiar, but still significant. They were killed fighting for something they believed in. "Dorian?"

"Yeah?"

I glance over his shoulder at the names, trying to figure out if there's any order to them. "My mother was Amalie Adeline; she died soon after I was born and, according to the Sindaco, fighting for the Night. I don't know much about my father—nothing really—except that his first name was Vincent. I overheard my grandfather say it once coupled with a swear, but otherwise Poppy's never spoken of him."

Dorian's suddenly stone-faced, not giving me the slightest hint of what he's thinking. "I'm not sure about your father, but..." He peers behind his shoulder to the back corner where a single light shines in the darkness. "Over here."

Dorian takes my hand this time. His touch sends a tingling warmth that travels up my wrist and back. He leads me to the orange glow of a torch that seems to burn with endless flame.

Just above it is the name *Amalie Adeline*, the words literally taking my breath away. It's so beautiful it could be a poem. Two simple words, when put together, would illuminate the page. But it's not a poem. It's my mother's name.

"What is this?" I barely manage to breathe.

"Moon help me, I didn't know." He turns to face me. "Please believe me, V. I've seen this memorial countless times, but didn't put your last names together until just now when you said it." He shakes his head. "I'm so sorry."

"It's fine . . . I believe you . . ." But I'm barely thinking on that. All I focus on is what scenario under the Sun could have ended with my mother's name being carved into this wall.

"The woman, Amalie Adeline—your mother, apparently—her death was the catalyst to the first war. She and a team of Night soldiers were on a secret mission to get intelligence on the Imperi, but were ambushed. She was caught, pressed for information that she never gave up, and executed by the Imperi. Like my parents, her remains, unfortunately, weren't recovered."

My stomach churns, sending warm bile up into my throat. "Where did this happen?" I choke the words out.

"We believe she was taken to the holding cells under the Coliseum. Secluded. With no one around to witness any of it. The Imperi couldn't risk Basso hearing word a revolution was brewing." He shakes his head, taking a long breath in. "She was the first of many, but the one who sparked our initial uprising, hence the special memorial." He glances at the flame illuminating my mother's name. "She was a warrior. A hero.

Your mother sacrificed herself so the other Night soldiers on her team could safely get away." He lowers his voice. "Maybe your father was one of them?"

"Maybe . . ." I run my fingers over the ornate letters carved into the stone wall. "Dorian?"

"Yes?"

"Why lie? Why not just tell me the truth when I was old enough to understand? Swear me to secrecy like my grandfather? Why the seventeen years of complete horseshit?" The back of my throat burns with anger.

He gives a stern, yet sympathetic nod. "I'd be thinking the exact same thing."

"I mean, it's not like I'd go and tell anyone, because I'd be putting myself and Poppy in danger."

Brow furrowed as if in deep thought, Dorian sets his jaw like he's worked something out. "I guess, this whole thing"—he glances around the room, then stares right at me—"you being brought down here now, when you've just turned seventeen, is exactly that. Finally giving you the truth and trusting you with it."

"Well, they sure did take their time."

"I know . . . I agree . . . But I can only assume it wasn't meant out of deception or mistrust but out of protection."

And it hits me, and I hate how much sense it makes, because I really want to be angry at all the lies. "The less I knew, the less that could get me into trouble." It doesn't absolve the deception, but it definitely puts it into perspective.

He nods. "I'd say so, wouldn't you?"

I lift an eyebrow. "I just did."

Dorian gives a slight grin.

But I'm unable to smile back. Instead I face my mother's memorial, run my fingertips across her name, a knot forming in my throat. "Thank you for showing this to me." It's like everything I thought was real has been pulled apart and I'm slowly puzzling the pieces back together in a new image.

He nods slowly, eyes heavy. "I wish I had more information to share with you. Something to ease the weight of it all." Taking a deep breath, I glance at Dorian from the corner of my eyes as something I hadn't considered nags at me. "Actually . . . I do have a question you can answer." His eyes flash to mine. "Why didn't you confide in me earlier? Up on Bellona? Why lie about who you were?"

Dorian sucks in a deep breath, runs his hands through his hair. "Technically, I didn't lie." I furrow my forehead but let him explain further. "I am Dorian Winters, nephew and apprentice to the glass-maker. I grew up on Bellona. I'm Basso and I can't fish to save my life."

"Oh, I see . . ." I snort. "So you just didn't tell me *everything*."

He shoves his hands in his pockets, shaking his head. "I wasn't sure I could trust you. And, honestly, what if I had been completely truthful with you? Told you *everything*?"

"I'd have punched you in the nose and then turned you in."

He laughs. "Exactly. Sure, trust has to be given to be received. But . . . it also has to be earned. Even with your closest allies. Though I have a feeling you get that."

I open my mouth to argue, but stop myself to really dissect his words. He must be referring to Nico. And even though Nico is my closest friend, I do keep secrets from him and, I'm sure, he keeps them from me. And what is trust anyway? Is it being able to expose all your fears and disappointments and desires to someone else? Or is it in trusting those things will be kept safe with that person if you do? And maybe it's not so much about the secrets. Maybe it's all about knowing you can tell another person anything. Knowing that you can be vulnerable and safe. Trusting— without doubt or fear.

I glance across the space at Dorian and he stares back. It's going to take a lot more than him letting me through secret doors to earn my trust. But it's a good start.

Finally, I answer. "I do get it, but trust goes both ways."

Dorian steps closer, gingerly takes my hand in his. After all we've shared here, so many layers beneath Bellona, the warmth of his skin against mine is everything. It's grounding and calming and exciting all at once.

It's as if we're suddenly realizing we've known each other all along. The way we relate, how closely we understand each other, it's like we've been reunited.

Like I didn't know I'd been missing him until now.

I place my other hand on top of Dorian's, lace my fingers between his, which sends my stomach reeling.

He takes a quick breath in as if he feels it too. "I promise you I will do all I can to earn your trust. Because, Veda, if you don't trust me . . . trust *us*"—he searches the room as if referring to the Night past and present—"this will all have been for nothing."

"THANKS FOR TONIGHT," I say when we reach my cave, stop outside the arched doorway.

"I'm glad I ran into you," he says.

"You were following me!"

"Details . . ." He flashes a crooked grin, waving my comment off with a flourish of his hand.

I'm about to enter the cave, but pause, one question plaguing me since my meeting with the Sindaco. "Dorian?"

"Yes, Veda?"

"If it's not the Night who's abducting the Basso and it's really the Imperi . . ." I pause, collecting my thoughts, unsure if I really want to hear the answer. "What *are* the Imperi doing with all of them?"

Dorian's face falls and he only shakes his head. "You don't want to know."

I don't want to know, but I must. "Please tell me." My voice strains around the words. I'm worried it's what I'm thinking. What I've feared.

He gives a slight nod, eyes somber. "We've found evidence they were Offered. Privately."

Heat turns my gut, warmth rises up my throat. Even though I assumed it, hearing the words sends me into a panic. I don't want to know what specific evidence they've found, but I can't help asking, "Even the children?"

Dorian shakes his head. "There's no way of knowing. Our hope is that some are being kept alive somewhere. But many"—he pauses to swallow—"have been killed."

"Sacrificed, the High Regent would say."

"Exactly. Somehow, he's justifying it, if even to his soldiers."

I think of all those names, photos of the missing. A flame lights deep in my chest thinking of my sweet Poppy still stuck up on that island. "How could they?" My voice shakes with emotion. Sadness and pure, seething rage. "It's not right."

Dorian steps closer, takes my hands in his. "If there are any alive, we *will* free them."

I nod, but I'm not confident. I've seen what the Imperi are capable of and, now, what the Night truly is. I can't begin to imagine a world where the Night can win this fight. It's a death wish.

"I know that look." Dorian breaks into my thoughts, and I'm instantly aware my face is tight with worry, my shoulders slumped. "It's a long shot. We're outnumbered and outweaponed. But with you"—he gazes over my shoulder and into the cave at the mural—"the hope you bring coupled with the fire we all have to defeat the Imperi . . . It won't be easy, but I know we'll defeat them."

THAT NIGHT I lie on my mat, images of the memorial room—my mother's name written in stone above the orange flicker of a flame—swimming around my mind, and I try with all I have to tap into some memory of my parents. I don't have any photos to reflect on; Poppy always said the few he had were long destroyed. Was that a lie too? All I ever had of my parents was a maybe-map and a pink crystal.

There's no telling if even those are authentic. Had Poppy just picked some scraps off the ground and placed them on my altar to give me a sense of real memories? That my parents had left these mementos behind for me when really they were someone else's trash?

Everything I thought I'd known, each memory I'd imagined based on Poppy's stories or that map and stone, I'd wholeheartedly believed.

And maybe some of it was true. The few things Poppy told me about my mother must have been; she was his daughter.

But the rest?

Or maybe he only lied about their deaths.

I close my eyes and conjure an image of my mother. Her hair is a few shades lighter than mine, but the same fiery amber. She wears a black Night uniform and wields an atlatl, busting into one of the Imperi's secondary army training facilities and freeing the Basso who then join the fight.

I breathe deeply, sinking more heavily into my pillow. It might not be steeped in truth, this story I've spun, but I'll hold the image of my mother dear. As hope. Motivation. Sun help me, I can't even believe I'm thinking it . . .

Yet, there it is. A tiny light, a flicker of the notion that maybe, possibly, I'm going to do this.

Follow in my mother's footsteps as a member of the Night.

What better way to honor her, to honor the life that was taken from us? The bond we'll never know. I'll never know.

What better way to honor her sacrifice than to fight the very people who took it from her?

And what better way to honor my future, the future of all Basso, than to stand up for what we deserve? For what's right?

I glance at the mural, the jagged pointed star that's supposed to symbolize me, and with the weight of a hundred boulders my chest grows heavy, doubt crushing all that hope I'd just built up.

How quickly possibility can be reduced to dust.

The truth is louder than the daydream: I'm not my mother.

I'm not so sure I've got it in me to be a member of the Night, much less their sacred Lunalette. Their symbol. Whatever that means.

Fighting, I get.

Freeing any Basso held captive? That I understand.

But being nothing more than a symbol? A good luck charm? Someone meant to motivate and inspire and do it all from belowground?

I don't think so.

The mere thought of such a responsibility throws me into an internal cyclone of pure doubt, icy fear.

Because I don't know what the hell being Lunalette looks like.

But it's definitely not me.

CHAPTER 15

What seems like mere minutes later, I'm shaken out of a deep, dreamless sleep by a panicked Bronwyn. "Veda, get up! We have to go!"

When I snap awake, she's pulling me up by the arms and I sit bolt upright. "What's happening?"

"Flooding . . . In the main cavern and moving fast. We have to get to higher ground now."

"Where's Dorian?" I ask, and the minute the words leave my mouth, the way Bronwyn pauses a fraction of a second, I realize it was probably the strangest question for me to ask. "I mean . . ."

"He's fine. With the Sindaco and the other officers."

I nod. *Really, Veda?* Instead of, *How can I help?* Or, *Is everyone safe?* Or, *Is there damage?* for some Sun-forsaken reason, I ask about Dorian.

Bronwyn and I sprint through the tunnels, the trickling of water growing closer and closer.

"Shouldn't we be running away from the flooding?" I ask.

"This is the closest way to higher ground."

Higher ground? "We're going up to the island?"

"No . . . It's not that bad yet. Just to the Crag."

The rock floor is slippery, at least half an inch of standing water turning the already smooth surface into slick stone, our boots sliding with each quick step. We run into several others along the same route and the narrow tunnel grows tighter and tighter, the air thinner and thinner.

Shoulder to shoulder, our boots collectively slosh through the low flood. There's a constant low chatter full of "What if the water rises?" and "What if we have to go up to the island?" and "We're not ready for battle!" Hell, I don't even know my way to the Crag.

I feel a tug on the sleeve of my shirt. "Will we have to go to the Upper?" one boy asks, looking up at me over the flicker of his lantern as we stumble through the damp darkness. "Is our army ready to fight the Imperi?"

And despite not having the faintest idea how to fight anything other than a fish on the end of a hook, I stop dead, lean down to his level, and lie. "Whenever our army has to go up, whether it's in five minutes or in five years, we'll be ready." I'm literally lying through my teeth because I have no idea.

Doe-eyed, slowly, he nods his head up and down, and I decide the lie was worth it.

Then I realize everyone's stopped.

All eyes are on me. A few appear near tears. Several smile. Most wear an expression of hardened strength. One I know well. It tells the story of someone who's fought in one way or another all their lives. I suppose you don't have to have physically fought to be ready for battle.

We're all warriors here.

The Sindaco's words about how I've been a part of the Night, their history, their family for years edges to the surface. I'm seeing it firsthand and it terrifies me.

While their belief in their Lunalette is heartwarming, it stirs the nausea already building in my belly, sending signals to my brain that shout, "Impostor!" and "Liar!" and "You can't do this!"

But before I shrink too small, we're back en route. Our feet are soaked and our breathing is labored and sharp, but eventually we reach the Crag and an enormous cavern full of what must be the majority of the Night.

It's cramped, but there's still room to breathe.

The space—nearly as tall as the volcano is wide—echoes and buzzes with organized chaos. Several officers are calling out orders, rounding people up in groups, assigning them tasks and rotating them out while others sleep.

Bronwyn and I are shuffled into a line with several of those around us. An officer assigns the kids in our group trash duty; the adults are tasked with gathering any and all dry bedding they can find, while Bronwyn, me, and the rest of our group are to refill canteens with fresh drinking water from a nearby spring and check on anyone who's missing or injured. All of us are told to get a few hours' rest after we've finished.

Only a handful of people were hurt slipping on the wet cave floors or scraped in the dark, but nothing life threatening. No one's missing, though one little girl claims she's forgotten her favorite blanket back in her cave. Bronwyn gives her one of Dorian's tiny glass animals—a cat. Apparently, she grabbed a handful on her way out of her cave where she has an entire menagerie stashed away, which only further endears me to Dorian.

Once we've made our rounds through our assigned section of the upper caverns and at least three trips to the spring and back, we're to rest until the lower tunnels and caves—where most of the living quarters are—are out of danger of flooding further.

There's one pillow and one mat for Bronwyn and me to share. We end up giving it to a woman with three young children and use our jackets for pillows, lying on the cold stone floor, which, honestly, is welcome after all the back-and-forth we've been doing.

Instantly, I drift off, but awaken to a loud crash. I sit up to find the noise was only the rumbling of thunder outside the not-so-thick walls of the volcano and that Bronwyn, who was right beside me when I fell asleep, is now gone.

Worried I must have slept through our next shift, I set out to find her. Why the Sun would she let me sleep?

Only a few days ago, anywhere I went, I caught straying eyes—questioning looks of speculation and longing gazes of admiration, both. Now? Here amid organized chaos? I'm just another member of the Night. But at the moment, no one's paying me any mind. And it's nice.

I weave in and out of sleeping bodies on the floor, members handing out food, smaller groups of two and three rushing here and there, carrying buckets of flood water and sand inside burlap bags.

When I return to the officer who initially assigned our tasks, some other soldier's taken his place. I ask a few people about Bronwyn, but no one knows where anyone is, much less someone not in their group. Though she can't be that far.

I leave through the same tunnel we used to get water and then head toward the spring.

But when I'm sure I'll see the small hole of fresh water around the next corner, I hit a dead end.

I retrace my steps, and somehow end up at a fork I know I didn't encounter before. I flip a mental coin and go right, snake back and forth down a long, narrow cave. This tunnel opens up, then descends down some rocky stairs where I trudge through a knee-deep puddle no one's cleared yet, making a mental note to tell someone about it once I find my way back.

From there, the cave goes up. And up. And up some more until I recognize where I am by the ladder before me and the mumbling of voices not far above.

The Sindaco's office.

I freeze, stuck between finding my own damn way out of here and not wanting to be caught looking like I'm eavesdropping.

I try my best to think back to when Dorian and I were here a few days ago . . . Which way did we go to get back? We definitely didn't go down where that puddle was, so if I keep going, I should find my way out.

Hopefully.

I'll chance it. I can always come back and ask for help if I need it.

Decision made. Two steps forward and I'm startled by the whack of metal on stone—a door opening—then, "Sir, you must tell her." It's Dorian, his voice raised, an angry edge to it. Surely, he's not speaking to . . .

"Please understand my position here." The Sindaco. "I need her to trust me—to trust us, the Night. I can't risk overwhelming her with too much at once."

"But, sir—"

"She knows she's the Lunalette." My stomach drops, that nausea reaching right up into my throat. "How could I possibly explain her father's still alive?"

I gasp, but thankfully swallow it down.

Dorian takes a deep breath. "I understand, I do, but think of how much more she'll trust and respect you—respect us, her role as Lunalette—if we're honest."

There's a long pause.

"I've thought long and hard about this, Dorian. She needs more time."

"She's heir to Bellona . . . What she needs is time to swallow that!"

"Enough."

"Please, sir, at least consider it?"

"I said enough!" Silence. "Now. We have flooding to deal with."

I know I should get out of there, run as far away as fast as I possibly can, but my feet are cement. I'm holding out. Hoping they'll say something more, clue me in to where my father is, discuss this heir-to-Bellona thing, which I can't even begin to fathom and causes me to run my hand over the scar on my chest.

But they've been quiet too long.

And before I can get out of there, Dorian's jumped the last several rungs of the ladder and stands before me.

"Did you just . . . ?" But I don't hear the end of his sentence because I turn and take off down the tunnel.

"VEDA, WAIT!"

I ignore him and keep walking. I can't deal with this right now. I just can't. If Dorian and the Sindaco have been lying to me about something this significant, I can't trust either of them.

I'm going to get answers from the one and only person I know I can trust. My grandfather. Now.

"Please stop. You have no idea where you're going," Dorian pleads.

"I'll find my way." Glancing over my shoulder, I see that he's not far behind me now.

"No. I'm serious, STOP!"

When I turn my head forward, there's only five steps or so of cave ahead and then . . . nothing. Blackness. I hold the lantern out before me. It's a drop-off. So steep, I can't begin to see the ground below.

I stumble back, grip the rock wall behind me, and then slide down onto the ground. "Someone should really block that off," I manage.

"There's nothing on this side of the volcano—no one ever comes out this far. Those who do know to avoid it."

I swallow hard, taking a shaky breath in. "My father's alive?" I finally say. Dorian nods. "Where the hell's he been all these years, then?"

Dorian doesn't answer, only stares, brow knit. Finally, "You didn't hear our whole conversation back there, did you?"

I glare at him. "Apparently not." He shifts his position, shoves his hands into his pockets, glances ahead into the nothingness. Stalling. "What aren't you telling me?"

Dorian shakes his head, then begins speaking so quietly that I have to strain to hear him. "I'll be going against his wishes—his orders—but you heard most of it on your own. I have no choice." He slides down the wall and takes a seat beside me.

Turning his head to face mine, Dorian makes eye contact over the slowly dimming lamp between us. He leans in closer. "Your father's alive. But you must believe me when I say, I swear, I didn't know until last night in the memorial room. I didn't realize it until we discovered who your mother was. I mean, I'd always known her memory was special, that the Sindaco held her in great regard for her sacrifice. I can't believe I didn't see it before." He pauses, lets a breath out. "I don't know, but you being here? It's like everything suddenly came together." I realize I'm leaning in too, that our hands are nearly touching. "Veda?"

"Yes?" I whisper.

"Your father's the Sindaco."

"Yeah, right." I shake my head, releasing a sort of snort-hiccup.

Dorian's eyes turn stern. "I'm dead serious. The Sindaco's real name is Vincent *Raevald*. You said they never married, which would explain why you took your mother's surname, another reason I never put it together. I don't think of the Sindaco as 'Vincent'; he's extremely private about his past, never speaks of it. I had no idea he was your father."

"Truly. You had no idea," I say, my tone monotone, body numb with shock.

"*Truly.*" He inserts the emotion I'm lacking. Well, not lacking so much as unwilling to muster. Incapable of exploring right now.

I pull my knees to my chest and try to rub the headache erupting between my eyes with my palms. Could it possibly be true? Dorian has no reason to lie. Especially about this of all things. He wants me to stay, and, if anything, he'd know this new revelation would push me away.

What had the Sindaco said? That he didn't want to dump too much information on me at once? That checks out too. He definitely wants me to stay and play Lunalette. Why push me away before I've had a chance to wrap my mind around the first shock by hitting me over the head with another?

I'm quiet for a long while, but don't realize quite how long until I see the lantern is fading and that Dorian has resorted to patiently pelting small pebbles against the cave wall like he's playing a game.

Raevald . . . If it's true and my father's last name is Raevald . . . "Wait." I finally break the silence. Dorian whips his head toward mine, dropping the handful of gravel. "So . . ." The word *heir* repeats over and over in my head until it's only noise. Nonsensical gibberish. "*If* my father's last name is Raevald, he's related to THE Raevald—as in, High Regent—which would make me . . ."

"His granddaughter. Your father—the Sindaco—is his son. The Imperi High Regent is your grandfather."

I'm shaking my head. It can't be. It's impossible. "Whether it's true or not I have to go back up. I've got to speak with my grandfather—my actual grandfather—Poppy. I need to hear this from him."

"I understand, I do, but you can't. Not now. The Imperi's planning another Night of Reckoning. It's too risky."

"What?"

He nods. "Tomorrow night." He squints at his hourglass. "I mean, tonight." He scrubs his tired eyes with his hands.

My Sun, it's all lies. All made up by the Imperi. "Then I definitely have to go back up and warn Poppy."

"Veda—"

I grab the lantern, stand, and—for once—tower over him. "Dorian Winters, either you show me how the hell to get back up to Bellona or your Lunalette will find her own way or die trying." I put my free hand on my hip. "Your choice, but I'm going this way." I walk past him.

I don't hear any sign Dorian moves, and then, suddenly, he's right behind me. "Fine." He throws his hands up. "You win."

"I'm sorry, what?" I can't help but say it, but my tone is dry.

Dorian sighs. "I said"—he holds his hand out for the lantern—"You. Win." I hand it over. "But only because, like an idiot, I promised you I'd take you back after and only after you'd given us a chance." He motions we take the tunnel to the left. "I'd say you've done that. Plus, I should check on my uncle, make some hourglasses, a few pantera fish."

"See? It all works out."

"Yes. *Perfect.* We just have to get past the Sindaco—he won't be happy." I quirk an eyebrow, purse my lips. "We'll deal with that later."

Dorian's words are strong. I do sense the tiniest hint of worry, but decide not to push him for answers. I'm having enough trouble with the information he's already given me. "Right now we need to focus on getting out of here undetected, which shouldn't be too hard in all of this." He shines the lamp ahead, highlighting the few inches of water we're sloshing through.

"Are we going to have to swim out?"

"Hope not. I'm thinking the worst is behind us. The biggest threat isn't so much high water, but of caves collapsing. The mudslides are unpredictable." I'm hit with the most terrible image of caves tumbling in, children running, mud crashing through walls. I swallow, blink my eyes to erase the sight from my mind. I note Dorian's slowed his pace and is watching me. "Everyone will stay in the volcano until it's one hundred percent safe," he says, his voice smoothed over as if trying to comfort me. It works. "As for us, we'll keep to the higher ground, the upper tunnels. Some of the exits are closed off, but I know a way."

"Guess I'll just have to trust you, eh?"

He laughs. "I've gotten us this far." Dorian gives me a small smile, and I can't help but wonder if the double meaning of our exchange is as evident to him as it is to me.

"I won't congratulate you until I've got the sea and the sky in my sights."

"I'd better get you that far—at least. It was one thing when you were simply the Lunalette, but now, being the Sindaco's daughter? He'd kill me. Literally. String me up and let the mud beetles and cave snakes feast off me."

I snort, being sure the cynicism comes through. "The Sindaco's daughter . . ."

Dorian catches my eye. "You'll see, V. You'll see . . ."

He drops the subject, rolling into an explanation of our general route, how cave snakes are afraid of fire, and that he'll send word back to the Sindaco after we're up on Bellona. From there, we walk quickly (for fear our lamp's going out) and in silence.

It's a shorter walk than I expect to the main tunnel, but Dorian was right. I'm sure not to mention it, but there's no way I'd have ever found my way out of this section of the Lower, much less back up onto the island.

Dorian leads as we traverse the labyrinth of twists and turns, stairs, tunnels that branch into other tunnels, until we've gone through several locked doors and have our feet firmly planted on the surface of the island.

It's dark as midnight. We stand still under the cover of the forbidden shadow of the Crag. The one Poppy's warned me of for as long as I can remember.

Rain mists lightly down from the sky, yet each drop stings with cold as it mingles with salty spray from the Great Sea. It's only been a few days, but winter's undoubtedly taken hold.

From across the island, high on Imperi Hill, a single bell rings. It's one o'clock in the morning. The devil's hour. Two things immediately seize my mind: I'm out after dark.

And I'm home.

Without a word, Dorian tilts his head to the right, motioning I follow him. From the darkness of the Crag and over the supposed land mines I'd been taught to avoid by threat of lost limb or two, we move toward the thick tree line. Sandy beach turns to muddy, root-laced, mossy woods.

Dorian leans in, and whispers, "Shortcut."

His lips graze my ear, sending a simultaneous shiver and jolt down my neck. I nod so he knows I understand. Ignoring it, unable to react (not that I would if I *was* able), I swear, Dorian feels it too. The way his eyes, reflecting like blue glass in the moonlight, linger a sigh longer than they normally would speaks more than words ever could.

Before I can reflect too long on any of that a whistle sounds from the other side of the woods. An Imperi soldier. I've heard those whistles countless times, but the sound's too distant to be for us. Still, Dorian quickens his pace and I'm sure to walk double time to keep up.

Like a couple of mice sneaking through a field, we're quiet on our feet, and thanks to the harsh wind, I can't imagine many forest animals are wise to our location, much less that soldier or any others who might be near.

Once it seems the whistler's moved on, I steal a moment to breathe . . . To take in the night version of a familiar landscape . . . Home. My Bellona. But the dead-of-night version. Here, the scents and sounds are so different from what I'm used to. Everything's cool, slick, and fresh with rain, so quiet save a chorus of crickets, an owl or two, and the *squish, squish* of the saturated, part-frozen ground beneath our boots.

It isn't long before we've reached the main pathway and the tunnel where, what feels like forever ago, Dorian helped me escape those Imperi soldiers. From behind the last copse of trees, we search for signs of anything from soldiers to vagrants to members of the Imperi version of the Night—the Not-Night. But there's no one.

"On three, we run for it," Dorian says so low I'm reading his lips more than hearing his words.

"On three," I repeat.

He holds up three fingers.

The entrance to the tunnel is only five, six strides away at most, a thick moat of fog the only obstacle. My heart speeds up.

One.

It's wet, the stone slippery. *Don't fall, Veda.* My breathing thins.

Two.

The light above the tunnel entrance flickers on, then back off, illuminating a familiar face on an unfamiliar posting. Raevald's eyes stare through the darkness, the words below him reading THE IMPERI NEEDS YOU!

I don't know if it's the shadows or my mind playing tricks on me, the words having all-new meaning, but I see something. An unshakable resemblance.

Three.

We run for it, but it's like a dream, my mind elsewhere, my body going through the motions. One foot, then the other. Repeat.

Once in the tunnel, we don't dare slow.

One foot, then the other. Repeat.

Raevald's image—one part the Sindaco, another part myself, the rest the Imperi High Regent I've both revered and feared all my life—hasn't left my head. There's no denying it. The resemblance is as real as the mangled five-pointed scar on my chest.

DORIAN AND I split up in the woods behind my cottage. He heads back to his uncle, and I enter through our back door to find Poppy's awake, sitting in his chair before the fire.

I bound toward him. What I expect of my grandfather is to be wrapped in a long, lingering hug. Then for him to check me over, be sure I'm all right. Then, of course, complete relief will smooth the lines on his face when he sees I'm safe.

Instead, "My Veda! What the devil are you doing here?"

"I . . ." I skid to a stop, halting about two feet away. "Wait, what?"

"You have to go back." He starts to push me toward the door. "Now!"

"Poppy!" I turn on my heels and stand tall, cement my boots to the floor. "I'm not going anywhere until I get answers. You owe me answers." Catching us both by surprise, my voice cracks and my eyes begin to burn. "Please," I barely manage, suddenly so exhausted I melt into the chair across from his. "Please," I repeat under my breath.

His tired, gray eyes bore into mine. Although he clearly wants me out of this house, safe and sound underground, he knows he owes me seventeen years' worth of explanations.

Finally, he exhales, relenting. "Yes . . . Of course." He smooths my hair from my face. "You're right." But before he sits back down, he runs around making sure every last curtain is drawn and every door and window is latched.

Then he sits across from me, elbows resting on his knees, eyes intent on mine. "Ask me anything, my Veda."

"Was my mother killed by the Imperi instead of the Night?"

He nods his head, gaze heavy, somber. "Yes."

"Did she fight in the first war?"

Nod. "In the very beginning. She was so brave."

I don't know my mother, I never met her. Yet, somehow, especially after the past twenty-four hours, I feel I know her. A strong knot forms in my throat. "And my father?"

Poppy's eyes flick to mine. "The Sindaco." He all but whispers the words like they're painful on his lips.

"His name is Vincent, isn't it?"

"Aye . . ." He stares, unblinking.

"I heard you say it once. Curse it, actually. I never asked you about him because I didn't want to upset you. I also assumed he was dead."

He shakes his head. "I would have had to lie anyway . . . But yes, Vincent Raevald, the Sindaco, is your father."

Hearing him say the words puts all doubt to rest. It also sends an aching to the back of my throat, one that stretches up into my eyes. I breathe deep and then shakily exhale. "So I'm . . . ?"

"You're the rightful heir to all of Bellona." He smiles in a sad yet proud way, the corners of his mouth twitching from either exhaustion or emotion. "Veda, you must know, Raevald will never stand for it. He'd deny it to his dying day that you, an orphaned Basso, are heir to his legacy, especially when, in his mind, your father's a traitor. A disgrace to his name and his position."

A disgrace. Of course. Bastard child of his traitor son. The Basso fisher girl with permanent mud staining her knees. But if it's true, if I'm really the heir, maybe . . . "If the truth got out . . ."

"Raevald will never let that happen. He'll die before he disgraces his family's lineage with the truth: that his son wasn't executed by the Night but is actually the leader. There'd be no trust in the name Raevald. He's made the Night out to be such monsters. Can you imagine if all of Bellona heard the truth? That not only had Raevald fabricated this ruthless, cruel version of the Night, sent his Imperi soldiers to do his bidding, but that his son was their true leader? They'd drag him off that Hill so fast, he'd never know what hit him. He'd lose everything." He scoots his chair closer, the legs scraping the wood floor. "Promise me, Veda. Promise me you won't tell a soul of this."

I finally have some power, a bit of control over our future, and I have to keep it quiet? I worry the inside of my cheek, trying to find a way around it, but as upsetting as it is, I know he's right. If anyone found out I'd be killed. Poppy too. "I promise." That aching in my throat now burns; my eyes prickle with heat.

Poppy releases a long sigh. "Good."

"Is that why you hid the truth from me all these years? Because, Poppy..." Speaking his name, I look into the familiar silver flecks of his eyes. He's the only parent I've ever known. The only person I've ever truly looked up to. I've hung on to Poppy's every word as gospel since I could understand them.

So, knowing what I'm about to say sends a heavy torrent of hot tears down my face. "You've lied." Of everything, that definitely hurts the worst.

Without a word, Poppy scoots out of his chair and onto his knees, wraps his arms around my shoulders. "It killed me to lie. My Sun, it killed me." He pulls away and finds my eyes, reflecting the sadness and anger and disappointment of my own. "But." Poppy straightens his shoulders. "It was what I had to do. For your safety. For the Night. For your father and, bless her, your mother." The undersides of his eyes swell with water.

All I can do is shake my head. Because I understand he had to protect me, that he was sworn to secrecy, but that doesn't make his betrayal any less painful.

"Veda, you must understand or I'll never be able to live with myself. If the wrong person had found out who you truly were—that you were a threat to the most powerful man on the island—you'd have been taken and killed. I lied for your life." He glances toward the fire. "Your happiness and your well-being. It's the *only* thing I'd ever lie to you for. Do you understand?"

I slide from my chair and meet him on the floor, wipe my face with my sleeve. "In my head, I do understand all of that, truly, I do. It's my heart"—my voice quakes—"that's having trouble coming around."

He grasps my hands in his. "It'll take time. I've always known this would be hard. My Sun, I've dreaded it for seventeen years. Forget the Night of Reckoning; it's facing you after all of this I've feared." Poppy finds my eyes, his bushy eyebrows raised, deep creases lining his forehead.

I can't help but give a hiccup of a laugh.

"Give it time, Veda. The one thing that's brought me peace is that I know you." He gives my hand a slight squeeze.

I throw my arms around him.

Because it's Poppy—mint leaves and soil and castile soap. Home. The one person in the world I could ever fully trust.

I'd lie for his life too.

I'd do it a million times over if I had to.

WE SIT ON the floor well into the night talking. It's not the first time we've had a long talk, far from it, and certainly won't be the last, but this is the most honest, most important one so far.

Poppy tells me of my mother, how it killed him to hide her true sacrifice, her true cause of death. How painful it was to concoct a tale about how no one knew where my father was and that I'd been left with Poppy after she was taken by the Night. That, by the grace of the Sun, I'd somehow been spared.

How he'd raised me in his daughter's memory. At the time, he explains, many were going missing—either truly joining the Night or being taken by the Imperi—and no one thought twice about a child being left motherless or the Basso woman who'd had me out of wedlock.

He had to pretend his own daughter had been taken by the Night and killed when it was actually the Imperi who ultimately took her from us. That, although Raevald never knew her identity, that his son ran off with her to join the Night and that they had a child, the truth couldn't be risked.

And when she was tortured for information all alone, secluded beneath the Coliseum, ultimately executed, she refused to give her name. For me. To protect me and Poppy and the Sindaco, the Night and the cause.

The Imperi killed my mother with no one around to see her sacrifice, to know the truth. The last thing they wanted was to make a martyr out of her. She died alone, not a witness at her side, by the hand of some nameless, faceless Imperi soldier. Simply a "traitorous member of the Night."

Poppy all but had to erase his daughter from history. For our protection, Amalie Adeline practically never existed.

Thankfully, the Night did know her identity. Amalie Adeline was a true hero, and one whose life and sacrifice wouldn't be in vain.

Unfortunately, their uprising didn't end the way anyone would have hoped. But with me, they have a second chance. Renewed hope.

Finally, the truth from someone I know is being honest. Someone I know no longer has any reason to lie to me. In this moment, despite the betrayal I logically understand but am still working through, I trust my grandfather without hesitation.

But Poppy's words are more painful than I expect them to be. It's like one truth after another is stacked on top of me until the weight is too much to hold. For fear of toppling, I stuff and lock all the information inside, push some of it to the back, dissect what I can right now. The simplest parts. And even those I break down, skin, and clean until it's only bones left to sift through.

The bones:

My father is the Sindaco.

My mother was a soldier, a hero killed by the Imperi.

Regardless of whether the Lunalette story is real, an entire society of people believe in me as if there is a prophecy. To them, I am their hope for revolution.

And I know quite well that believing in something makes it very real. I don't speak for some time as I sort all those bones of truth.

Poppy gives me the time and space to work through it all, but keeps glancing at the hourglass. I'm about to ask him if he has someplace to be, if he's taken on a lady friend in the few days I've been gone, when I realize I should be the one watching the time. I should be the one itching to get moving. We have two days' worth of work to do to prepare and only until vesper bells to do it.

Jerked out of the past and into the present, I speak loudly, quickly. "Poppy—the Imperi's attacking. Tonight. Another Night of Reckoning." I jump up, start packing things away, covering the furniture.

"Veda, I know already. Stop, stop." He stands, swatting my hands away from the blanket-covered chair. "I've known for days. The Imperi's posted warnings all over the island. Bragging their spies got word of the attack just in time."

"Just in time?" I ask. "For what?"

"For an Offering. Tomorrow." Yet again, Poppy glances at the hourglass on the table. "Today. A preemptive pleading to the Sun that he might shine through the night. Also in preparation for another Ever-Sol Feast."

I shake my head. So many lies. "Tell me," I say, changing the subject back to something that's been nagging at me since I first saw that mural of the Lunalette in my cave. "Did I really get my scar the way you've always told me?"

"Aye," Poppy says. "That was the day I truly believed. Before that, I'll admit, the Lunalette was a fantastic legend, but you never know with prophecies . . . So many things can thwart their paths." He guffaws. "Something as innocent as a gust of wind's been known to change the course of fate. Just ask your father." I raise an eyebrow, wondering where

160

in the world he's going with this. "Had fate not intervened, he'd be pre-paring to take over as High Regent. Instead he's leading a revolt."

"I don't know, Poppy... Do you *truly* believe in all that?"

He smiles wide and proud. "I've always said there's no harm in ques-tioning things." He has always said that. "But when, all of one year old, you wandered off that day—I'd only left you for a second and off you went! Down to the canal—always toward the water—and splash! You fell... or maybe you dove... right in. I wasn't the wiser until I heard your scream. Rushed out back, yanked you out by your ankle, and detached that pantera fish's jaw right from your chest. Damned thing took some skin with it." He shakes his head, staring in the direction of the canal. "I couldn't believe my eyes... The most jagged, gnarled, scar I'd ever seen, smack-dab over your heart. And curse me to hell and back if it didn't resemble a star. I knew right then..."

"Knew what?"

"Well, two things... That you'd be a great fisher and I'd better start taking you fishing more so you didn't sneak out on your own and get eaten by pantera fish." He smiles, that unmistakable twinkle in his eye. "And that fate, when not thwarted, is truth. Just look at the Lunalette legend. That star on your chest is an omen. I truly believe, had you not fallen in the canal, some other way you'd have gotten that scar. The mark was there all along; something just had to bring it to the surface. This Lunalette, your secret claim as heir, it's true. The whole of it."

We sit in silence as I think on that. That Poppy believes in it. In me.

"Now." He claps his knee, making me jump. "You have to go back."

"What?"

"It's not safe here for you, my Veda. With the Offering tomorrow..."

"Wait. Did the medallions arrive?" I glance toward the front door, the metal slot, then down to the floor. No medallions.

"Yes. Yours is in your room on your bedside table. No Sun."

"Okay. Good." I stare, brow furrowed.

"Mine's fine too." He waves my concern off with a flick of his wrist.

I let out a long, relieved sigh. "Don't do that to me, Poppy!"

"Sorry."

"I can't go back yet. I have to help you prepare for tonight." I glance around the house, note that nothing's been done. Nothing. "I promise I'll leave before vesper bells, once you're safe in the cellar."

"Veda . . ."

I place my hands on my hips. "I'm not leaving."

He narrows his eyes at me, crooked smirk dancing at the corner of his mouth. "I never could get you to mind me. Stubborn to a fault, just like your mother." He shakes his head as if imagining memories from long ago. "Fine. But once the house is secure, you leave, eh?"

"I promise."

CHAPTER 16

Poppy and I do all we can to barricade the cottage until daylight.

After the last Night of Reckoning and the red paint, Poppy's been stockpiling sheets of canvas, scraps of muslin.

"I have to see Nico before the Offering." I speak my rambling thoughts as we spread an already paint-stained sheet over the kitchen table.

"Of course, yes." Poppy's suddenly working more quickly. "You'll need to leave soon, then."

I take in the room. "But there's still so much to do. I suppose I could wait until—"

"No. Go now. I can finish this." He throws his arm out, motioning all around us. "Nico needs to know you're all right. I haven't seen him since the day you disappeared, but you can imagine he didn't take it well. He deserves to know you're safe."

Well, I can't exactly argue with that. "You're right."

"And take your time," he says. "You don't have to come with me to the offering. Go back to the Night after you see Nico. It'll be safer while everyone's at the Coliseum for you to get away."

"But you'll never get this done in time on your own."

"I can handle it. Don't worry yourself."

"Poppy." I look him straight in the eyes. "You're being too proud. I'm helping and I'm not taking no for an answer. Besides, I have to stay for the Offering anyway. I need to be there." He shrugs. "Think about it . . . Not only will I get to spend a little more time with you but I think it might be helpful for other Basso to see I've returned from the Night. Proof it can be done."

"Veda . . . Listen to your poppy for once, eh?" There's a pleading deep in his eyes, but I ignore it. He needs me here and just doesn't want to be trouble. I'm not falling for it.

I raise an eyebrow. "If anyone asks, I'll keep to the story that I escaped, but if I plant even one seed, light a small fire in someone, it'll be worth it. If one person is motivated to fight back tonight, to possibly uncover the truth about the Imperi pretending to be the Night, my being delayed is a small price to pay."

He heaves a long breath. "I suppose you're right."

"I'll see you in one hour. At the docks."

He nods. "One hour."

FROM THE BACK of our house, I follow the canal, my boots sludging slowly through mud and oversaturated ground where the channel has flooded. I'm in my old clothes, taking the same route I've taken countless times as if nothing's changed. But so much has.

Going over what I plan to say, what I'm going to share with Nico and what I'll need to keep to myself, I reach the small pond down from Denali Manor.

Up the hill, I see the back of Nico's home, the fence surrounding it taller than ever, but I think I can climb it.

I hike along rocks and steep ground until I'm face-to-face with the iron fence. It towers at least a foot above my head.

TWO DEEP BREATHS and I jump, my fingertips grasping the top rung, which is all cold, wet metal. Boots left with nothing to cling to, I slip and fall, landing on my knees, the pain stinging something fierce. After a moment to gather myself, I brush leaves and mud off my legs to reveal the holes in my stockings have torn even larger, my bloodied knees now in plain sight. I try three more times with no success.

"Damn it."

"Veda?" I hear Nico, his tone riddled with disbelief.

"Nico?"

"What the Sun are you doing?"

"Trying to find you. How'd you know I was back here?"

"You weren't exactly being quiet," he says, and I can tell he's smiling. Then, as if with zero effort, Nico hops over the fence.

"That was—" All set to say something sassy, I stop short because Nico's right there. A sprig of spearmint hangs from his mouth, and he gently places his hands on my cheeks. Nose inches from mine, he examines me.

"Where have you been?" He leans in. "It was the Night, wasn't it?" he hisses. "I've been going mad with worry and Poppy didn't know a thing and my Sun I'm so glad you're all right!" He wraps me in a perfectly warm, perfectly lovely, lingering hug.

If I thought Poppy's cozy scents of mint leaves and castile soap and earthy soil was home, this? This is heaven. I'm enveloped by all things Nico . . . The sweet of vanilla and the bitter of spearmint along with the freshly laundered wool of his scarf. I could stay here, my head resting on his shoulder, his warm breath grazing the top of my head, forever and then some.

He pulls away, eyes red around the edges. Nico stares, waiting for me to speak. Surely anticipating I'll spill every single detail of the past four days.

The Night is good, the Imperi is bad, no other details . . .

"I want to tell you everything, but . . ." I glance behind us. The Sun slowly rises higher above the horizon, reflecting off his windows. Imperi soldiers march on their morning drills on the other side of the hill, their boots clapping lowly against stone walkways. "Can we go somewhere else?"

"Of course. Yes."

Without so much as a word, we both head down the hill and to the pond and the bench that sits beneath a white wooden trellis. The small area—where we first met and have used as our secret place all these years since—is concealed by thick trees and plants and, in the spring, abundant wildflowers.

We sit side by side on the bench. The chill of the stone slowly sneaks through my layers and into my skin as I work out how in the Sun to begin. Where to start.

Nico moves to take my hand in his, catching my eye to make sure it's okay. I give a slight smile because it's always okay and lace my left hand with his right. He grazes my wrist with the pad of his thumb, arcing my skin back and forth. *Ad astra.*

The friction of his skin arcing mine sparks a tiny fire that spreads from my wrist to my chest and down to my belly, where it ignites an unsuspecting swarm of butterflies.

Heaven.

And as much as I want to avoid what must come next, bury everything deep, deep down, I force myself to jump right in because there's no other way.

"When we were caught the other morning and you told me to run, I did. But they chased me, so I couldn't go home and ended up at the main tunnel. Even though I was running fast as I could, they were right behind me. I was hoping to somehow lose them in the tunnel when someone stepped out of it. Dorian."

Nico leans in, brow furrowed. "The glassmaker's apprentice?"

"Yes. Him. When he saw what was happening, he took me down a sort of stoop. A den. A . . ."

"Devil's den."

I nod and pause a beat as Nico works over what I'm saying, putting some of the pieces together. And I see it the moment everything sparks for him. His eyes go wide and he opens his mouth, but I beat him to it.

"You can't say anything to anyone." Nico only stares. "Promise me, Nico. Promise me you won't tell a soul. If anyone finds out, I would be executed. Dorian too and, I fear, that would just be the start."

"I . . . Okay . . . I promise."

"And, please, no snap judgments?"

He nods slowly, silently.

"No arguing or commenting until I'm finished?"

Slow nod.

"Dorian's a member of the Night." Nico's expression hardens, but before he can say anything, I continue. "And they're good, Nico. Not at all like we've been told."

He releases his hand from mine. "What?"

"I know it's hard to hear. But you have to trust me. I've seen it with my own eyes."

"Then they're putting on a good show." He sarcastically spits the words out. "You've only been gone a few days, and you've already forgotten all they've done, Veda?" I'm shaking my head no. "Your parents? So many missing Basso?" He's staring at me like I've lost my mind.

I fold my arms over my chest. "It wasn't the Night." I turn my body so I'm facing him, gaze straight into those dark eyes of his. "It was the Imperi."

"Right." He almost laughs the word. "If you truly believe that, you've been brainwashed."

"How are you so sure?" My voice quakes, and for the first time ever, those dark eyes of his doubt me.

And maybe in this moment I doubt him.

"The Imperi takes care of us, protects us. They keep us with food and materials, health and happiness, all of that . . ." He trails off.

"They do that for you, Nico. For Dogio. Not so much for Basso."

He swallows hard.

He stays quiet, staring at the pond. Then, "You're right."

"What?"

"We live in different worlds." He glances toward the pond, and I can see the faintest shine of water in his eyes. "I haven't been a good friend."

"What?"

"No . . . I mean, here I am in a position of power; I should have done something long ago to help change things."

"How could you?"

"I don't know, Veda, I guess that's the problem." He looks into my eyes. "Because even I feel powerless most of the time." Nico sighs deeply. "And if I feel like I have no control, I can't imagine how you've felt. I can see how easily you could be turned against the Imperi, and I don't fault you for that."

"You don't *fault* me?" Brow furrowed, I take a step away from him.

"I didn't mean it like that . . ." He stumbles over his words. "Just that we've had completely different experiences. Based on that reasoning, it makes sense you don't trust the Imperi and I do."

"Well, your reasoning's stupid, Denali. That's obvious, even without the whole they've-been-lying-about-the-Night part."

Nico takes me in, chest swelling with a deep breath I know is him giving up, not wanting to argue with me. "Fair enough," he concedes, crooked smile quirking at his lips so that dimple deepens.

I smile back. "Fair enough." I decide not to push any further. I told him all I planned to tell him. The truth (most of it).

Nico checks his hourglass. "We should get going."

His words tug me back to reality, and I glance down at my own hourglass. "Poppy! Damn it, I promised him I'd meet him in an hour."

"When was that?"

"Nearly an hour ago."

I stand up and start to walk away.

"Veda?"

I stop and turn on my heels to find he's right behind me. "Yeah?"

"I'm glad you're home."

"Me too."

I take his hands in mine. But instead of holding on, clasping our fingers together like we normally would, Nico wraps his arms around the small of my back. Pulling me into his chest, our eyes connecting, unspoken words long overdue pass between us. Slowly, slowly, our mouths inch closer.

"I've . . . ," Nico breathes.

"Me too . . ."

Lips a mere sigh away, our foreheads touching, noses grazing, we kiss. I stop breathing.

I realize I've stopped when I can taste his breath, his lips, all things Nico. He's all warmth, mouth spiced of spearmint, one hand clutching my back, the other in my hair, twirling a long wave and then pushing it off my shoulder. My knit hat falls off as I put my arms around his neck, pulling him closer, closer, never close enough.

I've wanted this and evaded it for years.

Blurry. That's what it is. Nico and I, we blur together into one. Opening my eyes I steal a glance. Instead of the satisfaction, the triumph, I expect to see, he's hurting. His eyes are closed tight, and there's a tear teetering in each of the corners.

Then it's over.

The kiss, my first kiss, ends too soon.

"Nico!" a voice calls from above.

My eyes widen.

"It's Arlen. I have to go." He rubs his fist across his face, wiping the emotion clean in one movement.

"Oh . . . Right . . . Me too." I'm still lost in warmth, in spearmint, in the blur of what just happened.

"I'm sure I'll see you at the Offering."

Before I can get another word out, he kisses me on the cheek, scales the hill, and jumps the fence.

I run nearly the whole way to the docks, and by the time I get there, I've missed Poppy.

He's nowhere to be seen, but I'm able to catch the next boat, surely not far behind him.

As I stand at the front of the transport, hands gripping the wet metal railing, chilly, saltwater-laced wind whips across my face like icy needles. I stare out over choppy water, toward the dark silhouette of the Coliseum in the distance.

Another Offering.

I'm still light headed, confused as ever, and those butterflies in my stomach have turned to restless, buzzing wasps.

CHAPTER 17

The strong scents of sausage and cinnamon swirl along the breeze as the boat approaches the Island of Sol and the Coliseum.

I'm first off and make a quick beeline to the entrance where I instantly, unmistakably identify Poppy's bald spot. He's only a few Basso ahead of me in line.

"Excuse me," I say, "I need to get in line with my grandfather; he's just up ahead." I push my way up to him, but he's already heard my voice, the commotion, and is looking back at me.

"Veda . . . ," he says, clearly disappointed. Once I'm next to him, he leans in, nearly whispering. "I hoped you decided not to come."

"I told you I'm not doing that," I whisper back.

His eyes turn stern. "It's a bad idea. You still have time. Go—"

But we're butting right up to the Imperi officers at this point.

"Too late," I say, satisfied smile stretched across my face. I don't know why he's so concerned. Being so incredibly stubborn. Well . . . I suppose I do. He is my grandfather.

Poppy only shakes his head and audibly swears under his breath.

We take our medallions out, hold them faceup in our palms.

With only one Basso ahead of us, I look inside the Coliseum and toward the Sun mural, hoping to see Nico, wondering if he'll be sitting with us again today.

I'm scanning the crowd so thoroughly that it isn't until Poppy very loudly clears his throat that I return my attention to the line, the medallions . . .

Poppy tosses his coin into the box and I do the same. But he doesn't move forward. He's staring at the Imperi officer. When I follow his eyes, I see why.

It's Nico.

"What?" I whisper.

Nico shakes his head and his chest rises and falls. He leans forward, glancing back and forth first before he speaks. "I wanted to tell you, but . . ."

"You didn't."

"I'm sorry." He breathes through his nose, working his jaw like he wants to say so much more but can't. Only a moment ago we were in each other's arms. Now he's Imperi uniform clad, gold Sun embroidered over his heart, Imperi officer's crest on his collar, pressed sash cutting his chest in crimson. A stranger. One of them.

"Keep the line moving, please!" another officer calls out, and we're pushed forward just as Nico's saying, "And there's more—"

More?

But he's cut off and we're already inside, being ushered through the crowd and toward our section.

"Did you know about this?" I ask.

My grandfather raises an eyebrow. "No."

"Me neither." My chest burns and my face heats. How could he?

"Veda Adeline?" We're not even to our seats before I'm tapped on the shoulder from behind.

I turn around to find an Imperi soldier. He's about my height and stands unnaturally straight, a thin beard shading the bottom half of his face.

"You're to come with us." He motions to another, much larger soldier behind him.

"What is this about, please?" Poppy says, standing and taking a step toward the soldier.

"The High Regent would like to welcome Miss Adeline back and congratulate her on escaping the Night."

"How the . . . ?" Poppy swallows what I assume was going to be a decent swear. "Excuse me, I mean, I'm confused. She just returned this morning."

"Oh, we know . . ." The larger soldier practically spits the words. "News travels fast." He shrugs.

"That it does." Poppy takes another look at both of the soldiers. "Go on, Veda. What an honor."

"I'll be right back," I call, walking double time to keep up with the soldiers who're in a ridiculous hurry.

Poppy, his body rigid, strains to smile.

The soldiers swiftly guide me through a door that takes us into a tunnel beneath the seating areas. There are prison cells lining the walls. Most are empty, but I catch a few figures hunched in corners. Supposedly the worst of the worst criminals are sent here, often executed in private Offering rituals. My mother's fate . . .

The image flashes behind my eyes, but I push it aside as quickly as it comes, a bit of bile sneaking its way up the back of my throat.

At the end of the tunnel we ascend a tall staircase, then go through another door. Once at the top, I'm brought through a red curtain, and to a red-carpeted balcony, high above the others, just a notch below the High Regent's perch.

The soldiers leave.

I stand in the center. Fidgeting with my pockets, I turn in a circle, taking in the sea of Dogio red. Faces surround me from all angles, yet no one seems to notice I'm here.

Behind me there's commotion. I turn to look and see the same two soldiers open the curtain, High Regent Raevald entering. His black suit is crisp as coal, crimson sash around his black hat accenting the red cockade he wears under his Imperi badge.

I remove my hands from my pockets. Not knowing what to do with them, I clasp my fingers behind my back.

"Miss Veda Adeline, I presume?" He clasps his own hands behind his back.

I nod.

His silver-streaked hair is slicked back as usual, weathered skin like leather close up. "I wanted to congratulate you personally." The High Regent smiles. Then he leans in. "You slipped through the cracks. How did you escape?"

Slipped through the cracks. If he only knew.

"They . . . I . . . I don't remember." I try to sound natural but the more I try, the more I'm sure it's obvious I'm lying.

He cocks his head then adjusts his hat so it sits lower on his forehead, shadowing his face in darkness.

"They drugged me and somehow I ended up back home. I have no memory, not even of being taken. I think, at some point, I hit my head." It's quick, haphazard thinking. He seems to be considering what I've given him, staring into my eyes, his eyes dark under the shade of his hat, unreadable. The High Regent clears his throat, moving toward the curtain. "Well. Thank the Sun! Beyond all odds, you made your way home. The Sun truly works miracles, does he not?"

"Yes, sir," I say under my breath.

"The fact you escaped gives hope to others *like you*. And . . ." He raises his voice. "Gives me reason to believe the Night is getting a little careless!" The soldiers laugh along with Raevald until he clears his throat. "We are so relieved to have you back safe and sound, Veda. You're welcome to view the ceremony from here or go back to your grandfather."

"I'll sit with my grandfather." Always.

"Of course." He shakes my hand. The exchange is stiff, his grasp cold, concealed within a leather glove. Looking me in the eye and turning on his heels, Raevald disappears behind the red curtain.

That is my blood relation? My grandfather?

Another round of hot bile erupts deep in my throat. *Grandfather.* It's an insult to Poppy.

I make my way toward the edge of the balcony and squint in search of Poppy but can't pick his face out from the throng.

"Come on, then," the shorter soldier calls from the door, less polite now he's done his duty.

Once again, I follow the pair, this time to our seats. We're closer to the dome floor than last time.

But Poppy's not there. I look behind me, all around, searching the crowd for my grandfather's silver halo of hair, but he's nowhere and I'm suddenly concerned. What if he's ill? What if he's stuck in the washroom or decided to head home?

I'm about to leave my seat and search for him when Raevald's voice booms out over the Coliseum.

Everyone stands.

"Welcome, people of Bellona: Dogio." He raises his arm to the right. "Basso." He does the same to the left. "Before we bring out the Offered, that praiseworthy soul, I have an announcement to share." The crowd breaks into chatter and excitement, anticipation as those around me wildly speculate:

"Could he be remarrying?"

"At *his* age?"

"Is it the Night?"

"A draft?"

Raevald resumes speaking, the Coliseum instantly hushing. "It's good news, I assure you." The High Regent motions toward the arena floor. "After careful deliberation, I've chosen an heir."

If he only knew . . .

Barely, barely, his next words register: "Nicoli Denali."

A tall, familiar figure walks out onto the Coliseum floor. The arena erupts in applause.

All I can do is stare.

When Nico had said there was more, I thought, he'll be busy training or off to strict schooling as he learns a specialty.

But this?

This?

There's no way Nico could begin to pinpoint me out of the thousands of faces, but I swear, the way his eyes are slowly scanning the crowd, he's looking for me.

Once the excitement dies down, Raevald resumes. "Mr. Denali's first area of training will be as an officer, learning the ways of the Imperi army top to bottom. Some of you even handed your medallions over to him to gain entrance." He nods like it's some sort of remarkable thing. Like we should be impressed Nico, *heir-to-be*, was interacting with the rabble. "As your future High Regent, it's important he's familiar with not only the army he'll one day command, but his people as well."

My. Sun.

I can't begin to fathom it. To wrap my mind around Nico as High Regent. As one day being the one standing up on that perch saying things like, "Now, we shall pay homage to our god with the Prayer."

We recite the Prayer. As if nothing's changed. As if that announcement Raevald just made didn't turn my entire world inside out. As if the boy I've known and loved for a decade didn't turn into someone else overnight, didn't become the enemy before my eyes. It's routine as usual.

"As we bear witness to this sacrifice, we remember: 'A thriving Bellona is only as strong as the light that shines upon it. Blessed be the light.'"

"—Blessed be the light."

Same speech each Offering, hasn't changed in centuries. Will it with Nico? When he takes power will he still be powerless to actually change things? Will he even want to?

Raevald raises his arms, then lowers them, motioning that we take our seats.

The Coliseum obediently sits.

My knee shakes and my palms sweat.

Beneath the High Regent's balcony is the familiar cranking of the door. The canal that runs along the floor of the Coliseum fills with water.

Several more soldiers, a handful of officers, enter the arena. My chest tightens and a burning wave of nausea hits my stomach when I spot one of the officers. Nico stands at attention by the arched exit. I dig my fingernails into my leg.

The entire dome is still. Nothing happens. People look around, voices whisper, mumble over the unorthodox nature of what's happening. Or *not* happening. Why it's taking so long.

"The Offered." I'm a breath away from leaving my seat, bolting up the stairs and to the exit to find Poppy. "The *honored*, is . . ." The High Regent pauses, drawing it out. Once he says it, I'll leave. "Jac Adeline."

I hear the name. It comes out brisk and sharp, like a burst of winter wind, and encircles me a hundred times. The High Regent's voice still echoes in the distance: *Jac Adeline*. The name gravely repeats over and over until it's nothing but a wisp in my ear: *Jac Adeline*.

Poppy strides through the door and into the arena, two soldiers walking behind him.

No. I whimper, tears rolling down my face.

As if he knows exactly where I'm sitting, he finds my eyes. I shake my head.

He nods his once. *Yes.* So strong. So at peace.

I watch as Poppy is led to the middle of the dome floor, head held high, silver tuft of hair blowing to the side with the breeze coming off the Great Sea.

And with the breeze, I'm slapped awake.

"No!" I scream, jumping from my seat, running down the aisle and hopping over the railing. Several people shout in warning from the stands, but it's too late. I'm nearing Poppy and the soldiers, sliding along the gravel to a stop.

"Veda, no!" Poppy shouts.

"Why him? There was no mark on his medallion!" I look straight up at Raevald. "*No mark!*" The words are fire and singe my throat on their way out.

Calmly, he stands, leans over the railing, and addresses me and only me through the golden speaking-trumpet. "You should be proud, Miss Adeline. It is the greatest honor to be Offered."

I run toward Poppy, falling into his arms.

But as soon as I'm there taking in my poppy—all mint and earth and castile soap—I'm ripped away by two officers, their crimson sashes flashing brightly in my periphery.

"Veda," one says into my ear. It's a voice I'd know anywhere.

All I hear now is betrayal.

Pulled off my feet, I'm forced to watch from the wall as Poppy makes his way to the altar. Once there he places his medallion atop it. I can see the mark of the golden Sun from where I stand.

We did get a marked medallion. I just never saw his.

Damn it, Poppy. I don't know what he tossed into the box when we entered the Coliseum, but clearly it wasn't the true talisman.

Nico tries to shield my eyes, pulling me into him, but I push away.

Betrayal.

"Poppy," I whimper, trying to fight my arms free, unable to do anything other than kick my legs.

My grandfather drops to his knees at the altar. A soldier slices each of his palms and Poppy smears the stone with his blood. His final mark. Proof of his sacrifice.

"No . . ." My whimper now a sob.

Poppy's always been tall, strong. Bent over the altar, vulnerable in so many ways, somehow he still looks tall. Taller than I've ever seen him.

That's when the raft is brought in.

My grandfather walks purposefully toward it, steps aboard, then sits on his knees.

Gray eyes set on me, he gives the slightest of nods, eyes firm but heavy. *It's all right. It'll be all right.*

The hourglass is full.

A single bell rings.

The Sun directly above, shining down and illuminating Poppy's hair so it's a silver halo, he mouths, *My Veda.*

It's too much.

Too much.

Something snaps inside me. Nico must not expect me to keep fighting, because I easily tear myself free, once again running toward my grandfather.

"Veda, stop!" Nico yells.

I'm going to jump onto the raft, pull him off, and we'll swim for it. Swim forever if we must. As long as we're far, far away from this cursed island.

But I see it on his face, his eyes, the fear I'm going to get myself killed too if I keep fighting it, because there is no *away from here.*

And I'll expose the truth.

And everyone depending on me.

On the Lunalette.

This is bigger than you, Veda.

It's bigger than Poppy.

It's then that my grandfather reaches into his belt, removing the knife he religiously keeps tucked in the secret inner pocket.

Lifting the blade up over his chest, he looks at me and only me.

Poppy, no! But I don't say it because I'm running straight at him.

"Be strong, Veda. Be strong," he says as I approach. Then, eyes toward the Sun, he slams the knife into his own heart, falling back onto the raft.

The crowd reacts. Nico calls my name. Someone screams. But then everything and everyone is silent.

The soldiers scramble to finish the ceremony. As if what just happened didn't really happen, they cut the rope and the raft is set free, pulled along by the current.

But the boat's moving too fast. He's leaving too fast, the knife sticking up from his chest, his body bent over, bright red blood blooming through his white linen shirt. It's wrong. All wrong.

"Poppy," I say, mouth slick with tears.

Floating through the door, the raft carrying my grandfather drifts out to sea.

He's gone.

"NO!" I scream so loud, something splits in my throat and I'm pulled from Nico and escorted by two soldiers back to my seat.

Everything disappears around me.

The archway door cranks closed, the canal dries up, the crowd claps. Their applause is more boisterous than usual.

But it's all just noise.

Life somehow goes on.

Food carts are brought out. People visit the altar. Several stop before me and say things I don't hear or register. Several shake my hand, pat my back.

It isn't until I hear an urgent "Veda!" that I begin to come to. The voice is low, so familiar, but it's not Poppy's or Nico's.

I can barely see him through the tears in my eyes, but I make out his expression, the concern etched over his face. The light hair that's concealed underneath a hat, his uncle by his side. "Let's get out of here," Dorian says, beckoning to me.

Despite the fact that my legs are lead, each step heavier than the last, somehow I make my way toward him.

Still, the closer I get, the farther away he seems.

It's my longest walk ever, and when I finally reach him, I collapse.

Curled in a ball on the ground, I turn my head toward Raevald's perch, and I'm shocked to see he's there. Staring down from high. Watching me.

I wipe the tears from my eyes and he's vanished.

Only the Sun shines down.

The sole witness.

CHAPTER 18

TAP! TAP-TAP-TAP!

The noise goes from the front door to my bedroom window, back and forth. Unrelenting.

I sit straight up. It's dark. I'm in Poppy's bed. Had I dreamed it all?

"Poppy!" I shout. "Poppy!" I stand up and run from the room into the hallway, nearly smacking straight into Dorian, who flies around the corner from the kitchen.

I stop and double over, heaving breath, trying not to faint or vomit or both.

If Dorian's in my house, it wasn't a dream.

TAP! TAP-TAP-TAP!

It's coming from my bedroom window.

"Stay here. Please." Only capable of single syllables, I wave my hand in Dorian's general direction.

Stumbling to my room, I pull the curtains back and there they are. Those brown eyes.

I open the window but don't say a word, blocking Nico's way.

"Can I come in?" he asks.

"No."

"Please, Veda, I have to talk to you." The desperation in his voice, the longing in his expression, I almost break down. But I don't. In this moment, for the first time since meeting him nine years earlier, I close Nico off. He's not who I thought he was. I'm beginning to think I'm not who I thought I was either.

What I am sure of is that Nico is now on the same side as the people who killed my grandfather today.

And that's enough to urge me to slide the window shut. My chest burns and my eyes sting from the insides out. *Stay strong.*

Nico slams his hand under the window frame, stopping me. He sticks his head in. "I'm so sorry I lied. So sorry." He swallows what sounds like a sob. "So sorry about Poppy."

Slowly, he pulls his head back out. He's still wearing his Imperi uniform, his red sash now slightly creased from wear.

I shut the window.

We stand eye to eye, a thin pane of glass between us. I clutch the curtains but pause when Nico puts his palm to the glass. He mouths the word *wait.*

I glance away, then back to his eyes.

I open the window again and he leans in.

"You have to get out of here, Veda."

"What?" It's the last thing I expect him to say.

He's hiding behind the tree in front of my window, but still glances over his shoulder. "There's been talk of members of the Night acting as Basso. Spying." He speaks quickly, quietly, like he's sharing a dangerous secret. And perhaps he is. "I'm worried with what happened to Poppy today that somehow Raevald knows. Even if he doesn't, it's safer if you go back."

All I can do is nod. He's right. As much as I want to storm Imperi Hill myself, take Raevald down in a blaze of vengeance, even I know it's not possible.

Not yet.

He scans the path in front of my house again. "I'm on my way to an emergency meeting now. All soldiers and Imperi officers are required to attend."

I nod again, still dazed. Still so blurred.

"Veda," he says, louder, and I jump. "Are you hearing me? You have to leave the island *now*."

"Yes. You're right, yes."

He places his hands in his pockets. "I've got to go. I'm pushing it by being here at all." I begin closing the window, but he keeps talking. "Just . . ." He steps closer to my house, leans in, our noses only inches apart. "I need you to know this wasn't my decision, I had no control over being chosen as heir-to-be, but . . ." He pauses as if choosing his next words carefully. "I'd have joined anyway." I can't hear this right now, but don't have an ounce of strength left to argue. "That early morning you disappeared, just a few hours after we fell asleep on your floor after cleaning your room . . ."

"Yes, I remember," I say drily.

"That day you left with Dorian, when you joined the Night"—it's dark, but I hear the anger and sadness in his tone, the way he snaps the word *Night* out like it's a weapon—"it was the same day I got news I was in the running for heir. But I didn't care about that, not then. All I could focus on was getting you back. Finding you alive or killing every one of those Night bastards who took you from me. So I joined." He looks away, then back again. "I thought you were dead, Veda." The word *dead* quakes in his throat. "Don't you see? It was my best chance to either find you or get revenge on those who took you from me."

Heat prickles in my dried-out eyes. "I'm sorry, Nico, but I can't see that. Not right now anyway. I can't begin to see how you'd join *them* in order to help *me*. And now you'll eventually be in charge of them? *All of them?*" I shake my head, unable to accept the words even as they leave my own lips.

Nico opens his mouth to speak, probably to argue, but must decide against it because he doesn't say a word, closing his lips with a sigh.

Our eyes locked, tears filling on both sides, a mutual understanding passes between us, the darkness of night closing in all around us.

Things aren't so simple anymore.

They never will be again.

I slowly shut the window.

But he doesn't leave. Nico simply arcs his thumb over his heart. *Ad astra.*

I close the curtains.

Something tears in my chest.

I collapse to my knees, slowly melt into the floor. Lying on my side, I stare at the now closed window and realize how perfect the image is. Locked, covered, pulled tight. Like the curtain at the end of a play. A closed book. Finished.

But I don't want to be finished with Nico. Not now when I need him most. Not now when I've just lost everything.

Because Poppy's gone too.

What starts as a whimper explodes into unrelenting weeping. I curl into myself for fear I'll snap in two. I squeeze my eyes closed, locking up like a dam the tears building on the other side. Behind the rising tears, I search and find a memory of me and Nico. So many surface, but one image repeats one after another throughout the past nine years: him arcing his thumb over his heart. The sound, sometimes soft, quiet, other times rough, scratchy, depending on what he's wearing, if he has gloves covering his hands. But his eyes are always the same. Deep, thoughtful, conveying so much but mostly, *It'll be all right.*

The memories fade as quickly as they came when I realize I won't ever see that image again.

The dam breaks, and, beyond my control, tears fall heavily down my cheeks, pooling on the floor beneath my chin.

I lie in that position, curled up on the cold floor, staring at the window, until my cheeks are stiff with dried tears.

Devoid of emotion, I stand up and rub my swollen eyes. Lacing up my boots, putting on layer after layer of clothing, I know it's time to go. Get out of this place where everything's connected to a memory. Where too many conversations and laughs and tears are imprinted.

On my way to the front door, I stop dead when I meet Poppy's gardening boots all muddied and worn and sitting dutifully next to the front door. More ghosts. This house is suddenly so large, the emptiness so vast, it's suffocating.

"It's just me here, Poppy," I say to his boots. "Only me."

"And me." Somehow, in all the . . . everything . . . I'd forgotten about Dorian. He sits at my kitchen table, sharpening a blade.

Hearing his voice both startles and comforts me. Mostly, his presence is a pleasant surprise, a realization that kind of shocks me. But this small cottage was getting very dark fast. I thought I wanted to be alone, but my reaction, the slight uplifting of my mood, begs otherwise.

In fact, I'm so glad to see those peculiarly colored eyes of his that I open my mouth to mutter under my breath that I'll never rid myself of him. That he's like the sarcastic friend I didn't know I missed, when I spot a lone white envelope atop the table. My name is scratched across the front in Poppy's handwriting.

My Veda.

I tear it open as Dorian looks on, pausing his work.

> *My Veda,*
> *When you read this I will be gone, put back to the earth, the sea, the sky, by will of the Sun. And you, Veda, Lunalette, are the one who will set things right.*
>
> *I know this is a heavy burden. But you are strong. Brave. Just like your mother was. All you need know is in your heart. What's right? What's wrong? It's all there.*

"Yes, yes, Poppy, but why?" you're asking. "How do I do this?"

Think of fishing. You have to wait . . . listen . . . Do that and you will know when it's time.

You hold the world, the motion of everything, in your hands, in your heart. Wait. Listen.

I love you, my Veda,
Poppy

I look up at Dorian, forcing myself to hold the emotion back. It still feels as if Poppy's only in the next room. Like he only just jotted this note down and ran out for firewood.

Dorian's staring, his eyes sympathetic, as he waits for me to say something.

I swallow a hard knot, but my voice still shakes when I speak. "Nico says that the Imperi are meeting tonight. Possibly right now. And if they're all in one place, preoccupied, it's our best chance to get back to the Lower."

"That was generous of him, considering he's officially on the other side now," he says, eyes narrowed.

"If you're thinking it's some kind of trap, it's not. He was risking everything to tell me that. Nico wouldn't lie." I consider what I've said for a moment, thinking how he didn't tell me he'd joined the Imperi until I saw it for myself. "Not about this," I add.

"How can you be sure?" I know he's referring to all that's happened since we returned only late last night.

And, my Sun, it's been so much in such a short time. The mere thought sends a deep aching to my chest, unease and tightness turning my stomach.

I push it all down. Poppy. His Offering. Nico wearing that red sash. I look Dorian in the eyes and don't mince my words. "I know Nico. I'm sure." I motion toward the back door. "Get ready to leave."

"Wait. What? I'm the officer here," he says, giving me a half smile.

"Yeah, but you're in my house." I can't smile, but manage to raise an eyebrow.

His smile broadens and he shakes his head.

As Dorian prepares to leave, I take one last look around my home, one last walk through the hall, my steps leading me to Poppy's bedroom.

It's tidy, everything's in its place yet at the same time too lived in. Too perfect.

Poppy's gone.

Gone.

They took him from me.

With a deep, deep breath, I rub my fists into my eyes, taking my anger out on the tears that won't come.

Before I allow myself one final glance around the room, I grab the photo of us from the glassless frame on his bedside table. I pick up his pipe that's sitting on the chair. I pull out my knife and cut a scrap of the pillowcase from his bed, wrap the pipe in it, and tuck it in my pocket.

Last, I walk to the chest where his copy of *Ancient Maritime Navigation* sits on top. I thumb through it and, near the middle, in the section on following the stars, is the only photo of my mother. Carefully, I tuck it into my pocket.

Then I leave Poppy's bedroom, not looking back like I'd planned.

He's not there.

I walk through the kitchen and out the door of our home. Dorian follows.

I stop when we're far enough into the forest that it's safe but I know I can still see the front of our house from where I stand. I glance back. It's dark, not a single lantern illuminating the space, especially not the lamp over our porch. Without Poppy there to light it, it's permanently out.

As we make our way through the forest, I picture the High Regent's face, that look he gave me when he congratulated me on escaping the Night, on slipping through the cracks. He knew then that my grandfather was about to die. He knew and he didn't show any sign of remorse or sympathy. Not an ounce of decency.

I imagine his smug grin, the way his red sash was so perfectly positioned. I fantasize about shoving him over the balcony.

Tying his sash around his neck.

And a hundred other ways I could have gotten revenge had I known what was about to happen.

But I didn't.

So, I'll find another way.

For my mother. For other Basso like us. For Poppy.

The last thing I see before we descend to the Lower is the Sun setting on the horizon, melting into the Great Sea like fresh lemon custard on a fine blue glass saucer.

And how vast that blue glass extends.

I stop, pause a moment. Dorian stops as well but doesn't utter a word.

Staring out over the Great Sea, squinting hard as I can to spot that one point where surely the Sun and ocean must meet, even if only to brush past each other. It must be a magical place, one where all time and space stop.

I decide that's where Poppy is, where he'll rest. There, in the warmth of the Sun, the refreshing sea breeze rushing past him, and with all the roasted pantera fish and sunrise bread he could ever desire right at his fingertips.

Not forever lost—though it very much feels that way right now, the aching emptiness in my chest battling my mind for closure.

But no. It's Poppy and he'd never leave me. Not fully.

He's there—I squint—in that place where yellow meets blue, he's there.

Waiting...

Listening...

CHAPTER 19

Once we're back in the Lower, I take the lead. I'm tired of always following Dorian around. I'm staying a good two paces in front of
him, each stride taken with purpose. Determination. It's time I start
finding my own way.

Problem is, my intense desire to see the Sindaco doesn't extend to my
navigation skills. I don't know the way. Not yet. But I know where I want
to go. Who I need to see.

I hang a sharp right.

"That's an interesting choice," Dorian says.

"Yep."

"You do know I'm well aware you've got no idea where you're headed."

"Yep."

"Okay. Just checking."

But as much as I want to take charge after feeling so utterly helpless
the past twenty-four hours, I stop, look back at Dorian. "Am I even
remotely close to finding the Sindaco's office?"

"Well . . ." Exaggeratedly, he rubs his chin with his finger and thumb,
as if considering I might be close. Then he drops his hand, shoves it in
his pocket. "No." He leans in. "Not close at all."

He's being playfully cocky, which makes me want to laugh, but I don't have it in me. It's becoming a theme, Dorian making me smile and laugh. I like it.

Nico does—did—that too, but I suppose that's over now. Our friendship, years spent side by side, our kiss, it might as well have been a dream. Maybe it was.

"But," Dorian continues, "the Sindaco's not in his office."

I place my fist on my hip. "How do you know?"

"Well, it's Monday, and he spends Monday evenings in the map room preparing missions for the week." He says this like *everyone* knows this information.

"Map room?"

"Mmm hmm . . ."

"And are we close to this map room?"

"Yes."

"So I *was* on the right track. Just a little . . . misguided."

He eyes me, holding back a smile. "Misguided . . . Yeah, if that's what you want to call it."

"Yep." I slow my pace. "But, just to be fair, you should lead the rest of the way."

He throws a crooked smile in my direction. "Never thought you'd ask." He pivots and makes a sharp left.

"And in this map room," I start, "would there, by chance, be a map of, oh, I don't know, the Lower?" Sure would be handy right about now.

"Not a chance. No maps, no paper trails."

Of course.

A few more bends and we stop before a metal door. There's an open padlock hanging from the handle. The door's cracked open a few inches, golden lamplight spilling out into the tunnel.

Dorian makes an "after you" motion with his arm, but then steps in front of me. He whispers, "Are you all right?"

I just stare. He could be referring to about a hundred different things.

"Your grandfather, Nico, coming back here, it's been a heavy couple of days." I'm not looking at him, but when I do catch his eyes, he's looking straight into mine. He's suddenly all serious, no games, no jokes.

"Yeah, I'm all right," I say, knowing I sound unconvincing. He crinkles his forehead like he doesn't believe me, like he's waiting for more. "I'm all right . . ."

"I'm not sure repeating it is going to make it true." His words are gentle, his brow furrowed as he looks down at me.

I look up at him, meet his gaze. "Well . . . Okay . . . Not really. But for the first time in a long time, I'm not wandering. I'm passionate about something more than fishing—not that there's anything wrong with fishing." He laughs softly. "I mean, it's going to be hard. I still have a lot to process, but . . . I'm where I need to be, and I know Poppy would agree. So . . . With that . . ." I stare at the door.

I take a breath, straighten my shoulders, and push open the door.

Dorian wasn't exaggerating. In this room, which is really a medium-size cave, is a mural that extends nearly the entire length of the wall, a map of Bellona.

I know the Sindaco knows I know everything . . .

That Dorian sent him word of what happened, how I overheard their conversation about him being my father, and that we went back to the Upper. No doubt he's heard about Poppy.

From this point forward, no more secrets. I'm so tired of lies and deception even if it is meant to protect me. Especially if it is.

I stride across the space right as he glances up from the papers scattered on the table before him.

If he's at all surprised to see me, he doesn't show it. He does stand. Places his palms flat against the rickety wooden table and then steps around it, pauses, and walks toward me.

I'm flooded with at least a thousand emotions at once. Questions of *Why did you leave me? Force my grandfather to lie for you?* Thoughts ranging from *I can't trust you* to *I've missed you all my life* to *You missed my entire life.* But I try to

force it all down. This is delicate. Something that should be eased into. Most of all, he's a stranger to me. Someone I just met who hasn't given me any reason to trust him.

We're walking toward each other, set to meet in the middle of the cave. His steps are calculated, cautious. Mine are strong on the surface, unsure underneath. We both stop dead when there's about a foot between us. But the distance is so much greater.

The Sindaco lifts an eyebrow and dares a glance. He must know I'm angry with him. That I know the truth he's my father, that Poppy was killed. And if he doesn't assume I'm upset by all of that, he's an idiot or only concerned with himself, which is worse.

I catch his eye and blurt out, "You lied."

So much for easing into things.

He glances away for a moment, then turns back to me. "I did," he says. "I'm so sorry."

I refuse to say it's okay, because it's not. I wait for him to continue speaking. He's the adult. The Sindaco. The one who lied. I deserve answers not apologies. "It wasn't right." Again, he looks away. "But it was necessary." He steps a few inches closer, clasping his hands behind his back. "Please understand that, Veda."

My name, so familiar, doesn't feel right leaving his lips. "I don't understand. Not really." Maybe not at all. I look away, cross my arms over my chest, hold tight. "Why did you send me to be raised by Poppy?" I ask, my voice monotone. Robotic.

"Please, can we sit?"

"I'd like to stand." Somewhere behind me, Dorian shuffles his feet or kicks a bit of gravel or sets down his lamp. I'd forgotten he was there.

"Of course. And Dorian?" The Sindaco motions behind me.

"He can stay."

The Sindaco nods. He breathes deeply in, then back out. "I loved your mother. I loved her more than there are stars in the sky. More than life itself. When she died, I lost everything. Don't get me wrong, I had you, thank the Moon, but . . . I wasn't strong enough." He shakes his head, emotion softening his voice. "I wish I could have been. I did the best I could at the time. But for that—for not being stronger—I'm truly sorry." He pauses. "The reason I sent you to live with your grandfather instead of keeping you here was to protect you. The less you knew, the safer you'd be. Whether I was right or wrong, I'm not sure, but I stand by it. I knew you'd be loved, well cared for, and that you'd be raised with empathy and compassion, that you'd be taught valuable skills. Mostly, I was certain you were safer up on the island because your connection to the Night was undetectable. Your identity was safe. What I didn't foresee was the Imperi, that they'd turn to such ruthless lies and destruction. That I'd have an even harder time convincing you of everything when you returned here. So, you see, I may have physically left you, but, in my mind, never truly. It was always my intent to be reunited."

"Yes, but couldn't Poppy have at least told me you were alive? Explained how my mother died? Anything?"

He's already shaking his head before I finish. "My father is vicious, despicable. Thus far, you've seen a somewhat reserved Raevald. But I lived with him. Was raised by him. I know what goes on behind closed doors, and you now know an extent of it. I could never, *never*, risk exposing you to that. Had he found out you were my daughter, the child of his traitorous, embarrassment, coward of a son? He'd have killed you and Poppy immediately." He swallows hard. "I don't regret keeping all of this from you, because it was the only way I could ensure your protection."

"Well, it only half worked because he got to Poppy anyway." With the mention of my grandfather, that wall I put up when I walked in here starts to crack.

He furrows his brow, takes a deep breath in, and looks at me, remorse softening his eyes. The Sindaco takes a step closer and lifts his arm as if he'd like to pat me on the shoulder, console me, but isn't quite sure how.

I take a step back so there's no question where I stand in wanting his consoling. When I do, I feel the warmth of Dorian's hand on the middle of my back. It's only a fraction of a second before he removes it, but the reminder he's there means everything.

Just as my vision's going blurry thinking of Poppy, this horror of a day, I spot all the maps on the Sindaco's desk, possible battle plans. Then, farther back, displayed atop a shelf, is an atlatl spear. One I can only imagine belonged to my mother.

I steel myself.

"I want to fight."

The Sindaco counters my demand by taking his own step back. "No. Absolutely out of the question."

I step forward. "Because I'm the Lunalette or because I'm your daughter?"

"Both," he says, raising his voice considerably. "And because I'm in charge here and you fighting won't help our cause."

"What about *my* cause?"

"*Your* cause is predetermined. Fated. I can't change that."

Well, I can. "You're telling me the prophecy states the Lunalette won't fight?"

The Sindaco turns and walks toward his desk. "It's not that simple."

"He's right, Veda," Dorian says.

I follow. "Then explain it to me."

He stops behind his desk, turns to face me. "I thought we settled this your first night here."

I let out a low "ha" under my breath. "You settled it. I never agreed to anything." I can see Dorian, who's shoulder to shoulder with me now, staring right at me. Silently pleading I shut up.

The Sindaco sits, rakes his hands through his hair. "I see . . ." is all he says before he begins shuffling through the papers again.

I look over at Dorian, who shrugs, shakes his head. *Thanks a lot, officer.*

I step forward so I'm standing right in front of the desk.

The Sindaco peers up at me, takes a deep breath in, then out again.

"I will not allow you to fight in battle. If anything happened to you, it would be the end of the revolution before it began. You don't yet see it, you haven't been here long enough to believe it, but your presence here is everything." He stresses the word by staring more deeply into my eyes. "Veda, by coming to the Lower, by joining the Night, you've single-handedly put this revolution into motion. You've given the true soldiers—those who've been training to fight this war for years—renewed hope." He shakes his head no. "I cannot in good conscience risk that."

"Or is it because of what happened to my mother? How she was captured in battle?" As soon as the words leave my mouth, I know I've probably crossed a line. I don't look at Dorian. I don't want to see his expression.

The Sindaco sets his sights back down at his desk, rubs his chin again, this time more aggressively.

"I apologize . . . I know it must be difficult, but she was my mother. I didn't know her, but it still hurts she's gone, especially knowing how she died." My throat closes around the last word, images of Poppy's own execution flashing behind my eyes. I open my mouth to keep talking, but he puts his hand up as if telling me there's no need to continue. "It wasn't meant to sound so careless," I manage.

"I know." He meets my eyes. "But there's truth to it. You're exactly right. When your mother was killed, yes, it sparked the first war, fueled our anger and our vengeance, but it also drained every ounce of hope we had. I don't want to repeat that and certainly don't want you to lose your life."

I'm not sure if it's physical exhaustion or pure emotional fatigue, but my legs are suddenly jelly. I can't stand any longer and slide into the chair behind me.

Dorian's watching me the entire time and sits as well. When I look over he seems to check in with his eyes, leans forward, brow knit, like he's asking me if I'm okay.

I nod and he looks like he's about to speak when the Sindaco starts talking again. "I'm prepared to make a deal with you, Veda."

"All right . . ."

"You may not fight in battle—" I open my mouth to argue, but he beats me to it. "However, I will send you up on a mission. *With* Dorian."

"What kind of mission?" I ask.

"Information gathering . . . I haven't sorted all the details yet, but I'll let you know as soon as it's all set." I nod. "In the meantime, Dorian—"

"Sir?"

"We talked about it a while ago, but please get Veda trained on a weapon." He says it like there's some backstory between the two of them.

"Of course."

But before I can pry or ask which weapon, the Sindaco cuts the entire conversation off.

"Now"—he rubs his puffy eyes with the heels of his hands—"I've got so much to do . . . Missions to hand out . . . Information to sort . . . I've got a pile of coded recon data to decipher . . ." His voice is low, speaking more to himself as he stares at the stacks of papers before him, and I decide not to press him anymore. For now, I'll save the rest of my questions for Dorian.

As we're walking out the door, the Sindaco calls Dorian back, murmurs something I can't quite make out, except I definitely hear the word *weapon*.

The minute we're out of earshot of the map room, Dorian looks over, eyebrows raised. "That got intense."

I throw my arm in front of Dorian, forcing him to stop.

"What *aren't* you telling me?" I say.

Dorian's still staring down at my arm, dramatically rubbing the place my elbow slammed into his chest. "Gah—you could be gentler, you know." He looks me in the eyes, smile flirting at his lips. "Actually, don't. That'll come in handy in training."

I only stare.

"I can see you're not in a joking mood."

"Not even a little bit."

"And I assume you're referring to what the Sindaco said about your weapon?"

"I am."

Hands up in surrender, all pretense gone, Dorian says, "Listen, it's a secret—"

"But—"

"But a good secret. A surprise."

"I don't like surprises good or bad or in between."

"You only need wait another five minutes . . . The Sindaco told me . . . It's in your room." He singsongs the last part.

I sigh, roll my eyes, but I'm smiling on the verge of laughing at how completely ridiculous he can be. "Fine."

When we enter my cave, unchanged from how I left it, he lingers at the door, fingering the rough stones that line it like a frame.

"It's there, underneath the mural. A welcome-home gift from us to you."

"Us?"

"The Night, the Sindaco, me."

I glance over my shoulder, catch his eyes. He's watching me, waiting for my reaction I suppose.

I walk farther into my room and quickly realize Dorian's still lingering at the doorway. "Are you coming in?" I call without looking back.

"I thought you'd never ask."

He can't see it, but I roll my eyes. Not out of annoyance, but because I *knew* he was going to say that.

I immediately notice a package wrapped in brown paper leaning against the wall beneath the mural. I walk up to it. Stare down at it. My name is scrawled messily on it in black ink.

"Did you write that?" I eye Dorian.

"I did." Which I can assume means he wrapped the oddly shaped gift. I can't deny the thought of him sitting Sun knows where, trying to figure out how to cover this awkward, pointy thing, is equal parts funny and hopelessly endearing.

"Did you swear a lot while trying to wrap all that?"

He laughs. "Definitely." When I glance over at him his face is the slightest pink.

I sit down on the mat and he joins me. I pick up the package. It's heavier than I expect, and something inside clinks together like wood. I quirk an eyebrow at Dorian.

"My Moon, V, open it already!"

I laugh. "I take my time with gifts."

He breathes in through his nose. "It's torture to watch, just so you know. But I'm coming to you if we ever need an explosive removed."

"Noted." I grin, continuing to take my time. Even more so now.

I untie the string and remove it. Then, strip by strip, I unwrap the brown paper.

What I find beneath the double layer of wrapping is unexpected.

Exhilarating and terrifying at once.

A worn leather quiver of spears and a hooked throwing device, the handle adorned with a glass five-pointed star the colors of the Sun and moon combined. Sparkling flecks of gold and silver swim within the star, a length of black leather wrapped around the handle as grip.

An atlatl. My mother's atlatl. Instantly, my eyes prickle because I can't believe it. I grew up thinking this weapon was a thing of legends. Lost to the past, forever gone just like her. It's the one item I ever linked solely with my mother. This atlatl is to her like my fishing pole is to me. It's everything. A tool. A weapon.

I blink a few times. Stare at it on the floor before me when I realize I've not given off any reaction good or bad. I look over at Dorian, who's eyeing me right back, unsure.

"It's . . . ," I start, then stop to take a breath. "I've only ever seen one photograph of my mother. She was holding this weapon. I used to sneak into Poppy's room after he went to work and gaze at it for hours. I'd make up stories about going hunting with her. I'd fish and she'd catch game and then we'd come home and make stew and bake bread." I smile. "Long after dark, I'd often awaken to sounds outside. I'd lie frozen in my bed, terrified of the Night sneaking into my room and snatching me. But then I'd imagine my mother with her atlatl standing watch, and it would always calm me." I gaze back at it. Run my fingers over the smooth wood. "Poppy always told me she'd used it to hunt for food." I turn and face Dorian. "I'm assuming that wasn't true."

He shakes his head, slightly humored. "No." Still, he's watching me. "So, you like it?"

"My Sun, Dorian, I love it. It's almost too special to actually use."

"What?" He must think I'm serious the way his jaw hangs lax.

"I said, *almost*. This weapon was meant to be used. It would be a disservice not to use it."

"Right." Satisfied with my answer, he looks deeply into my eyes, which sends a buzzing from my chest to my stomach and back up again. "You'll get your chance tomorrow. First thing."

I move closer to get a better view of the weapon, and when I do, not only is my leg pressed against Dorian's, but my hand is now resting on his knee. I hear him take a breath in like he's about to speak, and I glance over. He's staring down at the place where my outer thigh is against his, then, when he realizes I'm watching, moves his gaze to the atlatl.

"Have you ever used one?" He motions to the weapon.

"No," I whisper, my voice suddenly hoarse. My heart is pounding in my ears because the heat from his body radiating into mine, even at the slightest touch, sends goose bumps down my arms. I'm shivery and too warm and my cheeks are burning and my stomach is fluttering all over the touch of his leg.

Instantly, I scoot away. "I should get some rest."

"Of—of course. Long day," he stutters, perhaps just as confounded and intrigued by all the sensations as I am. He stands up, starts for the door. "Sleep well, Veda."

"You too," I say, not looking back, still sitting in the exact same spot and position, working to regain my breath.

A moment later, when I glance over my shoulder at the doorway, he's vanished.

Without thinking, I run after him. "Dorian?"

He's only a few steps down the tunnel and pivots to face me.

"I never thanked you for being there for me . . . after Poppy. I'm glad I wasn't alone and I'm glad it's you who was there."

Something that looks a lot like adoration passes over his face, and my butterflies begin to stir. He steps closer. "You're welcome. I'm glad I was there too." His expression is soft, intense. The yellow glow of his lantern beaming up, casts him in a golden warmth.

If this were a fairy tale, it'd probably be the moment we'd kiss.

But this isn't a fairy tale.

I bite the inside of my cheek, swallow really hard. "Sleep well," I say.

He smiles shyly, like he knows what I've been thinking. "You too."

I force myself to walk away.

And like that first day we met, I glance back. He hasn't moved, eyes still intense, slight grin on his lips.

I return his look with a small smile, then walk straight back to my cave.

If I were at home, I'd throw myself onto my bed and think about how embarrassing and exciting that exchange just was.

Except I'm not at home, I'm in a cold, damp cave.

Instead, my thoughts busily consumed with the past few moments, I unpack the bag I brought along and place my things from home on the rock ledge next to the glass pantera and sun figures, the little girl's embroidery. Poppy's pipe, the photo of us, and the scrap of pillowcase all now line the shelf. An altar in its own right.

I don't immediately go to sleep like I should. Instead, I pull the picture of my mother and her atlatl out of my bag, lean it against the weapon.

Long into the night, lying on the wooly mat, I look at the photo, imagining fighting alongside my mother, working together to defeat the Imperi. Staring into her eyes, despite the image being fuzzy, I can see they're the same dark green as mine. But fierce, so much fiercer than I've ever felt.

Then I think . . .

Would *she* stand for being forced not to fight in a battle she was destined to lead?

I think not.

CHAPTER 20

Mere hours later, Dorian's at the door to my cave.

And I've been up a while.

I had a brief, but hard, sleep. Dreamless. A welcome respite from the overload of thoughts and emotions streaming through my head.

I woke up what would have been before morning bells, and with nothing to do and too many thoughts, memories of last night, running through my head, I prepared my atlatl.

I've no idea how to use the thing, but I needed the distraction, the monotony of working with my hands. I've only ever seen the one weapon in the photo and some Imperi soldiers carrying them. But I did what made the most sense. I sharpened the wooden tips of the spears, checked the leather binding to be sure the handle was secured. I even added my own talisman. For good luck, I broke off the already cracked end of Poppy's pipe, sanded the wood, and then strung some fishing line through the holes like beads. I attached them to the end of the handle.

When Dorian and I enter the training cave the space is abuzz with the echoes of arrows whizzing, swords clanking, and small explosions, the smell of sulfur and sweat permeating, a blue haze in the air.

The large cavern, same one we used during the flood, has been transformed. What was then a makeshift living space is now sectioned off into separate training areas. The "walls" dividing where Night members train are not walls at all, but a hodgepodge of items from warped sheets of metal to driftwood to bricks and large rocks. But it's effective. There are at least ten distinct training areas marked off.

And the movement going on within those areas? Complete and utter controlled mayhem. To our right, four soldiers work together, taking turns sword fighting. On the left of us, there's a line of metal cans and hay-stuffed, haphazardly painted targets. Two lines of Night members wait their turn to try their hands and aim with the pelters, handheld weapons that hold tiny versions of the blue-smoke explosive Dorian used on the Imperi soldiers the night he brought me here. Each time one goes off, my shoulders jump at the loud popping sound.

"They aren't deadly," Dorian leans in to say, "but burn like the devil. They're popular, but we only own a set of six we stole from the Imperi. We're working to find a way to develop our own ... No luck yet." At "yet," one of the soldiers shoots a bull's-eye and the entire crowd erupts in cheers.

"Ah, here we are." Dorian motions toward an empty training area straight ahead. It's marked off with a mix of metal sheeting and wood propped in place by large rocks like a rickety fence.

"You go ahead and ready your weapon while I set the course up, okay?"

"Okay," I say, not knowing how the hell to "ready my weapon." Sure, I'm okay with a blade and I'm excellent with a fishing pole ... I stare at the atlatl. It's about as long as my forearm. The spears are simple wooden stakes. A few of them are worn, clearly the originals, while the others are more newly crafted. The hook of the atlatl is made of carved bone.

I examine one of the spears more closely and see that the back of it is slightly hollowed. Perhaps that's how it fits into the atlatl itself? Using raw common sense, I fit the atlatl to my forearm, balancing it within the crook of my elbow. I then attach the spear to the hook so the point is uncomfortably at my wrist.

It falls to the floor with a loud *whack*.

Dorian's eyes snap right to me.

I raise my eyebrows, throw a hand on my hip like I totally know what I'm doing.

He smirks. "It's not fishing, eh, V?"

"No. No, it's not."

"Here." He gives the target he was setting up a final adjustment, then jogs over and picks up the spear. "You're going to put a hole through your hand holding it that way." Dorian takes the atlatl from my arm. "Like this." He removes his button-up uniform shirt, folding it over the nearest sheet of metal fencing. Pushing up the sleeves on his black undershirt—a light cotton tunic—I notice the ties have loosened to reveal a bit of his chest. I find myself distracted, and worse, he sees I'm distracted. The moment our eyes meet, a wave of embarrassment runs over me, then memories from last night, being close to him, invade my thoughts and send warmth up my neck and into my ears. "So . . ." He pulls me back into the present. "Place the atlatl like so." He positions it over his right shoulder, hook in back. "As for the spear . . ." Dorian then fits the sharp stake into the hook like I'd had it, but holds it in place with his right hand so it doesn't drop to the floor. "Then, *smoothly*, like you're casting your line, cock it back, throw, release the spear, and—most important—follow through." He mimics the motions and then demonstrates.

The muscles in his forearms flex and contract as he inhales, steps back, throws the spear while also releasing his breath, and sends it soaring right into the target. It's not a bull's-eye, but he's only three rings to the middle. Respectable.

"Now you try." He hands the atlatl over.

I nod, realize my shoulders are slumped, and straighten them. *It's like casting a line . . .*

Pulling a spear from the quiver slung over my shoulder, I place the atlatl on my right shoulder like Dorian did, gripping it in the place I noted when he demonstrated. I then insert the spear, securing it into the hook and holding it steady with my thumb and forefinger. I step back, cock my arm, and ready it for a hard throw. "Wait," Dorian says, cutting into my concentration. He steps so he's standing right behind me and adjusts the atlatl so it sits closer to the crook of my shoulder, his warm hand grazing my ear, sending a shiver down the back of my neck.

I remind myself to focus.

Then, placing his hand on top of mine, he moves my fingers along the spear, but more toward the back of it, and, I swear, when our hands touch there's a spark. Not the metaphorical kind, but a literal spark of static between us. Neither of us mentions it, but I know he felt it too because of the way he sucked his breath in, how he caught my sight from the corner of his eyes.

Dorian moves away, putting space between us, and clears his throat. "Have at it."

I hone in on the middle of the target, a brown dot painted on cotton fabric wrapped over hay. I cock my elbow back, bend my legs for stability and extra momentum. Then, breath steady, I throw my arm forward, release the spear, follow through, and . . . The stake flies a solid two feet before it slams point first into the stone floor.

"Huh," Dorian says right into the back of my neck. Except this time instead of igniting shivers, it actually lights a small fire of *I'll show him*.

I pick up another spear. Aim at a closer target. The spear goes a little farther, but doesn't get remotely close. Instead it hits the makeshift fencing next to it.

The next one flies so high it soars over the target and into the cave wall, where it cracks down the middle and falls to the ground in pieces.

"You tilted it too high. Try to focus, V. *Aim*."

My eyes dart to his.

Aim? As if that's not what I'm doing? As if I'm just tossing it like a ball?

Aim . . .

This time the spear actually flies straight but zigzags between two targets, missing both completely and ricocheting off the side of one of the frames.

"Better . . . ," Dorian says, not overly convincing.

With the next, I really try my hardest to aim more precisely, this time at a hay-filled dummy.

I shoot for the dummy's middle but hit it in the knee.

From the corner of my eye, I catch Dorian nod. "Nice one."

After that small success, I decide to stick with the dummy. Spear number six soars straight into its shoulder.

The next grazes the top of the dummy's head and hits the fence, bouncing off the metal and clacking onto the floor.

Another barely catches the dummy's middle, stabbing it in the side.

"If done right, that'd be a kill shot."

Speaking of kill shots, my last two attempts completely fail. One nose-dives right before me, and the other, after overcompensating for the first, flies the highest yet. So high that Dorian has to yell, "Watch your heads!" To which everyone within a twenty-foot radius ducks and then stares.

"Damn it," I swear under my breath as I quickly jog to retrieve it three training areas away where it's sticking point-first in the top of a pile of hay near the corner of the room.

I see it in their eyes too. *That's our Lunalette? The one to lead our revolution? At your service. Need some hay punished? I'm your girl.*

"It's your first try," Dorian says, handing me the rest of the spears he's retrieved from our course.

I take them, shove them into the quiver. "Thanks. I just need to practice." But my words fall so flat, I find them hard to believe myself.

"Hey." He runs his hands through the spiked side of his hair. "Why don't you fill your water while I reset the course? Take a minute, okay?"

My canteen is mostly full, but I nod and leave. I know that a bit of fresh air will do me good, but there is no fresh air here. Still, I wander down to the spring, splash water over my face, behind my neck. It's more refreshing than I thought it'd be.

When I return, the targets are in different positions, more dummies added to the course, a couple actually slumped over the fencing like corpses. I suppose he figures I kept hitting the walls anyway, so I might as well aim for them?

I thread the quiver back over my shoulder. I've got twelve spears.

"Ready?"

"Ready." *You're the Lunalette. People are watching whether you like it or not.*

"Just for fun, I'm going to time you this time. You have exactly three minutes to shoot all twelve. No exceptions."

"Fun." I'm doomed.

Turning his hourglass over, flipping it to the minutes side, Dorian counts down, "Three, two, one . . . Go."

One—I aim for a target in the back, bottom corner: The spear misses completely, sticking into a wooden slat a foot above the target.

Reload. I fumble. Drop the spear. Reload again.

Two—I decide to shoot closer. Front, center: I catch the bottom ring of the target, but the stake immediately falls right out.

Reload. I bobble, but manage to keep the spear in place this time.

Three—a dummy to our right, propped against one of the metal sheets: I get the foot by the toe. But again, the spear doesn't stick and instead falls with a *plink.*

"Shi—" I swear, stopping short by biting the inside of my cheek. Anger boils up from my gut and into my chest. Why can't I do this?

Dorian raises his eyebrows.

I breathe.

Reload. Better this time. Still awkward, but steadier.

Four—dummy, far left: I hit the knee, barely, but it stays.

"All right," Dorian says to my back.

Reload. It's a little easier.

Five and six—center, back: The spear pierces the shoulder. Middle, right: Total miss. Nosedive into the floor.

Reload.

Seven through ten: complete misses.

I'm about to fling the cursed atlatl across the room.

I can't do this.

"Come on, V. You've got this," Dorian says.

I look over at him. He's so calm, so confident in my abilities that are horribly lacking. Dorian just stands there, hands in his pockets, *waiting* . . .

Listening . . .

I take a beat. Breathe in. Try to refocus. Ignore the countless sets of eyes surely on me. Scrutinizing me. Sizing me up and watching me fail spectacularly.

I close my own eyes. Cock my arm back. Grasp the spear between my thumb and forefinger, memorize the ridges in the wood, the place where the spear stops and the atlatl begins, how it's light on my shoulder yet so sturdy, powerful.

"You can do it, Veda!" someone calls from across the room. I think it's Bronwyn. Then another voice chimes in, one I don't recognize, with, "Keep steady . . . Don't forget to breathe . . ." And before I know it, I'm surrounded by an encouragement and support I've never known. The soft rhythm of clapping begins to take hold. A "you can do this" cadence.

I focus on the beat, how it's in time with the rapping of my heart. Then I hear Dorian: "Just like casting your line . . ."

I open my eyes.

Release the spear. Follow through. Concentrate on my target—a dummy in the very back, middle—keep my arm straight and steady as I can.

Eleven—smack dab in the . . . ear. It only grazes the dummy and clanks the metal sheeting, falls to the floor.

The gathered crowd, thankfully, begins to break up, but a few stay, determined to see me succeed, which makes it even more stressful.

I reload my last spear.

Twelve—another target in the middle and to the left. It's a bad shot, but it sticks, right in the belly of the dummy next to the target I was aiming for, but I imagine Raevald's face on it.

Chest heaving, blood rushing in my ears, I lower my arms.

"Damn, Veda," Dorian whispers right next to me.

I glance at him, eyebrow raised, a smile playing at the corners of my mouth.

I play off the last shot like it's exactly what I meant to do.

TRAINING CONTINUES, and I try my hand at the sword, which is less successful than the atlatl. I do all right with daggers. Forget about the bow and arrow.

So. Atlatl it is.

Members come and go in shifts. Dorian and I eat the lunch he packed—two overripe bananas; dried, salted meat; and a hunk of stale bread.

Eventually space opens up and Dorian takes the training area a few down from mine. I stay to work more on the atlatl (which he "definitely thinks is a good idea"), but during a water break, I walk down to sneak a peek.

I've seen a few different sides of Dorian . . . the Night officer, the sassy-sarcastic flirt.

I'm not sure exactly what version he was last night, but I liked it.

When I step around the corner of his training block, I discover warrior-Dorian.

He stands in the middle of the station, sword outstretched, battling a hay-stuffed, man-size target on a poorly constructed metal track. Another officer pulls the target by a rope tethered to its middle. The target, wielding a stick that's been carved to a point, moves back and forth jerkily, its wood base groaning against the metal each time the other officer pulls it by the rope or kicks it back toward Dorian.

Every whack of the sword rings out as Dorian blocks the target's unpredictable movements, sweat beading his forehead, barely showing through the thin cotton of his tunic.

Lunging forward, the target lurches a good two feet at him, the sharp stick falling and jutting toward Dorian's middle. Jumping to the side, he stabs the target between the ribs, spilling hay to the floor.

In the back corner, another officer launches a ball over the top of a target. Dorian drops to the ground and rolls just before the ball explodes in a plume of blue smoke right where he'd stood. Burned sulfur fills the air.

Reaching over his shoulder, he pulls a throwing ax from his back and chucks it end over end into the target's head, splitting it down the middle, red clay peeling like sinew from within the canvas sack.

Just then two more officers come out of nowhere, yelling, "Attack!"

Dorian bounds to the weapons wall and grabs a long-speared polearm. He makes a run for it back to the center as the four officers pummel Dorian with mound after mound of hay-stuffed projectiles.

One after the next, a constant stream of motion, he obliterates the targets, stabbing and slicing them in a deadly dance.

With one target left—the one on the track having been resurrected—he sees I'm watching. Staring me in the eyes, Dorian jabs the polearm straight through the dummy's chest and out the other side.

The officers erupt in whoops and hollers.

Chest rising and falling, sweat glistening across his forehead, down his neck, he gazes up, so many emotions swimming in his eyes. Whose face did he imagine on that last dummy?

Dorian removes his shirt and wipes his forehead, the back of his neck with it. I don't want to look, but he's only a few feet away. It's impossible to miss his body; each ripple and muscle and angle is right there before my eyes.

I force myself to swallow and then to breathe. I'm frozen, temporarily mesmerized, and he catches me. Sees the blush that's overtaken my face and is creeping up into my ears.

He runs his fingers over the shaved side of his head and then shoots me his crooked grin. I'm not sure which version of Dorian this is, but deep down, I know I like it.

And as much as I want to shrink into the shadows, instead I smile back.

"Damn, Dorian," I say, stealing his words to me from earlier.

I walk away, the smile reaching up into my eyes, cheeks heated, flush so deep it extends down my neck and to my chest.

I want so badly to glance back.

This time I hold strong.

CHAPTER 21

Several days pass, and each day is the same, a strict schedule of train-ing, then briefings. The briefings and mission assignments are held in the main cave where the celebration my first night here was held.

The tapestry of the Lunalette leers over my shoulder each meeting, a reminder of the massive responsibility I've been dealt, as officers hand out tasks, training schedules, and I wait for my promised mission.

Today is different.

The Lunalette still leers, but the Sindaco is uncharacteristically in attendance. We line up according to rank (newest members up front), officers facing us. I'm in row one, and coincidentally (or not) Dorian stands across from me but avoids my eyes, all business.

"Welcome." The Sindaco speaks loudly, standing behind a pieced-together podium. "There's much to cover and very little time to do so, so please listen carefully." He glances at me. "Things are growing grimmer by the day, the number of missing Basso steadily rising." A nervous silence spikes the room. "I assure you that my officers and I are tirelessly work-ing on a plan of attack. We're uncovering new information daily, but it's not enough. Our spies on Bellona are having to be more discreet than ever. This is where you come in." He pauses, dark eyes stoic and his hands clutching the edges of the podium. "The time to act isn't on the day of the attack, but in these days leading up to it. Our first full-scale mission will be to take the Coliseum and the Island of Sol, seize and occupy them. This will send a clear and strong message to the Imperi that we do not accept their Offerings and their impersonation of the Night as an excuse or justification to oppress Basso.

"Leading up to that mission, we will send small teams to the Upper, all with specific tasks to gain information, an advantage. Some of you will receive assignments and, very soon, plans for our official day of attack. It's nearing and we're ready. Speed, strength, and the Moon be with you all." His eyelids are heavy as he nods, then walks away.

I look to Dorian.

He's staring at me but quickly glances away.

Officers walk down the line handing out missions left and right. They completely pass me by.

Dorian stares forward, watching, scrutinizing my every motion as I get more and more agitated over the Sindaco's obvious avoidance. He has no plan of keeping his promise. The man was only pacifying me. Biding time.

I'm about to step forward, tell Dorian I'm going to see the Sindaco when he steps forward first, hands me an envelope. "Your assignment."

I tear it from his grip.

He releases a small whistle but doesn't speak.

Opening it, willing my hands to stop trembling, I read the hand-written instructions. There's a location, a time, and a packing list.

It happens tonight.

At the bottom is a final note: I'm to meet with the Sindaco privately first. Dorian will escort me to the map room an hour before we're to leave.

I lift my eyes. Again, Dorian stares, but he doesn't look away this time. He nods instead.

I look away.

CHAPTER 22

I'm packed and dressed. I've gone over the list at least ten times. I'm ready, prepared for my first mission.

Logistically, anyway.

My atlatl is ready to go, but I'm not so ready to actually use it should I have to. Setting it to the side, being careful not to let it fall over, I sit on my mat.

I lean forward, making sure the laces on my boots are secure, that the ties are tightly tucked into the tops. When I glance up to stand, my own name stares back at me. It's in Poppy's script, jotted across an envelope. His final farewell. I added the letter to my cave altar a couple of nights ago.

My first reaction is to leave it be. I shouldn't get all teary-eyed right before Dorian meets me for our mission.

But . . . I stare back at the letter. Maybe I'm wrong. Maybe it's exactly what I need right now.

Sliding down the wall, I take a seat on the mat and pull my knees up against my chest. I open the worn paper, read it for a second time.

I take in the words as Poppy's voice plays inside my head, reminding me of who I am, what I need to do, what I'm capable of.

I can't help but see him that day of the Offering, those gray eyes bursting with all the love and hope in the world and even moments before he'd die.

Always so strong, so brave.

If he were here right now, he'd tell me to be the same. To muster the strength and courage I need. The bravery he knows is deep inside of me. That I wanted this. I demanded to go on a mission.

And he'd be right. My thoughts are clipped off by a knock at my door.

I fold the letter up, placing it in my inner pocket, next to my heart.

Then I open the door.

Dorian. Right on time. We're to meet with the Sindaco for his special instructions before we set out. "Ready, V?" He shoots a wide grin my way.

I breathe in, holding it for a few seconds, then let it out. His grin quickly falters. "Are you all right?"

"I'm fine. Really. Just thinking."

He moves closer.

The memory, and more, the image, of him training a few days ago flashes behind my eyes, and my stomach flits right when I should be focusing on the mission ahead, meeting with the Sindaco. Stupid stomach. Stupid butterflies.

"Thinking about the mission?"

I nod, half lying.

"Veda." My stomach does that thing again. "You're ready for this. You've been training nonstop. Studying. Honestly, you probably know more than I do at this point." He lifts an eyebrow.

I laugh, play along. "Oh, I definitely do."

Despite the joke, he must still sense my doubt because he asks, "Give and Take?"

"Huh?" I heard him, but, what? Now?

"Come on . . . It'll be fun."

"Fine. You know I'm weak to a game of Give and Take."

"Exactly." He gives a crooked smile.

BY THE TIME we're nearly there, Dorian's told me about his first mission—a huge failure and one that somehow left him bootless. "That's a story for another time," he finishes, slightly embarrassed, more like he's trying to leave me with a cliffhanger I'm sure to want to come back to.

"—What about your first time fishing?"

"—Did you—"

Dorian gets his question out first, so I'm forced to answer and he's officially winning, which I hate. Which he knows, playful grin and all.

"I was three the first time I actually did it on my own: baited my line, held my pole, caught a fish, and reeled it in. Poppy unhooked it and cleaned it, but he showed me how in *painful* detail. It wasn't more than a minnow, but I was proud and Poppy . . ." I swallow back a painful knot of emotion. "Poppy was exaggeratedly proud. He even cooked it."

"How did that work?"

"Not well."

We both laugh.

"And look at you now," Dorian breaks in. "You can probably catch a beast with your eyes closed."

"I have."

He raises his brow, not so much surprised as impressed.

And for a moment, a split second, we catch each other's eyes, the laughter falters, and what's left is an invisible energy between us. Something tethering him to me and me to him that I can't quite place because it's not exactly anything I've ever felt before. It's as if here, in this moment, in this cave, Sun knows how far beneath the earth, everything's all right. Safe.

Instantly, I think of Nico. Because I have felt this way around him. Right and safe in his presence until I didn't. Until another Dogio walked past, or an Imperi soldier's eyes found mine. Then, like lightning, the pendulum would shift to the other direction: fear, shame, confusion.

And I suppose that's the difference. The newness of this sort of familiar emotion.

He stops walking, glances ahead. "We're here." And he sounds almost as surprised as I feel.

"Oh. Right." The door to the map room practically appears before us.

"The Sindaco requested to see you privately, but only if you're comfortable with that. Otherwise I can come along. I was briefed earlier."

"It's fine. I can see him on my own."

"Good. Well"—he's already walking away—"I'm going to see if anyone else needs help preparing, but I'll meet you at the den. The Sindaco can tell you how to get there. It's not far."

"I'll find it."

He nods.

I knock on the door.

"Come in," the Sindaco calls from the other side.

Dorian turns and leaves, and I'm left with a strange feeling. Like I missed something that pushed him into officer mode. As if a switch went off in the few seconds between that moment of eye contact and now. Did something happen I'm unaware of? Is he feeling as confused with our . . . whatever it is we are . . . as I am?

I want to ask him, stop him from leaving and have him come with me, but the Sindaco opens the door and invites me inside just as Dorian rounds the corner.

I follow the Sindaco into the cave, that large map painted across the wall lit up by several lamps.

We sit on mats before the map of Bellona. When I glance toward the wall, I notice there are new markings on the mural, red Xs at various entrances and exits. Places, I assume, that will either be used or closed off when the Night attacks. The Sindaco follows my eyes.

"Are the markings to show closed-off areas?" I ask.

"Some, yes. Others"—he points to a green circle—"are good ways out, nice and hidden, less foot traffic on the other side." He stares from one spot to another. "It's just a bit of brainstorming I'm doing, plans for the attack. We've got to be more organized than usual. Precise. I'm having to pull on some of my much earlier training."

"Training?"

He nods. "Remember, the current High Regent is my father." Oh, I remember. "I grew up in the Imperi palace. Was groomed from birth to rule that island and in the way my father saw fit. Precisely. Relentlessly." He sighs. "My mother died soon after I was born. So it was just me and my father, whom I rarely saw. I barely know him, but what I do know is cruelty. Harshness. Someone who strives for perfection and advancing his own interests." He glances toward the map. "Thank the Sun for your mother. She saved me."

"How so?" Now this I'm interested in. I have seventeen years' worth of my mother's past, her personality, her history to catch up on.

He meets my eyes. "You . . ." He clears his throat. "You look just like her. It's remarkable." I feel like I should smile but chew the inside of my cheek instead, unsure of what to say. "Your mother worked in the palace. She gardened. She was actually the one who started the main garden down here. Each morning she'd put out fresh flower arrangements throughout the house. I'd never known anyone to find such joy in something so seemingly mundane. Cutting flowers and placing them in vases? I couldn't fathom how she always wore a smile. And, my Sun, what a smile it was! I came to look forward to it every morning. Eventually I found the courage to introduce myself. Then strike up a conversation. Then I noticed she was always placing the vase in the hallway outside my room at the same time. She wanted to see me as well.

"Before too long we were meeting in the garden, spending hours under the Sun, surrounded by nature, just talking. We were in love." He smiles so warmly it's infectious, and I surprise myself, probably him as well, by mirroring it. My mother and the Sindaco, young and in love . . . It's hard to imagine when the only scraps I've ever had to go on are a photo and a name. "We knew because I was Dogio, not to mention the heir, and she was Basso, we had no future. And because I didn't want to rule, especially how I'd be forced to—in my father's footsteps—we left. And we joined the Night. When my father discovered I'd left he told everyone I was taken by the Night. Brutally killed. His hate for the Night, revenge over my betrayal began years ago. Luckily, he never made it a point to know the people he employed, so your mother's identity, in turn yours and Poppy's, was safe."

"How did you both end up joining the Night?"

"Amalie . . ." He says her name as a sigh. "Your mother was a member. She was actually a spy, stationed in the royal palace, no less. And despite her loyalty, her commitment to the cause, she couldn't fight her heart just as I couldn't deny mine. When we decided to leave together, she resigned from her post and another gardener was hired."

"Wow." I release a long breath. "So my mother was a spy?" I glance over his shoulder at the single atlatl spear he has on display behind his desk. The one original piece of it he kept for himself.

"Not just a spy." He looks back at the spear too, then returns his focus to me, giving a knowing look. "She was our best spy."

"And Raevald knows you're here. He knows you're in charge?"

"He suspects I'm still here, that I'm still alive. He doesn't know I'm in charge, but he might assume that as well. His hate for me, for what I did, runs deep. It wasn't until I left that the stories of the Night began to surface. That we're evil monsters who prey on children and take people from their beds at night? That was all him. The fact Basso are disappearing in droves and it's being blamed on the Night? All him. He can't stand that I abandoned everything he provided me with for the Night. I mean, he was always power hungry. Always felt that Dogio, because of their station and influence, should be in full control of Bellona. Unfortunately, my betrayal gave him an excuse to do something about it." The Sindaco pauses. "I'm sorry . . . You asked a simple question and I dumped a whole history on you."

"No. I want to know all of it. Everything."

He laughs. "You've gotten the most crucial parts at least. But as of now, we have more pressing matters."

"Right." My mission. The one I demanded he give me. I'd nearly forgotten.

"The main reason I asked you here tonight, Veda, has to do with your friend Nico."

My heart skips a beat. "Okay . . ."

"We've had our eye on him for some time. From what I hear, he sounds a lot like me at that age. Confused. Conflicted between his heart and duty. Fiercely stubborn. But if we could get him on our side . . . if he joined the Night, I believe he could prove invaluable in defeating the Imperi. His family is the second most powerful on the island. And now that he's been named heir-to-be, with Nico on our side I've no doubt countless Dogio would follow."

My first thought is, *No. I will not drag Nico into this.*

But then I remember he's already in it; he just chose the wrong side.

"I'd do anything to have Nico here instead of up there. But I can't imagine any circumstance where he'd willingly join the Night."

He leans forward. "You're right. But what if we don't give him a choice?" I narrow my eyes as he lifts a small glass vial, a covered needle on one end, from his jacket pocket. "This is a highly concentrated amount of moonroot."

My eyes go wide . . . Does he expect me to drug Nico?

"It's most often used to make a relaxing tea." The tea I drank on my first night here. "But moonroot in its purest essence—this tincture—will render someone immobile and without their faculties. In short, it'll knock them out, cause temporary paralysis."

"You want me to give that to Nico?"

"Only to get him down here, yes. Then I'm certain we can convince him to stay. To join."

"I can't." I stand, ready to walk right out of there. "I won't." The mere thought turns my stomach, pushes a bit of bile up my throat.

"I know it's a lot to ask, but, Veda, please, just hear me out." He stands too. His eyes are gentle, his voice soft, soothing. "You're the only one who could ever get close enough to him. The only one he'd trust. He won't hesitate meeting with you alone. All you need to do is give him a hug and a tiny stick. It won't hurt him one bit, but the results will change everything. I believe he's the key to us winning this revolution. We need you—our Lunalette—but we also need him."

"I don't know . . ."

He continues. "Not only will having Nico on our side convince other Dogio of the truth, but if enough Dogio doubt the Imperi, speak out against them, it will terrify my father. Raevald can't stand the thought of his people turning against him. His power being threatened. While I believe in the Night, I'll do anything to help us win this, avoid mass bloodshed. And shaking up my father will only aid in that. Unfortunately, time is running out." He pauses. "It won't be easy, but I'm giving you this mission because I know you can do it. I won't force you though. It can only happen if you agree and if you're willing."

Could I possibly do this? Drug Nico? For the greater good? The Sindaco said it won't hurt him. And, just as I did, I know he'll fall in love with the Night. It might take a bit of time, but he'll see how wrong the Imperi is, how they've been lying to everyone. Lying and deceiving at every turn. My heart skips a beat. "I'll do it," I hear myself say. I have to try.

"Wonderful."

"But only on one condition . . ."

He lifts an eyebrow. "Anything."

"I am going to try to convince him first. Sticking him with that needle will be the absolute last resort."

He sets his mouth in a grim line, but nods once.

"Though . . ." I hesitate before I ask the question that's been brewing in the back of my mind. "What's to keep the Imperi from spreading a rumor that Nico was taken by us? That we're holding him hostage or something?"

He begins pacing. "You'll set up evidence to make it look like he's chosen to abandon his post."

"What kind of evidence?"

"Once you drug him or if you're able to convince him, his uniform jacket and sash, along with his weapons, are to be removed. The clothing should be folded perfectly, sword placed over the sash in military fashion, and left someplace only he would go, but someplace you have access to. A show he's deserted his post." Our spot by the pond in his backyard immediately comes to mind. "Leave it so there's nothing left open to interpretation. That he's switched sides." He must sense my unease because he leans forward, widens his eyes. "Would it be so unbeliev-able to his parents?"

"No." He's right. They know how much he cares for me.

"Good. I trust you and Dorian to finalize the details. He's not to be seen, but will be there for backup should you need it."

I nod. I don't allow myself to think of any circumstances where I'd need backup, but having Dorian with me definitely brings peace. Until it doesn't. It's suddenly quite glaring that Nico, Dorian, and I are going to all be in the same small space at the same time.

So many emotions and feelings are changing and weaving in and out between us that I'm worried I might need backup for my backup.

But this isn't about that. It's not my thing. It's *our* thing. All of us. Basso and Night. Plus, Dorian's professional (I think). And Nico's quite the gentleman (usually).

I check my hourglass. "I'm supposed to be at the den in ten minutes."

My mind spins and my palms instantly go clammy. Because I've sud-denly forgotten everything. Every rule and warning and protocol. Forget using the atlatl. I feel like I could barely say the word at the moment.

The Sindaco checks his own hourglass. "I've kept you too long. You best be going. Here." He hands me a small handwritten map and the vial. "It's a short walk."

"Okay." Carefully, I slip the vial into my inside pocket, turn, and head for the door.

"Veda, wait." I stop and look back. He glances toward the floor as if searching for the right words, then gazes back up at me. "I know it probably doesn't mean much—we're practically strangers. But . . ." He pauses to swallow. "Please be careful."

"I will be." I turn to leave, but stop and glance back once more. "Thanks."

He nods. "The Moon and the Sun be with you."

I give a motionless wave, then leave.

OVERWHELMED WITH INFORMATION and instructions, my nerves already on edge, I walk down a long, tall, rocky tunnel, my lantern swinging as each step I take echoes from one end to the other.

Once out of the passageway, I'm hit with nothingness. Stale, dank underground air surrounds me as if this den isn't used often.

The necklace Nico gave me several moons ago hangs around my neck for good luck while the vial the Sindaco handed over is safely tucked in my pocket. To have those items floating among all the ordinary things in my bag—extra socks, water, dried fruit—seems odd. Like they don't belong. Like they should be in some special compartment. Protected.

"You're late." The words come from behind me. I turn on my heels to see Dorian striding toward me.

"Actually, it would appear you're late. I'm walking in front of you."

"I went looking around. Assumed you'd gotten lost."

"*Really?*"

He smiles. "No. I'm late."

I laugh, but the moment turns serious when he asks me to check my weapon, be sure everything's secured. "You're on board with the Sindaco's plan?" he asks.

"Yes." Maybe. Hopefully.

"One hundred percent?"

"One hundred percent." Eighty. Tops. But I'm not about to admit it. Mostly for myself. I can't handle anything negative right now. Even if it's true. Especially if it's true.

"Well, all right." He checks his blade on his belt, eyes mine as well. "We'll be coming up near the canal, but we're traveling to my uncle's shop. It's the closest den that isn't still closed from flooding." Dorian checks his hourglass. "Ready?"

I nod, my mouth suddenly dry as sand.

"You can do this. We will do this."

I nod again, but my palms are sweating and my heart's racing double time.

"Oh, I almost forgot. Here." Dorian hands me a set of keys. "These are for the doors that lead out of the dens. In case we get separated, now you've got a set. Guard them with your life."

"I will." I breathe in a shaky breath.

We walk in the darkness a little farther, splashing through a bit of standing water along the way. I open the next two doors with my keys and lock them back as we go. Eventually, we hit a dead end. Dorian lifts his lamp to reveal a rope, which he pulls. A metal flap opens and he yanks a creaky ladder down, metal on metal screeching.

"It's a lengthy climb."

"Got it."

He starts up and I follow close behind. We climb what feels like forever, as if we'll never reach the top.

It's then Dorian stops. I can hear him breathing sharply. Something feels off. "You all right up there?" I call.

"Yeah. Just . . ." He takes in a short breath. "I'm remembering why I make it a point to avoid this particular den." Another shallow breath. "Heights aren't my favorite."

Gripping the ladder with one hand, I detach my lantern from my belt and hold it out to the side so I can get a glimpse of Dorian. He's white-knuckling the rung in front of him, opening and closing his eyes, sweat beading his brow.

"Hey, Dorian?"

"Yeah?"

"Give or Take?"

"Take. Definitely Take." I figured as much. "How'd you get your scar?" he asks.

"When I was one I wandered into our backyard, fell in the canal, and was attacked by a pantera fish. The result was a gnarly bite Poppy sewed up on his own and disinfected with gin."

At *gin*, Dorian sucks in a breath through his teeth. "Ouch."

"Yeah. Thank the Sun I don't remember it, but he claimed I drove the wolves out of the forest and into the ocean with how loudly I wailed. Thanks to his excellent stitching skills, how the wound happened to heal, it ended up most closely resembling a five-pointed star."

"*That's* how you got it?" His voice is lighter. Less strained.

"Wild, eh?" I see him nod before I reattach my lamp to my belt because I really need two hands fully committed right now. "I was terrified of water after that. Poppy said I wouldn't even bathe. That I stunk like a fish for a good year at least. I can remember refusing to go out in the rain, and forget about splashing in puddles. I was convinced a fanged pantera fish was waiting to pounce in any and all water."

He starts moving. "Well, you're obviously not afraid of water or pantera fish anymore."

"Oh, I'm still terrified of the ugly things. But I'm much bigger than they are, and now I know how to catch them."

Dorian keeps a steady pace, and I decide not to distract him by asking a Take question, even though he owes me one. Instead, we climb the rest of the way in silence.

Finally, the ladder ends. We crawl up onto a ledge of rock. The light from our lantern illuminates the space just enough for us to tell between solid ground and a horrible plunge over the cliff. Taking Dorian's hand, pushing my exhausted legs a little farther, once up and over the rock I grip the ground around me with my hands. Legs on fire, when I know for certain it's safe I fall to my knees, grateful to be horizontal again. Dorian falls onto the ground next to me.

"Thanks," he whispers.

"Anytime."

We lie still a few more seconds and then crawl down a short dirt-and-rock tunnel. Counting our paces, we stop at thirty where the den door should be right above us.

"A couple things before we head up," Dorian starts. "We've marked a route that shouldn't take us past too many Imperi soldiers, but it's not a guarantee. If we do get seen, we run to the nearest den, not to my uncle's. We can't give him away. And don't go back to your house. I have a feeling they're watching it."

"What if we're not near a den?"

He huffs a breath out his nose. "We run. If for some reason we get split up, hide. Use your training and your common sense. Most of all, if you can't find me, I'll find you." He places his hand over mine. "I promise."

I pull my fingers up so they latch with his. "Okay." My mind is suddenly swarming with what-ifs, all the possible outcomes both good and bad, but I'm sure to push them out before they take over. *One step at a time.* We have to get out of this den and to Dorian's uncle's.

Unhooking his lantern and a set of keys, Dorian hands me the light to hold as he releases the large metal lock securing a small, square wooden doorway about a foot above us. He sets the lock on the ground and reaches to his side, where he finds a long wooden pole. Lifting the pole, connecting it to a metal ring on the door, Dorian thrusts all his weight into it and the flap opens up. Several heavy objects tumble against the ground on the other side of the earth.

The minute we're out, I know I'm back on Bellona, familiar scents brushing my face: moss and sea and crisp winter air, wood-burning stoves. I'm so taken by the smells, Dorian has to nudge me into the present. And when he does, I see we're in the forest along the canal, not too far from the main tunnel.

We secure the hidden door, covering it back up with moss and brush and snow, several randomly placed large rocks, until the den's completely dissolved back into the ground. It was never there.

The moon, nearly a perfect crescent, is a silver lamp that lights our way through the snow-dusted woods. All goes smoothly until we hit a fence, one that definitely wasn't here before. It's separating the Basso village from the rest of town.

Plain as day, a posting hangs from the fence: BEWARE THE NIGHT. Familiar, ominous warning. Black as night and red as blood—how they used to strike terror straight into my heart. Ink on paper. That's all it is. Stories. Fables. One man's overactive imagination and penchant for control through fear.

And now he's fenced in our entire village? As if Basso are the trouble.

Beware the Night . . .

I pull my blade from my belt and slice the stupid posting right down the middle.

Then I move to graze my finger along the top wire of the fence, see how thick it is, because I'll tear the whole thing down. But Dorian grabs my sleeve, stopping me right before I touch it.

I whip my head around.

Hands up, he raises his eyebrows, then pulls out his canteen and pours some water over the fence.

It hisses and sparks, the water evaporating instantly.

My shoulders shake at the sound and a deep anger boils in my gut. They can pump electricity into a fence all night to keep the Basso village "safe," but won't power our homes most days?

Ridiculous.

Dorian holds a finger up like, *Wait a minute*, as he digs something out of his pack. Unfolding a piece of paper, with barely a sound, he plucks what's left of the Imperi's poster off the fence, dropping the pieces to the muddy ground, and hands me the improved replacement.

I stab it through the stake.

The new posting reads: JOIN THE REVOLUTION. THE MOON WILL RISE AGAIN. It's like the one on the back of the Sindaco's door I saw that first day.

He leans in, whispering just below the whistling wind. "If they're gonna pretend to be us, might as well make it more accurate, eh?"

I shrug, nod, and give him a slight smile.

This way, Dorian motions with his hand.

We follow along the fence and up to the main, paved walkway. From the tree line, I spot two soldiers standing at the gates to the market. They're enjoying a game of cards while all of Bellona is tucked in, hiding from the horrors of the Night. From what they think is the Night.

And Dorian and I are right here. Right under their noses. The real Night. For so long I saw the Imperi as godlike, unbeatable, impenetrable. Oh, how things can change when you truly see them for what they are.

Dorian motions for me to follow him deeper into the forest. I've just turned my back on the soldiers when I hear, "Hey!"

I glance over my shoulder to see a different soldier, whistle at the ready, staring back at us.

Dorian and I take off running.

Get to the nearest den or the other side of the canal or . . . run!

The guard's alarm whistle sounds, a high-pitched ringing breaking through the stillness of night like glass shattering on stone.

"Alert! Alert! Night members spotted!" the Imperi soldier yells. There's more whistling.

A shot rings out, followed by a bright light flashing right above the trees. A flare to call backup to his location, I assume.

But we're gone.

Dorian and I fly through the woods. Despite our boots slipping and skidding over the frozen ground, we run full speed. Jumping over roots, climbing then descending large mounds of boulders, grazing past closely positioned tree trunks, we don't stop until we've descended a steep ravine and nearly fallen into the icy canal at the bottom.

"Let's stay here until it's safe," Dorian whispers.

I nod.

But we barely get to catch our breaths when we hear, "This way! They can't have gone far!" The shouting, accompanied by several pairs of boots crunching over sticks and frozen leaves, heads right for us.

"Damn it," Dorian says, and he's already standing, tying down his gear, adjusting his pack so everything is secured.

I just stare, wide-eyed. Surely he's not . . .

"We're gonna have to swim. It's the only way to get them off our trail. They'll never suspect it—not since it's half-frozen." I'm shaking my head no, and it's like he's thinking back on my pantera story, as if that's why I'm terrified to do this. But it's not. I'm afraid of drowning, being caught by the Imperi, freezing to death, or being washed into the Great Sea. Pantera fish are the least of my worries. "It'll be all right, Veda. I won't let anything happen to you, and you me, all right?"

You wanted this, Veda. This is your mission. Your fight.

I glance toward the water, back at the Imperi soldiers closing in on us, then to Dorian. His eyes are intense, set directly on mine, confident of the words he just spoke.

And I believe him. We're in this together.

"All right," I say, connecting with his eyes. *You and me.*

"Ready?" Dorian stares through the darkness at me. I'm not at all ready. The water is freezing and, thanks to the flooding, higher than usual, the current rushing over rocks and carrying debris in white, foamy crests.

I double-check my pack is secure, then say, "Yes."

At that, he quickly loops a rope around his waist, latching it in the back and doing the same for me, but latching it in the front and then to his. This way, if we get washed away, we get washed away together.

Him and me.

In the distance, some ways down from where we're at the bottom of the ravine, a series of yellow lights approaches. The Imperi soldiers. And they've brought backup. What was just a few has ballooned into ten at least.

Swiftly, we enter the canal and the sharp chill instantly takes my breath away. At first, it's only knee deep, but soaks through to my bones quickly. As we make our way across, the water reaches to my chest, the iciness cutting into my lungs. My breathing is shallow, shaky, taking far more effort than it should.

Everything is weighed down and swollen, the canal so cold, my body's gone from tingly to completely numb. As the soldiers' lamps grow closer, Dorian and I sink lower so only our heads bob across the canal, icy water splashing over our faces, rushing up my nose and into my ears, engulfing all my senses. Everything is cold, fishy, and white-capped rapids.

The current is strongest in the middle. Dorian and I work together to keep each other from washing downstream, being spit out into the Great Sea. My hand is clutched onto the strap of his pack and his on the tether that connects us. My body burns from the chill of the water and the extreme effort of fighting against the current as my feet fail to gain purchase against the slick rocks along the bottom.

When we finally reach the other side, I've got nothing left. Scrambling up mud and rocks, I can't even feel my own legs, but, somehow, manage to get myself out of the water.

"This way!" a soldier shouts on the other side of the canal, the group of lights, like a swarm of fireflies, following his call, and barreling down upon us.

Dorian and I scatter into the brush and drop to our bellies side by side. It's here, with his arm heavy and wet, yet still providing warmth, hugged around my lower back, we make eye contact.

The sliver of moon above shines down on the thin layer of ice frosting the ground. We both breathe heavily. Dorian's lips are a mere blink away when he speaks. "You okay?" He rests his forehead to mine, and, the warmth of his breath grazing my cheek, suddenly I'm not so cold anymore.

I part my lips to tell him I think I'm all right, but I can't seem to find the right words.

We're breathless from swimming and running and freezing, and I'm shaking from fear and adrenaline, yet we're somehow at a standstill. All the world whooshes around us. An owl screeches, the sound quickly drowned out by wind howling through branches. It's as if we weren't nearly washed out to sea. As if we've been lying in the forest, huddled next to each other all along.

Imperi soldiers march in the distance, the canal rushes by, the moon and the night and the brisk wind all move on—yet it's silent.

Until something heavy cracks right above us.

I pull away with a gasp.

Dorian follows my gaze upward.

The heavy branch creaks again and part of it falls, missing us by mere inches.

There's another sharp crack, the tree shifts above us, and before I can get on my feet to run, Dorian, still tethered to my waist, lifts me up and rolls me over twice so I end up on top of him.

The branch, tall as Dorian, lands with a crash and a horrible thud in the exact place we were lying.

"I'm beginning to think"—Dorian's words brush my face—"you're bad luck, V."

All I can do is shake my head in disbelief. My heart pounds into my ears, the intensity of the moment only amplified by a stupid, broken branch, nearly flattening us to nothing.

We untether, I awkwardly slide to the side off his body, and we lie still, waiting to hear any sign of where the Imperi soldiers are, if they've crossed the canal too.

But after waiting and shivering from being soaked and chilled to the bone, Dorian finally risks a peek. Standing slowly, he scans the area. "I don't see them."

I half sit up and take a look. The swarm of fireflies is moving away, back down the opposite end of the canal and toward the Hill.

Dorian stands fully, lending a hand to help me up next to him.

The crack of a flare goes off too close to where we stand.

Once again, we take off running, but in the opposite direction, hiding tree to tree, searching for some sign of the thing—where it went off.

I tug on Dorian's sleeve the moment I spot it. The faint glow of the flare illuminates the night as a dim cloud of smoke on the other side of the forest near Imperi Hill, not at all as close as it sounded.

Another fires away, popping like firecrackers and then bursting into a flash of light. Then another and then nothing. Still, we keep going, treading carefully, to the only den this side of the canal.

From there, we travel through a winding tunnel until we come up behind the market, near the waste and refuse bins. Dorian motions his uncle's shop is to the right and, shadow to shadow, each step calculated and light, we make our way there. I immediately place our location—we're behind the glassmaker's shop.

Slipping in through the back door, we walk down the hallway and then directly downstairs to the cellar.

The second Dorian closes the door behind us, almost in unison, we breathe a deep sigh of relief. I lean forward, placing my hands on my knees, trying my damnedest to ignore how even one misstep could have sent us spiraling into Sun knows what horrible fate.

I feel Dorian's hand on my back, gently patting me. "Nice work back there, V."

I glance up, then stand fully, placing a hand on my hip. "You too."

Looking away, like he's trying to resist the grin pulling at his lips, he quickly succumbs, finding my eyes and giving me a grand smile. It's in this moment I realize he likes it when I'm sassy just as much as I like it when he is.

There's a small stint of silence when I think he's going to say something meaningful, but when we both spot that a fire, hot tea, and a loaf of bread await us across the room, the moment's gone.

Dorian and I immediately huddle before the fire, both of us convulsing from the cold. I'm pouring us each a cup of tea when his uncle descends the stairs carrying a pile of blankets.

He stops dead when he sees we're drenched. "Get a bit more than you bargained for, eh?"

"We ran into a group of angry Imperi soldiers and got to take a swim in the canal," Dorian explains.

"I see. Here . . . Wrap up, get warm, I'll put on more tea, bring some soup down." Dorian's uncle quickly introduces himself to me before he takes the stairs two at a time to get more blankets and dry clothes.

Dorian loads another log on the fire while I grip a mug of hot soup between my palms, sipping gingerly, basking in the warmth. It's his uncle's special chicken stew recipe. It's mostly broth, but I'd drink hot mud right now if it was offered to me.

The fire roars back to life as Dorian sits down next to me. He's wearing a pair of his uncle's pants that are about six inches too short and five sizes too large, plus a similarly ill-fitting tunic. Each time he reaches forward to stoke the fire, the tunic rises and exposes his midsection. Just a couple of inches above the waist of his pants. And, for the life of me, I can't help but look every single time it happens, which reminds me of that first day in weapons training when he was battling the targets. Shirtless. Sweating.

I'm suddenly quite warm, our bone-chilly swim a distant memory.

I've also donned a set of Dorian's uncle's clothes, a long button-up white tunic and some trousers I've cinched at the waist with a length of rope.

"So," Dorian says between sips of soup and bites of bread. "Nico takes the main tunnel when he's finished with Dogio meetings, about two hours after fishing's over? You're positive?"

"Always." But I consider that a minute. "I mean, it's what he's done for years. Things have changed though . . ." I stare into the fire, imagining Nico in his Imperi uniform. The image turns my stomach, and suddenly I'm not enjoying the chicken stew so much. Pulling my knees to my chest, I curl into myself to soothe it. "He and Arlen always have an hour of mentor training, followed with another hour of advanced government." Dorian gives me a look like *Why?* His brow knit. "I don't know." I shrug. "I suppose they learn how the government works . . . or how to run the government . . . or how to overthrow rogue governments."

"Fair enough."

"From there, they go their separate ways: Nico takes the tunnel back to his house, and Arlen takes the stairway up the ravine. They live on opposite sides of the Hill."

"He'll be alone?"

"He should be."

Dorian looks away. He's being short, distant. I'm not sure what's wrong with him.

He tosses a small stick into the fire, showing his midsection again. "Sorry, there's no way you'd know that."

"It's fine. But you're right, I have no idea. He's usually alone; though, like I said, things are different now." Now I'm being short with him and I'm not sure exactly why. It's been a long day. I suppose we're both tired. I gaze over at Dorian, who seems to be working things out, plotting our positions tomorrow in his head. Something occurs to me about our plan. "You can't go with me, you know. Into the tunnel."

Dorian's eyes swipe to mine. "What?"

"It'll be too risky. Too obvious. Nico will think it's a trap or something. And then what if he's not in the tunnel? We could both be caught."

"We'll just jump down the . . . Damn it."

"That den's flooded."

He breathes in then out. "Flooded." Dorian sets his mug down and stands, walking back and forth in front of the fire, surely trying to figure out how to get his way.

"It's the only option. Besides, this is my mission. You're backup, remember?"

At first his eyes narrow into mine and I'm worried I've insulted him, but then he softens, sits back down. "You're right. It's the best way. And it's your mission, your call."

"Really?"

"Really." He takes his last swig of soup. "We should get some rest. Big day tomorrow."

He's still being a bit cold, but I leave it alone.

We sleep on the floor atop scratchy wool quilts and beneath a double layer of blankets, but the chill of the stone still cuts right into me.

Dorian, an inch away, if that, manages to keep his distance.

I barely sleep.

Neither does he, based on the way he tosses and turns. Is he thinking about the mission? Or is he maybe remembering how close we were earlier right before that branch broke? The thought sends sparks down to my toes.

At some point, there's a lull in Dorian's motion. "You awake?" he asks.

"I am."

"I can't sleep."

"I noticed."

I turn from my back onto my side to face him. When I do, I find Dorian's eyes are looking right into mine and we share a long silent look, as if neither of us knows what to say yet somehow we understand each other.

My stomach's in a mess of knots over what tomorrow might bring. I wrap my arm around my middle so my left hand rests on my stomach, then curl the other underneath my pillow.

A mounting pile of worst-case scenarios builds in my mind, weighing on my shoulders and tightening my chest.

A headache's instantly formed a tight knot between my eyes. As if he senses it, Dorian places his hand over mine, the warmth welcome, soothing. With feather-light fingertips, he traces small circles back and forth. Back and forth in a spiral motion, the contact—so slight—sends a current of shivers up my arm.

He keeps up with spirals as he moves closer, the heat of his body now radiating into mine.

"Hey," he whispers like he just realized I was there.

"Hey."

He takes his hand off mine and pushes a rogue lock of hair off my forehead. "What're you thinking about?"

"Everything. Nothing." The mission, but not only the mission. Deep, deep down, I'm terrified to see Nico. A new Nico. Heir Nico. I've never been nervous or afraid of facing him. And, although I've buried the image of my best friend in an Imperi soldier's uniform deep down to avoid dealing with it, the closer it gets, the more it surfaces.

Dorian smiles. "Somehow, I know exactly what you mean." I don't say Nico's name, but I swear, Dorian senses it.

I return a slighter version of his smile. "Do you ever get nervous before missions?" I ask, shoving those feelings back down.

Dorian's face softens and he takes my hand and I lace my fingers between his, the soft warmth like heaven.

"Always. I mean, it's easier now after going on so many. But I'm definitely nervous for tomorrow, about how it'll go, if we'll be successful." He pauses. "I'm worried about you." He squeezes my hand more tightly. I lean up on my elbow, brow knit. "No, not like that. You're more than capable of taking care of yourself. You'll do great. But . . . things can always go wrong." He's kind of rambling and it's adorable. "Just . . . I sort of like having you around." He glances the few inches between our faces, crooked smile and all. Our breathing is in rhythm and the fire's still cracking, casting the room in a soothing orange glow.

I inch even closer. "I'm terrified," I mostly mouth the words.

"Me too." He speaks so lightly I'm reading his lips.

I shiver—I'm not certain if from cold or nerves or something I'll never place. Dorian must notice because he lifts the corner of his blanket and pats the quilt, inviting me to sleep next to him.

I slide in and roll over, my back to his chest.

Wrapping one arm around my waist, Dorian stretches his other arm beneath the pillow and under my neck, I nestle my head into his shoulder. Again, he finds my hand and over and over continues with those soothing circles.

Dorian's doing and saying all the right things, but it's Nico's image behind my eyes I can't seem to escape.

Because if things were different—if the world hadn't tilted just so and even one small event or detail hadn't played out as it did—it's possible it'd be Nico lying behind me underneath this blanket. Not Dorian.

My eyes sting but I squeeze them shut. Tight.

At some point, I fall into a restless sleep.

CHAPTER 23

I made Dorian swear on his favorite glassblowing torch that he'd stay at his uncle's until I got back. No matter what.

He refused "no matter what," but we compromised with "if I'm not back in three hours, you can come find me."

I imagine he's pacing a track into the stone floor of his uncle's basement. I'd told him to make something out of glass to keep busy. He completely missed the humor I was aiming for, but I heard him gathering his tools as I left so he must not have been too offended.

The Sun is high in the sky and people are out and about, living their lives. Through the thick foliage, I spot a group of Imperi soldiers harass Basso in between tacking up BEWARE THE NIGHT signs. Down the way, a woman pushes a rickety cart of eggs past a group of children sitting by a pile of rocks seeing who can stack the highest tower.

There are eyes everywhere. This couldn't be riskier unless I'd strolled through the market and then shown up at Nico's house, knocked on his front door. Yet here I am. Sneaking through the woods of Bellona in all black like a wolf stalking prey, shadow to shadow, tree to tree. Fortunately, most Bellonians are at the market, at work, or tending their homes. There's not much in these woods for anyone to be concerned with, especially in winter.

Dorian explained the best spot to duck into the tunnel from the woods was the same place we used the night we came back after the flood and I saw that posting with the High Regent on it.

When I reach the spot, just a few steps from the tunnel entrance, again I'm greeted by the poster of Raevald's face, this time in daylight. I wish I'd taken it down last time . . . Stuffed it in my pocket and used it as a target during training.

THE IMPERI NEEDS YOU! it says. I stifle a sarcastic laugh. I wonder how many Basso they've recruited into the army. What they're offering. I suppose it wouldn't take much. Basic living needs. Food. Bait for their families. Opportunity to find lost loved ones "taken by the Night" would be more than motivation enough.

Gripping my blade, I glance left then right. A couple of Dogio women walk past. I duck behind a tree and listen as they enter the tunnel. I'll have to wait awhile before I can go in and hope no one else does. My plan is to stand near the entrance and get a glimpse of Nico (or anyone else) before he enters. I'd spot his silhouette anywhere. If it's not him, I'll speed walk through and duck into one of the tight spaces where there's a drainage grate, wait until they pass. It's the best I've got.

I'm about to bound forward when I hear more footsteps crunching over gravelly snow. Pulling my black hood tightly over my head, I inch around the tree to get a peek.

Thank the Sun.

Nico.

He enters.

I look left, right, don't see anyone, and run into the tunnel.

I have no idea how I'm going to get his attention. I'd planned to say his name, certain he'd recognize my voice, but I'm suddenly unsure. It's been a while. What if he doesn't? What if he's not certain and ignores me? I consider whistling, but it could be anyone.

Then, thank the Sun, I know exactly what to do. I simply say, "Ad astra."

His boots skid to a stop. "Veda?" He says my name so lightly, like he's just heard a ghost.

"It's me."

Nico turns around, lantern held before him. He runs straight for me. For a split second I'm on guard—he's in his Imperi uniform and I'm breaking about five different laws, but he throws himself into me, wrapping me up into a tight, lingering hug.

And I'm home.

"Veda," he hiccups. "You scared the shit out of me."

We both laugh, but he's crying and then I'm crying and he holds me and kisses the top of my head and I kiss the tears from his cheeks and it goes on like that for some time as if we're lovers reunited after war. And maybe we are.

I wasn't expecting this. The emotion. Especially after spending so much time with Dorian. This is supposed to be simple. But I quickly realize it's going to be anything but.

Then it's like we suddenly catch each other.

"What are you doing here?" he asks.

While at the same time I say, "I have to see you."

"I'm right here."

"No. Later. Alone. Someplace safe."

"The pond behind my house."

"Perfect."

"But, Veda." He says my name like a secret as he searches my face over his lantern, concern lining the corners of his eyes. "You shouldn't be here. It's not safe."

"I know. I'm only here through tonight. To see you. I just need to speak with you."

"It's important?"

"Very."

"Are you all right?"

"Yes."

241

"Okay." Again, we embrace, my face is in his chest, and he's all Nico, spearmint and sandalwood and the crisp of winter. "The pond, after vesper bells. I'll have about an hour free."

"I'll be there."

That's when we notice someone else is heading from the other direction. Two lanterns bob like floating leaves atop the canal, rushing toward us.

"Go," Nico hisses and turns in one motion, walking straight for them.

I take off, but am sure to stay light as I can on my feet. As I make my way to the exit, I catch parts of their conversation . . . "Just a Basso girl . . . ," Nico says. "Questioning her about fish . . ."

"Always taking what isn't theirs," another says.

They must be Imperi soldiers or officers.

I know he's thinking on his toes, throwing them off my scent.

Still looking out for me.

Still Nico.

"HE CAN'T SEE YOU."

"Right."

"Can't even sense you're near. Understand?" I whisper.

"You've got it, V. I'm invisible," Dorian says to my back.

I turn my head around, narrowing my eyes. "Promise?"

He throws his hands in front of him, waves them about. "I'm a ghost."

I don't know why, but I have this horrible feeling Dorian's going to have a hard time staying still.

I want to smile but I don't have time for his antics and my nerves won't allow it anyway.

From Dorian's uncle's home, we had to get creative to avoid soldiers and fences, especially after the mess that was last night. Darting in and out of a couple of dens zigzagging through a tunnel, we manage it without much issue.

Now, only yards away, there's a bend in the canal and it's as good a place as any for Dorian to stand guard. I look at my hourglass almost the exact moment vesper bells ring.

"You stay here," I say, the words barely making sounds. "I'll be right over there." I point to my and Nico's spot.

He nods, crouching onto one knee next to a tree.

I walk on, taking in deep breaths as I do, the stale yet slight fish smell of the canal coupled with the woodsy tree scents tingling my nose. Taking a moment to peer at the darkening night sky, I see the crescent moon winking down on me as if for good luck. It's silver, shimmering against the cloudless, indigo backdrop, as the creases of Poppy's letter—slightly worse for wear after getting wet last night—push into my chest.

I check to be sure my necklace is around my neck, a reminder of our friendship, of the Nico that was. That, deep down, he's still himself just like I'm still myself. I have got to remember this.

My stomach pitches with heat and nausea.

I turn the corner.

Nico.

It's dark, though the tall lamps from the gates up above provide a gentle sheen of light.

He stands beneath the umbrella of trees, nervous, fidgety, tapping his fingers against his leg as I approach.

"You came," I say.

"Of course, I came." Nico looks into my eyes. "Veda . . ." My heart skips at hearing him say my name. He walks toward me and takes my hands in his. "I knew I missed you, but my Sun, seeing you earlier, out of the blue like that, I had no idea just how much."

"Me too." I've tried, *Sun have I tried*, but it's been impossible to erase the kiss we shared, our history, so many moments, from my memories. And seeing him now, looking into his eyes, mirroring his dimpled smile because it's still just as infectious . . . I'm swimming in all things Nico, and oh how I've missed him.

"Should we sit?" Nico glances at the bench beneath the trellis and I nod.

I sit down first, the stone hard and cold, seeping through to the backs of my legs. He takes the place next to me. Nico's uniform is pristine, freshly pressed, his Imperi emblem shinier than ever, and his red officer's sash has new patches and pins adorning it. Nico glances down at the sash. "I know it's strange."

I shrug. "A little." A lot.

Then I look down at my own clothes, all black, the new silver crescent moon pinned to my collar. I pull my hood off my head. "Me too?"

He smiles gently. "A little." Probably a lot for him too.

If I focus on his face, blur out the Imperi uniform, he's still my Nico, dark curly mane, deep dimple perfectly carved into his cheek. So gentle. So kind.

He leans in. "You shouldn't be here."

I take his hand in mine. "I know, and that's why I have to make this quick." Worry lines crease Nico's brow. The needle and vial sit heavy in my pocket. If things go wrong, how will I ever be able to go through with this?

"I need your help. More than ever."

His expression turns from curious to concerned, that dimple disappearing. "My help? How?"

This is my chance. Right now. He's given me the perfect opening, but I've got to go about this delicately. I can't afford to upset him or scare him off, but I also don't want to be too vague or he won't sense the urgency.

I take a deep breath. "Nico, do you know why I joined the Night?" He looks down at me, dark eyes softening. "Poppy." My voice hitches around his name. "How could I ever live in this place after that? After what happened? That wasn't an Offering, it was a murder. I know it. Poppy knew. And I think you know too."

Nico clasps his fingers in mine, pulls my hand to his chest over his heart. "I understand. I'd probably have done the same. What happened to Poppy . . ." Nico shakes his head, anger lacing his expression. "It wasn't right. That Offering felt different. I can't place it, but—"

"It *was* different." I see an opportunity and take it. "Deep down I think you might know what was different."

His eyes flash to mine. "Raevald?"

"Raevald," I repeat. "I'm not so sure Poppy's name was randomly plucked from a list as much as it was deliberately chosen." I lean my forehead to his. He half nods. "Nico . . . what if you came back with me?"

His brow farther knits and he shakes his head. "I could never, Veda. I can't see how that would solve anything." Yes, yes, but I've got to convince him otherwise. Now. Before it's too late.

My nose grazes his as I try to form what might possibly be the most important words I say tonight. "Having you on our side"—I stare straight into his eyes and he gazes back—"on *my* side, will spark revolution. Instead of more fighting, more death, together, maybe, we could change everything."

He pulls back. "War? Who said anything about war?"

I bite my lip worried I might have said too much. But, no. If he's going to end up on our side whether by choice or force, he deserves to know what's happening. "Yes, war. It's probably inevitable at this point, but if you join the Night—if the heir of Bellona joins the Night—others will follow. Dogio and Basso alike. Maybe some Imperi will even flip. Before we know it, Raevald will see he's fighting a losing battle. If he doesn't have the support of his people, he can't win."

"I think you might be overestimating my influence."

"Am I though?"

Nico falls silent for a moment, his gazing turning to the pond. "You understand how much that would cost me. My family. My standing. My inheritance." He looks back at me. "Possibly my life."

"I know. Trust me, I know." His eyes dart to mine. "But you have to understand where I'm coming from."

He turns to face me and I face him, pull my legs up and cross them in front of me on the bench, rest my elbows on my knees.

"I know you better than I know anyone," he says.

"Do you though?" He nods, but I can tell he's lost some of his confidence. "Knowing someone and understanding them are two very different things. I'm Veda Adeline. I'm Basso, was raised by my grandfather. I like to fish and I have an ugly scar from a pantera bite on my chest." He nods. "None of that is news to you."

"No."

"Now. Try to understand me. I'm still Veda Adeline. Still Basso. I've always been told my parents were taken and murdered by the Night. This was a lie. I know for a fact my mother was killed by the Imperi as a traitor." For a split second I consider telling him about the Sindaco, but quickly decide it's not the time. Not the place. "For the majority of my life, Poppy and I sustained our hunger on dried seaweed and salted fish, onion stew. When it was really bad—if I couldn't fish or Poppy was ill and didn't work—we actually ate our bait." Nico's face falls. "Worms. Poppy'd boil them in onions and water. He'd joke it was an improvement to the usually bland onion stew." I pause to smile. "Those onions—cheap, available, and the onion farmer always needed bait, so trading was successful. Poppy could eat one whole and raw like an apple." I shake my head. "When you're hungry enough, you do what you must."

"Veda, I—"

But I know what he's going to say. "When you're hungry and poor, the last thing you feel comfortable doing is asking for help. I know you'd have helped us and I know you did." He glances away. "It was you, wasn't it? A bag of potatoes left on our doorstep? A pound of rice mysteriously shows up on our back porch? New fishing hooks?"

He gives a sheepish smile. "I knew you'd never take them if I offered. I used to sneak and buy bait from Poppy when you weren't working, but my father forced me to stop when he caught me giving it away to Basso. Said I'd throw the balance of things off. That people should work for

what they have, not be given it." He grits his teeth. "I argued how much easier it was for us to say that when we're surrounded by everything we could possibly need. He took the rest of the jars of worms and threw them into the canal." Jaw flexed, he glances down at his uniform. "I can't pretend I'll ever understand your life, Veda, but I know I care for you more than I've ever cared for anyone. I know that love means sacrifice, and I know that I can do more good from inside the Imperi, one day, Sun willing, as High Regent, than I can from underground. Maybe I can change the rules . . . The system . . . Get people to understand more fully . . . Maybe."

"Maybe. Years, decades, from now. I can have hope in that. But for now? In this moment? The foreseeable future? I'm afraid the system is too broken to change."

"I have to try." I can't argue that. It's the same thing I'm doing this very minute. And I can't give up either.

"Think of all we could change if working together? Instead of being up against everyone—the entire Imperi—you'd be surrounded by people who want the change you seek—*we* seek. The Night believe in it so much they're willing to die for it."

"So am I. But from a different vantage point is all. Think of what we could do coming at it from both sides."

Nico's wrong. I don't want him to be wrong, but he is. There's no changing the Imperi. No reasoning with Raevald. He's too blinded by his pursuit for power and revenge. "I know you believe that, but I just can't. There's no time to change the system, Nico, it must be taken out. Overthrown."

We mutually pause, take a breath. Going back and forth the way we have, it's like we're circling the same planet but from slightly different axes. So excruciatingly close to coming together but missing by a hair each time we pass.

"When?" he finally says, and for the first time I'm concerned I might have given him too much information. Because *what if*? Nico is technically the enemy after all. I'd never in a hundred years think of him as that, but . . . *what if?*

"I don't know," I say quickly, but it's the truth. I have no idea.

"Soon?"

"Possibly."

"Veda . . ." Nico squares his shoulders so he's sitting straighter, no longer leaning in toward me. But it's not his sudden distance that strikes me, it's his eyes. His lack of a dimple. He sees what I'm doing, that I don't fully trust him for the first time in forever.

And he's right.

My Sun, he's right.

And I've got to do the only thing I can to get him down to the Lower. Not only for the cause but for his own safety. If he stays, especially as an Imperi officer, soon to be directly under Raevald's thumb, what if the truth comes out about who I am—it's no secret we're close friends. We've not shied away from pushing the bounds of our society in the past. He could be labeled a traitor, sympathizer to the Night, untrustworthy— he could lose everything anyway.

If I could quickly and fully convince him of that right now I would. But I can't. It's clear he's not coming with me. Not tonight and certainly not willingly.

With a deep breath, I steel myself. I become Lunalette, the one who's foretold to set the revolution into motion, bring the Night to victory. The one like my mother, fighter and spy. Perhaps this is how I become her. Perhaps this is my first act. And act I must.

"Nico . . ." I speak softly and scoot closer, bridging the space he created between us. "If I knew when, I'd tell you." *Only if you joined the Night.* "Truth is, I have no idea. We're not near as organized as the Imperi, not close to as battle ready." *It's not a huge secret.* "I'm so sorry . . ." *I am.* I inch even closer, take his hand, my other already in my pocket, gripping that cold glass vial. "I'm pushing you too hard." I place my forehead to his.

Our noses grazing, he says, "It's all right." I pull my right hand out

248

of my pocket, glass vial tucked against my palm, needle sticking out between my middle and forefingers, the cap still on, but easily popped off with the slip of my thumb.

He wraps his arms around my waist. "I believe in us," he whispers, and he's so close his words wash over my lips. "We can both do good. Apart, yes, but also together." He places his hand just above my heart, runs his thumb in an arc. "Ad astra." Nico places a barely there kiss to my lips. Again, "Ad astra. I believe in us." A couple of layers below where his thumb makes a constant arc, back and forth, my scar tingles.

But my act, my mission is compromised the moment Nico pulls me in, wraps his arms around me, and kisses me like it's our first and last kiss ever. His lips are warm, soft, laced of spearmint. When I wrap my arms around his neck, Nico clutches the back of my jacket, pulling me even closer.

"Veda . . . ," he whispers against my lips as I run my fingers up the back of his neck, into his hair, kissing him more deeply, my head completely spinning. Everything around us a blur.

I'm caught off guard by how much I don't resist. By how quickly I pull away from my mission and *this is bigger than me* and *Lunalette*, all for the boy before me and *ad astra*.

Truth is, I can't simply throw my cares away *to the stars*. Not this time. For once with Nico, it's not so simple.

Neither is drugging him to convince him to join my side of this revolution. It'll never work. He'd never trust me again, much less come around to our side.

What was I thinking?

As if waking up from a trance, I abruptly pull away, hide the syringe up my sleeve. I plan to shove it back in my pocket. But as I do, my fingers get tangled in Nico's jacket and I drop the vial. It clanks against a clump of stones on the ground and shatters.

Nico jumps and pushes me away. He stands up. Glancing all around, he sees the broken syringe and looks back and forth between it and me.

He's frozen, staring straight at me, betrayal and anger and hurt written in the way he shakes his head. How he doesn't say a word. So quiet. Too quiet.

"Nico . . . ," I say, slowly getting up from the bench, "it's harmless. Only meant to . . . I mean, I wasn't going to—"

"*Stop.* I don't want to know. I can't know." He glances back at the shards of glass, the liquid spilling, slicking the rocks beneath it. "You shouldn't be here." He peers up toward his house. "It's not safe." He gazes across what feels like endless space between us. "For either of us."

I nod. My hands are shaking and I force them to my sides. Caught between the shame that I nearly attempted it and the disappointment that I couldn't find some other way to convince him to come with me, pain pricks behind my eyes.

And the pain, the burn of fresh tears trying to surface, isn't so much about the failed mission. It's Nico. Behind his anger, his betrayal, I see the same pain that's about to double me over. Together, we're coming to the same realization. Peeling back something I think we've always known but refused to admit. And the truth of it, the hurt below the truth, is enough to split me in two.

Because despite our differences, despite that we had the world stacked against us, I always hoped, believed, something would magically change. That it would somehow, eventually work out for Nico and me. That the stars would align and the seas would calm and we'd be there to see it all. Together.

I now understand that'll never be.

And that's what I can explain to the Sindaco when I go back. Nico and I aren't like him and my mother, because they were on the same side. We're not.

"I'll go," I barely manage.

"Good." He backs away.

But wait! I want to shout. *Please! Come with me! Trust me!*

He tightens his jaw, shakes his head, and takes another step back. "It'll be better this way. We can't—"

But I don't get to hear what "we can't" do or be.

Dorian bounds out from around the corner, a single sharp needle in his hand.

Nico makes to pull his sword from its hilt, but before he can, I throw every last ounce of strength I have into my legs and slam my body into his, sending him tripping over his own feet and into the pond. Dorian halts, steps toward the water after Nico, but stops short when a soldier, shining a light through the thick trees in our direction, shouts from the top of the hill. "Denali! That you?"

I jerk the needle from Dorian's hand and throw it against the rocks so it shatters next to what's left of the first syringe. We run for it.

Two vials of moonroot wasted.

Without Nico.

Both of us seething with anger, out of breath and in a cold sweat from sprinting through the snowy forest to get away.

But we do get away.

We run straight for the same den we came through yesterday. The soldiers continue sounding the warning, but their whistles grow fainter the farther away we get and I wonder if Nico somehow stalled them. Would he even?

I'd do it for him.

Of course, maybe not if he'd just tried to sedate me. My stomach sinks even lower.

Dorian doesn't say a word. I stay a good couple of feet behind him, pretending to enjoy the silence.

In fact, he ignores me our entire journey and I ignore him right back. But beneath the blaring silence, my mind's roiling with all the things I'd like to say to him.

Did you think I'd fail? Is that why you brought your own needle?

Back through the forest, shadow to shadow, tree to tree—not a single word spoken.

Or were you jealous of the kiss Nico and I shared? Is that why you came running out when you did?

Around the electric fence, we pass THE MOON WILL RISE AGAIN posting—not a glance is shared. *Remember that? Remember when we were on the same team? When you trusted me to make the right call? Or was that only then, when tacking papers up on fences was the task?*

If he's anxious or afraid during our descent back down the ladder, he doesn't show it.

I'm forbidden to fight. Not trusted with missions. Do I have no say in any of this?

Dorian and I return to the Lower as we'd planned had our mission been a success.

And with each section of earth we pass below, each layer we descend, I grow angrier. At myself. At Dorian. At the situation and the Sindaco, the Imperi and Nico. I curse the Sun and moon, both.

Because the mission was a fantastic disaster.

But it was my mission.

I failed.

But I'm not about to admit it to Dorian. I don't have to.

"Are we going to talk about what happened back there?" We're heading toward the map room, and Dorian says his first words since we left Nico.

Anger wells up as heat from my chest. "What?" I say through a clenched jaw. "I've been waiting for the same from you."

He stops dead. "You completely botched the mission."

Heart pounding, breath heaving, I squeeze my hands into fists so tightly, my nails dig into my palms.

"You had him, Veda. You had him."

"And you . . . The Sindaco . . ." I nudge my head just ahead, toward the map room. But when I open my mouth to continue, to really let him have it, I'm suddenly without the words. Without an excuse.

There isn't one.

"I did what I had to do." His words stream out through gritted teeth and they burn. I wonder if I accidentally show my disappointment on my face when he looks away, allows his shoulders to soften.

Because I did fail. Regardless of it being wrong in the first place, I agreed to it. I justified it. And I botched it.

But he's not blameless either. Had he not tried to "fix my mistake," who knows? I might have been able to convince Nico. Maybe.

Instead, I shove past Dorian. I won't allow him the first word on this with the Sindaco. Marching past, I walk through the map room door and straight up to the rickety waist-high table the Sindaco stands behind. I slam my hands against the wood and the whole thing wobbles, several maps falling off the side. He doesn't flinch.

Forcing my voice steady, I simply state, "The mission failed."

He glances across at me. "I see." If he's upset, he doesn't show it. "And was Dorian able to—"

"No." I cross my arms. *Yeah, I know you sent him with his own needle. You didn't trust me. You assumed I'd fail.*

Suddenly, Dorian is at my side. "I apologize, sir."

"For the failed mission or . . . ?" He glances toward me.

"All of it. I should have acted sooner. As the highest ranking on this mission, I take full blame."

"That's ridiculous," I say. "*I* take responsibility for the failed mission. *I* made the call. *I* know Nico." I pause, carefully considering my next words. "It wasn't right to force him here. That's not the way."

"Veda . . . This is why I wasn't sure . . . Why you shouldn't fight. Why as Lunalette—"

"Don't do that. Don't say I'm better off being a symbol. If Dorian hadn't jumped out of the bushes with a needle, maybe I could have convinced Nico."

"There's no way—" Dorian cuts in.

"Maybe not. But you didn't help. Not at all."

The Sindaco sighs. "It was too much to put on you. I see that now. You're not trained for missions. It won't happen again."

No. "What?" I say the word through a clenched jaw. Taking a step back, I shake my head in disbelief, but not completely surprised either. "I'm being punished. For choosing what was right. For making the call on my own mission."

The Sindaco scrubs his face with his hands. "This is what you don't understand." He looks me in the eyes. "Sometimes battle, war, isn't about what's right, but what's best for those you're fighting for."

I open my mouth to argue, but then I realize there's truth to what he's saying. My mother recognized this. It also got her killed.

The Sindaco continues, "Dorian having his own vial wasn't meant to be a slight at you, nor did I doubt you. It was simply a backup plan. Extra assurance. When setting out on a mission like this, you just never know." He pauses. "Most important, you're both safe and we now know that at some point, Mr. Denali could be an ally to us."

Not after we attack Bellona and unravel his entire world.

"And, as you found out, sometimes your only hope is to act on instinct." He gazes across the table at me, points to a single word in the margin of a page surrounded by countless maps that says *Lunalette.* "I trust your instincts. Just not in battle."

That last part stings.

Mostly because I'm terrified he's right.

ONCE OUTSIDE THE MAP ROOM, I'm not sure what to do with myself. I need some time alone. Something to take my mind off everything. Normally I'd fish. Walk the beach with Nico. Sort worms into jars. A few days ago I'd have asked Dorian if he wanted to do some weapons training.

But I can't take one look at my atlatl much less Dorian right now.

So I do the only thing I can when stuck Sun knows how far underground.

I wander.

Without a plan or a map, I traverse the tunnels and caves aimlessly, working to gather my thoughts.

I know my way around well enough now that I'm confident I won't get stuck or completely lost. I plan to get a little lost, but not so much they'll send a search party or I'll waste away into dust.

I move at a steady pace, up rocky stairs, down a metal shoot, past a door I know leads to one of the dens. The one Dorian and I used when we came back here after Poppy's Offering.

I pass by the door labeled GARDENS, and soon find myself in a familiar series of tunnels branching off other tunnels. The labyrinth. And soon, the once-mystery door to the memorial cave.

A dead end.

I hear Dorian approaching.

I assume the Sindaco told him to check on me. Be sure I didn't do anything reckless like try to leave.

If I had a key, I'd lock myself in just to get away from him. I glance over my shoulder and make eye contact so he knows I see him.

"Veda," he calls after me. "It's locked."

Of course it is. I turn to face him, lean my back against the door, and then slide down it so I'm seated. Dorian approaches and sits next to me.

Searching the ground for something to pick at, I'm pleased to find a scattering of gravel on the cave floor. I pick up a handful of pebbles and then drop them. Over and over.

Out of nowhere, Dorian blurts, "Pebble for your thoughts?" He holds a small rock atop his palm.

I look over at him, scrutinizing his face, unsure whether to laugh or slap the stone out of his hand. "You've literally been with me for two days. Do you really not know what I'm thinking?" I say.

He raises his eyebrows. "I assume you're angry with me?"

"A bit."

"It's fair. Warranted. I shouldn't have overruled you, and I got a mouthful from the Sindaco about it if that makes you feel any better."

"It does."

Dorian laughs under his breath. "Good." He glances over at me. Narrows his eyes. "But there's more, isn't there?"

I only meet his stare.

"Is it Nico?"

I shrug, my insides cramping with guilt and disappointment. I couldn't begin to delve into all of that right now. Still, I answer honestly. "Nico's on my mind, yes."

"I know you're close to him. I imagine facing him like that, the idea of drugging him, dragging him down here was hard. On several levels."

I nod. Several levels is right. But does Dorian know I'm developing feelings for him? Does he have feelings for me? Last night . . . Sleeping next to him . . . I'd have never admitted it, not even a few hours ago, but within those hours everything's changed. Dorian's becoming more and more comforting. A source of laughter and happiness. A bright flicker in all this darkness.

And I don't know if my heart can take the confusion. The pulling in two directions as I lose Nico, yet gain Dorian. And I have lost Nico, haven't I? To the Imperi. To duty. To everything I always knew would eventually tear him away from me.

We both know it. That look we shared after our kiss confirmed it. The memory tears an invisible hole through my chest, makes me want to curl up into a ball. The place he held in my life used to be so full of light and love and everything Nico. But now it's empty. Dark.

"It's hard seeing him this way . . ." I take a deep breath. "So much has changed. I've known it for a while, but it feels so final now."

Dorian glances over at me, dropping the sarcasm, any and all pretenses. "What feels final?"

"Nico and I . . . Our friendship . . . It feels finished. And maybe it was

256

always doomed." I'm saying it for myself, but also, I think, for Dorian to hear too.

He scoots closer. "I'm sorry, Veda, I really am sorry. For the mission. For you and Nico . . . For . . ." His words trail off, but I can see he means it. All of it.

I take a deep, shaky breath and I pat the top of his hand. "Thanks."

Dorian nods, then turns his head, looks me in the eyes, and I realize how close we're sitting to each other. When he speaks, his breath grazes my ear and despite the weight of the moment, my heart quickens. "You love him?"

My answer is automatic. "I always will."

"I understand." His words are soft, genuine, and at the same time he says it, Dorian pulls back, puts a bit of space between us.

I'm a little worried he took what I said the wrong way. I love Nico, but it's not so simple. So far from simple, I'm not sure I'll ever understand it all. But back at the pond, just after our kiss, that was goodbye.

We both saw it, both undoubtedly felt it.

I turn my head to look at him. I'm about to explain this when he asks, "Do you want me to walk back with you?"

"Thanks, but I think I'll stay here a bit longer. I'll find my way."

He gently pats my hand, then stands. "Hey, I'm sorry again. For everything."

"Me too." I nod.

I sit for a good five minutes pelting tiny rocks and staring down the dark cave, the empty place where Dorian had been sitting next to me.

The place where, in another life, Nico might have been by my side.

I'M LOST.

I'll find my way . . . Those might have been the most idiotic words I've said in a while.

I have absolutely no idea how to get back to my room. I've given it a good go, but I'm certain the path I'm on is taking me farther into the endless labyrinth. Everything looks the same: tunnels, unmarked doors, stone and dirt, darkness. I take yet another set of rickety stairs only to hit yet another fork.

I flip a mental coin and choose left.

And I thank the Sun because I did find my way.

Eventually.

In a big circle back to the map room.

I march right by—I definitely know the way from here. But despite my mind trying to will my feet forward, I skid to a stop only a few feet past the door.

As if that isn't enough, I knock.

Then enter.

The Sindaco glances up, motions I come inside. He's in the same place as when I left, but instead of standing behind the table, he's sitting on the floor, papers spread out all around him like fallen leaves.

I sit down across from him, narrowly avoiding several maps.

After a short beat of silence, not looking up, he says, "I understand your frustration, you know." The Sindaco jots something down on the page before him. "My entire childhood, much of my young adulthood, was spent with choices always being made for me."

"So, you know how used I feel?"

The Sindaco looks up, meets my eyes. "Yes." He releases a sigh. "But . . ." I raise an eyebrow. "It's not the same."

"How so?"

"My father, those around me, all they wanted was to control me."

"And this is different?"

He nods. "Veda, you don't see it now, but you will . . . You are the opposite of powerless here. You are the power. The influence."

"You keep saying that, but it doesn't feel that way."

"Be patient. Be open. Sometimes you have to read between the lines, so to speak. Refocus to truly see." He sits up straighter. "All of this . . ." The Sindaco shuffles his papers. "It's just details . . . Important details, but

258

details nonetheless." He leans forward, speaking more lightly, but with emotion accenting his words. "Your task, *your destiny*, it's superior to details."

"Maybe . . . But it doesn't help I'm so in the dark to the details either." I shrug. "Shouldn't I have some information? I mean, how am I supposed to be Lunalette when I know less than everyone around me?" Honestly, it makes me feel naive. More like a child and less "legendary savior to the revolution."

He looks across the space at me, seems to consider my words, then digs through one specific pile of papers. Plucks a page out and hands it over. It's a map, ink lining different routes, X's marking specific spots. "We're attacking in six days, during the next Offering."

I glance at the large mural of the map on the wall, as if it holds answers. "How?"

"We're going to attack the Hill. It's the perfect opportunity. They'll never see it coming. When most of Bellona is on the Island of Sol, we'll make our move and take control."

"Will there be casualties?" Nico . . .

"Some. Likely many. It's the cost of war. A war we're waging, but a war that's years in the making and long overdue. Once we get Raevald they'll surrender. That's the goal."

"Who's getting Raevald?" The strap of my pack slips off my shoulder, the atlatl falling from the quiver into my lap, then onto the floor with a light clunk. Instantly, I think of my mother, try my best to invoke her warrior spirit. The Sindaco's eyes go to the weapon. Her weapon.

"Raevald's mine," he says. I follow his stare toward the atlatl before me, his tone taking on a severity I've yet to hear.

From my mother's weapon, he glances up at me.

"I know you want to fight," he says, quiet yet stern. Again, he focuses on the atlatl, then the quiver of spears. "You're more like her than you'll ever know. She'd be so proud." His voice snags with the last word. "And *she* would insist you stay behind. Not fight. Be the symbol of the Lunalette."

"Fighting would be easier . . ."

"I understand. Being Lunalette is a heavy role to take on. A huge responsibility. But don't overthink it. You'll know what to do when the time comes." It's sort of his version of "ad astra" or Poppy's "wait, listen."

Maybe I will know what to do. Or just be more confused than ever.

"I'll try."

"It's all any of us can do, eh?" A smile plays at his lips as he looks down and surveys the piles of papers before him.

"I should get back," I say.

"Me too." He motions toward his work but pauses. "This is for the force briefing tonight." He studies my reaction. "Would you like to attend?"

"Yes." I say it too quickly, too enthusiastically.

He appears to hold back a smile.

"But *only* as Lunalette—to observe. To be less . . . in the dark." His repeating my exact words doesn't go unnoticed.

I nod.

"In one hour."

Nod-nod. "Thanks. I'll be there." I pivot toward the door.

"Hey, Veda?" he says, and I turn back around and face him. "Tell me something about yourself? Something I wouldn't know. Something outside of all this."

I think for a second. "I love the snow, how it sparkles in the moonlight. I used to get on to Poppy for smoking his pipe, but now, beyond all reason, I miss the stink of it." I pause. "I love to fish, but hate gutting the slimy things."

I look over at him, see he's smiling.

"What about you?" I ask.

"Hmm . . ." He looks toward the ceiling. After a short stall, he answers. "I collect maps . . . old . . . new . . . fantasy . . . nautical . . . sometimes I create my own. I'll admit, I've been known to have a celebratory pipe from time to time. And . . . I can't catch a fish to save my life. Never could."

"Did my mother fish?"

"Not one bit."

"So that I get from Poppy, eh?"

He nods, eyes crinkled at the edges under a wide smile.

I return the smile, but it doesn't reach my eyes. Not nearly. There's still this distance between us. I'm not sure whether it's seventeen years' worth of absence or the weight of everything hanging over us or something I'll never know, but it's there. It might always be there.

Again, I turn to leave.

"You forgot something."

Glancing over my shoulder, I see that he's holding one of my spears. It must have fallen out when I set my pack down.

I walk back to get it and reach out for the smooth, sharp wood. Under the firelight, it holds the faintest sheen of gold.

"Thank you." I grin, but it's a sad smile.

The Sindaco stares up at me, expression somber, and nods once.

Walking across the room, watching the lamplight reflect and flicker across the door, distorting it as I exit, something hits me. How under the intense candlelight of the map room, the spear had morphed from wood to gold. Then, in a blink, right back again.

Maybe there's something to that. Maybe I've been looking at this whole Lunalette thing the wrong way. Under the wrong light. I've been shining all the rays of the Sun over it, putting so much pressure on myself, been caught under the spotlight of it all, when I should have gone dimmer. Like the candlelight in the map room.

Even though these spears, this weapon is probably made of the finest wood, well taken care of and preserved for so many years until it reached my hands, there are visible blemishes, snags, the corners worn. It's not perfect, and I imagine neither was my mother.

She wasn't heir to anything. There was no Lunalette star staining her chest.

She was a fighter.

261

A soldier.

She held her head high and her atlatl even higher. She fought for what was right.

And isn't that enough?

Shouldn't it be enough?

"Yes," I say.

CHAPTER 24

That night, the Sindaco gives the entire force a briefing that includes charts, graphs, and maps marking team movements and high-value targets.

When the Sindaco invited me here only an hour ago, he was clear it was only as Lunalette, symbol of hope and revolution. Not to get any grand ideas. That my presence is purely for morale and to appease my desire to be "less in the dark."

Regardless, I'm taking it all in. Every detail is being committed to memory. And I'm secretly jotting down notes. Just in case.

Every thread is gone over point by point. The specific phase of the moon the night we attack. Which dens will be open and closed. Officers speak. Movements and alternative plans, if-all-else-fails scenarios are sketched in charcoal and paint on the cave wall.

By the time the briefing's through—hours later—and everyone is dismissed, I'm ready to scale the dens, storm the Hill, and take out the Imperi even if on my own.

But based on the Sindaco's last word on the matter, it won't happen.

When I turn to leave, there's a tap on my shoulder.

Dorian stands before me, holding out a folded piece of paper. "You dropped this."

When I look down, I see it is indeed mine. I'd been using it to hide my notes, folded it around the smaller scrap of brown paper where I wrote down dates and times and circled which den exits to use. This paper, thankfully, is only marked with a small sketch of the Bellonian coast. I figured I should have something to show for all my scribbling if someone walked by and glanced down.

I'm about to tell him I don't need it—when I catch a bit of writing that isn't mine along the edge. "Oh, thanks." I take it from him.

His eyes linger on mine for a beat before he's called away. But when I sneak a glimpse over my shoulder as I leave the room, I catch him looking at me.

I hurry out of there before he sees how my face has gone flush.

DORIAN'S MESSAGE ALONG the corner of the paper reads, "V—after dinner, meet me outside the door to the garden."

I've read it a few times to be sure of the time and place, and maybe to study the quickness of his pen strokes, the way the first line of the V is hard and the second, upward stroke is light and curves at the end.

My cheeks heat at the thought of our last meeting, how I'd spoken so honestly about my feelings for Nico and how he'd given me the space I needed. I'm suddenly the tiniest bit light headed, a bit queasy, my nerves on edge. The walk to the garden from my room doesn't help at all. I'd hoped I would calm down, but I'm more and more anxious with each step.

What if Dorian decides he could never compete with my feelings for Nico, our long history?

I mean, I get it. What Nico and I shared . . . it'd be impossible to duplicate. I'd never want to. Sure, it'd be a hard relationship to follow, but I'm not looking to re-create what I had with Nico with Dorian. That would be wrong. Ungenuine.

Hell, I'm not even sure where my emotions for Nico stand, where my budding feelings for Dorian begin and end.

Dorian and me . . .

Is it even a possibility? We're great in so many ways but also not.

I breathe deep. Dorian and I have had to learn to trust each other, we've trained and been on missions, he was there after Poppy died.

It's true I haven't known him as long as Nico, but there's still a solid foundation there. If Dorian and I decided being more than friends was too hard, we'd still have that.

I hope.

And it's no secret we've both felt it. Both been witness to silent moments alone in close quarters when our hearts quickened. When the brush of a hand sent warmth up into our faces.

But what if . . .

I bite the inside of my cheek and force myself to stop because I'm quickly tumbling down an endless hole of *what-if*.

Go with your gut, Veda. It's all you can do. Wait, listen. Then act on what feels right. Simple.

When I'm one turn of the tunnel away from the garden door, my palms are sweaty and my heart's pulsing much too fast for the rate I've been walking. Not quite so simple.

It's just Dorian, I remind myself.

Then, of course, *It's Dorian*, slaps me right back.

When I come around the corner, Dorian's there. Hands shoved in his pockets, when he notices me walking toward him, he pulls one hand free and waves.

I smile. My stomach buzzes with a mix of wasps and butterflies.

He pulls his hourglass from under his shirt. "I thought you'd stood me up."

"Well, your note wasn't exactly brimming with details—it only said, 'after dinner.'" I shrug.

He nods, catching my eye, a grin dancing at the corners of his lips.

"So . . . ?" I ask. Begging myself to please *be normal. Act normal.*

"Oh, right. Do you have some time to spare?"

"I do."

"Good." He frees one hand from his pocket like he's going to offer it, but quickly changes course and points ahead instead. "Come with me?"

I shove my own hands into my pockets because I can't for the life of me figure out what the hell to do with them. "Okay . . ." I drag the word out, my curiosity getting the better of me.

"What?" He knits his brow. "You're not worried, are you?"

"Well . . ." I smile. "You do have a sordid past."

"Ah . . . ," he says, nodding. "True . . . True . . . If it helps, it's nothing dangerous or to do with rocks or birds."

"In that case . . ." I take a step forward so I'm right next to him. "Lead the way."

Once down a questionable set of stairs, we stop at a dark door leading to an even darker, more precarious stairway leading down to who knows where. "It's still a good distance walk from here," Dorian says.

"You realize we've already walked a good distance, yes?"

"Yep."

"Don't I at least get a hint?"

"Nope. Come on."

We walk through caves, wind along tunnels, descend a narrow passage, until finally, we're at a red door.

We stop.

Dorian looks over at me and breathes deep. "First, let me tell you, not a lot of people are allowed down here. You have to promise never to bring anyone here."

"I couldn't if I wanted to."

He laughs. "Ready?"

"I am."

Pulling a ring of keys from his pocket, he finds the correct one and opens the door. We go down a short passageway and reach another door exactly like the first. He opens it.

Before us is a narrow waterfall that flows down over the entire cave entrance like heavy rainfall.

"I'm assuming we're going to have to walk under that?" I raise my eyebrows, so intrigued I'm ready to jump right through it even if he says no.

He looks me straight in the eyes. "I go to battle in six days . . . I'd say, a good distraction is in order—you up for it?" But before I can answer, Dorian walks forward, a thin mist splicing off his shoulders and brushing my face with a light spray. It's cool and refreshing.

"V?" Dorian's voice is muffled, but his hand peeks through the sheet of water.

Without thinking, I grab his hand, lace my fingers with his, close my eyes, and walk underneath the falls.

It's warm like bathwater and fresh as day, obviously a part of the springs that run like veins throughout the caves. Once on the other side, I rub the water from my eyes and ring out my hair, but stop short when I take in the cave before us. It's like one gigantic geode. "Whoa . . . ," I whisper.

"I knew you'd love it."

Light flickers and sways throughout the cavern in a shimmery luminescence even though the cave is lit only by a single large lamp in the middle of the floor. But it's all the light needed.

Surrounding us, floor to ceiling, are crystals. They're mostly differing shades of blue and green, but there's a cluster of bright pink here and there, and when I walk up to one, I realize I know it. "Rose quartz?"

Dorian nods.

"I have a small piece of rose quartz that belonged to my mother."

"It was her favorite, so I'm told. Supposedly, she spent a lot of time down here."

"I can see why."

But as I continue taking in the room, something occurs to me. "Does the Sindaco know you brought me here?"

"Not . . . exactly."

"First the memorial room and now this . . . ?" I swear his cheeks blush and he grants me that rare genuine smile of his—the one that reaches his eyes. My stomach twirls, the butterflies awakening. Apparently, they're not too concerned with *wait, listen*.

We continue walking along the edge of the cavern and I take in the gems. Each is unique, not one having the same points or angles or speckled surface.

When we've taken our time walking, noting it's not only rose quartz here but also citrine, amethyst, and lapis lazuli, we stop about halfway around the circle.

"Some Night members who live double lives like me use the gems for trade," Dorian explains as he sits on a flat stone.

I nod, sitting down next to him. He looks over at me, his eyes . . . happy. Less intense than usual. Content.

"Have you found it hard?" I ask, "Living down here and up there?"

He shrugs. "Sometimes. Especially when I've missed my sister. But once I was old enough, I learned how to come and go undetected." He grins, brushes some dirt off the knee of his pants. "Don't get me wrong, I've had some really close calls getting caught."

"Really?"

"Too many to count. Most of which my uncle and the Sindaco know nothing about."

"You sound like me with Poppy." I smile. "Sneaking out before morning bells, I've had some terrifying run-ins with Imperi soldiers that, had one thing gone wrong, could have been bad."

"And you never told your grandfather."

I sigh. "Never." I take in the cave from this new vantage point where, from here on the ground, the gems seem to shimmer even more brightly against the ceiling and walls. "Thank you for this. It's magical." I meet his eyes and smile but he's all serious. Not the usual Officer-Dorian serious, but a different kind. One I feel has something to do with me. One that reminds me of that moment after we escaped the Imperi soldiers through the river and we were huddled in the woods, so close, hearts racing from adrenaline and fear and his breath grazing my cheek.

"Here—" He faces me and reaches into his pocket. "A good luck charm." Atop his palm is a round of glass. At first glance it doesn't look like much, definitely not nearly as intricate as the other treasures he's sculpted for me.

I take it from him and hold it up toward the light. Within the orb, which is flecked with oranges and yellows and pinks, reminding me of the sunset, is a bubble filled with water. Each time I flip it over, the water flows as small waves.

"You told me to keep busy yesterday by making something of glass. So, I did." He flashes an impish grin. "It's water from the Great Sea."

"How'd you get it?" I ask, flipping it back and forth, mesmerized.

"There's a path through the woods from the glass shop that leads to a small tide pool. I sneaked out and snagged it. Took several tries and more foul language than I'd care to admit to figure it out." Dorian places his hand on my shoulder. "I wish there was some way to give you more of your grandfather, something more tangible to remember him by, but I figured, the sea . . ." His words trail off.

"He's a part of it now," I say.

Dorian nods, clearing his throat.

I bring the token to my heart. "It's the most precious thing anyone's ever given me." With that thought, I'm hit behind the eyes with the memory of Nico's necklace. It's been sitting on the ledge in my cave. Neglected. All but abandoned. But as quickly as it came, I shake the image from my head. I don't want to get caught up in that right now. I can't.

Instead, I wrap my arms around Dorian's neck, embracing him. His cheek against mine, my face buried in his chest, it's like I'm surrounded by him and it's everything right in this moment. His earthy, woodsy scent—something he bathes in. His warmth. His body—all strength and speed—the memory of him training instantly flickers behind my eyes.

I glance upward to find him looking down at me. Drawn together by some invisible force beyond our control, we've inched toward each other's mouths.

I wait.

"Veda ... I ...," he whispers, the heat of his words hitting my lips.

I listen.

"I know..." I nod and my forehead grazes his. "Me too ...," I say, moving in closer.

And the closer we get the stronger the pull until he's there and I'm there and we're kissing as if it's what we were made to do. Like we should have been kissing all along.

Like we belong.

And it's right.

"I've wanted this so long ...," Dorian whispers between kisses. "But I wasn't sure ... You're hard to read sometimes ..."

"I have ... Really, I have ... Just didn't realize how much ..." I begin explaining myself, but the pull is too strong, too far beyond my power to resist. I continue kissing him, his lips soft, so gentle, it's all so very clear and not at all blurry.

Dorian laughs lightly at my response but keeps his lips to mine with a wonderful, continuous string of kisses.

I silently pray he never stops. That I can stay here under the glow of rose quartz, surrounded in all that's right in the world.

But I know it'll end too soon.

Everything good does.

CHAPTER 25

In the briefing earlier, the Sindaco warned us that from tomorrow morning it's nonstop prepping for the attack. But tonight? Tonight, I lie on the mat in my cave, staring up at the mural of the Sun and moon at war, the star, symbol of the Lunalette, joining them in the middle.

Candlelight flickers across the painting, gleaming and reflecting like fire, popping like tiny explosions and destruction and war. The five points of the star are pulled by shadow, stretched between the two sides but also sharp as blades, cutting the Sun down the middle and shaving the moon into a perfect crescent. Just barely, the star holds together, yet so close to slicing in two itself.

Herself.

Myself.

I sit straight up.

Stare at that crescent moon and muse over how I'd thought it was winking down at me for good luck just before my mission. Winking, indeed. Smirking, more like. As if it knew something . . . I didn't . . .

With the memory, several things cinch together for me. Moments and conversations from the past twenty-four hours come barreling back.

I stand, pull the handkerchief the little girl gave me off the shelf. Open it up and study the embroidered phases of the moon: new, waxing crescent, first quarter, waxing gibbous, full, waning gibbous, last quarter.

Waxing. Crescent.

"Damn him," I say under my breath. Back in the map room, the Sindaco had told me we attack in six days, yet in the briefing, the notes I took . . . I swear . . .

I dig into my pack, pull the folded scrap of paper out from the front pocket, and squint through the darkness. The words *waxing crescent* next to *day of attack* stare back at me.

He lied. *Six days . . .*

I was just up there, and the moon was nearly a perfect waxing crescent then. In six days it'll be—I stare at the handkerchief again—at the first quarter or past.

He knew I'd try to fight, so he lied.

Of course he lied.

Which means Dorian lied too.

"I go to battle in six days . . . I'd say, a good distraction is in order . . ."

My chest fills with heat and my throat aches with anger and betrayal.

But, no.

Focus.

I have to get to the Upper ahead of the Night.

Warn Nico before we attack.

Then I'll fight.

To hell with what the Sindaco or Dorian or anyone else thinks I should do.

Quickly, I throw what I think I'll need together. Quiver with my atlatl and spears slung over my shoulder, blade in my belt, pack on my back, I'm ready.

But first, I have to be 100 percent sure.

Once I am, I'll leave a little something behind for "my father."

WHEN I ENTER the map room, all is dark save my single lamp.

No Sindaco.

I'd assumed he'd be gone, and thank the Sun I was right.

My plan is to leave the handkerchief of the phases of the moon on the table. I've no doubt he'll put the pieces together.

Once I'm at the table, I start to dig. I've got to find something that has tomorrow's date, something to assure me I'm not making a huge mistake.

Shuffling papers, moving stacks from one side of the table to the other, I can't find one line of scribble that gives a date. I'd even settle for a doodle of the phases of the moon with the waxing crescent circled.

But there's nothing.

From the table, I move to the desk farther back in the cave. There's more maps, pen and ink, blank paper, a pile of crumbled mess-ups in the trash bin. There are two drawers in the desk. The first is empty and the second is stuck.

I pull with all I have, but the thing won't budge, and the harder I try, the more convinced I am that exactly what I'm looking for must be inside this stubborn drawer and oh, how that crescent moon is smirking down on me now.

When I pull out my blade, shove it in the small space between the desk and drawer and give it one hard jerk, the thing breaks loose. The wooden drawer slips out of the desk with a crack, and knocks the metal trash bin over in the process.

Of course, the drawer is completely empty except for some blank paper, but I've already moved on. When the trash bin fell over, something underneath it knocked loose.

A key.

Moving quickly now, sure that the Sindaco or Dorian or some officer's going to walk in and catch me digging through the map room, I scour every inch I can looking for a keyhole. But aside from the desk, a chair, and the table, maps hanging from the walls, a few thick books stacked on the floor, the cavern is barren. Starker even than our home back up on Bellona.

I stop, sit down in the middle of the room.

It's got to be in here, because why would the key be in here, then? Of course, I'm thinking about how that'd probably be exactly what I'd do: keep the key and whatever it opens in different rooms, when my eyes settle on a paper map of Bellona hung on the far wall.

There's a small red X marked over the Coliseum. That alone isn't suspicious, but the fact that the map is bowing slightly, one corner a hair crooked, that part's strange. Every other map in here is meticulously straight, almost in pristine condition, but this one's been taken down and put back up, by the looks of it, many times.

I walk over to it, gently pull the top right corner off its nail. When the flap falls forward, I find there's writing all over the back of it.

It's small, lightly jotted with graphite, nearly invisible, especially in the dark, but it's there.

And once I pull the whole thing down, look at it under the light of my lantern, there in the upper corner, next to tomorrow's date, are the words: *Mission Waxing Crescent.*

Below are battle plans . . . Soldiers' movements . . . Who's leaving through which dens . . . Much of what he explained at the briefing, but to my ears, at least, he'd been vague. Did everyone else know he was lying to me?

How is it not one soldier mentioned attacking tomorrow?

Was there some predetermined code word? *Appease the Lunalette . . . Make her think she's being let in on the fight . . . Speak in code . . .*

My mind spins with endless deceptive possibilities as my fingers clench the sides of the map. Marching to the table, I set the map facedown, place the handkerchief with the phases of the moon on top, then go to grab my blade to skewer it all together for the Sindaco to find, but . . . I can't leave my blade behind.

I need a sharp shard of rock, a nail, anything . . .

Yet again, I'm searching the cave. Rushing, haphazardly checking behind maps and under papers, my palms beginning to sweat as more and more, I'm worried this is all a huge waste of time, that someone could walk in any minute. Still, I somehow rationalize it with the fiery anger welling in my chest. This is important. The Sindaco needs to know he didn't win. He didn't pull his lie over on me.

After a failed attempt to pull a nail from the rock wall, nearly slicing my fingertip on the jagged thing, I stall. My eyes scan hopelessly from one corner to the next.

As if he knew I'd need something, there's nothing.

Knowing I've already been here too long, I settle on stacking a few books around the map so at least it doesn't fall off the table.

The Sindaco will see it, that's all I need.

I grab three of the thick volumes and set them on the table, but the last one gives an unexpected jingle.

There's a small lock holding it shut.

Fishing the key from my pocket, I try inserting it, but it doesn't fit. The stupid key's too big and probably for the door, some other box of the Sindaco's secrets.

Dropping the book onto the floor, I stomp on the lock with my boot, breaking the hinges off in one try.

I open it up.

And inside . . . Inside . . .

It's not what I expect.

The book is hollowed out. Not a great shock, but I was sure I'd find coded plans, a top-secret battle agenda, signed statements by every member of the Night to keep the date of the attack a secret.

But what I do find is a thin, small copy of a child's storybook.

The book is bound in red leather, and printed on the front is a golden eight-pointed star, the title: *The Solvrana*.

The story reads . . .

Once upon a time in a far-off land, there lived a girl of limited means. She was kind and generous, thoughtful and loyal, but very poor.

An orphan, the girl longed to one day have so much more than she possessed, which wasn't much: a doll to hold, a single quilt to warm her, and the birthmark over her heart to remind her she was special.

You see, the girl knew of things no one else in this land knew. It was a secret and one that kept her going even in the darkest of days when hunger and war and death ravaged her once peaceful land.

For she was the only soul who knew of her birthmark.

However, everyone in lands far and wide, across the Great Sea and back, knew of the prophecy of the sun-child: the Solvrana.

Legend foretold that one day a girl with an eight-pointed star upon her heart would rise up and save their land. She would bring peace and hope and end the fighting. Restore joy.

Unfortunately, it was not so easy. On her tenth birthday—

The rest of the pages are torn out, the binding left unraveling, but I don't need to read further.

On the back inside cover, bright as the Sun striking down at midday, is the word *Lunalette* and a jagged drawing of a five-pointed star. It's unmistakably the same writing as the Sindaco's notes. No doubt inscribed by him.

More lies? More deception?

My chest tightens and my scar tingles. I squeeze my hands into fists, planting my feet to the spot to keep from running to the Crag and busting through the Sindaco's door.

It's all just a story. Made up. Horseshit.

I stare down at the place where my scar sits jagged and shiny just below a few layers of clothing. Was it even a pantera fish? Or was it given to me some other way? By someone's hand? All to fulfill a stolen child's story.

A legend.

A revolution.

I have to remind myself to breathe despite the heat coming up from my chest like fire.

Glancing down, the word *Lunalette* stares up at me. Taunting me. The letters screaming of lies.

I slam the book shut. Set it atop the map, next to the handkerchief with the phases of the moon and the lie of a name Lunalette embroidered on it. Mocking me.

I take a deep breath.

So, I'm not heir. Maybe by blood, but not legitimately. That's Nico's role now. And he can have it.

But I'd come to rally behind the idea of the Lunalette.

And I'm not that either.

I'm not Lunalette.

I have to repeat it once more: *I'm not Lunalette*.

The corners of my eyes sting. My throat and jaw sting. And just below my jagged scar, which is simply that and nothing more, my heart stings.

Not only did the Sindaco lie to me, he lied to the people who trust him most. And for what? To rally them behind his revolution? Behind a false prophecy? The stinging turns to burning, and I realize I'm gripping the handle of my blade so tightly, my fingers itching to pierce a hole right through this book.

But no.

It's not enough.

I walk behind the desk and remove the lone spear from my mother's atlatl the Sindaco has on display. I march back to the table, and then slam the stake point first right into the book and through to the wood so it sticks straight up.

Unavoidable. Impossible to miss.

He wanted a symbol?

"There's your symbol."

MY STEPS ARE fast and hard, my feet racing to keep up with my mind, as I try my best to reverse the route Dorian and I took through the caves just yesterday.

I tighten the quiver more securely over my shoulder. Think of all the ways I'll get to use my atlatl tomorrow. How completely shocked the

Sindaco will be when he hears I showed up on the battlefield. To fight for the Night. *With* the Night.

I grip my atlatl, think of my mother, the warrior.

The Sindaco, my so-called father—the word sends hot nausea coursing through my stomach, up my throat—he's no better than the High Regent. Because despite pretending they're doing right by their people, they're only working for themselves. Shoving everyone else beneath them to take the fall or fight the battle.

The sad part is I've no doubt they'd have rallied behind him without it. They'd have supported me regardless.

And Dorian . . .

I can't begin to sort out where I'm at with Dorian, but if the stinging from my heart moving up into my chest is a clue, it's not good. Because he lied too. He knew when the attack was, knew I'd been told differently.

Maybe he knew the truth about the Lunalette too.

The back of my throat is tight. On fire. The burning spreads to my ears and into my eyes, but I can't.

I scrub my eyes with my fists.

I refuse to cry. I will not cry.

Because I can't do anything about any of it now.

It's done.

I'm not Lunalette.

I'm just a Basso girl from the south village who can fish and now kind of use an atlatl.

And I'm still going to lead this revolution.

But first I have to warn Nico.

CHAPTER 26

I climb out of the den door, quiet as possible, silently thanking the Sun that Dorian trusted me with a set of keys.

I'm now on the upper side of the earth, large boulders and overgrown plants hide my location from view. I didn't come up the den I'd intended, but I'm not too far off. I'm in the woods that sprawl like jungle behind our house. Nico's home is only a short walk away.

It's dark, that crescent moon winking down at me again. Snow heavily blankets the ground so everything's lit up like midday—both helpful and not.

I walk along the canal, boots crunching over ice, and round the corner where the canal turns from smooth rock around the edges to snowy dirt.

But something's new.

A fence has been added.

The same kind Dorian and I encountered last time, but on the other side of the Basso village. I pick up a small mound of snow and toss it at the wire. It hisses and I swear back at it.

Up ahead, I see the faint outline of houses along the ridge above me. The lights from the gate separating Dogio villages from Basso villages shine bright.

I can either jump into the canal and swim around the fence or risk being seen by taking the main road and sneaking through the gate.

I look to the water. Parts of it are frozen, but not solid. I'd get wet like when Dorian and I had to swim it, but it's much colder now. I'd freeze.

Sneak through the gate it is.

I step light as air, keeping low and behind the trees. When I near the top, I have a perfect line of sight to the entrance. Two Imperi soldiers sit to each side of the stone wall, a metal gate between them. One naps while the other watches the road. His eyes are heavy and it's as if he too is asleep, just with his eyes open.

I move closer.

Closer.

I duck behind the last tree before there's a small field and then the road. No change in the watching guard. Still lazy and bored. Half-asleep. A spot near the gate catches my eyes: Where the electric fence stops is a small section of stone wall. It's low enough I should be able to jump it at the place before it snakes up, joining the pillars flanking the gate.

I consider throwing a rock to create a diversion, but the soldiers are so close and half-dead anyway. Instead of causing a commotion, it's safer to sneak.

I take three steps.

One of the soldiers coughs.

I freeze.

If he turns his head to the left, I'm done for.

Adjusting himself on his stool, he leans back against the wall, assuming his position, lowering his eyelids.

I don't dare breathe.

Two more tentative steps.

The wind blows, shuffling frozen leaves, nature's diversion. I walk faster.

Three steps.

Almost there. Two more strides.

Step.

Step.

The guard might as well be a statue because he doesn't so much as twitch.

I climb the stone.

Then, over the other side.

I breathe.

Almost too easy.

"What's that?" a guard says from behind me.

I drop to the ground.

"What?" the other says, now clearly awake.

"On the ground, just there, do you see it? Something shiny."

Shiny?

I pat my back pocket and immediately know what it is. The tin-wrapped dried fish I'd shoved in before I left.

Now it's on the ground.

Damn it.

I crawl back down the ridge toward the canal and into the forest. They stomp toward the object, but that's it because I'm out of earshot in seconds.

My pulse and breath do double time as I sprint as quietly as possible until I hit it. Our spot. The small pond, now encircled in an umbrella of snow-covered trees. To my left sits Nico's home, one light shining through a solitary window, a beacon among the many darkened windows that make up the rear of his home.

I'm doing this.

I hike up the ridge, stopping at the back fence.

Eyes straining through the dark and distance, I can barely make out a pennant hanging on the wall: the Dogio school crest embroidered in gold against the charcoal background.

It has to be his room.

Hands shaking, I pick up a small pebble, and breathe . . . one . . . two . . .

It hits the glass with a *plink*.

"Oh!" I gasp. A tall figure stands in the window, but disappears before I get a good look.

It could be anyone.

Do I run? Do I wait?

There's an unmistakable *creak* and *click* in the distance: the back door.

My heart thumps in my throat, beating so fast I'm out of breath. I slide down the fence and huddle into myself. Hidden. I hope.

Footsteps.

I start to fling my body down the hill, but . . .

Knife at my throat.

I pull mine from my belt and thrust it to their wrist. One move by either of us and we'll both be spurting blood.

Breath wheezes in my ear. "What the hell are you—"

He drops the knife.

I drop mine.

"Veda?" It's a pained, horrible whisper. "How the . . . ? Where did you . . . ?"

Exactly.

"I had to see you, warn you," I say.

He nods. Scans the area. "It's not safe here."

He looks back at his window, nudging his head toward it.

"Inside?" I say.

"It's the safest option. My parents sleep like the dead and in the opposite wing."

He throws his arms around me. "I'm so sorry," he says into my neck.

"I know." My throat closes around the words. "Me too."

He pulls back. "Come on."

I follow him around the fence and to the other side. We enter through a gate he has to unlock.

In slow movements, Nico opens his back door, guides me in, then shuts it, locking several locks behind him. Something about it gives me the impression of being both secure and imprisoned.

The empty, nighttime version of Nico's home is cold, lonely, such a stark contrast from the jubilation and splendor of the Ever-Sol Feast. How the place was packed at the seams and lit up like sunrise what seems like a lifetime ago.

But Nico's bedroom is different.

There's nothing lonely or cold or remotely sterile here. It's home. Nico.

The room smells of the forest, a burning fire in the hearth against the outside wall, a small pile of clothes slung over a chair at his desk, a book left open on his unmade bed. I move toward his dresser. Several items line the top against the wall: a fishing hook, a rock, a button, a coil of metal, a scrap of fabric, an autumn leaf, a piece of tree bark, and several other trinkets, scraps of debris.

I glance over at him.

He stands at the door, watching me. "Just a few memories . . ." Memories? "The fishing hook is from the day we met when I caught you at our pond. The button fell off your sweater at some point. It was cracked"—I swear his face is the slightest bit flushed—"so I figured you wouldn't want it back." He peers at the dresser. "The metal is from your window—it was sitting on the outside ledge. I picked it up the last time I visited you there after Poppy . . ." He stops there and nods. "Just stuff like that. Memories. For some reason, I can't bring myself to throw it all away."

"And the fabric? Is that from my skirt?" I turn my head toward him. I know for a fact it is and exactly when it snagged and tore.

"Oh, that . . . Yeah. I think it caught the corner of the bench the night we kissed." Nico inhales deeply, holding the breath in and shrugging his shoulders. "Feels like so long ago."

"A lifetime ago."

He nods, face pained, lines creasing his forehead. He exhales. "Veda—why are you here?"

"Two things, actually." I look away, then back to him. "Well, maybe three." Suddenly, I'm terrified about warning him of tomorrow's attack, telling him about my father, who I am and who I thought I was. Because when I do, everything changes. Right now, if only for a moment, all I want is to be here with him. To simply be Veda and Nico instead of all the other things others expect us to be. "You're not like them, Nico. You're not an Imperi officer. Not like the ones we used to scoff at as kids. The ones I used to hide from for fear of punishment. Certainly not the next Raevald."

He looks down at the floor. "I don't know what I am anymore," he says quietly, running his hands through his hair. Somehow, despite being on opposite sides of the earth, I know exactly what he means.

"You could have reported me, had me arrested or worse by now. But you didn't. You should hate me after last time. Yet here I am." I take a couple of steps toward him. "In your bedroom for the first time."

He shakes his head. "Do you know how long I've wanted to show you this room? My home? I've been to yours a hundred times at least." He stares out the window as if looking toward my and Poppy's cottage. "I asked my father once if you could visit." He looks back at me. "I told him how wrong it was that you were my best friend and not allowed to stand inside our house." Nico releases a breath. "I won't tell you what he said, but it had something to do with keeping to my place, being reckless and stupid." He moves closer, eyes intense. "Pretty sure I'm somewhere in between right about now."

"But it's more, isn't it?"

"Maybe . . ." He stares into my eyes, his eyes somber, serious. "Why else are you here?"

"I'm here because . . ." I pause for breath, to attempt to calm the buzzing of my nerves. I came here to warn him, to explain everything, and suddenly, I can barely remember my own name.

I gaze across the lamp-lit room at him and he gazes back and I can't help the words that leave my mouth in a desperate flurry. "I know you, Nico." I close the distance between us. "I know you like I know myself. Like I know a fishing pole or Poppy's old, wrinkled hands." I step closer and briefly I think of Dorian—Dorian who's been working with the Sindaco on high tales of attack dates and Lunalettes and prophecies—but swiftly push him out of my head. "I think of you often, especially these past days, maybe more than I ever have." I place my hand on his chest. "Yes, a lot has changed, but deep down, we're still just Nico and Veda." I run my thumb over his chest in an arc. *Ad astra*. I meet his eyes. "Aren't we?"

Nico's eyes don't veer from mine, but his breathing speeds and I'm so close now, I can feel his chest rise and fall. "Yesterday I'd have probably said no." His words brush across my lips. "But right now, here with you, I feel more like myself than I have in a long time. More than ever."

I want to trust my instincts. Our history. I want to share everything with him from the Sindaco to Lunalette to the atlatl strapped to my bag to how I knew he'd picked up my button when it fell off my sweater last year to the impending attack. That we'll be fighting each other come sunrise. On opposite sides of a revolution. How could I ever fight Nico? Raise my weapon toward him?

My heart raps like a war drum against my chest, and my mind's a mess of memories and confusion.

I can't tell him any of that when only the thought sends my nerves on edge, makes my eyes burn.

I wouldn't even know where to begin.

Where to end.

And everything in between would ruin all Nico and I have been through up to now.

Instead I wrap my arms around his shoulders, nestle into his body, place my lips at his neck.

Nico's breath catches. He pulls away for a moment, but then he's leaning in too. I kiss the soft place just under his ear, breathing in all things Nico: the forest and spearmint and sandalwood, all that is home. He leans his head back, exposing his neck, and it's there I enjoy more kisses, tasting the warmth and salt of his skin against my lips.

I steal a peek. His eyes are shut, closed too tightly, like they were during our first kiss. Bringing my hand to his face, I smooth his eyebrows with my thumb, softening the lines on his forehead.

Nico clasps his hands around my waist, urging me up toward his mouth. We kiss.

Everything rushes.

It's like we're out of time before we've begun. Like our lips can't get enough of the other's. Quick movements and fast breaths, and hands, hands, hands all over.

Until somehow we're lying down. I don't know how. One second I'm standing next to his dresser, the next I'm beneath him on his bed and his room is dark save for a single, dim lamp next to the door and the light flicker of firelight. His bed that's so soft and white and clean and scented of lemon and juniper.

It's nothing but lips and hands and skin and quickened breathing and everything . . . blurry.

Nico shakes his head back and forth so slightly; the softness of his nose grazes my ear like silk. "Veda . . . ," he breathes.

"I know," I breathe right back. I know it's not like that. Not now. This is closeness and lost time and hello and goodbye and *why?why?why?*

I'll tell him everything. Just not yet.

WE'RE ON HIS BED. The room is still and dark. The world at rest. Nico's shirt is unbuttoned and his chest, the same shade as sunbaked sand and everything warm, is pushed against my back. My tunic, having loosened and slightly fallen, reveals my bare shoulder.

Nico runs his fingers back and forth, sending a shiver of goose bumps over my arm, down my back, and then up my neck. His mouth is at my ear, and the way his breath hitches, it's like he wants to say something but keeps stopping himself.

I beat him to it. "Nico?"

"Hmm?"

"There's something I need to tell you."

"Is it the second thing or the maybe-third thing?"

"I don't even know anymore."

"Does it have to do with why you're here?" He kisses the back of my neck. "You never answered my question."

His arm, wrapped around my waist, rises and falls as I take a deep, shaky breath.

There's no way to spin it casually. No reason to drag it out.

I'm just going to say it, blurt the words out, and then we'll deal with it whatever it means. Whatever it ruins between us.

"The Night is going to—"

An unending series of loud bangs and knocks steal my words.

The front door.

Both of us bolt straight up, eyes wide as we stare at each other.

"No," Nico says, the word near silent.

Hurried, bare footsteps pad down the stairs.

I shake my head.

"It'll be all right," he whispers, his hands on my shoulders.

We jump up, still staring at each other, no idea what to do or where to go.

Knocks and bangs blast from the floor below.

The front door opens, slamming a wall. Something shatters.

"What in the—" Nico's father shouts.

A chorus of murmured voices breaks out in confusion.

Several pairs of boots march up the stairs.

Nico and I scurry to find our things, to find a way out of whatever's about to happen.

He's lacing up his boots and I'm throwing on my jacket, reaching for my atlatl, when—

Loud knocks bang against his door like it's the end of the world.

It very well may be.

Nico grabs my arm before I can reach my weapon and drags me to the closet, shutting me in.

The bedroom door swings open, hitting the wall behind it.

"Where's the other one?" a guard yells.

"Who?" Nico answers.

"You know exactly who!" the guard shouts.

"I have no idea what you—"

There's a punch . . . Knuckles hitting flesh . . . A pained grunt . . . Then someone I assume is Nico falls against what must be his dresser, because a dozen trinkets scatter like marbles raining down on the wooden floor.

Items are tossed, picked up, and moved. Furniture scratches against the floor and bumps the walls.

The closet door flies open.

A soldier with a broken front tooth stares right into my eyes.

His large hands clutch my wrists, and he yanks me from the closet. My feet trip over the mess on the floor, our memories wrecked and strewn about like spilled garbage. My eyes move from the fragments to Nico. His face is swollen, bruising before my eyes, and he struggles to get up off the floor, a broken chair taking the brunt of his fall.

I'm sorry, I mouth. This is my fault.

He shakes his head.

"I came here on my own. He had no idea. It's my fault. He's not to blame. He told me to leave, but I refused!" I shout.

"Veda, don't—" Nico says.

"I'm telling the truth!"

"It's not us who need convincing," the soldier standing over Nico growls. "The soldiers at the gate tipped us off. We're to take you straight to Raevald himself."

"Both of you." The broken-toothed guard holding on to me raises an eyebrow while tsking Nico, heir to Bellona.

Nico and I lock eyes.

We're in this together now.

CHAPTER 27

I shouldn't have come.

I should be preparing for battle.

I accused the Sindaco and High Regent of only thinking of themselves, and wasn't that exactly what I did?

I didn't think of Nico.

Or the Night.

That I might ruin the surprise attack.

I'd shout the words, but my voice is hoarse from screaming at the door to my cell, my throat raw like fire.

Back flat against the gravel floor, I try to suck the pain from the fresh wounds on my knuckles. When the screaming didn't garner anyone's attention, I moved to punching the door instead.

Then kicking it.

All I have to show for it is exhaustion, sweat, and blood.

I don't know what's happening.

I don't know where Nico is.

I was dragged from his house. Rowed across the Great Sea and to the Island of Sol and, without ceremony or explanation, thrown into this, one of the many prison cells beneath the Coliseum. The place where criminals and those set to be Offered are kept.

The Sun's now nearly risen.

I've been in this tiny stone cell for hours. No word.

I dig my boots into the gravel and bury my eyes into the heels of my hands.

I failed at warning Nico—what will he think when he realizes I know? I can see his expression now, disappointed, hurt.

I failed at being there for the Night. I imagine the little girl who embroidered the moon phases on the scrap of muslin for me, the lettering she worked so hard on. What will she think when she hears there was no Lunalette? When I don't return?

Lunalette.

I wrap my arms round my middle, curl into myself.

I even managed to fail a fake destiny.

My sight blurs as my eyes prickle with heat.

A guard sticks his nose through the barred window of my cell door, taking me from my thoughts. I'm almost thankful.

He clears something thick from his throat, spitting it on the ground. "Put these on," he orders, pushing a white bundle through the compartment at the bottom of the door.

The mound thumps against the stone floor. When I look back up at the bars, he's gone.

I sit up and make my way to the pile. I reach for the clothing, hands trembling, because I've just received my answer.

Unfolding the mound, one by one, I lay out a white tunic, white pants, and white boots.

Same thing each Offered wears.

I won't wear it.

I pick up the clothes and toss them into the muddy corner of the cell.

This isn't my sacrifice. If I'm executed as a traitor, I'll do so in my Night uniform, not under the guise I'm doing some favor for the people of Bellona to please the Sun.

I stand, staring through the bars in the door, waiting for anyone who might give me some information. Or better, who might open the door so I can punch and stab and kick my way out of here.

No one passes. I'm alone. Weighed down by endless thoughts and memories.

Just me and the stone and the smell of rot and the drip, drip of something not too far off.

But then there's something else mingling with the sounds of nothingness. Something far worse.

Even from a distance, I know his silhouette, his stride, the tilt of his hat and the way his red sash is pressed, creased like new.

Raevald opens the door to my cell, locking it behind him, two soldiers appearing from nowhere waiting outside.

He looks me up and down, then stares at the soiled, once-white clothing in the corner. "Do the garments not fit?"

I don't say a word.

He smirks, nodding knowingly.

I run straight for him and throw a punch that misses spectacularly, my knuckles landing into the door for the hundredth time in several hours. Pain and fresh blood burst across my fingers.

He strides toward me, stopping when there's no space between us, his nose an inch from mine.

I shove him in the chest to push him back, staining his gold sash with a spattering of blood from my knuckles.

He grabs my wrist, twisting my arm so it burns and threatens to tear in two.

I lock my eyes on his, refusing to be intimidated.

"*Tt-Tt-Tt*—" He clicks his tongue against the roof of his mouth. "Save that for the Coliseum. The crowd will *love* it." Still squeezing my wrist so tightly my hand's going numb, he jerks farther, my elbow burning. "I knew you'd be special. *The only one to escape the Night.*"

I struggle for words. "Why am I being Offered? On what grounds?"

He laughs under his breath. "Treason, of course. Just like your mother. Funny how things come full circle."

The High Regent lets go of my wrist. I pull away, rubbing my hand back to life.

Eyes wide, all I can do is stare. Hope I can somehow turn my hate for him into fire, burn him to cinders.

"So, you're my bastard granddaughter..." His eyes search over me, disgusted, like he's looking down at an insect he's about to smash. "So much like your *mother*."

And he knows about me too.

Raevald walks across the cell until his sculpted eyebrows, his leathery skin, are in my face again. "I've said too much. But... you'll see. I'd hate to spoil the big ending."

"You're *not* my grandfather. You'll never be half the man he was."

"Yes, well, I guess we'll never know, will we?" He sneers.

I spit in his face. Without expression, he pulls a red handkerchief from his breast pocket and wipes it clean.

Turning on his heels, he leaves.

The door locks.

I slide down the wall, bring my knees to my chest, and curl into myself...

TIME PASSES AND doesn't pass. It's as if I'm in a trance, staring at the grit between the stones in the floor, trying to think of something, anything I can do. What I should have and shouldn't have done. But there's nothing. It's over.

It goes on like that until I snap out of it, the roar of the crowd gathering above, awakening my body and mind.

I jump up, try to see out of the small opening in the door of my cell, but it's all shadows. All I can do is listen, the sounds of the Coliseum so familiar and at the same time completely foreign, masked with echoes from down here.

One thing is unshakably clear: The Offering is about to begin.

My heart rushes as it beats faster, rapping against my chest, into my neck, pounding at my ears. It won't stop. It doesn't stop.

Pounding.

CHAPTER 28

I walk down the hall, hands bound at my waist, a guard on each side jerking me along.

My eyes are drawn down, focused on my boots and how they shuffle with every forced step like they're someone else's feet.

My head could explode any minute. My heart, still in pieces, works too hard pounding for its fragments to hold strong.

We reach the door.

Raevald's voice echoes, magnified, over his speaking-trumpet, but I can't make out his words, just a string of murmurs, then applause.

Murmurs.

Applause.

I force my ears to work harder, but I'm only able to make out: "Special treat... Offering... the Night... a fine show... unfortunate... traitor... begin!"

I'm thrust through the door.

Applause. Whoops. Hollering. Whistling. Boos.

The Sun blinds me, glinting off the snow. I shade my face with my tied wrists, hiding from the spectators.

Here I am, shuffling along, kicking up snow-covered gravel, taking the long walk to the altar.

Hands still hovering at my forehead, all I see is the white ground, the

Sun reflecting into my eyes, until the altar is at my waist, the cold of it pushing through to my skin like ice.

My eyes are pulled to the brown smudge atop the stone; the place where the Offered give their blood is so bloodied, it's no longer fading back to stone.

It's then I notice another body. I glance up.

The pounding of my heart stops completely. My heart is nothing, an empty, useless cavern, all blood from it dried out, cracking, falling to dust.

Nico stands before me, blade in hand. Face unreadable. But his eyes. His eyes scream at me to run. To find a way out of this. *Fight, Veda, fight!* they shout.

"What a show this is going to be!" Raevald speaks from on high, a satisfied humor in his voice.

The crowd erupts with applause.

Raevald motions to Nico now. "As your heir, Mr. Denali will stand by as we Offer this traitorous former Bellonian. But first, he will open the ceremony by performing the altar ritual. Oh, how the Sun will reward Bellona today! Now, I give you your Offering."

The arena thunders with excitement, but Nico doesn't so much as flinch. He's being punished, I know it. I can see it in the way he's gripping the blade before him, his knuckles white around the handle. Raevald knows we were together, and he's going to force Nico to watch me die.

And afterward?

What will Nico's ultimate punishment be? I purge countless horrors from my head just as Raevald's words from moments ago come bounding back. *You'll see. I'd hate to spoil the big ending.*

This punishment is for both me and Nico. Me for being a traitor, for slipping through the cracks, for being Raevald's bastard granddaughter and almost costing him his crown. Nico, for his association with me.

I glance up at Nico. His eyes still scream, *Fight!*

Fight, how? I ask.

"It is time for the Offered, a traitor among us, to give her blood back to the Sun."

The crowd goes quiet.

I'm shoved forward and stumble several steps, tripping over my own feet. When I look back up, another soldier stands at the altar next to Nico. Arlen. He doesn't give me a second glance and is quick to grab my hands, hold them down as Nico, keeping his eyes on mine, looking into me, right through me, pushes the point of the blade into my palms.

And he's slow about it.

Slice.

I wince.

He's trying to bide us time. Figure out how to get out of this. But there's nothing.

A second slice.

No way out.

A second, more pained wince.

Nico places my palms against the altar, where my fresh blood blossoms atop the rusty stone. He catches my eyes; his pained, red at the corners, so powerless.

The crowd cheers.

I picture my mother, the soldier. Poppy, so strong. Countless lost Basso faces who never had a chance.

It's time.

I don't know how, but I must fight.

Whipping my arms around, I swat the closest soldier—one right behind me—against the ear. Blood dribbles from it, and his fist comes toward me, landing at my jaw.

I stumble into the altar as blood bursts in my mouth.

The other soldier, the one who helped drag me out onto the Coliseum floor, jumps toward me as I struggle to my feet.

They aren't used to the Offered fighting back, but the shock is long gone. "No, she's mine!" says the soldier I hit.

The rope around my wrists loosens, but I can't get free, so I jab him as hard as I can with my elbow in the eye. He squeals in pain, doubling over, both hands covering his eye like he's trying to keep it in his head.

That's when I see his knife, how it's large and jagged and dangling from his belt. I dodge for it. The other soldier bounds toward me, catching me around the waist. But the knife. The knife is just within my reach.

I grab it with my fingers by the tip of the handle.

Clasping it between my hands, I bring it down, shoving the blade into the thigh of the second soldier, now behind me.

He screams, letting go of my middle. I lunge forward, jabbing the other one in the shoulder, the blade catching onto something as I yank it out. He yelps in pain, falling to the ground.

The crowd is split: half booing, the other half cheering for more fighting. More blood.

I look to Nico. He dives for Arlen, knocking him down, and scrambles to reach for his sword. But he doesn't see the two guards rushing up behind him.

Nico's lifted up off the ground and dragged away kicking, arms straining against the guards' tight grips.

Now free of Nico, Arlen charges toward me.

"Get her, boy!" a man yells from the stands.

I work to cut my hands free.

"Put her in her place, the traitor!" another hollers.

"Finish her!" rages over the speaking-trumpet. I glare at the balcony. Raevald's hands are folded under his chin as if in prayer, golden cone he yells through slung over his finger.

Nico shouts my name and one of the guards punches him so he slumps forward, still slung between them.

But he manages to lift his head. Find my eyes. His eyes are still his. Still Nico.

Arlen approaches me.

I free my hands, then hasten backward, knife shaking. Both soldiers writhe on the blood-splattered snow. Arlen steps over them like they're rocks, a part of the landscape.

A mass of clouds moves in front of the Sun, giving everything a gray tint, shading Arlen's face, distorting his expression.

More Imperi soldiers and officers gather at the doors around the Coliseum floor. One carries a large hatchet. Walking past us, he leans it against the altar. I expect him to join the fight. He doesn't and, instead, returns to his post.

Then it begins.

"Come on!" Arlen yells.

I flinch.

"Come on, traitor! *Fight!*"

The crowd loves it. They squall and holler. "Fight, fight, fight!" they chant.

Nico, still dazed, still within the soldiers' tight grips, looks at the crowd, then back at me. Despite the threat of another fist to his face, he yells, "*Fight, Veda!*"

As much as I want to run to him, find some way to get us both out of this, we're far outnumbered.

And he's right. I've got to keep it going. Stall as long as I can.

If I don't fight back, we've got no chance. I'm biding my time. For what, I have no idea.

I run full force, slamming both my fists into Arlen's chest. I lay him out flat on his back, all the air knocked out of him. But he jumps to his feet like it was nothing and comes for me, shoving me to the ground, the back of my head hitting it with a thud.

Stars haze my vision.

I kick him in the stomach hard as I can.

He falls back, but is above me again before the stars in my head have disappeared. My cheek is against the ground, the snow. Arlen lifts his foot up over my face. He brings it down. Nico somehow manages to get free and runs toward us. He screams "No!" but is just as swiftly pulled back toward the wall again.

Everything draws out like I'm watching it pass me by in a string of pictures.

Crack.

My jaw.

The snap echoes between the walls of my skull as white-hot pain shoots down my throat and into my ears, pushing water from my eyes.

One shaky whimper flees my lips. Just one.

His boot—now a vise with the ground—clamps my cheeks between the hard grate of its sole and the sharp, icy gravel beneath me.

Snow drifts down, sweeping me with cruel, frosted kisses.

The Coliseum is taller, more menacing, than ever. This time, I'm the cause of all the commotion.

Down here, the large stone arena orbits me—the traitor—mocking the Sun instead of honoring it. Each towering arch surrounding me is an ashen rainbow, cracks and all. And below each arch, the stands are crammed, stippled with faces like small dewdrops piled on grass. The Coliseum is strong as always, but today, it's suffocating, the unbreachable walls yards away yet closing in on us.

We're positioned front and center, the main attraction: a Basso girl, her executioner, and her closest friend, Bellonian heir, forced to look on. Our stage: snow and dirt. Our audience: the blood-hungry citizens of Bellona. Hungry for a show.

And a show they'll get.

I'm numb and frozen and burning all at once. Long strands of hair stick to my forehead and hang over my eyes. Blood trickles thick from my nose down the back of my throat. It tastes of tin. I spit it out. Blood sprays the snowy ground.

The crowd cheers.

"More!" several shout as one.

"Traitor!" a woman calls out.

300

A child lets out a high-pitched "Off with her head!"

Mass laughter ensues.

They lust for this, are entertained by it, feed on and frenzy over it.

But all of that is background noise. At this moment it is only me and one other—Nico, who's somehow managed to drag the two soldiers struggling to pull him back several steps toward me. He holds me with the intensity of his eyes. Each fleck, each shadow. I know so much and so little of those eyes.

Together.

Tears collect in my own, blurring his image. Bloodying every memory. It's better. I can't stand seeing him witness this. My heart breaks for all that's in store. Everything that's to come once my part of the show's over.

As if on cue, the gray clouds break. The Sun shines down, casting a fiery ring around Arlen and me; a spotlight illuminating the place where I lie and he crouches over me, his boot at my jaw like a hunter with fresh-killed game.

The Coliseum quiets.

A newly hung banner flaps in the wind. The red words IN SUN'S NAME, THE IMPERI WILL PROTECT YOU FROM THE NIGHT distorting with each whipping gust.

"Veda . . ." My name cuts through the silence as a whisper in my ear. As if by magic, Nico's at my side.

I strain my eyes to see past his exterior. To find the boy I know so well within the enemy uniform. But everything's a blur, and hard as I try, I can't begin to pluck a single piece of him from the fray as Imperi soldiers barrel down on us.

In the background of chaos I hear one word.

"Wait—" Raevald says. The soldiers stop in their tracks; they glance up at the High Regent.

My sight settles on the altar, on Arlen, bloodlust in his eyes, the stone pedestal to our right, the large sacred hourglass suspended above. Red sand fills the bottom bulb.

A single bell rings.

It's time for the finale.

Nico kicks Arlen's boot off my jaw, throwing him off-balance so he falls flat on his back. I don't see what happens next, but I hear knuckles to skin, a pained groan, and Arlen lies still not too far from me.

Nico picks me up. My body's heavy, limp. I can't move.

From Nico's arms, I see the hourglass dangling above—all red.

He sets me down, resting my head on the altar.

Staring at the red, I watch as Nico's shadow reaches for the blade.

"It'll be all right," he whispers.

Everything goes dark when my head's covered with the canvas bag.

"I'm getting us out of this." His words barely register or maybe I'm imagining them.

As if in answer, the unmistakable brushing of Nico's thumb runs across my back: a long drawn-out arc: *ad astra, to the stars.*

Time stands still; the entire island, the Great Sea, all the world falls silent.

"Listen—" Again, Raevald speaks a single word that reverberates out over the Coliseum. I wait . . . No blade slices my neck.

Next, I listen . . . Silence. Then . . . An explosion not too far off. Objects whiz through the air, pelting the ground all around us.

Nico yelps out in pain.

His body falls, dropping hard and heavy onto my back.

Screaming.

Yelling.

Scrambling.

More zipping, the sound like a thousand birds diving from the sky.

I remove the bag from my head.

I'm barely able to move, but manage to sit up. I turn around, find Nico's eyes, which are someplace between intense pain and relieved contentment. I hold him into my chest.

There's an arrow in his back.

I pull it out.

He yells and whimpers at once.

My blood-stained hands shake as I throw the bloody arrow to the side.

"Nico!" I search his face. Blood soaks through the back of his uniform. "Oh my Sun," I whisper, staring into his eyes. My Nico. Always with me.

"Get . . . out . . . of here," he manages.

I finally look up.

The Coliseum is under attack. There are Night forces everywhere: in the stands fighting Dogio; on the dome floor fighting Imperi soldiers and officers alike; bodies falling in pools of blood; blades clashing; arrows flying.

"Get out. Veda," Nico pleads.

"I'm not leaving you," I say.

Together.

Over the High Regent's speaking-trumpet, an Imperi guard shouts, "Bellona! We are under attack—"

But he's cut off.

Up in his balcony Raevald is taken by his security council and disappears behind the red curtains.

"Veda! Please!" Nico says, shouting as best he can, his brown eyes begging me to leave him.

It's then I have no choice. From behind, I'm lifted by the underarms, Nico's body flopping to the ground.

Dragged away, my feet kicking, slipping in the snow, I screech a final, "NICO!"

He turns his head to look at me. We hold each other through our eyes.

Then, an explosion, like the end of the world, consumes the Coliseum.

All goes black.

CHAPTER 29
NICO

When I wake up I'm surrounded by shadows, the low flicker of light. Wherever I am, there is no Sun. No Veda. Only sharp pain in my back and chest. Darkness. And one, maybe two, dim orbs of orange light floating in the distance.

As my eyes focus, a shadow comes into view. Two shadows? Three?

"Nico?" It's a low voice. Not one I recognize, which instantly sets me on guard and sends my nerves on edge.

I try to sit up, throw my fists toward whoever might be near enough for me to punch, when I realize I'm tied down. Strapped to the bed.

"Give him some space," the voice of a woman breaks in from behind my head.

Barely . . . Slowly . . . I force my eyes open more fully. Blurred but standing over me is Dorian and an older man. There are others, more blurs, but I can only make out that they're all dressed the same, wearing black.

Glaring from one face to the next, I see. I begin to remember. I put the pieces together.

I scream the only name I can think. "Veda! Where's Veda?!"

"Shhh . . . ," the woman, peeking around a mound of bandages—a nurse, I think—soothes.

I'm not interested in any of it.

"Veda!" I pull against the ropes holding me down. I kick, jerk, nearly send the whole bed tumbling over.

"Not yet," the man, the one who's not said a word until now but refused to take his eyes off me, says. The one who holds a distinctive air of authority.

"Please, Sindaco, he deserves to know," Dorian says. The man seems to consider his request and then gives a curt nod.

"Nico," Dorian says. "Veda was captured by the Imperi during the raid. It was chaos. We tried to get to her, but with the blast, the confusion . . . it was too late." He breathes through his nose, jaw flexed.

"What?" Again, I try to sit up. "No!" I use every last ounce of strength to fight the restraints holding my arms down. "We have to help her!" I shout.

"We have soldiers out on missions to find her. We'll bring her back. *I'll* bring her back." Dorian's eyes are puffy; he looks like he hasn't slept in days.

"No." I shake my head, and the movement sends a sharp pain down my back. "They'll kill her. Raevald will kill her." Pain be damned, I thrash against my bindings. "I've got to find her! I need to go to her!" I shout. "Please!"

"Is this necessary?" Dorian asks the man, eyeing my arms, the burns I can feel are quickly surfacing under the rope.

"It's as much for his own safety as it is ours," the man in charge says without emotion. He steps closer to my side. "Nico, your injury's significant. You've got to rest." And he motions to someone standing behind me. From the corner of my eye, I watch as the nurse approaches. A flash of silver and glass passes my periphery. Then, a hot, fiery sting plunges directly into my neck.

"Veda . . . ," I say, the voice barely my own. "I need . . . to save . . . her . . ."

"So do we," Dorian says quietly.

I open my mouth, a thousand questions to ask, but everything in the room spins, blurs, and goes dark around the edges.

Then, like vesper bells ringing inside my head, the older man's low words echo, "We'll find her. I promise."

Ad astra.

It's all I need to hear.

ACKNOWLEDGMENTS

ACKNOWLEDGMENTS ARE ALWAYS one of the parts of publishing a book that I both worry over (I *know* I'm going to forget someone!) and enthusiastically anticipate (it means the hardest parts are behind me and I get to be all gushy and sentimental!). It's also a part of the book that I realize is often skipped over by readers, so I feel perfectly fine using this line to say things like *SHMIFLY!* for my husband, Wade; *You clod!* for my daughter, Sierra; and *Windows . . . are the eyes to the house,* for my oldest daughter, Ainsley. They'll know what I mean.

In my debut novel's acknowledgments, I listed my sweet family last (but not least), so I decided here I'd thank them first. Without my daughters, Ainsley and Sierra, I'd never have been inspired to write, and without my husband, Wade, I wouldn't have had the time and space to truly explore what writing a book is or how to do it (also, he's been a real champ over my coffee-shop bill!). It's undoubtedly through my family's unconditional love and support that you're reading this book today.

I am forever grateful and thankful to Swoon Reads and Jean Feiwel for taking a chance on me and this story and for giving so many YA authors the opportunity to publish their words on SwoonReads.com.

A triple-chocolate-covered-in-rainbow-sprinkles-with-a-unicorn-on-top THANKS goes out to the readers at SwoonReads.com. I am forever humbled and honored they took the time to read my words and critique my work. Honestly, if it wasn't for their insightful feedback and passion for this book, I'm not sure you'd be reading it today. The story has changed a lot since it was up on the website and I hope you all love the final product as much as I enjoyed creating it!

There isn't thanks enough for my amazingly talented editor, Kat Brzozowski. The manuscript Swoon Reads originally chose to publish has evolved beyond anything I ever could have imagined and blossomed into the book you now hold in your hands. This wouldn't have been possible without Kat's keen eye for details, unwavering support of me and this story, and her overall vision for the project. I'm not even kidding when I say editors wear many hats: reader, cheerleader, flowery prose police, and drill sergeant to name a few. Fact: I hit the editor jackpot.

A huge thank-you also goes out to Lauren Scobell, director of Swoon Reads, who, along with Kat, saw the potential in my writing and was a partner throughout multiple revisions and the ultimate molding of this story. Lauren helped me connect a lot of dots (and delete several that weren't necessary), which ultimately helped *Beware the Night* truly come together in the end.

A big, squishy thank-you to Swoon intern Ruqayyah Daud and former Swoon intern Rachel Diebel for their invaluable insight and spot-on feedback for this story. You gals are truly the cat's meow and I'm forever grateful.

To the rest of the wonderful Swoon Reads staff: publicist Madison Furr, production editor Alexei Esikoff, production manager Raymond Ernesto Colón, designer Liz Dresner, and marketing associates, Ashley Woodfolk and Teresa Ferraiolo—thank you for turning my story into an actual, physical book. Without you all, *Beware the Night* would just be a mountain of words on a screen.

Special thanks goes out to artist Elen Winata. With her special illustration magic she was able to encapsulate not only Veda as a character, but also the symbolism, mood, and setting of *Beware the Night*. Elen's gorgeous cover art left this author speechless and misty eyed. It's quite honestly one of the most beautiful book covers I've ever seen.

Gigantic hugs to my critique partners and early readers of the many versions of this story: Dani Bird, Megan Cordaro, Fiona McLaren, and Sarah Stith. Thank you for always being enthusiastically willing to read my words.

There isn't enough thanks (or chocolate) in the world to express my gratitude toward my critique partner/writing BFF/doppelganger/right-hand gal, Jeannette Smejkal. It's an understatement, but I'm so glad we met during that blog hop so many years ago. I seriously don't know what I'd do without your moral support, sense of humor, and overall CP-badassery. This definitely calls for a *DORIAN!!!*

Last, but certainly not least, a big, lovey thanks to my mom and dad for always fostering an atmosphere of *follow your passions*.

On a personal note, I wrote *Beware the Night* (it was titled *The Offering* back then) in 2011, not too long after I sustained a traumatic brain injury from a sharp jerk of a metal window frame. When I look back, I'm honestly not sure how I was able to write an entire book during that time of fatigue, depression, and anxiety. But writing gave me a wonderful escape, as it still is, and the characters, per usual, were extremely insistent I tell their story. Despite the fact I could only sit and focus for so long, I wrote this novel in a matter of months—a bit of magic all its own. I made quick work of it while the rest of my world sort of chaotically spun around me.

Still, it was important to pause every so often to wait. And listen.

FEELING BOOKISH?

Turn the page for some

Swoonworthy EXTRAS

A COFFEE DATE

WITH AUTHOR JESSIKA FLECK
AND HER EDITOR, KAT BRZOZOWSKI

GETTING TO KNOW YOU (A Little More!)

Kat Brzozowski (KB): What was the first young adult novel you ever read?

Jessika Fleck (JK): I can't remember which one specifically but it was DEFINITELY a Sweet Valley High novel! I learned so much alongside those mischievous twins and their shared shenanigans.

KB: I am a huge Sweet Valley High fan. Who is your favorite fictional couple?

JF: I adore Todd Hewitt and Viola Eade from Chaos Walking by Patrick Ness.

KB: Do you have any hobbies? What do you do when you're not writing, or when you're avoiding writing?

JF: Lol—I would *never* avoid writing! I love to knit, read, drink lots of coffee, go on walks and hikes, travel, spend time with my family, and snuggle with my two-year-old mini labradoodle, Opal.

KB: If you could travel to any time period, what would you pick and why?

JF: Oh goodness . . . Probably the 1950s. I've always been intrigued with the mid-century (maybe beginning with my obsession with *Dirty Dancing* and *Grease*)—the clothing and styles and music—how simple a time it seemed. Can you tell I've been binge-watching *The Marvelous Mrs. Maisel*?! It's so good!

THE SWOON READS EXPERIENCE

KB: How did you first learn about Swoon Reads?

JF: I actually learned about Swoon Reads from Katy Upperman, who was in my 2017 novel debut group. I remember seeing her post about cover voting and I was so blown away by the response and how fun it was.

KB: Thank you, Katy, for sending Jessika to us! What made you decide to post your manuscript?

JF: I had recently parted ways with my first agent and decided to try something different. Lucky for me, I had a manuscript all ready to go that seemed like a good fit for Swoon Reads' catalog so I took a chance. I'm so glad I did!

KB: What was your experience like on the site before you were chosen?

JF: I was a newbie to the site upon posting my manuscript, so I hadn't done much reading or commenting. But after I posted and started exploring, I found the most amazing community of readers and writers (and so many wonderful stories!). I'll be forever appreciative to those who read *Beware the Night* (titled *The Offering* back then) and gave such helpful feedback.

KB: Once you were chosen, who was the first person you told and how did you celebrate?

JF: Well . . . I tried to get ahold of my husband but he was at work (womp, womp), so the first person I told was my critique partner—which, actually, felt quite fitting, lol. My husband called me back soon after and then I told my daughters. We went out to dinner and my family gifted me a lovely antique copy of *Jane Eyre* (one of my all-time faves).

THE WRITING LIFE

KB: When did you realize you wanted to be a writer?

JF: You know, I didn't discover my love for writing until later in life. I'd always looked at writing as more academic than creative because that had been my experience. But when my girls were babies and I was spending my days at home with them, I found I needed a creative outlet (I'd previously painted and sculpted but life with two kids under three just didn't allow for that kind of setup): enter writing.

KB: I love that. Do you have any writing rituals?

JF: Coffee + music = writing. If I'm at home, I'll sit by the window and light a candle. If I'm at the coffee shop—where I do much of my writing and editing—I'll still try to sit by a window but I'll sort of tuck myself into a corner and block everything else out. Sometimes I'll have a chocolate chip cookie.

KB: Where did the idea for this book start?

JF: Oh boy . . . Way back in 2011, after the horribly devastating tsunami struck Japan, an idea sort of hit me (as they usually do): I pictured a girl and her mother trying to survive after a near-apocalyptic massive flood ravaged their land, leaving it an island and cut off from the rest of the world. Obviously, that's not the story that ended up being *Beware the Night*, but it was the catalyst for my brain spinning and weaving a bunch of thoughts and ideas into what became this story.

KB: It's interesting how the idea is so far from what the book became. Inspiration can come from anywhere! Do you ever get writer's block? How do you get back on track?

JF: Sometimes. Though, I think it's more a mix of procrastination and distraction. I'll take my dog for a walk, have a second (or third) cup of coffee, chat with my critique partner, or do some stream-ofconsciousness brainstorming in a notebook. Sometimes, if possible, I'll give myself a few days off. Honestly though, for me, oftentimes it takes reaching a deadline or a "tough love" self-pep-talk to get my brain thinking clearly and my fingers typing.

KB: What's the best writing advice you've ever heard?

JF: "Block out the noise and make the thing." Thanks to author Lance Rubin for sharing this insight. It's gotten me through many writing challenges.

THE SWOON INDEX

KB: On the site, we have something called the Swoon Index where readers can share the amount of Laughter, Tears, and Thrills in each manuscript. Can you tell me something that always makes you laugh?

JF: The show *New Girl*. I love how adorably dorky Jess is (probably because I share a lot of that dorkiness). Book-wise: an awkward meet-cute.

KB: Makes you cry?

JF: The ending of *The Book Thief*. Every. Time. Heartbreakingly beautiful.

KB: Sets your heart pumping?

JF: A good rom-com. The 1996 film adaptation of *Romeo and Juliet*. A great new song. Candles with scents that remind me of lovely memories. The perfect cup of coffee + a crisp autumn morning.

BEWARE THE NIGHT

DISCUSSION QUESTIONS

1. The island of Bellona is a secluded, self-sustaining island society. It's not an easy life, but like anywhere else, there are positives and negatives. Would you want to live on a small island? Why or why not?

2. Bellona has a lot of rules its citizens are expected to follow. But some circumstances force Veda to bend the laws. Do you feel she's justified in breaking the rules of Bellona? Why or why not?

3. Dorian is apprentice to his uncle, the island's only glassblower. He enjoys his craft but would much rather make his own creations than hourglasses and kitchenwares. If you could ask Dorian to make you one of his miniature glass trinkets, what would you want him to craft for you?

4. Bellona is a society that worships the Sun. They show this through altars and prayer and ceremonies like the Offerings. Many societies throughout history have worshipped nature deities. If you could create your own nature-based society, what entity would your society worship? What would be their traditions?

5. Which character from *Beware the Night* would you most like to meet? Why?

6. Which places in *Beware the Night* would you most like to visit? Why?

7. Veda finds herself caught between Bellona and the Night, the Sun and the Moon. Are you drawn more to the sun or the moon? Why?

8. If you could read *Beware the Night* from another character's point of view, which would you choose?

9. When Veda finds out she's the Lunalette and the truth of her parents' fate, she has a lot to process and even more questions to explore. Do you feel she handles the news in a believable way? How would you have handled such information?

10. Share a favorite quote from *Beware the Night*. Why did this quote stand out?

11. Because of her circumstances, Veda is faced with complicated feelings for both Nico and Dorian. Do you believe she handles her feelings fairly? Why or why not?

12. Are you team Nico, team Dorian, or team neither? Why or why not?

13. They say not to judge a book by its cover, but what do you think of the cover for *Beware the Night*? How well does it convey what the book is about?

14. If you were to write *Beware the Night* fanfic, what kind of story would you want to tell?

15. There are several unique foods included in the world of Bellona: sunrise bread; star and moon cookies; candied lemon; and carnival-type food that is served after the Offering. If you could try any of the foods from the book, which would you want to try and why?

In this electrifying sequel to
BEWARE THE NIGHT,
Veda is captured and leveraged against her
best friend, who fights for the opposing force.

DEFY
·THE·
SUN

JESSIKA FLECK

Keep reading for an excerpt.

CHAPTER 1

VEDA

I t's been minutes.

Hours.

A day maybe.

Since I lay at the foot of the Coliseum altar, as all the world crumbled down around me.

Everything hurts.

My eyes are swollen.

My jaw is on fire.

My body broken.

My heart? It's not much more than a shell of something resembling a heart at this point. I do know it continues to beat because everything has its own throbbing pulse. Each thump pains me more than the one before.

My mind? A blur. Strange snippets of memories and nightmarish images haunt me day and night. I can't begin to pull reality from fantasy from dream.

All of that and the best I can do—the only thing keeping me sane—is run my tongue along the jagged tooth in my mouth. The one Arlen cracked with his boot.

It's sharp. Pricks my tongue with the point of a thorn. Draws a bit of blood.

It's a different sort of pain than the throbbing. It's the kind that stings up into my ears and reminds me I'm alive.

I'm alive.

I didn't die like Raevald wanted. I ruined his big finale. It's the only thing that almost, barely pulls the corners of my mouth upward.

My Offering was stalled by my fighting, then slowed by Nico, and ultimately hijacked by the Night.

The Night . . . my dear people.

The same ones who left me on the bloodstained gravel of the Coliseum floor as they dragged Nico away.

With an arrow through his back.

A different pain consumes me now. The worst kind. It's the one that has no cure. No amount of adjustment or consoling will quell it. This pain reaches from my toes to the top of my head and then down into the very deepest depths of my being.

But I can't get lost in those depths. Not now. Not anytime soon.

It's futile, but I try to shake my head. Toss the thoughts, the terrible pain out because if I dwell too much on Nico . . . that arrow . . . I'll fall down a horribly dark hole. I'm already surrounded by enough darkness—I can't take any more.

I have no idea where I am.

Possibly hell.

The ends of the earth where all is darkness.

I do know one thing: I will not die here.

I'm certain Raevald isn't too far away, and I refuse to give *him* the satisfaction of my death.

CHAPTER 2

VEDA

Days pass.

Some wounds heal.

I gain a semblance of time and space and realize where I am, how much time has passed.

Twelve days ago, Nico lay in my arms bleeding.

Dying.

An unforgiving arrow stuck out his back.

The Coliseum, all of Bellona, crashing down around us.

A mere twelve sunrises ago my hands were in his, and then they weren't.

Eleven days ago I woke up on fire.

I'm still surrounded by darkness, but instead of hiding behind the safety of swollen eyes, the black space squeezing in on me is now reality. Drowning and ever present.

The prison floor is cold and callous. Forever damp and smells a mix of mildew and straw. There's no window. Not even bars. No fresh air or sunlight or moonlight.

Nothing but four walls, a door, a small grate in the ground, and a single lamp. It's lit what I assume to be each morning and burns for six hours give or take. Once it goes out, the only light in my world comes in unpredictable flickers from a crack underneath the cell door. The space—a few inches tall—is just wide enough for a meager tray of food to slide under. Twice daily—morning and night—I'm fed. Once daily—midday, I've convinced myself—I'm allowed to bathe. The time of day is arbitrary, I know this, but I've lost all concept of night and day. So even if I'm wrong, thinking there's some structure to the endless hours brings me a stitch of comfort.

And every once in a while a cold gust snakes under that crack in the door. Then something—what I've come to refer to as *Death's shadow*—shuffles its way across the floor in front of my cell like a broom. It clicks and swishes, breathes a deep sigh, and disappears as mysteriously as it arrived. I'm convinced it's either the ghost of someone who met their untimely and gory end down here or, more likely, Death himself checking to see if I'm ready to take a journey.

The cell door unlocks. Creeps open.

Instinctively I scramble to the side, push my body against the equally cold, damp wall.

I don't want to meet Death just yet.

A dim bucket attached to the same Imperi soldier who's tended me since I awoke from darkness comes into view. All shadows, bright lights framing her form from behind, she enters like a dark apparition. The guard sets the bucket on the ground beside me. Cold water overwhelmingly scented of lemon and pine sloshes over the side.

When the dark silhouette turns to leave, I ask her the same thing I asked yesterday and the day before.

"What's your name?" Gingerly, unsure of her reaction, I crawl forward just enough so the light from the hallway shines across my face. I need her to see me as human. As a girl and not a traitor. As a person and not the evil that is the Night.

But she stays still. Eyes on the door.

As I do every meeting, I give her a small measure of myself. "Each year, on the Night of Reckoning, I used to bake a loaf of sunrise bread for me and my grandfather. I'd layer the middle with candied lemons so when we cut into it there was a lovely ribbon of bright yellow." For the first time in forever, a smile makes its way to my face. It sends a wave of pain across my jaw but it's no matter, because the memory is too sweet to spoil with agony. "Poppy would always try to gobble it all up in one sitting, but when he couldn't, we'd cut it into slices and share it with the neighbors. Of course, not before he'd dig into it and pull several candied lemons out, hide them in a cupboard. Such a sneak. But he loved those sticky lemon slices."

I expect her to ignore me, tuck her short, dark hair back behind her ear, and leave and lock the door behind her as she always does. But today she's stopped. Stayed long enough to actually let me finish my story. This afternoon, she's paused momentarily in her automatic actions. Halfway to the door, her back to me, she looks over her shoulder.

I chance moving an inch closer, making eye contact.

The soldier—an officer, I notice for the first time, or maybe she's only now wearing her red sash—stares. There's hate and anger in the way her eyes set on mine, unblinking, narrowed. But then, as she scans me up and down, her expression wavers. Softens for the briefest of moments. Curiosity? Pity? I can't be sure.

"Your name?" I plead as if the slightest communication will somehow satiate me. "Please?"

She straightens her posture, lifting her chin slightly, adjusting her crimson sash. "Down here a bucket of clean, soapy water is worth its weight in gold." She shakes her head as if disgusted. By my presence or the conditions I'm not quite sure. "Consider yourself lucky. The High Regent gave special orders for *you*. He wants you healthy and strong so you can face your punishment properly." She lowers her gaze as if speaking to the bucket now. "Wash up."

She then nods like she and the bucket have made an agreement and leaves without another look or word.

Damn it. I pushed too far. Got too greedy by asking her name. One step forward, two steps back.

It's become my battle march, and it's infuriatingly useless.

The thick, metal lock bolts shut with the sort of finality I've come to expect.

I glare at the door.

They want me healthy so I can die with dignity? I release a snort under my breath. As if that's some sort of consolation or comfort. Not that that's the point either. They'd never wish anything close to dignity for me. Not unless they're about to strip it away for the sake of cruelty.

Because I'm the enemy. Possibly their most prized prisoner, short of arresting the Sindaco himself, of course.

But that officer . . .

I can't quite figure her out. I've not had any contact save my meals—what I can only describe as pig slop, one step above fish bait—and my baths. It's then and only then she graces me with her company—a total of one to three minutes each time (I spent one full day counting the seconds, marking the minutes and then the hours with a hunk of gravel I found on the floor).

She'll return, but she won't say a word, only pick up the items, be sure I ate and cleaned myself. It's my job to put everything back where it was left. If I don't replace the tray or bucket respectively, I won't see my next meal or bath. And despite the bitter mash and grimy water and the cold silence of an Imperi soldier, I've found it's better than nothing at all.

I can tell by the way the lantern hanging in my cell dims that it's quickly drying out of oil and that, once again, I'll be locked in darkness.

I'd find it poetic, maybe even humorous, if I wasn't being driven mad by it. How, not too long ago, it was the night, the outside world after sunset, I feared. Anything indoors, light or dark, prison or home, meant safety.

Now, I'd do anything to be out there instead of in here.

The monsters live indoors.

Among us.

I'M NOT IN the prison below the Coliseum, of that I'm confident.

This one is quiet, as if I'm the only one down here. Or, at least, there are very few of us. Maybe high-level prisoners? Ones they know others might try to get to, either to free us or kill us themselves.

I'm also fairly confident I'm underground, and I can't help but wonder: If I were strategic, might I figure out where in Bellona I am? Dig my way to one of the Night's tunnels? Get home?

Impossible, of course.

But I've got lots of time to muse and pray. Make wishes I know won't come true. Especially here in total blackness where my eyes play cruel tricks on my brain. Where shadows become ax-slinging executioners and the breeze that intermittently sneaks in tickles over my shoulders like mice skittering across my skin.

Sometimes I lie down next to the door and peek through the crack. There's never anything to see. Just a stone hallway. An hourglass on a small empty table. The soft flicker of light.

I now crave light like I used to crave sunrise flowers and candied lemons, Nico's dimple, Poppy's speckled hands, Dorian's sheepish grin. My goodness, how simple life seemed when sneaking around for mud beetles before morning bells was the scandal of the day.

Try as I might to avoid it, I think the words, see the unavoidable images and memories because everything's all wrong now. Poppy's gone, Nico might be dead, Dorian's fate is unknown, and I'm set to be executed any day now.

Even the sunrise flowers are long wilted and the mud beetles are hibernating from the harsh winter cold. There are no lemons to be candied.

It's silly, but somehow it's that last thought that sets my eyes watering and my nose stinging.

Check out more books chosen for publication by readers like you.